BREAKING HIS RULES

THE BILLIONAIRE HART BROTHERS BOOK TWO

VH NICOLSON

Boldwood

First published in Great Britain in 2025 by Boldwood Books Ltd.

Copyright © VH Nicolson, 2025

Cover Design by Lori Jackson

Cover Images: Ren Saliba Photographer, Adobe Stock and Shutterstock

A CIP catalogue record for this book is available from the British Library.

Paperback ISBN 978-1-83678-646-7

Large Print ISBN 978-1-83678-647-4

Hardback ISBN 978-1-83678-645-0

Trade Paperback ISBN 978-1-80656-058-5

Ebook ISBN 978-1-83678-648-1

Kindle ISBN 978-1-83678-649-8

Audio CD ISBN 978-1-83678-640-5

MP3 CD ISBN 978-1-83678-641-2

Digital audio download ISBN 978-1-83678-644-3

This book is printed on certified sustainable paper. Boldwood Books is dedicated to putting sustainability at the heart of our business. For more information please visit https://www.boldwoodbooks.com/about-us/sustainability/

Boldwood Books Ltd, 23 Bowerdean Street, London, SW6 3TN

www.boldwoodbooks.com

This one is for all the girls who crave the thrill of the chase but love to let themselves be caught.

1

MAX

"Have you heard from Ms. Bradshaw yet?" I ask Tate from across the table if his lawyer has been in touch with him this morning, doing my best to keep the annoyance out of my clipped words. It's almost impossible.

"Nothing." He dips his chin and sways his head, having checked his phone for the twentieth time.

"Can you two be civil to one another for a few minutes?" My eyes volley between Tate and his soon-to-be ex-wife, my client, Stella.

"I have zero plans on talking to my husband," Stella replies coolly, making Tate scoff.

"If I had known divorce was the only way to shut her up, I would have filed for one a long time ago," he mutters under his breath.

"Enough." I point at him. "She's the mother of your children. Have some manners, Mr. Young."

Screw marriage, and to hell with the kind that ends in divorce. It's ruthless.

How two people can go from loving each other deeply to

being unable to sit in the same room is brutal and, honestly, baffling. The way love can rot into hate is something I'll never fully understand. That's why I am never getting married.

Fuck to the no.

"Excuse me." I push my chair back, remove myself from around the boardroom table, and fake a smile. "Let me check if my secretary has heard from Ms. Bradshaw," I say, desperate to get away from them. I can think of a million better ways to spend my morning than with a couple who can't even look each other in the eye. The air is so thick with acrimonious hostility, you could cut it with a knife.

Why I decided to become a divorce lawyer is anyone's guess, yet here I am in the thick of another messy divorce. But, truthfully, I love my job. It reminds me of all the reasons I will never get married.

I whip open the boardroom door and storm down the corridor in the direction of my office. "Find out where she is," I instruct Louise, my secretary, as I round the corner and point at the phone. "Get her on the line right now and put her through." Rage burns through my veins as I move into my office, slam the door, and wait for the phone to ring.

Who the fuck does Paige Bradshaw think she is, keeping me and my client waiting again? Hell, she's even keeping her own client waiting.

I have back-to-back settlement conferences all day. I don't have the time for tardiness, and I'll be lucky if I even have the time to take a piss between meetings.

Resting my hands on the desk, I drum my fingers against it and pin my eyes to my phone as it sits idle, staring at it as if summoning it to ring.

Inhaling a deep breath, I prepare myself for the conversation with Paige, the woman who gets under my skin more often than I care to admit.

A divorce lawyer, like me, she turns heads without trying too hard, and she's so strikingly sophisticated that I often find myself forgetting what I was saying mid-sentence. In meetings, she's as sharp as a razor, and I hate that she's always one, if not three, steps ahead of me.

Is she ever on time, though? Nope. Recently, she has been working in her own time zone and makes me wait for her. Every. Single. Time.

This is the fourth time she's been late in the last few months. Now I think she's doing it on purpose. Although when she eventually does show up, she's always apologetic, but seems frustrated with herself and everything around her.

Her most annoying trait is that she seems to see right through me. She's immune to my charm, which my ego hates, and I know she tolerates me solely to put on a show in front of our clients. We've handled many divorce cases where we've represented opposing spouses so I'm familiar with Paige and how she operates. I'm not sure if anyone else has ever noticed how often she paints on a smile, but I always do; it gives her away every time. It's subtle, and you've got to be quicker than divorce papers getting filed to catch it, but I've seen it enough times to recognize the difference between polite and performative.

She may look like a fucking goddess, but she's so detached and emotionally shut off, I'm sure she eats the hearts of small children for supper.

Finally, the red light on my phone blinks, followed by the ring that fills the room. Maybe it's just my imagination, but it sounds agitated, like me.

I lift the handset to answer, and before I have a chance to

talk, Louise informs me that she has Paige on the line and puts her through.

"Max. I'm—" Paige blurts out, but I don't let her finish.

"Late," I state firmly, walking over to the window. "You are half an hour late." Even that's a lot for her.

The faint click-clack of heels, mixed with car horns and the sound of traffic, drifts down the earpiece.

Out of breath, she says, "I got held up. My secretary was supposed to call you. Move out of the way, asshole," she chastises someone.

A mental photo of her frantically weaving her way through morning commuters comes into my mind, and I secretly love the fact that she's already having a shitty day. She's messing with mine, and it's not even nine o'clock yet. Serves her right.

"Well, she didn't call," I inform her, looking at the San Francisco skyscrapers out of my office window.

"Someone's getting fired today," she states matter-of-factly, as if that won't mess up her entire week.

"You fired one last month, too." How many has she had?

"Can people not just do their job?" she asks, now panting.

"I could ask you the same thing. You had one job to do at eight thirty this morning."

"Please let me explain..."

I pull off my tie, which I hate wearing, before cutting her off. "Have your secretary call mine to reschedule. Again," I add to make my point. "And if mornings are too difficult for you, because you seem to have an issue with getting your ass out the door on time, then maybe you should schedule an afternoon meeting instead." My tone is thick with sarcasm, then I follow up with, "Tate is going to fire you if you keep this up."

"He won't, he's already paid up-front. And let's face it, who else would take him on?"

Of course he did. He throws money around like confetti to get what he wants. His cutthroat reputation in the investment banking world is notorious.

She adds more reasons why she's representing him. "Also, I didn't have a choice. I was told I had to take him on."

That's because her firm knows Paige is the only lawyer who could handle him. Smart move.

"Did you hear about the uncompromising position he found himself in at work?" I ask, curiosity zipping up my spine. He's been screwing practically every single woman in the city behind his wife's back. I hope Paige isn't another one to fall victim to his actions.

I know Tate, so I wouldn't put it past him to pursue her, but I think Paige has more self-respect. And not that I've been keeping tabs on her or anything—well, maybe I have—but what I do know about her is that she generally keeps to herself. She rarely attends lawyer lunches or networking events that we get invited to. I also know she's single. Something Louise told me, because every secretary from every law firm across the city seems to know everyone and everything.

If Paige is still single, I guess it's because she's too busy keeping her broomstick warm.

"Personal feelings aside, I'm just doing my job, Max."

"He's a handsome motherfucker; I'm surprised you don't find him attractive. Maybe after the case, you know, I thought you two..."

She barges in with, "Hell no." Her voice rises by three octaves, informing me that I've rattled her cage. "I have standards, Max. You're a fucking asshole," she fires back.

"Just checking." This might be the most fun I've had with her.

I know it is because Paige Bradshaw doesn't know the

meaning of the word. This is also the first time I've heard her swear.

Usually a vision of calm, right now, she sounds anything but.

A disgusted noise down the microphone informs me that I've riled her. "Well, for the record, Max, it's a flat-out no. I would never go near him, not even if I were desperate. He's a client, not that it matters to you. Knowing you, you're probably fucking Stella already. Poor woman. You should inform her that she needs to take herself to the walk-in clinic. She'll need a full range of tests if she's been with you." She spits venom into the earpiece, even more breathless than she was before.

Chuckling at her saltiness, I reply, "I've never slept with a client." I suddenly don't feel annoyed anymore. I'm quite enjoying screwing with Paige. "And careful, you sound jealous."

"I'd rather slay a dragon than sleep with you."

I burst out laughing. "Well, that would be easy for you, given you're a witch and could easily find one of those."

A gasp is followed by her question. "A witch?"

"Sorry, I meant bitch."

"Fuck you, Max."

"You wish."

"Never." She makes a gagging sound down the earpiece. "If contracting an STD was on my bucket list, maybe."

I fight to suppress my amusement but then find myself imagining what hate sex with Paige might be like. She's all curves, with an ass to fucking die for, legs longer than the Golden Gate Bridge, long blonde hair she wears in a severe bun, and a snark level that could cut glass. She's sharp, unapologetic, and somehow still manages to dress like she has just stepped off a *Vogue* cover.

That smart mouth of hers is fucking begging to be stuffed

with my cock to shut it up. Hell yeah, I could get on board with that. My cock jumps in my boxers in agreement.

Fuck, that's never happened before.

Ice queens aren't my thing. That is, until now.

And hate sex: I think I just unlocked a new kink of mine.

"I'm outside your office," she drawls.

On high alert, I push my shoulders back, stand up straighter, and then look behind me.

She adds, "I'll be up in two minutes."

And with that, she ends the call.

Fuck, we only have twenty-five minutes to discuss alimony. I needed an hour for that.

Fucking Paige Bradshaw.

Equal parts exhausting and entertaining.

She's a beautiful fucking wildfire.

The kind that can burn everything to the ground, and when she's gone, I'm left sifting through the ashes, replaying every spark she lit and every hard-fought argument she won.

2

PAIGE

"It's so good of you to join us," Max says dryly as I enter the room, feeling like I need another shower.

My whole morning has thrown me for a loop.

Max states the obvious. "Let's be quick, I have another meeting to attend." Then he jabs the knife in. "And my client will not be billed for my time today; instead, I will be charging you directly, Ms. Bradshaw," he adds casually before I've even had the chance to sit down.

I already hate this stupid day.

"Consider it paid." Screw you, Max Hart.

I pull out a chair around the boardroom table, take a seat, remove the case file from my workbag, and open it flat on the table. "I'm sorry I'm late." My eyes shift between Tate, my client, and Stella, his wife. Well, soon-to-be ex-wife. I feel sorry for her. Life with Tate must have been dreadful. Why she went on to procreate, four times over, with the cretin, I will never understand. I apologize further. "It won't happen again. And as per my conversation with Mr. Hart, we will schedule any further meetings for the afternoon."

It'll be easier for me that way.

Since Alfie, who is now one year old, arrived, my mornings have been total chaos. I honestly can't remember the last time I managed to leave the house on time. It took two outfit changes and Emma, my nanny, arriving late because she got stuck in traffic, before I finally headed out the door. Only to realize I had forgotten my laptop and had to turn the car around to get it. Then, to make things worse, I got stuck in the worst traffic imaginable.

What a day this is turning into.

"As long as afternoons suit my client, then we'd be happy to accommodate," Max replies, a faint smirk shaping his lips.

Max Hart can fuck off. The last thing I need is his stupidity this morning.

"I prepared these in advance to save time." I lift the proposal out of the case file that I agreed on with Tate yesterday and slide two copies across the table, one for Stella and one for Max. I fake a smile. I'm nothing but efficient and Max knows it. "As you'll see from our alimony proposal, Mrs. Young will receive indefinite support, given the eighteen-year duration of the marriage." I then proceed to list how the property they own will be divided. "We propose discussing child visitation further at the next settlement conference."

Stella and Max study the proposal before Max lifts his eyes to me, one brow rising as if impressed that I made Tate agree to it all. "On first glance, this seems satisfactory, but I will need to go over this with my client in private," he states.

I nod my head in acknowledgment, feeling smug. I know they'll accept. It's the least Tate can do for his wife, considering that he cheated on her throughout their marriage.

If she ever trusts another man enough to remarry, it will be nothing short of a miracle.

Trust.

It's such a small word, and yet it's heavily weighted with promises.

Max Hart is another one not to be trusted. He's San Francisco's most eligible bachelor.

According to the office grapevine, he's like a grasshopper, jumping from one bed to another. I don't know how true that is, and I shouldn't make assumptions, but there you go, I have, based on the rumors.

He told me once that he would never settle down during one of our many heated arguments. Something to do with me being too argumentative, and reminded him of why he was single, or something equally predictable. I mean, apart from him being a complete pain in the ass, the guy has everything going for him. Naturally attractive, moves in high-status circles, has an adventurous lifestyle, but he's also emotionally unavailable. Having worked in this job for a long time, you become cynical about love and if he's anything like me, he probably doesn't believe in lasting love either; it inevitably ends in disappointment and messy breakups.

So, yeah, when it comes to Max Hart, I understand why women get hooked on the chase. He's a guarded Lothario with an air of mystery around him. Devastatingly handsome, though, and I see the appeal. Sometimes, Max makes me forget what I was about to say because I get too distracted by the way his sculpted muscles flex under his crisp white shirts. He rarely wears a tie and always leaves just enough buttons undone to push the boundaries of PG. What can I say? I'm a sucker for a hairy chest. Don't judge. His skin is sun-kissed all year, making him look healthy and wholesome, and his wavy hair, longer on top and sitting just above his shirt collar, only enhances his chiseled jaw and makes it look even more defined.

He's a distraction I don't need. One I don't want.

Never.

But it's hard not to look at him when he looks the way he does: Godlike and one of the most handsome men I have ever set my eyes on.

Not that I'd ever go near him; venereal diseases aren't my thing. Also, he'd never look twice at me. Not only does he represent pop stars, movie stars, and models looking to untie the knot, he dates them, too. I know this because he's practically a fixture in the gossip columns, always snapped on the arm of whatever celebrity is trending that week. Somehow, his divorce settlements always come with a happily ever after... not always for the couples involved.

There I go again with my assumptions, but if he's photographed with them, it must be true, right?

The last I heard, Max was dating the fire chief's daughter, although she's not just the fire chief's daughter; she's an influencer with over five million followers on Instagram. Beautiful, influential, and a celebrity in her own right, she's exactly his type: high profile, high drama, and sufficiently high status enough, sitting above everyone else to make him feel like he's winning.

"Thank you for this. Your proposal seems reasonable enough," Stella says, breaking me from my stupid thoughts about Max. She fumbles with the paperwork and shuffles in her seat, looking everywhere but at her husband.

"Are we done?" I ask, my gaze moving between Max and Stella.

"For now." Max stretches his neck. The thick veins running down his skin that disappear inside the collar of his shirt don't get overlooked by my obsessed eyes. He even has a nice neck. How is that possible? And I'm ashamed to admit that this isn't the first time I've noticed that. It's thick from working out at the gym. Hard-earned.

We lock eyes for a second, and that roguish smirk returns when he catches me staring, highlighting his perfect cupid bow and causing his dimples to make an appearance.

God, what is wrong with me today?

I really need to get laid.

It's been far too long. Years.

I turn my attention away from my nemesis, ignoring the weird feeling I don't understand in my stomach, and check the time on the large clock on the wall, then point to it. "And we still have time to spare."

I'm a little pissed at that. Today wasn't enough time to fulfill my perv quota staring at Max Hart, but it will have to do.

"Thank you," he replies.

His pleasantries don't surprise me. Around everyone else, he's polite and professional, but when it's just the two of us, we verbally spar, which I both enjoy and hate equally.

I push myself to my feet at the same time Max does and extend my hand for him to shake. "Again, I'm sorry for being late. It won't happen again."

Max takes my hand, and then turns to Stella and Tate, asking, "Could you two give us a minute?"

"Of course," they both reply at the same time.

Stella and Tate awkwardly leave the room, avoiding eye contact. Hell, they're even trying to avoid the air they breathe. Not that Tate cares, but I see the hurt in Stella's eyes. She's in pain and hates every minute of this.

Divorce is a lot like grief.

Unless you're completely blind or oblivious like Tate, it's obvious she's grieving for a family life she's losing: vacationing separately, Christmastimes apart. Then there are the friends and family who have to choose sides. It's exhausting for everyone, and we shouldn't forget the guilt of not being able to make it work.

Max mutters under his breath just as they close the door behind them. "I hope she doesn't kill him out there."

"I wouldn't blame her if she did," I reply, acutely aware that Max's hand is still in mine. I instantly release it like it's scalding my skin and apologize, feeling slightly awkward before sitting down. "Do you want to change the time of the next settlement conference?" I ask, opening the calendar on my phone that runs every minute of my life.

He sharply bites back, "No. I want to know why you didn't give me a heads-up on your alimony proposal. If you already had it, you could have easily sent that by email yesterday."

I slide my gaze away from my cell phone to look at him and say, "In-person conferences are my preference." I prefer seeing him every week to simply torture myself. "And off the record"—I drop my voice to a whisper—"I want Tate to see how much this is hurting Stella. Have you seen how much weight she's lost? But don't worry, she will be well taken care of, as will their children."

"Did your heart suddenly start caring?" Max taunts, his smirk making a reappearance.

Ignoring him, I counter with, "Those kids deserve stability, and that is something only Stella can give them. I'm a divorce lawyer, Max, I'm not dead inside. You know how compassionate I am." I don't tell Max, but Tate knows he's the one in the wrong, and I've prepared him for the consequences. Give Stella what she wants and needs, and he'll still walk away with his penthouse along with several of his sports cars. That's all he needs. It's all he asked for. Oh, and his yacht. He wants to keep his *baby*.

Heartless bastard.

I watch Max as he eyes me suspiciously.

My conscience wins every time; that's what makes me a great lawyer. I'm fair to everyone involved, and Max knows it.

Confidently, he sits straighter, squaring his shoulders. "My client and I appreciate your cooperation."

"You are welcome. Now..." I close the file laid out in front of me, then lift my bag off the floor and stuff it inside. "...about the next meeting?"

"I'll have Louise contact your secretary," he replies, then adds, acting like he's a fucking comedian, "That's if you still have one."

"One more job to do." I sigh, suddenly dreading the thought of hiring a new one.

I'm surprised when Max offers, "I could find someone for you. Or why don't you ask Joseph at reception," he adds. "He knows everyone, and everyone knows him."

"I can find someone myself, it's fine," I snap.

He holds his hands up in mock surrender. "I was only trying to help."

"I don't need your help." My voice is sharper than I intended. I've been doing just fine on my own for years. Although if he'd offered me his assistance six months ago in helping me find a nanny, I would have welcomed it with open arms because that was the toughest decision of my life. Hiring a nanny was not something I thought would be on my to-do list this year. And it was the ultimate curveball. One I wasn't prepared for.

Max raises an eyebrow, amused. "Wow. You need to work on accepting kindness without drawing blood."

I bite back. "And you need to work on minding your own business."

"That's my cue to get the hell out of here," he says as he

scoots his seat back, grabbing his paperwork and laptop from the table. "Have a great fucking day, Ms. Bradshaw, and maybe sometime today you can find a way to loosen up. You make a mannequin look relaxed."

"Well, at least I have things going on in my life to be stressed about." If only he knew why I'm constantly wound tighter than a rusty bolt on a boat. Clueless idiot. "I guess the only thing you need to worry about is who is going to keep your bed warm tonight." I'm sure he has more names in his little black book than anyone I know. At forty years old he's still chasing tail and causing women's panties to disintegrate with just one look.

The girls at my firm get themselves in a tizzy when Max is scheduled for meetings with me or fellow colleagues, appearing in their conversations more often than I'm happy with.

The blabbermouths speculate a lot. The hot topic always comes back to one thing... They assume that because he has a body to die for he could go all night.

Yeesh.

Although being fucked by a man, specifically Max, who knows what he's doing, is something I know I would enjoy but have never had the pleasure, or displeasure, of experiencing. But since Alfie entered my life, the dating game has sailed away from me, leaving me stranded on my own little island, waving it good-bye. It's long gone, and has disappeared beyond the horizon.

Being single sucks, but hey, Alfie is the only thing that's important in my life right now. He's my priority, and I love him in a way I can't even begin to describe. That brown-eyed dumpling in a diaper has stolen my heart, and I pray to the powers that be that they don't break it.

Shaking myself out of my side thoughts, I glare back at the man who is shooting me death stares.

He sneers. "Well, at least one of us will be warm tonight.

Scorching hot, actually. Unlike yourself. Fuck." He shivers, shaking his shoulders in exaggeration. "Whoever shares your bed must get frostbite. You're like a glacier with a fucking heartbeat, although I'm not even sure if you have a heart."

My fists clench so tight, they whiten at the knuckles around the handle of my workbag. Blood surges like wildfire through my veins, threatening to wipe out everything in its path as I fire back, "And anyone who sleeps with you must be brainless, or they lost a bet."

Knowing he's pushed all of my buttons this morning, a grin shapes his lips, and with that, he walks out of the boardroom with an air of smugness I hate without saying goodbye.

I close my eyes and take a deep breath.

During kickboxing classes at lunch, I'll pretend it's his face instead of the punching bag I'm pounding. That'll make me feel so much better.

Sweeping my bag off the table, I head out the door, relieved that I don't have to see Max for a few more weeks. It's a pity, but also a blessing. If he just kept his mouth shut, he'd be the perfect man.

I walk into the reception area on the top floor of Hart Law and greet Tate with a bright smile. "Tate," I say, distracting him from his cell phone. "Let's grab a quick coffee to discuss what comes next." It's probably the same thing Max is doing with Stella in his office right now. Or fucking her on his desk. The latter is more than possible. Although he did tell me earlier that he's never slept with a client, and for once, I believe him.

"Great." His whole face lights up as if I just suggested we go out on a date, something he asked me when I agreed to represent him.

To clarify, I say, "It's just coffee. We need to discuss custody of the children."

"Pity," he says with a widening grin.

Presumptuous idiot.

Roll on going home time.

3

MAX

I'm unplugging my laptop to take home with me so I can work tonight when Cole, my youngest brother, strolls into my office.

"Good day?" he asks, making himself comfortable on the sofa opposite my desk.

"Started off terrible and went downhill from there." I need to remind Louise to ignore me the next time I suggest a full day of meetings. Now I have case notes and paperwork to finish that will keep me busy for over a week. "Do you want to go for dinner, or do you have plans tonight?" I had a quick lunch at my desk between meetings, and coffee isn't enough to keep me going, not after the exhausting gym session I did before work this morning.

"As free as a bird," Cole replies, looking unhappy about that.

"Still not found the one?" I wrap air quotes around my last two words for emphasis.

He blows out a long, heavy breath, slackening off the knot in his tie. "Dating in San Francisco is shit."

"I have no complaints." I slide my laptop into my leather workbag and fasten the metal clip to secure it.

"You're not fussy."

"And you're too fussy." I wag my finger at him, then point to the cell phone in his hand. "Dating apps suck, you'll never find the love of your life on there." I only know this because after years of using those apps, he's still unhappily and frustratingly single. He has struggled to find love since splitting up with Stephanie three years ago. They were college sweethearts, and he still maintains she was the love of his life. If she was the real deal, Stephanie would never have cheated on him with his best friend, breaking his heart and destroying his self-confidence. Poor bastard.

Cole places his cell phone face down on the sofa as if he's annoyed with it and puts it in timeout. "Whatever." He runs his hands through his dark hair. Why he's still single is a mystery since he's a handsome motherfucker.

He's younger than me by eight years, and I notice the way the women in the office ogle him. According to Louise, it's his gray stormy eyes that they all love for some reason. It gets them hot and bothered beneath their desks.

There are plenty of women lining up to date Cole, but none of them *feel right* according to him.

"Should we ask Eli and Nathan if they want to join us for dinner?" Cole asks. Unable to keep his hands off his cell phone for more than a minute, he picks it up again when he receives yet another notification.

"Nathan is too loved up to join us." I state the obvious. Since Arianna stormed into my older brother's life like a full-on hurricane, he's become pussy whipped. I don't blame him; she's beautiful and funny, a complete contrast to the salty old goat that is my brother, and perfect for him.

"Nathan and Arianna are off to buy furniture for the nursery," I say, confirming his evening plans. With a baby on the way and a wedding only a few months away, my workaholic brother has no choice but to take time off work. He'll never admit it to us, but he's totally into the whole dad- and husband-to-be thing. I can see how invested he is in organizing the wedding and how excited he is about being a dad. He practically bought the entire bookshop out of baby books.

Surprisingly, I'm happy I'm going to be an uncle. It's something I never thought would happen, considering how my brothers and I have always prioritized work over relationships. Honestly, I never imagined Nathan would be the one to start a family. And as for me? The idea of becoming a dad still feels completely foreign to me. Commitment is a terrifying word. It makes me want to run for the hills.

But Nathan has shown me something unexpected: if a grumpy bastard like him can find love, maybe there's hope for Eli and Cole, who might find love again too.

"And what about Eli?" Cole asks, referring to our other brother, the one born between the two of us. Four boys. My mom was a sucker for punishment.

"He's out for dinner with the head of the company who is hosting our annual staff team-building day this year."

"Sounds boring."

"According to Sapphire it will be an enlightening experience." I draw a rainbow across the sky, just like she did when she came to the office earlier to pick up Eli.

"Who's Sapphire?"

"She owns the company we hired." She's far out, kooky as fuck with multicolored hair, and the only other way to describe her is *bright*. I swear she was high as fuck. Or maybe she's just a lover of life. Something Eli struggles with. The guy is so uptight that his butt cheeks squeak when he walks. I laugh at the ridiculousness of the two of them waiting for the elevator together.

Sapphire was in full-on talk mode, not taking a single breath or giving Eli a chance to speak when he usually has an answer for everything.

"So, it's just the two of us tonight?" Cole asks as he stuffs his phone into the top pocket of his suit jacket.

"Looks like it," I reply, wishing Paige could see me now to prove her wrong. See, I don't always have someone warming my bed at night. However, that might change depending on where Cole and I end up after dinner.

I haven't had my dick sucked in so long that I've forgotten what it feels like. Although, since I split up with Juliette, I haven't been interested in anyone. According to Eli, I'm going through a *dry spell*. More like a drought, but whatever.

Cole stands to his full height of six feet five, two inches taller than me.

The guy has everything going for him: estate lawyer, dark features and hair, penthouse apartment, sports cars, and more money than he knows what to do with. His single status makes no sense. "Why did your day start off shit?" Cole asks, stretching his arms above his head to unwind his tense muscles from sitting behind a desk all day.

"Two words. Paige. Bradshaw." I still fucking hate that she prepared an ironclad alimony proposal. If I had to guess, I'd say it seems like she's trying to present Stella in a more favorable light than her client.

"Yikes." He shudders. "That woman makes my balls jump inside my body."

"I think my balls have yet to come out of hiding," I lie.

Usually, she has the same effect on me too, but today... well, today was different. My dick got hard thinking about having hate sex with her.

Fuck, what was that all about?

I hope that never happens again.

* * *

"I needed that." I wipe the corners of my mouth with the napkin and lay it on top of my empty plate.

"Me too." Cole pats his stomach, which is covered in tattoos beneath his black shirt. "They make the best steaks here," he says, looking around No.33, the steakhouse we regularly dine at.

"And the new waitress is fucking hot," I point out. Our server has already slipped me her number, which I have no intention of calling. She's a bit too young for me.

"She's not my type." He scrunches his nose up.

I scoff, unable to comprehend him sometimes. "What the fuck are you looking for exactly? What is your type, then?" I push my plate away from me, fold my arms on top of the table, and lean forward.

"I want more than just looks, Max. I need someone who can connect with me without even speaking, someone who will support my dreams, and someone who laughs at my shitty jokes even when they aren't funny. Damn, if I had that, I would love them with everything I've got."

It's what he had with Stephanie, or so he thought, until she screwed his bestie.

I listen closely as he continues sharing words he hasn't admitted before: "I want someone who sees me for me. Not my job, the money, and the cars, or the high-profile cases I work on. I also want someone who looks past my looks and charming personality." He lazily grins at the last two items he mentions, messing with me a little, but I understand what he means.

Owning the largest law firm in the city has its challenges. Cole's recent trials have drawn a lot of media attention, but not because of the case itself; it's his looks. He went viral on social media after someone filmed him walking in and out of the courthouse. Now, he's become an American heartthrob, and his DMs are flooded with women eager to date him, but like he said, that's not the type of woman he's looking for.

He wants someone who doesn't exist—someone who will fit seamlessly into our work life. Difficult, given how busy we are. When our dad was diagnosed with dementia and Parkinson's, all four of us took over running the firm our father spent a lifetime building.

As the older brother, Nathan seems to think the success of the business weighs solely on his shoulders, but that couldn't be further from the truth. We share the burden equally, and we all play our part.

As brothers, you would think we would fight all the time, something we did do when we were younger, but my three brothers are my best friends, and I couldn't do my job or run the firm without them.

For a while, when things fell apart with Arianna, it made us doubt each other. After Mom brought us together, she showed us that no matter what, we stick together and support each other through good times and bad, unlike my clients, who can barely make it through a few months of marriage.

Cole shifts the spotlight to me. "Anyway, what about you? Have you been on any dates recently?" he asks.

I hate to admit it. "No," I reply firmly, pushing my hands through my hair in frustration. "I have my plate full with work." I'm juggling too many cases to consider a social life. That's my excuse, and I'm sticking to it.

"So, the fire chief's daughter is off the table." It's not a question; he already knows it is.

"Something like that." I'm non-committal with my answer.

Like all the others, after a few months, she started talking about the future, diamond ring settings, and babies.

Nope. Never happening.

Being a fun uncle will be enough for me.

"So, you ghosted her, that's what you're saying without saying it." He reads between the lines of my response.

"I've been busy."

"You ghosted her," he repeats as our server appears to clear our plates, saving me from a roasting from my brother. "Thank you," he says, looking up at her. "Compliments to the chef."

The beautiful brunette's lips shape into a curve, shooting Cole a dazzling smile. "I'll be sure to pass that on, sir. Would you like to see the dessert menu?"

I hold up my hand. "Not for me, thanks."

"I'm good, thank you, just the bill when you have a minute," Cole says, lifting his cell phone off the table as he receives another notification, making his eyes light up. He ignores our server as she clears the rest of the table and scurries away.

What the hell is wrong with him? "She's perfect, you know." I throw my thumb over my shoulder. Same age as him, all legs, with beautiful brown eyes.

He glances up briefly and examines the back of her. "Nah." He shakes his head in disagreement. As he opens something on his phone, his eyes widen before a smirk spreads across his lips as he scans his screen. He turns his cell phone around to show me what has caught his attention. "Have you heard of The Velvet Rooms?"

"Yeah." I take his phone from his hand and scroll through the website he's viewing. "It's a sex club." My friend Timo, who owns the biggest construction company in California, is a member.

"An exclusive, members-only one. You can't get access into it, unless you have an invitation. Which I do."

"Who the fuck sent you this?"

"Libby."

My head snaps up. "Libby? As in Libby, our law librarian?"

"Yeah."

"But she's..." I trail off, unable to find the words I'm looking for.

Cole helps me finish my sentence. "A wallflower."

That's exactly who she is. "Is this what she's into?" I ask, my curiosity at an all-time high.

"She's been trying something different. Like me, she's had enough of using dating apps. We've gone on a few dates together. Well, not exactly together; I mean, we go out with our own dates, but we just coordinate the times and places, then share notes afterward. She's cool."

Cool. Right. If this is what she's into, I kind of love the fact that she's a librarian by day who unleashes herself at night. I never would have suspected this is what she's into. But now that he mentions it, at first glance, she ticks every librarian stereotype: buttoned-up blouses, tailored skirts, hair in a neat bun. But her blouses always cling to her body a little too well. It's clearly not accidental, and the slits in her skirts often verge on the risky side. The deep red lipstick she wears every day is a bit too bold for someone so quiet, too. Behind those tortoiseshell glasses she wears, she's hiding secrets best left unspoken in daylight. She's not just cool; she's a silent siren.

"She's been on their waiting list for a while but became a member a month ago."

I raise my eyebrows in question. "How can she afford that? She's not at the director level yet."

"She comes from money. Old money. She doesn't need to

work, but since high school, she has wanted to study law. After college, she got an internship with us, and that's when she decided she didn't want to become a lawyer because she loved being in the library instead. And her position with us gives her independence, something to call her own, and freedom from her controlling father." Cole shifts in his seat, looking uncomfortable.

"You seem to know a lot about Libby."

"We talk."

I look at him suspiciously.

"Anyway, moving on." He pulls at the collar of his shirt. "She's permitted to invite three guests for the special events they host. She invited me." His grin turns devilish, as if he's already imagining himself there.

"To go with her as her plus one or tag along?" I'm a nosy bastard and want to know everything.

"Oh, it's not like that between Libby and me. We're just good friends."

I question him some more. "You sure about that?"

With firmness in his tone, he replies, "Yeah, I swear on Mom's life we aren't like that."

Pushing him will only force him to push back. I'm certain there is more to the two of them than just friendship, he just can't see it for himself.

"Libby would be more than happy to add you as her guest. If I go, will you come?" he asks, his face deadly serious.

"No," I'm quick to answer, and I hand him his cell phone.

"Oh, come on. They do this dating in the dark night for singles looking for a connection without seeing what the other person looks like. No one will see you. Sounds like fun." He lets out a puff of air. "I could seriously use some fun. Fuck the dating game." He tilts his head, examining more of the images on the website as he continues scrolling. "Let your senses guide you, with no pressure and zero judgment. Be whoever you want to be in the dark." He reads the description out loud. "'Awaken your darkest desires, ignite your curiosity where touch, sound, and scent will help you paint your own picture.' Sounds hotter than hell. I'm in." He moves his fingers across the screen of his phone, and I can only guess he's RSVPing to Libby, confirming his attendance.

I squirm in my seat, uncomfortable with the prospect of going to a sex club with my brother. We're tight, but not that tight. "It's a hard pass for me." That's my final answer.

"Well, I'm going tomorrow night, if you change your mind."

"I won't change my mind." But I might check that website out again when I'm alone later. Fuck knows why I feel compelled to do so, but I do. It feels like a bit of a rush using touch, sound, and taste without sight. Knowing you can hide your identity while exploring a desire sounds erotic; sensual, even.

I park those thoughts and leave them there to revisit later.

"I hope you have fun." I lift my glass of premium aged whiskey with a hint of honey. I finish it, letting the rich oak and syrupy sweetness fill my mouth with complex flavors, providing me with a gentle buzz.

Yeah, whiskey is what I need.

Not a date in the dark.

4

PAIGE

"C'mon, gorgeous boy, time for the sandman." I snuggle a sleeping Alfie into me one last time. I lay a soft kiss against his thick head of blond hair that smells like sweet milk and vanilla powder, then gently place him in his crib in his nursery I spent hours decorating. "Love you, little man."

One day, he'll appreciate how much I love him and the sacrifices I made for him.

Just like I do every night since he arrived, I perch myself on the edge of the rocking chair and enjoy the moment, simply watching him, observing his adorable movements as he stretches his arms above his head before opening and closing his pouty little mouth.

That adorable little boy with the button nose has changed my world. He turned everything upside down, but now that he's in my life, I can't imagine him not being here.

"Night, night," I whisper with a smile, quietly moving from the chair to leave the nursery, lifting the baby monitor off the dresser before I exit and close the door, but not fully.

Tilting my head left and then right to stretch out the tension,

I turn on my new best friend, a baby monitor with a video display, so that I can watch Alfie; it's my favorite TV show.

"What a day." I talk to myself as I head down the hallway, then go down the stairs and summon whatever last bit of energy I have left. I enter the messy kitchen that looks like it's been hit by a Tasmanian devil, grabbing a chilled bottle of water out of the fridge. Long gone are the nights I'd sit around my dining table in my immaculate home working late into the night with a glass of wine, but now that Alfie is in my life, I prefer to keep a clear head just in case he wakes up in the night.

I hook two fingers through the strap of my workbag and lift it off the floor, its weight pressing down on my shoulder as I head for the dining table.

Fumbling with the baby monitor and my bottle of water, I place them on the table, nearly knocking them over in the process. With a sigh, I unzip my workbag, start pulling out the papers I need, and dust off the dinner crumbs from the seat before sliding into the chair.

Yellow light from above pools over a sea of legal briefs. Tomorrow's hearing casts a long shadow, and I can't afford to show up with a foggy head. Not now. Not with my place at Moore & Associates already on thin ice. The partners have noticed the late arrivals and the unexpected absences since Alfie's appearance in my life. While they've been supportive, I've promised many times that it won't happen again. But working long nights and making promises don't mean much when Alfie is ill or the nanny calls in sick again.

But this is my reality now.

I grit my teeth, push through, and give everything I have, even when it never feels like it's enough, not for Alfie, not for work, and not for me.

My life would be easier if every divorce I negotiated was

amicable, because that's exactly what I need right now. Simplicity. Not two successful adults who can't even agree on who gets custody of the dog, let alone their own children.

Cutting through the silence and the low static hum from the baby monitor, my cell phone chimes, alerting me to an email as it often does at this time of night. I don't mind answering emails outside of regular business hours. It works to my advantage and means I don't have a longer-than-necessary to-do list before I even have my first coffee in the morning.

"Let's do this." I get to work, open my laptop, then my emails and exhale a tired puff of air. Even though I'm exhausted, I know that diving into work now will help me sleep better. If I don't go through my emails and get some reading done, my mind will race the moment my head hits the pillow, and I'll just end up reopening my laptop in the middle of the night anyway.

Hours later, I'm pleasantly pleased with myself for zipping through my workload in record time. I'm almost finished when an email drops into my inbox from Max Hart.

I check the time: 11 p.m. What the hell does he want at this hour? Max might be a lot of things, but he's respectful of my time and never sends unnecessary emails or makes demands late at night. I think that's because he knows I won't tolerate any crap from him, or anyone else for that matter.

I read the subject line, *Alimony Terms Agreement – Tate Young/Stella Young*, and hope Stella agreed to the proposal I know will support her for the rest of her life.

Clicking the email to open it, I scan my eyes down the screen and give myself a virtual high five. Stella Young agreed to everything.

Without hesitation, I hit reply and write back, my inner smugness doing a happy dance.

From: Paige Bradshaw – Moore & Associates
To: Max Hart, Esq. | Hart Law
Subject: Re: Confirmation Alimony Terms Agreement Acceptance – Tate Young/Stella Young

Mr. Hart,

    Thank you for your rapid response. I'm pleased to hear that your client has accepted the proposed alimony terms. I will proceed with drafting the Marital Settlement Agreement and will forward you a draft after the Child Custody Agreement has been agreed upon, which we will discuss at the next settlement conference.

    Regards,

    Paige Bradshaw, Esq.

    Moore & Associates

I hit send and rest my back against the chair. Now I need to sleep.

Just as I'm about to shut my emails down, another one arrives from Max.

From: Max Hart, Esq. | Hart Law
To: Paige Bradshaw – Moore & Associates
Subject: Re: Re: Alimony Terms Agreement – Tate Young/Stella Young

Ms. Bradshaw,

    You shouldn't be working at this time.

    Max Hart, Esq. | Hart Law

    Hart Law, A Professional Law Corporation

Confusion hits me, and my eyebrows furrow. I don't know

why I hit reply and engage with the insufferable prick, but I find myself typing before I can stop.

From: Paige Bradshaw – Moore & Associates
To: Max Hart, Esq. | Hart Law
Subject: Re: Re: Re: Confirmation Alimony Terms Agreement Acceptance – Tate Young/Stella Young

Why not?
  Regards,
  Paige Bradshaw, Esq.
  Moore & Associates

Once I've pressed send, I regret it. Feeding the self-important jackass will awaken the bitch inside me, and it's too late for this bullshit. I have an early start tomorrow, and I like to get up an hour before Alfie. I drum my fingers on the dining table, waiting impatiently for him to reply.

After five minutes, nothing arrives.

The prick is keeping me waiting. Until, ping, here we go...

From: Max Hart, Esq. | Hart Law
To: Paige Bradshaw – Moore & Associates
Subject: Re: Re: Re: Re: Alimony Terms Agreement – Tate Young/Stella Young

Because you go to bed too late, and it's clearly the reason you've been late for every meeting and court date for the last six months. You're beginning to get a reputation for yourself.

However, if you go to bed now, you might make it in time for your meetings tomorrow.

Get to bed.

Max Hart, Esq. | Hart Law
Hart Law, A Professional Law Corporation

My pulse races as if it has a life of its own. No one tells me what to do. He's really riled me up. My fingers quickly hit reply and tap against the keyboard as I furiously type out a new email and hit send before I overthink it.

From: Paige Bradshaw – Moore & Associates
To: Max Hart, Esq. | Hart Law
Subject: Re: Re: Re: Re: Re: Confirmation Alimony Terms
Agreement Acceptance – Tate Young/Stella Young

You know for someone who is supposed to be a well-connected insider, I'm surprised you don't know what has made me late for the last six months.
I guess the secretaries don't tell you everything.
Regards,
Paige Bradshaw, Esq.
Moore & Associates

If only he knew I've been struggling to juggle this new life that has been thrust upon me. Having a six-month-old left on my doorstep was not something I was expecting.

But that's where I am.

I'm trying to do everything in my power to make it work. However, it looks like I'm not. Even Max Hart has noticed how tardy I have been lately. This is terrible.

I need to try harder, but that feels impossible when I am already stressed to the limit. I've reached my maximum level of coping.

My eyes survey the still messy kitchen and the laundry pile

higher than the laundry washer, and I groan at the chaos of my life.

Tomorrow I'm hiring a housekeeper.

As well as finding a new secretary. I had to let go of the temporary one I had today after she failed to inform Max that I was running late. It was the last mistake in a long list of errors she made.

From: Max Hart, Esq. | Hart Law
To: Paige Bradshaw – Moore & Associates
Subject: Re: Re: Re: Re: Re: Re: Alimony Terms Agreement – Tate Young/Stella Young

What is that supposed to mean?
    Max Hart, Esq. | Hart Law
    Hart Law, A Professional Law Corporation

Faster than a bolt of lightning, I respond.

From: Paige Bradshaw – Moore & Associates
To: Max Hart, Esq. | Hart Law
Subject: Re: Re: Re: Re: Re: Re: Re: Confirmation Alimony Terms Agreement Acceptance – Tate Young/Stella Young

It means, if you don't already know, then mind your own goddamn business.
    Goodnight, Max.
    Regards,
    Paige Bradshaw, Esq.
    Moore & Associates

I close the lid of my laptop with a thud, cutting off this

annoying conversation that's getting too personal. At least now I have the confirmation I needed that all the secretaries I hired in the past haven't revealed the most private part of my life: Alfie.

Let's hope it stays that way.

Except for the partners at work and my very close friends who know, he's been my little secret for so long, and I've treasured every moment we've shared in our quiet little bubble. The reason I never told anyone about Alfie is because, when my sister left him on my doorstep with nothing but a note tucked into his blanket, no bottle or change of clothes, I truly thought it was a joke. Only, the punchline never arrived.

Since that night, I've lived every day half-expecting her to come back and take him away. Not that he's mine to claim, but God, it feels like he is. At the end of this month, I'll have cared for him longer than she ever did.

I've been there for all his milestones: his first words, the first time he crawled, the moment he first pushed himself up to stand. And when he grinned at me with those first tiny teeth, it was the kind of joy I'll never forget. These are the memories I'll cherish for the rest of my life.

And I'm praying I get to keep creating memories with him. That's why I've already filed the adoption papers, something I couldn't legally do during the first six months. But now that we've passed that point, and my sister has left Alfie in my care without offering support or declaring her intention to come back for him, it's clear she intended to abandon him. That gives me a strong case. A very strong one.

More than anything, I want Alfie to be safe, and I know I can give him the life my sister never could.

My sister, Marin, hides her chaos behind a polished exterior. By night, she works as a dancer in a strip club in Las Vegas, something I only found out about a month ago when she told me in a text message. By day, she's locked in a battle with addiction and instability. From the outside and to everyone around her, she probably looks healthy, composed, maybe even thriving. But it's all smoke and mirrors. I know my sister well. She's a master of manipulation and a high-functioning addict who hides behind a veil of lies. That's why my mom and dad disowned her years ago. The never-ending stream of excuses became too much for them, along with stealing their prescriptions and lying about her expenses. If they had kept track of how many times she said "It wasn't me" and "You're overreacting" out of her gaslighting mouth, they'd probably be millionaires, I'm sure of it.

Since she left Alfie with me, she's been like a ghost, only showing up in the occasional text, just enough to remind me of the wreckage she left behind.

She won't be winning Mother of the Year, or Sister of the Year, for that matter. And while I may never forgive her for what she did, I've made peace with one thing: I'm stepping in to set things right.

Alfie will never want for anything. He'll be loved and have stability. I'll make sure of that.

Eventually, everyone will know about Alfie, especially when the adoption is finalized, but for now, I'm enjoying having him all to myself.

My phone chirps, and I jump, my instinct coiled and ready to strike. I feel it, a readiness thrumming just beneath my skin, following my irritating exchange with Max Hart. Add to that the prospect of dealing with my sister via text, who doesn't care what time of day it is, and I'm battle-ready.

Reluctantly, I pick up my phone and immediately relax, the tension leaving my body in droves when I realize it's not my sister messaging me, but my friend Catalina, or Cat as she prefers to be called.

Her text has me shaking my head with a no before I've even hit reply.

CAT

Are you free tomorrow night?

ME

No.

CAT

Sorry, I'll rephrase that. I'll pick you up at eight tomorrow night. Be ready. Dress up or down, whatever you're comfortable in. We're going speed dating!

ME

Absolutely not.

CAT

It wasn't a question.

ME

I won't find a babysitter this late. And my nanny needs forty-eight hours' notice for evenings.

CAT

I have that covered. I booked SanFran Sitters to take care of Alfie. They are the absolute best. Paisley will arrive at your place tomorrow night at six to give Alfie time to get used to her. She'll also do bath and bedtime to give you time to get ready before I pick you up. She's CPR-certified, specializes in early childhood education, and is lovely. I interviewed her myself.

I stare at my phone, too shocked to reply. Cat knows me better than anyone I know and has been my friend since my sophomore year at college. She knows I haven't had a night out, not even a simple dinner with friends, since Alfie arrived. My evenings used to be spent dining at fancy restaurants, but now they involve my silk work blouses being splattered with mushy food by a very fussy eater named Alfie. Not that I would change anything; he's my world now.

Cat fully understands how special Alfie is to me. I don't trust him with anyone else, and that's why she hired the best sitter service in the city. Arranging a sitter for me forces me to be brave, and she knows I wouldn't book one on my own.

Trusting someone other than myself or Emma, the nanny, with Alfie has my palms breaking out in a sweat, but it's something I should have done a while ago.

This is a big step.

Huge. The first of many more to come.

CAT

You're welcome.

ME

I hate you right now.

Meddling minx.

CAT

You'll love me when you find out what we're doing.

ME

I hate dating.

That's why I don't do it, and it's not just because Alfie is in the picture now—it's because I gave up looking for Mr. Right after the worst date I ever had. Being two hours late to pick me up, taking me to a dive bar, and then waiting outside my house afterward, just in case I changed my mind about sleeping with him, put me off dating for good.

> CAT
>
> It'll be fun. It's just one night. Let's get you back in the dating game.

That makes me feel sick to my stomach. Dating is not something I'm good at. Give me a courtroom any day; it's where I thrive. But when it comes to small talk with someone I have zero chemistry with, I'm out the door with my sneakers on, running for the hills.

> ME
>
> It's a work night.

> CAT
>
> I'll have you home before midnight. I promise.

> ME
>
> Okay.

> CAT
>
> Yes! See you tomorrow. And bring ID. Oh, and your results of having a clean bill of health. *wink emoji* From the one you did last month to renew your health insurance.

> ME
>
> What? Are you referring to my sexual health certificate? If so, why do I need to bring that?

> CAT
>
> That's the one and it's just a formality.

> ME
>
> Are you sure?

> CAT
>
> Yes. Chill!

That included everything, even my sexual health results. I'm clean. I didn't need an examination to tell me that. I'm practically a born-again virgin at this point.

What the hell have I gotten myself into?

I have no intention of hooking up with anyone.

Drumming my fingertips against the wooden tabletop, I consider all the excuses I can think of to prevent myself from going when another text arrives.

> CAT
>
> And don't even think about cancelling on me.
> You're coming.

Oh, screw it. "You're going, Paige." I smile to myself and for the first time in months, I feel butterflies dancing in my stomach.

I'm excited.

But speed dating.

What happens at a speed dating event?

I google it to find out and my palms immediately feel clammy as I read the words on my phone screen: conversation, timer, scorecards.

Oh God, what the hell has Cat signed me up for?

And why do I need my sexual health certificate?

She's up to something.

5

MAX

"Good morning, Louise." I sidle up to my secretary at the coffee station.

"Morning, Mr. Hart," she replies brightly as she stirs creamer into her coffee. "You don't have any meetings scheduled for today. I pushed some of your appointments to later in the week after yesterday's busy schedule. I thought you needed some admin days to catch up."

Hallelujah and thank God for Louise, my office angel. Hiring her was one of the best decisions I ever made. For five years we've been working together, and she never misses a beat. She gets me and knows what I need, and when.

Louise lifts the coffee off the counter and passes me the steaming mug. "You're just in time. This is for you."

"Thank you." Gratefully, I reach out and wrap my hands around the mug before taking a sip, welcoming the caffeine that hits my bloodstream. "What would I do without you?" I ask her.

She double pats my shoulder as she passes me on her way back to her desk. "You'd be screwing every temp at your desk during lunchtimes, firing them when you got bored, then repeating the same scenarios all over again two weeks later."

I almost snort my coffee out of my nose as I take a bigger sip. I would never do that, but she sure does like to wind me up.

This is the reason I love Louise. She's blunt, efficient, and, more importantly, she takes none of my bullshit and shoots from the hip. I love her.

And if she weren't happily married to San Francisco Giants first baseman, Austin Porter, I would marry her myself.

Obviously not, because, you know, marriage isn't for me and all that, but I love a strong woman who knows her own mind and isn't scared to speak out, like Louise, and her husband loves her for it. She doesn't need to work; she can afford not to, but she loves her job here at Hart Law and has even said that if her husband gets traded, she will work for me remotely.

She's clearly a glutton for punishment.

A thought comes into my mind. "Hey, Louise, can I ask you something?" I walk with purpose toward her as she turns around.

"Anything. You had better be quick, though; I have a date planned with a Dictaphone, and he'll be mad with me if I keep him waiting," she says deadpan, keeping a straight face.

Another thing I love about Louise is that she's funny without trying. "Oh, don't worry, it won't take a minute," I say before looking around to make sure no one is within earshot, then ask her, "What do you know about Paige Bradshaw?"

Her mouth downturns as she lets out a humming noise and puts her memory to work. "Well, she's like your work twin because she's a great divorce lawyer, if not better than you. Why Moore & Associates hasn't made her a partner yet, I will never understand because she knows her stuff and I like her because she gives you hell." Her lips curve into a smile.

Wicked woman. Brilliant. But she teases me way outside the norms of acceptability.

I don't care; it makes work more fun.

I stop Louise in her tracks before she reels off more of Paige's career track record. "No, that's not what I meant. I mean, do you know what's going on in her personal life?"

"Not a thing." She shakes her head.

"But she's single?" Why the fuck I am asking is anyone's guess.

"As far as I'm aware, she is, yeah."

"Mmmm," I hum, pondering what the hell she meant last night. *I'm surprised you don't know what has made me late for the last six months.* "So, you don't know what happened six months ago?" I ask.

Louise's brows pull together. "No, why?"

"It's probably nothing, but she mentioned that the reason she's been late for almost every one of our meetings is because something changed for her six months ago. Is she sick?" I wonder out loud.

"I think we would all know if that was the case, and would she still be working?"

My grip around my mug tightens, annoyed that no one seems to know. Asking Nathan was a dead end, as was Joseph, our top-floor receptionist who knows everyone and everything happening inside the building and at every law firm in the city.

I sigh, surrendering to the inevitable: I'm searching for an invisible ghost. "Maybe I misinterpreted what she told me in her email."

"Most likely." Louise thumbs over her shoulder. "Gotta go, Dictaphone date."

"Enjoy." I follow her down the corridor in the direction of my office.

"Oh, Cole stopped by before you arrived to tell you that he's in court all day. But if you want to go out with him tonight to that place you discussed last night, he'll meet you outside the venue at nine."

I tut, annoyed that he didn't take my first answer as my final one. "Thanks, Louise." I have no intention of going with him tonight.

Walking into my office, I settle behind my desk and turn on my laptop. While waiting for it to wake up, curiosity takes over, and before I can stop myself, I open my cell phone and go to The Velvet Rooms' website.

On the events tab, I hit the promo for tonight's Dating in the Dark.

I read the words I saw last night instead of just scanning the page; this time, I absorb each one.

Whispered words.
Velvet cloak of darkness.
Tentative finger brushes.
Breath like warm caresses against the skin.
Slow burning desires.
Pulses quicken.
Electric encounters.
Feel soft laughter like tiny vibrations.
Where shared silences ignite connection.
Sensual magic.
Let your body come alive in the shadows.
Let your heart connect beyond appearance.

Fuck. I've already got a semi just thinking about it.
Sounds fucking wild.
But it's not for me.

Nope.

Leaving my cell phone open, I wheel my chair further under my desk to get closer to my screen. I swear I need eyeglasses. Note to self: book an eye exam.

Opening my emails, I brace myself for a day of admin work, phone calls, and endless email chains and paperwork. Unless the building is on fire, I won't leave my desk.

One minute later, my eyes flick toward my phone, which hasn't gone to sleep yet. The Velvet Rooms' website glares back at me, begging me to take another look.

Like a moth to a flame, I can't tear my gaze away.

Nope, I'm not going.

I return my focus to my laptop, but again, not even five seconds later, I find myself sliding my eyes to my cell phone again.

"Fuck it." Before I second-guess myself, I'm texting Cole, informing him I'll meet him outside The Velvet Rooms tonight.

6

PAIGE

"Are you sure I look okay?" I haven't worn a dress this revealing in God knows how long.

Looking down at myself, I adjust my boobs to give me a little more cleavage.

I'm more curvaceous than most of my friends, and this is when wearing figure-hugging dresses works in my favor. My black silk dress contours perfectly to every curve of my body, and the black silk and lace bra I splurged on last month is keeping my girls in place.

"You look sexy as hell." Cat's grin is wide and has an undertone of devilment about it. "I'd fuck you."

I chuckle out loud as I leave Cat's private limo, then remember the first thing she said when she elegantly floated into my house, smelling like a perfume shop. *We're riding in style for tonight's night of debauchery.* I really hope there's no fucking or debauchery. Speed dating is one thing; debauchery is a whole different evening altogether.

I glance up at the deep-red velvet-looking sign with subtle

black lettering embossed into it: The Velvet Rooms. I've never been here before. "What the hell is this place?"

"Sex club," Cat says casually, like it's the place we visit regularly for coffee every day.

"What? No," I exclaim. "I'm not going in there." I'm going through an adoption process, and I can't have anything jeopardize it. Alfie needs me. I need Alfie. My heart's thudding so loudly it drowns out any noise around us. "I've worked too hard fighting for Alfie to ruin it. One wrong move and the agency could pull everything. What if someone sees me? What if there are cameras? What if it leaks somehow?" My voice cracks. "They already questioned me about being single. This would be the nail in the coffin." I point to the club.

"Yes, you are going inside." Cat drops her voice as we look up at the sign. "This is an exclusive club. It's a respectable and ethical members-only space. I've been a member for a while and everything is discreet. No phones, no cameras, no social media." She steps closer. "As a member, I've been heavily vetted. I can invite up to three guests. Only guests I trust. You're my guest." She gives me a look. "There will be masks. No names. No one will know who you are. The people inside have more to lose than we do, they protect confidentiality like it's religion." Then, more gently she adds, "I know this adoption means everything to you. But you're allowed one night. One night to not be an adoptive-mother-in-waiting. You're not doing anything wrong, and you're not alone. I'll be right beside you." She steps in front of me, searching my face. "And I promise you, this won't jeopardize your adoption. I wouldn't bring you if there was even a one percent chance of that happening." She pauses. "You're not breaking any rules. You're not doing anything illegal. You're just breathing for a minute. And you deserve that. This isn't about risking him, it's about holding onto yourself and remembering that you have needs too."

"Members only?" I ask, quietly.

"Yes. This isn't like your sister's world, this isn't some seedy backroom sex club." She takes my hand in hers as her limo drives off, meaning I am now stuck here with a dilemma: to take the plunge or not. "It's one hundred percent safe, Paige. Confidential and discreet. This place is vetted, protected, and light-years from the place your sister works and has worked in," she provides calmly and without any unease in her voice. "And again, I swear to you, nothing about this night will touch your adoption file. It won't even leave a fingerprint. They have strict security protocols and encrypted data protection software. Also, you are not your sister. Far from it, Paige. Her career is something she does to fund her lifestyle." She sighs. "And I know how much that upsets you, but I promise you, the only reason I brought you here tonight was to have fun. That was all."

She's right, I'm not anything like my sister, and everything she said has reassured me. This is fun. However, nothing she said stops me from being stunned by her membership so, with my mouth open in astonishment, I stare at her. Cat is stunning, a picture of sophistication. She's gorgeous and exudes quiet confidence that commands every move she makes. Success clings to her like glue, which is why she runs the most successful health supplement business in North America. Not only is she lithe, but she's also elegant and so graceful, I'm sure she could command the ocean to part for her. As the winner of the executive of the year, she's unstoppable, and when she's around, it feels like you're breathing the same air as a legend.

That's why I ask, "What the hell do you need a membership to a sex club for?" Powerful and ambitious, she's the sexiest woman I know. With the snap of her fingers, she could easily have any man she wanted.

Smoothing her blunt black glossy bangs with her perfectly black manicured nails, she dismisses my bewilderment with a quick shrug. "Excitement, fun, sex with no commitment, no awkward afterglow, and cuddles." She shudders. "Here, there is no expectation to follow up with unnecessary calls to arrange another date, and there are no feelings involved. This suits me perfectly." She gestures to the sign with the tilt of her chin.

Oh my God, this is crazy. "We're doing speed dating in a sex club?" I squeak, still standing gawking at the sign, my mouth opening and closing like a fish gasping for breath on dry land.

"Okay, so I told a teeny tiny itty bitty white lie." Turning toward me, we look at each other face-to-face. At this moment, I don't recognize my friend. She hoodwinked me into thinking I was going speed dating in one of the many swanky bars Cat regularly frequents, and instead, she's brought me to a sex dungeon where I'm going to be tied up, whipped, and I'll be made to have sex with a stranger.

Holy. Fucking. Shit.

I can't do that.

The pasta I ate earlier is threatening to make its reappearance, tension coiling, my temples pulsing.

"It's dating in the dark," she finally says.

"What even is that?" I'm not sure I want to know.

"We step into a darkened room meant only for singles where you can interact with a group or with someone you feel connected to. You can touch, listen, talk, whisper, use a fake accent, be whoever you want without being seen—that's entirely up to you." Her voice remains steady and calm, unlike the panic I'm feeling right now. I think I'm sweating.

I point to the ominous red door with my sparkly silver

clutch. "But what if there is someone in there I know?" I let go of Cat's hand and lay my hand over my heart. Yup, my heart is beating so fast, I'm sure I'm having a heart attack.

Unaware of the mental image playing out in my head of me jumping onto a magic carpet so I can get the hell out of here, Cat replies deadpan, "I already told you, it will be dark and you will wear a mask, and let's be honest, Paige, what is the likelihood of that happening?"

Well, now that she's asking, I have no idea what the probability of that is. I try calculating the population of San Francisco and the percentage of high-flyers who can afford this kind of membership, then divide that by... what? Hell, I'm lost. One in a hundred thousand, maybe? God, yeah, that makes me feel better. It's slim. Almost zero.

Cat eases my spiraling thoughts. "In the twelve months I have been a member, I have yet to meet anyone I know. Everyone is vetted, they only let a handful of members join every quarter, and it's expensive. The joining fee alone will put a lot of people off."

I dare not ask how much it is.

Stepping toward me, Cat grabs the top of my arms. "Breathe, Paige. It's going to be fun and I'll be there."

"But what if you meet someone and you leave me alone?" Although, maybe this is how I overcome my awkwardness with dating. Surface-level chatter is not my thing, and dating in the dark seems like it offers less pressure to perform, worry about what they might think of me, or how I look. A chance to go deeper, perhaps without any social filters.

This might be fun after all.

"What if, Paige," she says slowly, "you meet someone and you leave *me* alone?"

Oh, I never thought about that. I remain quiet while Cat stares at me with a mischievous look.

To hell with it. "Let's have some fun." I summon all the confidence I can, taking the first step toward the doorway that doesn't look quite so scary now.

"Ready?"

"No. But I'm here and ninety-nine percent sure I'm going to throw up my mac and cheese, but I've done less with more anxiety, so yes. Let's go."

Cat chuckles by my side. "Just remember to breathe."

I think that's all I will be capable of. "I might need to use the restrooms." Before I pee myself from fear.

"To freshen up your kitty. I like your thinking, Paige."

Jesus fucking Christ. "That's not what I meant."

Completely unflappable, Cat ignores my strained response and takes a black card from her purse with gold writing on the front before tapping it against a hidden reader on the wall.

I flick my long blonde hair over my shoulder.

Holy shit.

I'm really doing this.

7

MAX

The Velvet Rooms is not at all what I imagined.

It's better.

It's dark, warm, decadent, and the low music drifting through the speakers is so faint, it's more like a whisper.

I'm still trying to find answers and figure out why I've never thought about becoming a member before now. This place would meet my needs perfectly: fucking without the commitment or promise of anyone wanting more or catching feelings. Stellar.

We are currently in a private holding room with just my brother, Libby, and me. Once we put on our mask-like disguises, only then will we be allowed to enter the main room, not the entire club. After the event, we have to come back into the same room to take off the masks, and that's when we can enter the main club for the rest of the night if we choose to.

After thoroughly verifying both my and Cole's government-issued IDs and current sexual health test results, something we regularly do, and we're cleaner than freshly fallen snow, we were granted access to a private room, but only after agreeing to a strict set of rules, which I memorized by heart.

We're not allowed to exchange names or cell numbers. If we want to connect with anyone, we have to inform the club, and they will find a way to put us in touch with one another.

- No physical contact without verbal consent.
- We're not to discuss appearance.
- Physical intimacy is permitted but only if consent is given by both parties.
- We've got to mingle.

More like fumble our way through the dark, but whatever.

- If we feel uncomfortable at any point we can leave through the same door number we arrived through which will light up thirty seconds after we close the door behind us.

To protect our identities, I assume.

- Trained staff are on hand to guide us through the event.

And lastly, the rule I love the most...

- Everyone is required to wear a mask provided by the club.

Mysterious and erotic by design, the neon pink-and-blue line detailing will glow under the UV blacklight. The women wear sleek black plastic bunny-ear masks that frame their eyes and sit lightly on the bridge of their noses, making each breath easy and every glance a tease. Meanwhile, the men wear matching masks: smooth, shadowy fox masks that mimic the same shape, adding a subtle hint of mischief and allure. Together, the masks set the tone: playful, anonymous, and undeniably charged.

Everything sounds simple enough, and I'm all in for whatever happens, happens.

While half of me is shitting myself, the other half is excited.

I've never taken part in anything like this before.

My anticipation is increasing with each second, like I'm about to enter a haunted house at a carnival. Still, at the same time, I'm eager to jump in because I need to get inside, feel the rush, get my adrenaline going, anything to confirm this is real and true. But it's terrifying as hell. Still, I'm ready.

I keep telling myself it's just a one-time, never-to-be-repeated event, so what do I have to lose? At this point, nothing.

I'm not dating. I'm single, and to be honest, my hand and cock have become best friends. Something I plan on putting an end to soon. Maybe tonight. We'll see.

"Fuck, I'm nervous," Cole says, putting his mask on at the same time I do.

"Don't be. You'll have the best time," Libby pipes up like a ray of sunshine, helping Cole tighten it at the back to secure it in place.

"We never speak of this again, or you're fired," I warn, pointing at Libby, which only causes her to laugh at me.

I haven't spent much time with Libby outside of work, so I didn't really know what to expect. But she's fun and lighthearted. And that red satin dress she's wearing leaves nothing to Cole's imagination.

He didn't think I noticed the way his eyes drifted down her body when she arrived at our arranged time outside the club, but I did. The poor guy became tongue-tied as soon as she stepped out of her cab to greet him. Much to my amusement, it was borderline comical.

Just friends, my ass. He likes her, but he's too scared to admit it.

Of course, I was only joking with Libby about firing her. It turns out she loves her job at Hart Law, is dedicated to her role, and aspires to become a legal research manager within the firm, overseeing research teams and assisting with litigation. She's ambitious, which I like, and I plan to talk to Janice, our human resources manager, to discuss her chances of promotion.

Before I brought it up and before we even entered the club, Libby reminded me that the NDA she signed for work covers personal information related to employees, managers, the executive team, and basically every shareholder at Hart Law. She also assured me that she would never disclose personal information, as her job at Hart Law is her dream position. She then told me that the firm was her top choice for employment after college.

All that aside, if Cole trusts her and she works for us, then that's more than enough for me.

"Right, let me put these on you both." Libby places a tiny heart-shaped sticker in neon pink on Cole's mask just above his right eye.

"What are these for?" I ask, wondering what the reason behind them is.

Sticking her tongue out to the side in concentration, she then does the same to my mask. "Because the last thing I want to do is hook up with either of my bosses. I might not know anyone else other than you two in there, but in the dark, and as my guests, this will distinguish you from everyone else for me. All members have been advised to do something to help them tell their guests apart from everyone else."

That makes sense, I suppose, although Cole doesn't look too happy about that.

Libby steps back and puts the same sticker on her bunny mask, then looks at us. "You'll be able to recognize me too. No tonsil tennis for either of you this evening." She breaks into peals of laughter that only make Cole scowl more.

"Let's go." He nervously tugs at the cuffs of his black shirt. I know Cole, and right now, I can see that his anxiety is at an all-time high, his fidgeting giving him away.

And me? Well, I'm going all in and having a full-on fuck-it moment. I'm here now and I plan to enjoy every single fucking minute of whatever awaits us beyond this holding room.

For me, this isn't about finding everlasting love. Having never found it before, it's something I've never truly believed in anyway. This event is fun, a new experience, something to tell my brothers about for years to come. Nothing more.

I clap my hands together and rub them enthusiastically. "Let's do this."

Cole watches Libby's every move as she hands us our preordered drinks that were waiting for us here.

She winks at Cole. "Loosen up, big guy." She gently pats his upper arm before turning to me. "And you, well, you just keep being you." She gestures up and down my frame.

"What the fuck is that supposed to mean?" I grin wickedly, knowing precisely what she's going to say.

"Max, everyone knows you're a commitment-phobe and completely unavailable. This type of night suits you, so just be yourself." Libby rolls her eyes as if she finds me exhausting.

I wink at her because I'm not offended; she's right, so who am I to argue?

And I have no plans to change who I am anytime soon.

8

PAIGE

"That guy over there is begging for some kitty Cat action." Cat points at someone I didn't even notice, wearing a T-shirt with luminous teal writing across his chest that reads, *Ask Me Anything*.

"What are you going to ask him?" I enquire, knowing Cat won't struggle for ideas.

"If I can sit on his face."

Called it.

That woman's mind and tongue are sharper than a Hollywood prenup.

Laying her hand on my thigh while I laugh against the lip of my wine glass, she checks if she can go to him. "Will you be okay if I leave you here?"

Holding on to her as if she's my life raft isn't healthy, and cutting the cord to let her explore is what's needed. "Of course, go, and enjoy yourself." It's something I am struggling to do myself. Even if I'm not having fun yet, I'm not stopping Cat from having some.

I'm at war with myself. I want to relax and have fun, but I'm battling the chaos within. From the minute I stepped into the main event, I've been desperate to return to the holding room where we had to leave our cell phones and purses inside a secure locker.

My nerves aren't just from being in a dark room with strangers, but from worrying about Alfie's well-being. Restlessness and protectiveness are stopping me from getting on the fun bus with Cat. I should be using my senses, the mask to hide my identity, and the dark so I can enjoy tonight, but instead, all I care about is the safety and well-being of my little man, who is at home with a stranger. I know she's not a stranger, but that's how it feels. And I know Alfie's not mine; I didn't go through all the pain and give birth to him or carry him in my womb; however, some days, it often feels like that. Never have I experienced a love quite like it.

Crossing one leg over the other, I nervously bounce my foot up and down. If I could quickly check my phone or check in with the sitter, maybe then I'd be able to relax.

"Don't you dare leave without telling me," Cat warns.

"I won't."

"And if I see you running. I'll know it's you because of your tattoo."

Having a UV glow-in-the-dark tattoo last year doesn't seem like such a bad idea now. As I approached the big four-o last year, I decided to get a tattoo. Cat said it was due to me having a midlife crisis; maybe I was, but I loved it then, and I still do. While I'd always wanted to have a tattoo, I also wanted something more discreet that wouldn't stand out on my pale skin. That's when my tattoo artist suggested a UV one. You can still see it in the daylight; it's just more discreet, but it comes alive under the light on evenings like tonight.

Cat kisses me on the cheek before she strides across the

room with purpose. All eyes are on her, and I can't help but admire her confidence as she wiggles her hips, exaggerating the sway at the guy whose focus is glued to her. I don't think she needs to do that. Whoever that guy is already looks like he wants to eat her alive, maybe even devour her.

Wearing a neon-yellow bandage dress tonight was a smart move on her part. She looks like a human glow stick under the UV blacklight. At least that means I'll be able to find her easily before I leave, which I plan to do in the next ten minutes if I don't gather the courage to talk to someone.

I clutch the drink in my hand so tightly I half expect the glass to shatter and slice into my palm, which, honestly, sounds like a much better option than being here. I've never felt so wildly out of place.

It's like I've stumbled into an erotic dreamscape, where everything is charged and alive with energy, and every shadowed glance carries weight. I hazard a guess that hidden touches and conversations with a hint of naughtiness about them are lurking in every corner as the low murmured chatter continues to fill the room.

Neon flashes from the masks, furniture, and the clothing worn by the patrons cut through the nearly dark room, causing bright jolts of motion and color to deepen the surreal atmosphere.

I'm captivated watching elegant female figures drift by in bunny masks traced with pink lashes, while fox masks, with eye holes lined in an electric blue glow, make them look like they're on the hunt.

It's official; I'm totally out of my depth. I have no idea why I thought this was a good idea because all I want to do is get the hell out of here. It doesn't matter that no one knows who I am; I do, and this dating in the dark stuff is so not for me.

I'm fucking petrified.

"May I take a seat?" A gruff voice attached to what looks like a floating head, because he's dressed all in dark clothing, appears out of nowhere, making my shoulders stiffen even more.

I'm so unprepared for this. I shouldn't have come.

"Yes, sure." Why not? Once he starts talking to me, he'll realize how boring I am and hightail it out of here. Then I can go home. I shuffle along to let him sit beside me, noticing the tiny neon-pink love heart above his eye that no one else has.

What do I say?

Hey, I'm socially awkward when it comes to dating, I've decided I don't like dating in the dark, I'm shit at small talk, more like hate it, and I want to curl into a ball and rock myself to sleep somewhere over in the corner of the room.

Hell, that makes me sound like a flaky female, which I'm not. I'm one of the top divorce lawyers in the city, and I fight for what is right.

Pull yourself together, Paige.

"Good evening, Bunny." He cuts the tension I was feeling in one sentence. I already feel better.

And is that a British accent I detect?

It has an American lilt, so maybe I'm wrong. Cat did tell me I could disguise my voice if I wanted, but I'm not faking who I am. If I do this, I'm going to be myself tonight. Unfiltered and real.

"Good evening, Mr. Fox," I purr. Actually purr. My voice sounds sultry and drips with a sexual undertone I didn't think I was capable of. "Do you like what you see?" I jest, which makes him burst out laughing, and an odd sensation twists in my gut. His laugh is so genuine and hearty, it's contagious, and I find myself joining in. It sounds familiar, but it can't be.

All men sound the same when they laugh, don't they? Every Monday morning at Moore & Associates, they hold a partner meeting, and I'm not kidding when I say this, but it's a total sausage fest. The women are heavily outnumbered. When that team does laugh, it sounds like a booming clap of alpha thunder that could shake the entire building apart.

Mr. Fox's gravelly voice cuts through my side thoughts. "I'd love to tell you how beautiful you look but I can't see for shit," he joshes.

"Neither can I," I whisper, keeping my voice low.

"This is, like, weird, right?" He twists in his seat, as if wanting to see me better, so I cross one leg over the other and turn to face him too.

There's something about his British-style accent that confirms to me he's faking it. The use of the word "like" plants him straight back in the Bay Area, as does the intonation rise at the end of his sentence. That's okay, I get it; he's protecting himself, and I respect that.

"It's a little weird," I admit. This event is more than a little weird. It's hugely bizarre.

"You smell great, Bunny." Oh, he's good, and I like the instant nickname he gave me.

"I'm wearing Tom Ford's Vanilla Sex." Hell, why does my perfume sound so boring? I can even feel myself blushing under my mask.

I follow the silhouette of his hand as he places his drink on the table. "There's nothing vanilla about tonight," he says.

"It's scary," I concede, feeling like I'm swimming in unknown waters and I set my glass next to his.

"Don't be scared, little bunny. I've got you. Just relax."

"I'll try," I agree. "Thank you for the compliments about my perfume. You don't smell so bad yourself, Mr. Fox," I say as seductively as I can, keeping my tone low so I don't give too much away. He smells like amber, black pepper, and something else I can't quite put my finger on—it's woody with a floral edge, maybe vetiver. It's heady with a hint of lemon, and I like it. Maybe a little too much. And I'm certain I've smelled it before.

Lifting my drink off the table that glows with a purple hue from the UV blacklights beneath, I take a big gulp of my chardonnay, needing the liquid courage to make this conversation go more smoothly.

"Is that real? Your tattoo. Or is it temporary for tonight?" Mr. Fox's attention drops to my ankle.

That slow drawl and lilt returns, giving his Californian accent away again.

"It's real. I got it during a moment of insanity last year when I turned forty." Shit, was I supposed to say how old I am?

"We're the same age," he informs me as I place my wine glass on the table.

"Thank God for that. The last thing I need in my life is a man who is younger than me and still needs his mommy to do his laundry."

"Well, you'll be pleased to know, my mom taught me well, and I can do my own laundry." He casually shifts the topic back to my tattoo. "Tell me about your tattoo." This guy's a natural at chatting up women; I can tell how comfortable he is keeping a conversation flowing. No one has ever asked me about my tattoo before, so this isn't small talk. Unless he asks me about the weather, it's game over.

Not that he can see me clearly, but I point to my tattoo anyway. "It's a Virgo constellation. My zodiac sign." That's not revealing too much of myself. I have a few friends who share the same sign as me.

He takes a minute to consider his next question before he asks, "Can I touch it?"

"Yes," I agree, excited by the thought that his hands will

touch my skin. It's been years since that happened, and I've almost completely forgotten what it feels like to be touched by a man.

Bending down, he lifts my ankle in the air and gently wraps his large hand around it before running his thumb over the intricate design of thin lines and the Virgo symbol decorated with tiny triangles, dots, and stars. "And the glow isn't temporary?" he asks, continuing to rub my tattoo, causing goosebumps to rise across the bare skin of my legs. Well, that's new.

"It's UV ink they use." I gulp loudly, because I can't understand why my skin is tingling and feels hypersensitive. "It glows in the dark depending on what level of lighting it's been exposed to, or on nights like tonight, it looks really vibrant under the LED blacklights."

"It's beautiful. And unique. I've never seen one of those before." He lowers my ankle then lets go of it.

Part of me wishes he was still holding on to me.

"Thanks." Shyness overcomes me as butterfly sensations I can't quite work out take hold in my tummy.

What the hell is happening to me?

"Can I hold your hand?" he asks, clearly seeking the same connection I feel we are missing, his Brit-style accent mismatching his California pacing.

Without seeing each other visually, it's hard to read body language. And with barely any eye contact to gauge emotion or even smiles, at least holding hands might help us understand each other better, to see if there's an attraction. I believe there is. It's dancing around us like a flirty little siren on the outskirts, just begging for us to ask her to sing.

"That's much better." He intertwines his fingers with mine then gives my hand a gentle squeeze.

I squeeze his back, welcoming his touch. "You have warm hands."

"I run hot."

"Me too, but my feet are always freezing. Bad circulation from sitting at a desk for years."

"So, you're a desk worker?"

Shit. I said too much. "Yes." That's all he's getting.

"So am I." He shares a snippet of his work life.

"I would ask you what you do, but I know we can't."

He hums, as if pausing to think, and the way he brushes his thumb across mine doesn't go unnoticed. "Let's just say," he starts, "I help people end things so they can start a new beginning."

"And I help people to untie knots."

"Cryptic, I like it." I sense the brightness in his whispered tone. "I like your vibe. You seem very chilled."

I giggle, fucking giggle, like a teenager, and I'm flirting. Holy shit, I didn't know I was capable of it anymore. "You really don't know me very well at all. I have a very stressful job that demands most of my time. Some people think I'm uptight." Add a baby into the mix to keep me on my tense toes, and what you have right there is the circus that has now become my life. Only, I'm not that great at juggling and it's taken much longer for me to adjust than I thought it would.

"I want to get to know you more," he says, his voice cutting through the charged air between us that feels heavy with things unsaid, curiosity, yearning, and a tension that hums just below the surface. There's a spark leaping, electric and undeniable, like static waiting to catch fire.

Continuing with my side-of-stage voice, I ask, "Have you been here before?" I cringe at my cliché question. "That sounded so much better in my head, sorry."

"Don't apologize; this is nerve-wracking. And to answer your question, no, I haven't. I'm not a member." There's no hint of humor in his reply, only that low and rough raspiness that sounds dangerous, even sexy. He consumes the space between us, moving closer.

I murmur, "I'm here as a guest too, but do you think you'll come again?"

"I don't know. The club intrigues me, though," he replies, every word heavy with unspoken want as he lightly traces his fingertips up my wrist and forearm, moving to my shoulder. I dare not stop him; I'm enjoying it far too much, and I appreciate his honesty about the club. I'm curious too because traditional and online dating have proven unsuccessful for me. Not that I've been searching for love, but it would be a good way to meet my sexual needs without becoming attached.

I have Alfie to think about now. He comes first over everything, and introducing a man into my life doesn't sit well with me. It's not something I want to explore. Not now, maybe never. We'll see.

"That feels nice," I admit, enjoying the way his touch brushes my skin as he explores my clavicle. There's so much heat in the way he touches me, it feels like burning desire laced with sparks of energy strong enough to set off a blazing inferno.

His ghost-like touches drift up my neck, and when he draws circles across the sweet spot behind my ear, I gasp, every hair on my body standing upright, my skin tingling with anticipation.

Desperate to gauge his body size and frame, I reach out and fumble clumsily, my palm landing on his thigh. Over his dress pants, I can feel how strong and steadfast he is. There's no way he has those athletic thighs from sitting at his desk all day; he works out. I'd bet on it more than once a week too. He's disciplined and dedicated.

"Your skin is so soft," he murmurs.

"I moisturize." I moisturize? Where are my sexy words and confidence? Come on, brain cells, hop on the fun bus with me.

He chuckles dryly. "Relax, Bunny. Tell me, how would your friends describe you in one sentence?" I think he's secretly enjoying the way I am squirming.

"Resilient. And you?" I counter.

"Unshakable."

Shadows move around us, but it only feels like it's just us trapped inside our own little bubble, isolating us from the rest of the room.

"You seem very confident. Are you always this comfortable in the dark?" I ask.

He answers, his faint whisper deliberate and low, "That depends."

"On?"

The silence that follows doesn't worry me; instead, I welcome it in. It tells me he's thinking and not just jumping into any old reply to appease me.

No one can see us, but inside our invisible bubble, our legs brush enough to make me crave more closeness. More touches. More of everything.

Eventually, he replies, "It depends on the woman I'm with."

"And is that a lot of women you've been with? Or..." My question trails off.

"More than I care to admit to you."

I'm not a fan of players and guys who sleep around, and yet I can't help but lean into his touch, which feels like it's lighting me up from the inside. I'm so drawn to whatever is happening between us. The connection feels different. It's something new and exciting.

I let my fingers glide up his thigh toward his groin, causing his breath to hitch in his throat.

He murmurs, non-judgmental, just intrigued, "How long have you been single, Bunny?"

"Four years."

"That's a long time."

It feels like that. I'm starting to see myself as a Christmas elf left on the shelf. But it's not a Christmas shelf I've been left on, it's a dating shelf, and right now, it's a lonely, bleak place.

After Chris, my ex, cheated on me all those years ago, the dating scene proved unsuccessful, and I kind of hoped love would find me instead of the other way around.

"And how about you?" Now I'm wondering, because if he sleeps around, then he most likely doesn't date, and that's a huge red flag for me.

But hell, this is just a bit of fun, right?

I ignore the alarm bells in my head and let myself enjoy the night that's taken an exciting turn for the better.

"Let's just say, I tend to keep things casual." He's non-committal with his response.

Who am I to judge when this is just a little nighttime amusement to pass the time, maybe boost my ego a bit? Or maybe I just want to feel like someone still desires me and sees me that way, even if only in the dark.

"You're still touching me," I point out in a low murmur.

"You keep giving me reasons to, and for some fucking reason, I don't want to stop," he confesses, the soft T's in his words betraying him. The whispered accent he's faking is slipping.

That's some big words right there. But he's right. There's an undeniable pull, drawing us closer. Every nerve-ending is tuned to his scent, voice, body, and every infinitesimal movement he makes.

It feels like we're under a spell, powerless to resist what's happening. Every touch defies logic, but we do it anyway. It's thrilling; my nerves are alive and fluttering deep in my stomach, while adrenaline races through me like a live wire. It's been so long since I've been touched, kissed, or even acknowledged, and now everything is driven by pure instinct. Raw and primal, the hunger climbs up my spine, wild and unrestrained. It's been locked away for too long, and now it's breaking free.

"Tell me something you've never told anyone before." The heat is simmering, and his velvet voice is raw and soaked with lust.

"I haven't kissed or had sex with anyone in the four years I've been single."

"Showing you what you've been missing sounds like fun." The warmth and darkness in his whispered directness should scare me, but instead, I find myself running toward him.

There's no space between us now; the desire growing between us and his huge body are everywhere.

"Sounds like something I might enjoy." Holy. Shit. Who am I right now?

Our mouths are now barely millimeters apart; his hot breath dusts the skin of my lips. "I guarantee you would."

An ache I haven't felt in so long hums between my legs, the throbbing sensation cheering him on to make his next move.

I uncross my legs and squeeze his upper thigh, my hand almost touching his cock.

"Can I kiss you?" he asks, his voice soft yet rough around the edges, as cool as a Californian surfer.

I'd be a great detective. This guy isn't British at all; he's a Bay Area native through and through.

I don't reply; instead, I eat up the small distance between us and crash my lips against his, giving him the answer he was looking for.

9

PAIGE

Like a rocket launching to the moon, my sensory receptors erupt when our tongues touch. Every lick, every taste, every tangled movement feels like a blazing inferno that burns with need through me, extending out into the intergalactic planets and beyond.

I finally reach out to touch him, fully, threading my hands into his hair, to discover it's longer than I imagined.

Searching with my fingertips, wanting to feel all of him, I dip them into the neckline of his shirt and follow the contour of his collar to his front. When I realize his shirt is unbuttoned, I let my hands drift down over his collarbone to his chest, and I smile against his lips when I discover he has a hairy chest. Not too short, not too long. Just perfect.

"What made you smile?" he asks on a series of pants and heavy breaths, the rough whiskers of his beard tickling my chin. I'm going to suffer and have beard rash tomorrow; my sensitive skin isn't used to his bristles.

"I love a hairy chest." My confession rolls off my tongue.

"I'm hairy all over, Bunny."

Oh God, that pet name is doing serious things between my legs. Mainly making me wet. Kissing has never had this effect on me. It's incredible, life-altering even, and has my head revolving like a spinning top.

Unable to resist, he presses his lips against mine again, and we kiss in what feels like a never-ending assault on our senses, and I can tell he wants this as much as I do. It's messy and dirty, almost sinful as we moan and groan into each other's mouths.

He roughly pushes his fingers into the hair at the back of my neck, pressing my mouth harder against his to deepen our kiss, and I'm grateful that the masks don't cover our noses, or it would make it impossible for us to kiss freely. An intentional detail made by the club, I guess.

Eventually, as our kiss slows down, he shifts his focus to the side of my mouth, then my cheek, kissing it softly before tracing a trail of ghost-like kisses along my jaw toward my ear, where he whispers against it, "I'm so fucking hard for you."

I shove my good girl into the freezer, locking her away and tossing the key, just to stop her from interfering with what I'm about to do. I don't give myself a moment to question it. Instead, I ask, "Can I feel how hard you are?"

"Touch me." He sinks his teeth into my neck at the same time I cup him over his pants and rub him.

And he's not just hard, he's rock solid, and holy shit, he's a big boy.

"How tall are you?" I ask, making him smile against my skin as he nibbles, his hands tracing down my body, shaping my waist and moving over my hips.

"Six-three," he answers, then throws me another compliment. "You have a beautiful body."

"You haven't seen it out of this dress." I'm not as toned as I used to be.

Squeezing my ass, hard, he says, "I don't need to see. I can feel everything through your silky dress. Your curves are fucking driving my dick wild."

The way he's touching me in such a public setting feels unhinged, almost freeing, because the dark hides us, although the low UV blacklight doesn't disguise everything. When I look over Mr. Fox's shoulder, I swear a couple are fucking in the corner of the room. God, this is so hot. I give his thick length, which is impressive enough to break the zipper of his pants, a firm squeeze before I get handsy and begin to explore the contours of his body beneath what feels like a dress shirt. Not only does he have a monster cock, but he's also big everywhere. Unmistakably defined and lean.

Using both my hands, I feel every hard inch of him over his shirt, the fabric taut, working hard to contain his large biceps. Moving south, I run my hands over his firm pecs, which he flexes, as if showing off how disciplined he is and the strength that lies beneath the surface. He feels like a statue of a god brought to life, sculpted with precision, strength etched into every chiseled muscle. He flinches when my fingertips explore his six-pack stomach, or maybe it's an eight-pack; whatever it is, I'm certain I could do my laundry on it and use him like a washboard in the same way they did back in the 1800s.

One thing's for sure: he's athletic and undeniably strong. I just wish I could see him.

"You feel amazing," I say in a secretive tone, reaching up to cup his face in my hands, loving the feel of his fuzzy beard against the tip of my thumb.

The heat jumps between us like an electrical charge, buzzing and tempting us to go further.

Raking his hand through the hair at the back of my head, he

pulls his face back to mine and devours me with his mouth again.

"You're perfect," he mumbles, between kisses as his lips work mine. "I could kiss you for hours."

It's the same for me; kissing has never felt so natural. That makes no sense, because we're strangers, and yet there's something so familiar about him. It's a nagging feeling. Something is gnawing away, like I already know him, but that can't be right.

My thoughts drift back to the conversation with Cat outside the club. The one where I asked her if she might know someone here tonight.

One in a hundred thousand.

That possibility is like winning the lotto having never even bought a ticket. I think I'm safe.

All the fear I had before now feels like an overreaction, because dating in the dark isn't nearly as scary as I thought. Kissing this guy beats winning any case I've ever had, even that divorce case that turned into a court battle with Max Hart last year. That man really does know how to push my buttons, and not in a good way.

Heat ripples across my skin like a shockwave when Mr. Fox runs his hands up my bare arms again, up over the spaghetti straps of my silk dress. "You're shivering."

I lower my voice and tell him the reason why. "I was just thinking, what if you were the guy who winds me up and who I have to work with sometimes?"

He stills for a beat before saying what he's thinking. "Shit. I never thought about that."

"Do you have someone you work with that ruffles your feathers?" I inquire, eager to learn more about what, or who, gets under his skin.

"Yes and no. She doesn't work with me but I work alongside

her sometimes. Any romantic involvement breaks not only ethical rules, but it's a serious conflict of interest, and possibly grounds for having my license revok—" He clears his throat then rephrases what he was about to say, unaware I've figured out his accent isn't fooling anyone. "I'd get fired from my position."

I figure out he was about to say he would have his license revoked, setting my mind off on a tangent, and maybe he's not a desk worker after all.

Doctor, physio, counselor, psychologist, teacher... He could be any one of those that could lead him to having his license revoked if he were personally involved with someone romantically.

I try to reassure him. "Before we came tonight, I did the math, roughly, and figured there was maybe a one in a hundred thousand chance I'd know someone here."

"I think we're safe then."

My lips curve into a giant smile, feeling more relaxed. "I think so too."

10

MAX

"I think so too." She sighs, sounding satisfied, and I can tell she feels relief at my reassurance that there's no way we could know each other. It's just as well because I'm enjoying this way too much, and I know from the few kisses we've shared, no one I've ever been with has felt so lush, soft, and just so damn perfect.

The entire experience has been both erotic and provocative. I'm on the precipice of moving this further along and asking her if she would like to continue what we started in a side room.

As I lean in to kiss her again, because I just can't help myself, a woman's sensual voice drifts through the overhead speakers, making the low murmurs and deep breathing around us fall silent. I swear someone just over my shoulder is fucking.

Good for them.

"Beautiful darkling lovers," the voice begins. "Good evening, and welcome to our dating in the dark event. We hope that by now you have experienced what can only be described as heightened desire through anonymity, and that you have learned that what you feel is far more powerful than what you see. Tonight's experience is about surrendering the senses...

letting touch, breath, and sound guide you. In just a few moments, the live show will begin."

Live show? What the hell is that? As in, sex show? Holy fucking shit.

"We invite you to watch," the voice explains, "as two strangers do what comes naturally. Let the dark do what the dark does best. In a few short moments, we'll switch off the blacklights and give you a front-row seat to something deliciously uninhibited. Our featured pair have kindly agreed to do what many of you are possibly thinking about, or might already be doing, and yes, you're very welcome to explore yourselves while you watch. Please, darklings, enjoy the show."

"What's happening?" Bunny asks, sounding like a scared rabbit caught in a snare.

"From what I can gather, there's going to be a live sex show." The website never mentioned that.

"Oh God, no, I'm out. Thank you for... Just thanks." My skittish little bunny is already on her feet and heading straight for the line of doors at the back of the room, the ones we came through at the start of the night.

I don't miss a beat and chase after her like a reckless Romeo in a dress shirt and pants. I need to know who she is, I have to, before I fucking lose it.

Having never believed in soulmates or the idea of being meant to be together—like swans that mate for life and form unbreakable bonds—I'm now seriously doubting that belief because something happened back there when we were kissing. And I don't mean how quickly I got hard; I mean, something changed. It was as if time shifted, and something snapped inside me. In that moment, her scent, her touch, her little whimpers—I know there's something more at play here. It's bigger than me, bigger than her, bigger than us. I feel it. I feel her everywhere.

My compass whirls as I walk faster toward her, stumbling blindly and weaving through the crowd in her direction, following her glow-in-the-dark ankle tattoo. My inner compass needle stops suddenly, pointing directly at her when I reach out to grab her.

She gasps when I loop my arm around her waist from behind and whisper in her ear, "Chill, Bunny." Fuck, she smells so good. It's warm and sweet, like vanilla and sandalwood, and makes my chest ache with something unexplained.

"I can't stay, Mr. Fox. I've never watched anything like that before." She hesitates and then adds, "It feels wrong to watch, you know?"

"Okay," I agree, because who am I to tell her she's not allowed to leave? But more than anything, I want her to stay, so I suggest, "But what if you stayed just for the first five minutes to see what it's like, then, if you don't like it, you can leave. I know you'll only hate yourself if you leave right now. It might make your night even better." My words sound desperate because I am. I want her to stay, and I'm struggling to maintain the stupid fake British accent I put on trying to disguise myself.

I sound like a fucking loser.

"I've already had a great night," she counters, making me feel like I'm ten feet tall and filling my confidence tank back up that she almost shot to pieces when she ran off.

When I told her I was unshakable, I was mistaken. This woman, whom my arms are wrapped around, has me trembling in my Gucci loafers. My balance has toppled.

"Then stay, please, Bunny."

Uncertainty flickers in her trembling whisper, a low-key level she's kept all night. "Okay. Five minutes."

If she could see me, she would see how large my smile is. It's larger than a crater on the moon. I'm sure of it.

Slowly and tenderly, with her back turned to me, I turn us around as the blacklights go out, plunging us into total darkness.

Noticing a slight tension in her shoulders, I tell her to relax, then gently squeeze her waist and kiss the shell of her ear. I don't usually do romance, and I much prefer fucking over kissing, so it's anyone's guess how I'm actually feeling right now.

Aliens have possibly abducted me. Or maybe she spiked my drink with a love potion.

Either way, I'm screwed, and not in the way I usually like.

From across the room, a faint, infrared glow appears along one of the walls where the live show must be happening. While that room is lit, ours remains cloaked in darkness, with only the red light reaching a few feet in front of the glass box set into the wall. It's not bright enough to give anyone away, but it's more than enough lighting so the audience can see the performers clearly without spilling into the seating area. Shame. I'm desperate to see what the jumpy little hopper in my arms looks like. Is she blonde, brunette, maybe a redhead? And what about her eyes? Are they green, blue, or brown? I want to know every-thing, but we're not allowed to reveal anything about who we are.

After the event, we will be asked to fill out a questionnaire, share our interests, and provide any details we think are impor-tant to identify ourselves, information we've also given to the person we connected with. Only then, and only if there's mutual interest, will the club facilitate contact. Even then, there's no guarantee she will choose to follow up. My mind is already made up; I want to meet outside of this room.

Fuck, I really hope she does too. Because not knowing is already getting to me.

The music streaming out of the speakers changes to a sexier, rocky tune. It's mellow, but at the same time, it's menacing and makes me want to sway in time with the beat. While everyone shifts closer to get a better view, we hang back, leaving no one around us.

A concealed door at the back of the voyeur box glides open and a man and a woman step through, hand in hand. He leads with unhurried confidence, the picture of control, while she follows, barely dressed in a whisper of lace that clings to her like a secret. The light catches the soft curve of her hip as they ascend to the circular bed in the center of the room, perfectly staged beneath the watching eyes.

Bunny stills in my arms, transfixed, watching every minute, and that hitch in her breath didn't go unnoticed by me when the couple entered the room.

Bunny.

At first, it seemed like a stupid name to call her, but it fits perfectly, like a rabbit, always alert. Her fight-or-flight instinct runs deep inside her.

She lays her hand over mine, which is still wrapped around her waist, then rests her head against my chest, settling in to watch the show.

I hope she likes it, really likes it, and wants to stick around for the whole performance. I've never been into watching other people have sex before, but I'm desperate to see how my very own flirty, timid Thumper reacts. If she enjoys a bit of watching, well... that's something new for both of us.

In front of us, the man, who is built as fuck and has abs I can only ever dream about having, crawls up the woman's body, wearing only his boxers, kissing every inch of her, teasing her, a preview of sorts of how good he can make her feel without barely touching her. She's writhing already, squirming as he kisses her pussy over her lace panties, sticking his tongue out exaggeratedly as he licks up the fabric from back to front before flicking his tongue over her clit.

Her moans fill our darkened room, the noise just enough to make the stunning woman in my arms wiggle her ass against my growing hard-on.

"Do you like what you see?" I shoot my shot.

She nods on a hum as if unable to form words, and I take that as a sign she's enjoying the show.

"Would you like me to do that to you?" I ask her, pushing the boundaries of our previous conversation.

Gasping, she replies in a hushed tone when the man pulls the woman's panties to the side, "Yes."

Through the glass, with one hand, the woman grabs her nipple through her bra, and with the other, she threads her fingers into the guy's hair so she can ride his face. He sucks her clit into his mouth, making the woman arch her back off the bed and cry out. "Oh, God, yeah, just like that." She tells him what she wants.

Fuck that's hot, but I wish I was doing that to the woman who has reached up and threaded her hands into the back of my hair.

"Kiss me," Bunny instructs, and I do so willingly, because fuck, when it comes to her I just can't say no.

Kissing along her shoulder, I glide my hand down her waist and hold it there for a moment before lowering it to rest on her hip.

My dick is fucking aching, leaking precum like a tap inside my boxers.

Peering upward, I bite and nibble at her skin as the man and woman continue to give us the show of our lives.

I watch on, mesmerized by the way the man inside the transparent chamber pushes one finger, then another, inside the woman's body before licking her clit in a slow rhythmic pace. While we can't see everything, it doesn't matter because my mind is filling the gaps, imagining that it's me and Bunny up there.

"Touch me," my bunny begs on a moan as erotic sounds drift through the speakers and from all around us, filling the sensual space. It seems like my girl isn't the only one who is turned on by the show.

It's tempting, arousing, and almost feels forbidden to watch something so beautiful and vulnerable without being vulnerable myself. Risky, breaking rules, yet at the same time, it's empowering. A raw, thrilled energy that piques my curiosity. There is no doubt in my mind that the stunning woman in my arms is staying. She's stuck to me, like Velcro, and I never want to let her go.

On a mission to make her crave me and make her forget any other man before me, I ask her, "Where do you want me to touch you?" I need her to be specific.

Her hand finds mine, and to my utter surprise and fucking delight, she directs my hand over her silk-covered hip toward her center.

"Are you sure?"

"Yes." Her fingers dig into mine to show me what she wants, pressing them firmly against her pussy.

I groan like a wild man, because I'm a fucking goner for her, and want to make her feel good.

As I rub her through her dress, she bucks her hips to chase her pleasure as I push my fingers into the thin barrier and between her pussy lips. She's swollen and ready, already needing the release.

"I want more," she moans, her voice heavy with need.

Carefully, I gather the thin fabric into my hands and slide it under the silk flimsy layer so it falls back down, hiding my hands and arms, ensuring no one can see. Not that anyone is paying attention to us or even near us, but the last thing I want is for her to feel like she's the one on show. She's all mine, and this is only for me and her.

I trace my fingers along the soft skin of her hips before dipping my fingers inside the waistband of her panties. "Are you sure?" I double-check that I have her consent.

"Yes. Touch me." She twists her head back ever so slightly to find my lips in the dark. Like a desperate woman, she smashes her mouth against mine when I move my hand fully inside the skimpy fabric and touch her pussy for the first time.

I'm no longer paying attention to the live show taking place in front of us. My dick presses into her ass, making more precum leak from my slit as I slide my fingers between her swollen lips, causing a little gasp to break free from her lips.

I rub her swollen clit in slow, languid strokes, teasing her, working her into a frenzy before filling her with a thick finger.

"Foxy," she cries.

Unable to stop herself, she moves her hips in time with my rhythmic strokes as I push in and out of her wet channel, rubbing the palm of my hand against her clit and driving her crazy. "You're fucking soaked, Bunny."

"Only for you," she murmurs against my lips.

Holy fucking shit.

While my fingers busy themselves to fuck her like I know she needs, I move my other hand upward on the inside of her dress. I palm her tit in my hand, then pull the cup of her barely there bra down and pinch her nipple, hard, making it pebble and pucker into a hard peak.

She lets out another soft whimper into my mouth, and a grin spreads across my lips. Knowing this is what I already do to her, and how to make her feel good, gives me such great satisfaction. My little temptress is so responsive, I'm already hooked on her little sounds.

I knock her legs open with my foot, roll her already sensitive nipple between my fingers, and push another finger inside of her, the walls of her pussy clamping around my digits as I hold her against me.

Rubbing my cock against the crack of her ass, I have to stop myself because the last thing I want to do is come in my boxers in a fucking sex club. Not cool.

An inner battle takes hold, and I'm struggling because I'm about to come myself. I can barely control myself because this girl is driving my dick mental.

I need her. Like the air in my lungs.

Everything around us becomes a blur, as if we're cocooned in our own quantum tunnel where nothing else matters but us.

"I'm gonna come," she whispers as I fuck her with my fingers much quicker now, causing a shiver of excitement to run up my spine and my cock to pound harder in my boxers.

"Oh, fuck yeah, Bunny, come for me." Her juices flood my fingers, proving how much she's enjoying this. The way she's bucking her hips, desperate to come, makes me want to tease her longer. It's a fucking massive high knowing how much control you can have preventing someone from having an orgasm until they're begging and pleading with you. But I don't want to do that to Bunny tonight. Because she's the sweetest fucking thing I ever met, and I don't want to scare her off.

Not yet anyway.

Tonight, I want to play, and with her, playing is even sweeter.

"Yes," she agrees, bowing her back, pushing her ass into my throbbing cock.

Knowing she'd say anything at this point because she's a

woman on the edge, about to explode, I ask, "Tell me how good I make you feel."

"So good. Harder. Please." The way she begs for me to stuff her beautiful cunt with my fingers has me pumping them in and out and rubbing the palm of my hand against her clit even harder to the point of being brutal and punishing. But she loves it and wants more.

"Come for me. Now," I growl like an unhinged madman against her mouth.

She lays her hand over mine and pushes my hand against her pussy, tilting her hips, showing me how she likes it, digging her nails into my skin.

"Oh, I'm coming." She pushes her tongue through the seam of my mouth as she comes undone, coming around my fingers, soaking them with her orgasm that's dripping down my knuckles.

Thrashing her hips, she bites my lower lip, hard enough to draw blood as her orgasm hits her in wave after wave. The sharp, metallic tang of my own blood fills my mouth, but I don't care because it tells me this is real and it's happening and not just some stupid fantasy I dreamed up. This feels so surreal but it isn't, it's a living, breathing event, a timestamp in my life I will remember forever. A core memory of the time I met someone who shook me to my very being.

Our kisses become much slower, her grip on my hand loosening as seconds pass, her body going limp as if she's boneless, while her breathing steadies again.

"I came embarrassingly fast," she says shyly like it matters.

When none of it does. It's a bigger turn-on for me knowing what I do to her and that she trusted me to do that with me here tonight.

If she really knew how much of a jackass I can be, she would most likely tell me to fuck off. But here we are. In the dark. Like this. Two perfect strangers with no clue what we really are or what we will become.

It's as if I got a clean slate and the chance at a new beginning.

Shut up, Max. You sound like a hippy.

"I think your five minutes was up ten minutes ago." I drop a soft kiss on her bare shoulder. I'm so happy I convinced her to stay. Those little whimpers and moans of hers will be what I imagine in the shower tomorrow morning before work. Maybe after work too. Hell, every day.

"I'm staying," she says, sweetly.

You don't say.

11

PAIGE

Descending from my orgasm, the one where I saw stars behind my eyes and I possibly blacked out for a minute, I arch my neck to the side, letting the afterglow fill my body with joy as he kisses my shoulder, then my neck. It's soft and caring, romantic-like, and it's sort of throwing me for a loop.

This isn't something I usually do; let someone I don't know touch me. But tonight, it feels dangerously thrilling in all the right ways. Mr. Fox, the guy whose real name I don't even know, had me come in record time with just his fingers.

The darkness has unleashed something primal in me, sharpening every detail. Even though I can't see a thing, somehow the world seems brighter.

As he removes his fingers from my pussy, my inner walls spasm, little aftershocks jolting through my body, and I love the way he gave me the best orgasm I've ever experienced. I whimper at their loss, wishing we could do so much more together.

Gentlemanlike, he repositions my panties, making sure

they're in place, then removes his hands from under my dress, allowing the delicate fabric to fall to my knees again.

Unembarrassed, with my mask still firmly in place, I turn around to face him, the live sex show continuing to go on behind me. It might have ignited the flame that longed for him to touch me, but that doesn't interest me anymore; it's only him I want.

He leans forward, finding me in the dark.

What little light there is gives no fucks in giving me any clues about what he looks like. In fact, in this light, he doesn't look like a fox; he looks like Batman. Dark and mysterious and a huge brute of a man.

God, he's beautiful.

As is tonight. It's also scary because, after being closed off from men for so long, I'm leaning in, feeling the fear, and doing it anyway, because everything feels amazing with him.

I want more; I want all of him.

"I want to taste you," I confess.

"You've already tasted my lips, Bunny."

"That's not what I meant." I reach for the buckle of his belt as the sounds of people around us pant, sigh, moan, and groan, creating a cacophony of feminine and masculine grunts and whispered words of encouragement to chase their release.

Being oblivious as to what they are doing, hidden in the dark behind a veil of black, is heady and addictive. It's deliciously depraved, and I never want this experience to end.

He stops me from unbuckling his belt, making my heart stutter in my chest because he's had an erection since we started kissing, and I thought that this is what he wanted, what he needs. It's what I want to do, and it's not to thank him in return for giving me an amazing orgasm, it's because I actually enjoy giving blow jobs. Weird, perhaps, but it's the best feeling in the world knowing that you have control over someone else's pleasure. Just like he did with mine.

"You don't have to do that." His words are deliberate and measured, telling me he means it.

"But I want to."

He thinks for a moment before removing his hand, granting me permission.

I make light work of his belt, then his button and zipper of his pants, pushing them down his hips, along with his boxers, just enough to give me access, allowing his cock to spring free.

With his gaze fixed on me through the thick darkness, the sex show continues both in the looking box and all around us, and it gives me the confidence to lose myself in him knowing that no one is paying attention to us because they can't see anything we do.

I'm so turned on, I could easily come again.

And doing this with him, in such a public place, is pushing me outside my comfort zone, but, for some reason, I want to venture into the unknown and beyond, then do it all over again. He's potent and addictive in a way I can't even begin to explain.

He's like catnip for my pussy.

I lick my lips in anticipation. I'm desperate to taste his impressive cock I felt over his pants. Moving at speed, I drop to my knees before him and wrap my hand around his hard length, which is thick and warm in my palm. I rub my thumb over the head of his cock, pulling feral-like sounds from his chest. Slowly, I move my hand down his shaft, then begin stroking him back and forth, making more precum bead from his slit. I wish I could see him, see his cock and every other hard inch of his body.

As I lean in, my nerves and sense of anticipation run through me much quicker than they did before.

"Squeeze my cock." He lays his hand over mine to show me what he wants.

I do as he asks, and I can tell he's loving it already when he squeezes my hand firmly in approval. "Fuck, yeah, just like that." Moving my mouth closer to his tip, I smile to myself because the fake accent he put on earlier is long gone.

Together, we move our hands up and down his thick shaft. "Fuck, Bunny, yeah." He exhales sharply, his cock becoming harder with every downward stroke.

Releasing his grip around my hand, he lets me take control, and when I take the head of his cock into my mouth and taste him for the first time, he threads his hands into the hair at the back of my head, so tight, I almost freak out because I don't want my mask to slip off.

"Your mouth is like heaven's gate, Bunny."

Hearing the effect I have on him boosts my confidence, and I lick his head and lap at his slit, enjoying every moment. More precum leaks from him, and the salty taste makes my mouth water for more.

I keep my hands positioned firmly around his shaft, moving them up and down his cock in tandem as I pull him in and out of my mouth.

"Fuck, you're so good at that. I'm not gonna last," he grunts, thrusting his hips into my mouth, making his cock hit the back of my throat, causing my eyes to water.

I suck much harder this time, and he groans long and low in appreciation.

"Jesus, fuck," he cries out in a whispered curse.

Roughly, he places both of his hands on either side of my head, holding my mask firmly in place, and fucks my mouth, thrusting hard, bucking against my lips, showing me the pace he likes, and it sends heat between my legs, so much so I have to squeeze my thighs together to dull the ache.

I struggle to breathe around his length as drool spills from my lips because I can't swallow, but like a fucking champ, I tease the head of his cock with my tongue and take him deeper.

"Aw, fuck, baby." His fingers hold me in the position he likes, and he roughly fucks my mouth as he's on the verge of completely losing it.

I groan, my pussy pulsing, enjoying every hot goddam minute of what we are doing, and I gag when his relentless thrusts cause tears to leak from my eyes and run down my face, which I have no problem with. This is so hot, connecting us in a carnal way I never thought possible.

Hungry for more, I suck him until he's panting hard, and my jaw aches from his size.

And when I grab his heavy balls and roll them between my fingers, he fucks my mouth faster. His grip moves to my jaw, his fingers tightening around it, the slickness between my thighs evidence of how aroused I am. I moan in pleasure, letting him hear how much I am enjoying this, and reach up, pushing my hands under his shirt, then running my nails down his washboard stomach, causing his muscles to twitch beneath my fingertips.

I flick my tongue across his weeping head, and with his restraint long gone, I flatten my tongue to the underside of his cock and tug on his balls, hollow my cheeks and suck him until one of his hands drops to my shoulder and squeezes it as if telling me he's going to come and if I don't pull out now he's coming down my throat. But that's okay. I want the full experience.

With his other hand, his thumb moves back and forth slowly as he dusts my cheek, and it's such a gentle contrast to the power behind his thrusts as he fucks my mouth, making butterflies dance in my belly.

Another few strokes and it's not long before he's moaning louder, giving us away in the darkened room. On a deep guttural moan, in a rush, his hot cum hits my tongue as he spills himself into my mouth and loses all control.

And like the good bunny I am, I swallow every drop of him down, loving the taste of his sweetness mixed with saltiness that I want more of. It's so unexpected and thrilling. Everything about tonight is exhilarating.

His hips punch forward a couple more times, jerking the last of his release into my mouth, his grip easing on my shoulder, while his other hand continues to gently hold my jaw.

Removing his cock from my mouth, I drop a gentle kiss on his tip, making him spasm, and in a moment of tenderness, he strokes my hair, once, then twice.

"You just blew my mind, Bunny." He searches for my hand in the dark to help me to my feet.

"And you just blew in my mouth," I joke.

Before I'm fully upright, I pull his shirt up slightly, just enough for me to kiss his laddered abs. "You have a beautiful body." I want to see it.

"And you have a fucking wicked mouth that can do deplorable things. Your mouth shouldn't be legal." And yet, it is, if only he knew I'm a kick-ass lawyer who can outwit any defending counsel and can wipe the floor with whoever stands in my way with my words alone.

When I stand to my full height, he tucks himself into his boxers, then quickly sorts his pants out. In one swift move, he then takes my face in his hands and kisses me, deep and long.

When I open my eyes, I realize there are no lights on at all anymore. The show must have come to an end.

I tell him, "I want to get out of here."

For a moment, he doesn't say anything until he cuts through my wayward, tension-filled thoughts. The ones that had me assuming he didn't want to meet me outside of this room. "I know this breaks all the fucking rules, but can I meet you outside the club tonight, now? I want to spend more time with you and get to know you better."

Whispering, I reply without hesitation, "I'd love that."

"I need to find my brother and tell him I'm leaving."

Curiosity snakes up my spine, making me tense. There's something about that particular whisper I recognize, but as soon as I try to grasp what I heard, it disappears again. "You're here with your brother?" I ask.

"One of them, yeah. He has the same love heart sticker on his mask as mine to identify us for our employee we are here with. No sex with the boss. That's the rules."

"Right," I say, and my head tries to piece together the puzzle. He owns his own company with his brother.

I love an ambitious man and a family man. He's ticking all the boxes.

His voice is gentle yet commanding when he orders, "Wait for me. Outside." He's eager, I'll give him that. I understood him the first time though; he didn't need to repeat himself.

"I will," I assure him. I'm not running away like Cinderella.

I try looking through the dark and decide on the spot that I'm not going to look for Cat, otherwise I'll just embarrass myself if she's deep down and dirty with someone like I just was.

"My door number is twelve. I just need to grab my purse and cell phone." The soft tremble of nerves flourishes in my stomach again as I realize I'll finally get to see his face and meet him for real.

"If you run, I'll only find you," he says, the darkness and longing in his tone evident.

"The hunt is half the fun," I counter.

"Yeah, but you're far too tempting to let escape. Run if you want, Bunny, but it will only make me want you more."

Oh, I like this game. "You'd have to know who I am first before you find me."

"I plan to. Now scamper. I'll see you outside." He plants a soft, lingering kiss on my lips before he slaps my ass, making me yelp, and I giggle at the absurdity of my night.

Then he leaves through the dark to find his brother.

Excitement causes me to run, and I instantly regret it when I trip over something. "Sorry," I whisper through the dark to apologize to fellow darklings, which is what the voice-over lady called us.

I finally locate door twelve, and after thirty seconds in the holding room, the light turns on, indicating I can now remove my mask.

Looking at myself in the wall mirror, I almost scream in horror. I look... well... I have that just fucked look about me, and my mascara has run down my face. My lipstick's also long gone. Hell, I barely have a scrap of makeup on at all.

Running my finger under my eye to remove the worst of the mascara, I do my best to fix myself and try to make myself look halfway decent. Then I grab my purse from within the locker that automatically unlocks when the lights come on, before leaving the holding room.

Dashing down the corridor toward the exit, I look behind me, double-checking I haven't been spotted by Mr. Fox already.

I promised I would meet him outside, so that's what I'm doing, and I'm not sure how long it will take him to find his brother in that room.

Opening my purse, I pull out my cell phone to find I've missed several calls from the new sitter.

Mild panic and adrenaline take over, and I immediately hit the call button. "Paisley?"

"It's Alfie. I think he's got chicken pox. He's covered in spots. It's like they just appeared out of nowhere, and he keeps crying. His temperature is through the roof."

"I'll be right there." I start running, past the hostess guarding the door, and rapidly tell her I have to go as my baby is unwell and it's an emergency. Without question, she unlocks the door, tells me she'll sign me out when I frantically give her my name, and when she shouts at me about something, I don't hang around to ask her to repeat herself when I don't catch what she says as I step out into the night where I wave a taxi down within seconds.

"Where to, ma'am?"

I give him my home address. The place I should have been all along. When I look down at my phone again, I realize I'm still holding the black plastic mask. "Shit," I hiss under my breath. That must have been what the hostess was shouting at me about, but in my rush to get away, I ignored her.

Holding it out in front of me, I take a closer look, and suddenly, laughter bubbles up in my chest before it escapes. Self-conscious, I quickly cover my mouth so my driver doesn't hear me.

What a night. The mask is a bittersweet reminder of this evening's events.

All the joy that consumed me in the club dissipates into the air, leaving me with a sense of disappointment. How stupid of me to think I could let my hair down for the night when I have a sick baby to take care of.

If you run, I'll only find you.

Too bad, Mr. Fox. I can't afford to get caught in your trap because I have responsibilities, and tonight was highly irresponsible of me.

And just like that, the fun I had becomes a distant memory, floating off into the wind as if it never happened, and I drive away.

12

MAX

A glimpse of sweeping black silk and long blonde hair is all I see dashing out the main entrance of The Velvet Rooms.

Is that her? Bunny?

If that's her, she's a bit taller than I thought, and from what I can see, her curves are fucking perfect. She's wearing that silk dress like it's her second skin.

With desperation, I hastily walk toward the entrance, but before I think I'm in the clear to leave, the hostess at the door stops me in my tracks. Shit.

"Sorry, sir, everyone must sign out before they leave." She taps her long red nails against the screen of the electronic tablet sitting in a cradle in front of her, indicating where I should sign.

"Sure," I agree, even though my feet are itching to run outside and chase after the woman who rocked my world tonight.

"Name please?" She stares at her own screen.

"Max Hart."

She takes a moment to find my name. "You can sign your name now."

Using my pointer finger, I sign the screen. It's the worst signature I've ever seen and bears no resemblance to my actual penned signature I must write at least twenty-five times a day on legal documents.

"I hope you had a pleasant night, sir."

It was more than pleasant. All other dates are forgettable. "I have no complaints."

"Glad to hear it. If you ever consider becoming a member—"

I interject because my patience is wearing thin. "I've to apply on the website. Yeah, I know." Adding myself to that waiting list isn't something I'm remotely interested in anymore. "Now, if you excuse me, I have to go."

The hostess nods in acknowledgment, not offended by my abrupt words because I think she can sense that I'm in a rush. "Just your mask then please, sir, and you'll be free to leave." She makes a gimme gesture with her hand, beckoning me to pass her the disguise mask, which I gladly hand over.

Goodbye, Mr. Fox, it's time to be myself. A sudden thought hits me like an eighteen-wheeler truck. Hell, what if she doesn't like me?

Who am I kidding? Everyone loves me, except maybe Paige Bradshaw, because she thinks I'm a fucking asshole. That's what she called me on the phone the other day.

"Good night," I say in haste, pushing the door open and storming out into the night like I'm about to hunt something down. More like someone.

I hit the sidewalk and freeze, eyes darting left, right. Nothing. Where the hell is she?

I spin around, take a few steps one way, and then the other. No sign of her.

I look behind me, then across the damn street like she might materialize out of thin air.

She's not here.

My hands tear through my hair, gripping hard at the back of my neck. The pressure does nothing to stop the surge building in my chest.

"Fuck."

She's gone.

I spin back around and bang on the door with my fist. "Open up. I forgot something," I lie.

It automatically opens for me and, relieved that it worked, I race in to find the hostess again.

I'm out of breath now for no other reason than I'm exasperated. "Excuse me, miss, I know this isn't following protocol, but the woman who left just before me, did she say anything at all?"

"I can't discuss other patrons with you, sir."

"No?" I eye her suspiciously in a stare-off. "And what about now, Storm?" I pass her two Benjamins, calling her by the name on her badge.

She slides the two hundred dollars toward her before folding them and stuffing them between her deep cleavage. "Her kid had an emergency, and she left so fast, I had to sign her out."

"And her name would be?" I draw out my words slowly, even though I'm a man on the edge.

"I can't tell you that, sir."

"So, you have nothing to tell me?"

Storm smirks wickedly. "I can tell you only a few things. She was blonde, with the bluest of eyes, very pretty."

Fucking pointless. But she sounds beautiful.

"I advise you to fill out the Hook Me Up form we send tomorrow via email, sir. And if she does the same, then and only then will we connect you."

That's so disappointing; I wanted to know her name and see what she looks like now. Not tomorrow. Or a week from now.

Now. I'm not a patient man, and my patience is already on thin ice. "Okay. Thank you." I nod a farewell.

Just as I'm about to walk out of the door, Storm calls back to me. "There was one thing."

"What was that?" My chest fills with hope.

"She took a bunny mask by mistake."

That isn't helpful to me.

"Do people ever fill out the Hook Me Up form?" I ask reflexively.

"Yes. More often than you think."

Optimism stirs beneath my ribcage. "And if she does want that? What happens next?"

"Then, with permission from you both, we organize a date, either here or at a place of your choice."

"Until then, it's a waiting game?"

"Yes, sir."

This is bullshit. "Thank you for your time," I say, completely deflated.

I push open the door, then text my driver to come pick me up.

While I'm waiting, I stuff my hands into the pockets of my dress pants and look to the sky for some help. Fuck it. I'll never find her there.

She has a sick kid so I get why she fled.

But chase after her? I never do that.

And commitment? That's not for me.

I've built my world on focus, success and being the best, not distractions. I try to justify why I shouldn't care.

Never does my head turn or my heart beg.

I like being alone. I don't need her; I never did.

She's got a kid.

Fuck, that's a curveball right there.

And I sure as hell don't do kids. Never will.

That's a life I don't plan to sign up for. Diapers, school runs, coming second to someone else's past, and complicated relationships with ex-partners? Not me. Not ever.

That's not cold, that's me being honest with myself. I know what I want, and it's not built around someone else's family.

Nope. I don't need her...

Then why does it feel like I've already lost something I never even had?

13

MAX

"And that was five weeks ago?" Nathan asks about the night I attended the dating in the dark event at The Velvet Rooms.

"Yeah." Five long fucking weeks of not knowing.

"And you've not heard from her since, not a peep?" Cole asks again, even though he already knows the sequence of events.

I scratch my beard and stare at my three brothers sitting on the sofa across from my desk, like vultures from *The Jungle Book*, eager to pick every bone of my flesh for any piece of information.

"Yeah. Like magic, she was there one minute and the next, poof." I make fireworks gestures with my fingers, making them look like they are exploding. "Her kid got sick."

Eli gives me a hard stare. "But you hate kids."

"I don't hate kids," I admonish.

Eli scoffs and reminds me of what I said. "Okay, maybe that's a bit harsh. But what you did say to me when Juliette suggested having kids was that they weren't part of your plan, and that you didn't babysit but build empires and that you had rules. No commitment, no relationships, no mentioning forever."

Fuck, I sound like a jackass.

Nathan jumps in like he's the fucking king of memories. "You also said that you weren't the white-picket fence, settling-down type and had zero interest in playing daddy. And you said it was breaking one of your many stupid rules. Then there was the no chasing women, no falling in love and no dating single moms or something equally narrow-minded."

Fuck, I did say that.

Cole adds his two cents' worth. "Just yesterday I heard you talking to Louise about how kids bring chaos to people's lives, and strollers didn't look cool."

I hate that my brothers' minds are like steel traps, which often makes them seem like know-it-alls. I'm also uncomfortable with how easily my brothers rattle off the things I've said in the past and use them against me. Assholes.

"My kid's going to have a cool stroller. It comes with cup holders and all sorts of shit. It's like a fucking space machine." Grinning proudly, Nathan looks down at his phone, tapping at it to find what he is looking for, then shows Eli and Cole his screen before turning it to show me a photo of what looks like a fucking mantrap.

It's a stroller, but fuck to the no. That's not for me.

"Cool as hell." Nathan brims with pride, sounding lovestruck with a stroller.

My solid, steadfast brother is turning soft. Pussy-whipped motherfucker.

Lucky bastard, perhaps.

Strollers?

My body tenses involuntarily.

No thanks.

"And she still hasn't completed the Hook Me Up form The

Velvet Rooms sent out?" Cole asks, double-checking if anything has changed since he asked me the same damn thing he's been asking for weeks.

"No." My short word is firm and tense. If she had any intention of finding out who I was, she would have done it by now, surely. "Nothing." I side-eye my email inbox as if a new email from The Velvet Rooms is going to appear from my want alone magically.

Nathan stands up, already bored with this conversation. "I would forget her. Move on."

"Great advice, never thought about that," I reply dryly, flipping him the bird. We might be the best lawyers in the city, but as brothers, we behave like we did when we were kids: childish and ridiculously petty.

He straightens out his suit jacket and rebuttons it. "Why do you even care, anyway? You never get like this over a girl."

I want to tell him it's because something was different about her and for once I gave a damn. It was subtle, but deep. I was drawn to her, and now it seems as if I'm tethered to her by an invisible thread. I don't admit any of that to my brothers, though; instead, I hide my emotions to protect my dented ego and go with, "It was the best blow job of my life."

Cole and Eli both roll their eyes at the same time.

Nathan sounds annoyed when he says, "You're shallower than a shot glass."

"Five words," I say, counting my next words with my fingers. "One. Night. Stand. With Arianna."

"Hey, that was different and you know it." His retort is firm and final.

"Well, the girl I met felt different." I speak before I think, and it's too late.

Nathan grins wickedly like a conspirator, shifting his gaze from me to my brothers and back again.

I'm as obvious as a neon sign. My brothers know me, and they know I wouldn't be wasting energy over someone who never looked back if I didn't feel something. There is no explanation for wanting someone I don't even know the name of.

This is fucked up.

Nathan's brow lifts, a question there, before he pushes me. "So, it wasn't just about the blow job? You felt something for her."

"Shut up. Get out of my office," I bite back, exposing my truth, which only makes Nathan sit back down. The greedy bastard wants blood and the truth.

As the state's best personal injury lawyer, Nathan doesn't switch off at the courtroom door. He'll peel the truth out of you like it's crucial evidence.

He's right though, I did feel something; I still do, but what exactly? Recognition, an unspoken understanding, familiarity, a sync of energy? Hell no, that sounds far out, and a bit woo woo, and I don't believe in any of that universal manifestation shit. Fated mates? Nah, fuck that. But I can't deny the pull between us that happened and how I dropped my guard, even if it was just by a few inches.

Even in the dark, I felt seen, and since then I can't stop thinking about her. Her fragrance, voice, touch, and all those fucking whimpers and little moans of hers hit me harder than anyone before. Like a punch to the chest, she's consumed me for days and I can't shake her out of my system even if I wanted to.

"And you're sure it wasn't just because it was in the dark? While it sounds hot as fuck, I think maybe your judgment's been clouded and that's what is making this mysterious girl so attractive to you." Eli, our voice of reason and the most level-headed out of the four of us, tries to play devil's advocate.

"Maybe." I sound skeptical. There was more to it, I know there was.

Cole pulls out his phone and taps the screen at lightning speed. "So, what do we know about her? Let's make a list." My youngest brother is the picture of efficiency. He thinks it's because his star sign is Virgo. Fuck knows what that has to do with it, but if that's what he believes, then who am I to disagree with his beliefs?

That reminds me. "She has a tattoo of the Virgo constellation on her ankle because that's her star sign. It glows in the dark under UV lighting, and she said it looked different in daylight." Doubting if that was true, I looked it up online and discovered she wasn't lying. "She has a kid." I list the one thing I'm uncomfortable with, and yet that's still not stopping me from running a mile. "She celebrated her fortieth birthday last year, which makes us the same age."

Cole continues to take notes.

"She said she helps people to untie knots." I give him another thing to add.

Cole looks up from his phone, confusion wrinkling his brow. A similar look adorns Nathan's and Eli's faces.

"What?" I ask, not clued in to what they are clearly thinking.

"She's a divorce lawyer," Nathan states confidently.

I reject his suggestion and recoil immediately, too shocked to say anything other than a sharp, "No."

"Yes." Eli nods enthusiastically.

I press my lips together, unimpressed with their detective work.

"What else could she be then?" Nathan challenges me.

If Cole thinks he's great at making lists, I'm even better when I reel off a notepad's worth of occupations. "Yoga instructor, physiotherapist, masseuse, counselor, therapist, sailor."

"A sailor? Shut up," Eli scoffs, waving off my ridiculous suggestion.

I want her to be anything other than a fucking divorce lawyer because there's no way I managed to attract someone my age who does the same job. That's impossible.

"You don't fucking know that. She might own a boat." What a stupid thing for me to say. I continue with more suggestions. "A mountaineer, a rock-climbing instructor."

Nathan sighs. "Now you're just being ridiculous."

"Fuck." I scrub my palms over my face. "She said she was a desk worker." The likelihood of her being a divorce lawyer now seems extremely high. I wish I had figured that part out myself.

"Desk worker." Cole adds another thing to his list. "Could be a divorce lawyer." He talks out loud as he types. "What else?" He's fucking loving this. His analytical brain that pieces together evidence like Sherlock fucking Holmes astounds me sometimes.

I lean back in my chair and recall more details. "Blonde hair." It was silky and long. "The hostess at the club said she had blue eyes. She took a mask by mistake, and put down on your list that she had a kid. I called her Bunny; she called me Mr. Fox."

"This is great, we could write a fucking romance novel based on this shit," Cole says with a huge smile painted across his lips.

Why the hell I'm entertaining them is anyone's guess, but I need help if I want to uncover my secret stranger.

I ignore the amused looks from The Three Stooges and keep sharing more facts. "It was her first time at The Velvet Rooms. Her perfume was called Vanilla Sex by Tom Ford. After she told me the name of the perfume, she said it matched her sex life because she's been single for four years and abstinent for the same amount of time."

"Four years?" Eli asks, sounding shocked. "She's practically a virgin."

"You four neanderthals are disgusting." Paige Bradshaw's clipped tone pierces the air, bringing an end to our conversation.

14

MAX

Paige continues her verbal attack. "Do you not have anything better to do, like, oh, I don't know, work, defend people, and be out there saving the world instead of talking about virgins?"

Shit, she heard that. But how much did she hear before that? Hopefully, none of it.

"What are you four egos in suits talking about anyway?" Her eyes dart from me then to each of my brothers.

A quiet chuckle bubbles inside of me. Sometimes, just some-times—okay, maybe always—I fucking love that smart mouth of hers.

Shut up. No, you don't. She's the enemy and works for the competition.

"We are working on a case, if you must know, Ms. Bradshaw." Nathan stands up again to his full height and stares her down. "Hunter versus Hare. Have you heard of it?"

We all titter like naughty schoolboys at Nathan's quick-witted answer.

Paige shakes her head vehemently as if annoyed, her bun so tight and firm, not a hair is out of place or comes undone. In every way, Paige Bradshaw is unshakable, something I told my sexy stranger I was. It couldn't be further from the truth; since that night, I've been shook.

"No?" Nathan asks. "Well, I'm sorry, I can't tell you anything about it then, unless you accept the job offer I made you last month."

Nathan offered her a job? What the fuck? "I'm sorry, what?" This is the first time I've heard about this.

My eldest brother glares at me. "You know it makes sense, Max." He gestures to the air between us. "If you two co-counseled, you would be formidable."

"That's a terrible idea," I retort. "I'd rather eat broken glass."

"And I'd rather French kiss an alligator," Paige drawls, sounding bored with this conversation.

"Sounds kinky," Eli interjects. "Or is that code for something else?"

"What the fuck could that be code for?" I snap, biting Eli's head off.

"I don't know." He shrugs, not offended by my razor-edged question.

"I hate coming here." Paige sighs, walking to the sofa. "It's like stepping back in time into some bizarre Hart brother time zone where you all become ten years old again. Weirdos."

Why the hell is she sitting down?

"What star sign are you, Paige?" Cole asks out of the blue, throwing me sideways.

Without hesitation, she replies, "Virgo, why?" She reaches down to pull paperwork out of her workbag, and when she sits back up, she realizes we are all staring at her.

No fucking way.

Impossible.

A rush of adrenaline sets my chest aflame and my stomach

twists, but deep down, a strange fascination grows, pushing Cole to ask more. Instead, there's this long stretch of silence bouncing between us all.

"What did I say?" she asks.

In a low monotone chorus, we all reply at the same time, "Nothing."

Leaning forward, I drop my attention to her feet, trying to catch any small glimpse of a tattoo on her ankle, to be met with spiky black heeled ankle boots that would look sexy as fuck on anyone else but Paige.

I'm lying about the sexy part. Paige Bradshaw has this innocent, elegant look, like a swan gliding on still water. But get too close, and she's fierce as hell. Just like a swan, she'll bite you when you least expect it, and I secretly like that about her. Hell, part of me fucking loves it. And those boots would look better wrapped around my ears.

Never. Going. To. Happen.

Unfortunately for me, the length of her ankle boot covers the area where my bunny had a tattoo.

She can't be Bunny. Paige is the last person who would go to a sex club. Fierce, yes, but she's beautiful, sexy, and I can't imagine she's short of offers on the dating scene. Also, she doesn't have a kid, so there's no way it's her.

My shoulders relax with relief and my brothers notice my change in demeanor, as if they know I figured out it's not her. I subtly shake my head from side to side just to make sure they get the message.

Nathan throws me a wink and walks to the door, talking over his shoulder as he leaves. "Call me if you change your mind about the position here, Paige. Or inform Max."

"I'm good. Thanks, though." She's quick to reply.

I hope she doesn't change her mind.

"And remember, your last fitting for your tuxedo is next week. That applies to all of you," Nathan shouts back over his shoulder, reminding us of our best man duties.

We had his bachelor party two weeks ago. It was the first time I've ever seen Nathan drunk to the point he couldn't string a sentence together. I will continue to applaud Cole's idea to have Nathan take a shot every time he mentioned Arianna's name. Fucking idiot should have known better.

"Right, I gotta go." Cole rakes his fingers through his hair before removing himself from my office sofa. "I'm off to inform a family that their father bought hundreds of properties behind their backs and unfortunately didn't leave a will to decide who gets what."

"Sounds like fun," I say dryly.

Cole loves the complex stuff. "It is. The ranch next to Mom and Dad's is one of those properties." He's by my office door in two long strides.

I blow a descending whistle. "That's got to be worth at least three million."

"He owns numerous ranches, plus commercial and residential properties throughout the state."

Paige inserts herself into the conversation. "Lucky family."

"They will be if they agree to my proposal," Cole agrees.

She asks, genuinely interested, "Will it go to court?"

"Most likely." Cole taps the doorjamb before pointing at me. "Meet you later for dinner."

I nod, confirming I'll meet him at Taboo, a new place in town that's just opened.

"Paige, a pleasure as always," Cole lies, and I almost burst out laughing because that woman scares my brother shitless. She scares most men, if I'm being honest.

Eli is the last to leave, but before he exits my office, I ask,

"How did it go with Rainbow Bright?" I can't remember her name, but I'm sure it sounded like a *My Little Pony* cartoon character that Louise's daughter brought into the office one day. She had multicolored hair just like it too.

"Rainbow Bright?" he asks, puzzled.

"The team-building woman," I clarify. "From a few weeks ago?"

"Oh, Sapphire."

I slap my desk, now remembering her name. "That was it. How did it go? Did she have good ideas?" We all want this year's staff conference to be better than last year's disaster. When emergency maintenance on the runway at the airport caused three of our speakers' flights to be canceled, we decided to use local speakers and event organizers going forward.

"I'm not sure her company is right for us," Eli informs me.

"Really?" The website and team-building activities they offer were the best when we compared them to three other local staffing event companies.

"I swear she'd been smoking pot or sniffing something." Eli's brows draw together. "Dinner was loud."

Paige clears her throat, then asks, "Is that Sapphire Feelgood?" Her curiosity hints at the fact that she knows who she is.

Eli nods, his brows dipping, making him look like he's in pain. "Yeah. Do you know her?"

"Yeah. And she's not high, that's just the way she is." Paige gifts us a rare smile, softening her usually stern features. She really is fucking beautiful when she loosens up.

Hell, where did that thought come from? That's not good.

Paige shares what she knows. "Her mom and dad met at Slab City, and I believe she grew up there for a while until they moved to San Francisco once Sapphire got a little older."

Slab City is the only place that self-polices itself in California. I admire the simplicity of their remote and off-grid lives they choose to live. It's not for me personally, but each to their own.

Paige beams, sounding in awe of her. "Sapphire is amazing."

"She never shuts up," Eli tells her, throwing me a quick glance. I know Sapphire has thrown him off balance.

Eli is usually outspoken, but from the sounds of it, it seems like Sapphire has got the upper hand and he's finally met his match.

"She sure does like to talk," Paige confirms in a way that tells me she's fangirling over her. "She hosted our staff conference last year, and it was the best one we ever had. Her keynote speech was"—Paige places her fingers on her mouth and kisses them—"Chef's kiss. She made me want to open my own law practice."

I pick up the pen sitting on my desk and start to doodle. "Do you still want to do that?" There's no real reason to ask, but I seem to have become a nosy bastard, and this is the most civil conversation we've had.

Her reply is heavy with melancholy. "Now is not the right time for me unfortunately. But one day. Maybe."

"Why is now not the right time?" She's single, no kids, free as a bird and she would get clients lining up asking her to represent them.

Nathan is right about one thing: We would be a powerhouse if we co-counseled. But she would much prefer to wrestle a porcupine by the sounds of it than work with me.

My usual magic charm doesn't work on her, and I hate how much I like that.

She's not just different, she plays an elite game in another league all together, one I am not worthy of in her eyes.

"I need the financial stability of a job at the moment." Blushing, she looks uncomfortable and quickly changes the subject.

"Anyway, I need to talk to you about something regarding the Young versus Young case. I was in the area and thought it would be easier to discuss it with you than over email."

From behind my desk, I nod once in reply and silently wave goodbye to Eli.

Just the two of us now, Paige begins to work through a list of terms I proposed for child custody.

"That's everything." Her eyes flit left and right from her notepad to the proposal in her hand once we are finished. "Thank you for seeing me at such short notice."

I respond with a quiet nod, completely speechless that she sounded sincere. Usually, she thanks me then makes a cutting remark to try and undermine my confidence.

Her cell phone pings with a message, and as soon as she reads it, her face turns a paler shade of white.

Whatever has happened, it doesn't look good. "Everything okay?"

"I have to go. That's my nan— nana."

What was she about to say?

"Is she unwell?" I ask.

She continues to stare at her phone, then looks up at me, her eyes slightly glazed and panicked.

I'm on my feet and kneeling in front of her before she can blink. I glance downward for a brief moment and catch a glimpse of a faint tattoo on her ankle just below the low rim of her boot.

What the hell? No way.

Fuck.

Fuck.

Fuck.

Also, not now; Paige needs you, Max.

Focus.

"What's happened? Is everything okay?" I ask again, concerned as my brain goes into overtime.

Shaking her head, she waves me off, dismissing me. "Nothing. It's nothing." She wipes a quick tear away, her eyes becoming bloodshot as she tries to hold back her emotion.

"Paige." I say her name more firmly to bring her out of her momentary glitch.

"I have to go." She lays the palm of her hand on her forehead as if being hit by a sudden thought. "Shit, I walked here because my car's still in the garage."

I catch another look at that tattoo hiding beneath her leather boot.

What the fuck?

"Wherever you need to go, I'll take you there." I'm desperate to find out what's happened to someone she clearly cares about and spend time with her.

And ask her if she's Bunny? Along with another million other questions.

If she's Bunny... then... what?

I don't know, but I'm desperate to find out.

Surprisingly, Paige doesn't fight me; instead, she agrees to let me drive her, and within minutes we're in my car.

15

PAIGE

In silence, Max is driving me to my house because I don't have a car and Marin's here.

When she should be in Las Vegas.

Instead, she's here in San Francisco.

Standing outside my gated house and reading the riot act through the security camera on my phone app.

If anyone is going to start a riot, it will be me.

How dare she show up unannounced, demanding to see me when she hasn't even bothered to ask how Alfie is in over six months.

The only time she has contacted me by text was to ask for money.

For months, I've ignored her requests. For months, I've secretly prayed that all she ever asks for is money because losing Alfie will destroy me.

And her being here now can only mean one of two things. She's either here to ask for money, because that's what she does when she's desperate, or she's here to take Alfie back.

My stomach rolls, and I place my hand over it. "I feel like I'm going to throw up." If Marin wants Alfie, she'll have to get through me first. She doesn't have a permanent home to keep him safe, nor money to feed or even clothe him.

"Do you need me to stop?" Max asks, sounding concerned and showing a caring side to him I didn't think he was capable of.

"No. Thank you. I just want to go home, as quickly as possible, please." My voice is weak and small, uncertain even. I don't know what I'm about to come face-to-face with when I arrive at my house, and the last thing I want to do is discuss it with Max Hart.

Max and I don't engage in idle chitchat. Never. When we work on divorce cases, we are either professionally civil in front of our clients or clashing behind their backs. There is no in between. Any contact between us is minimal, mainly to protect our sanity.

Unbeknownst to him, I hate every minute of being in his car because it means I'm opening the door and dragging him into my personal life. But that's okay; I'll just tell him to drop me off and leave. There's no reason for him to stay.

Only my close friends know about Marin and when I told Emma, my nanny, about the circumstances around Alfie being my nephew and not my own baby, it made me feel exposed and vulnerable. I didn't want anyone to know that my sister had abandoned her own son, and I feared being judged by association. I'm still not sure who I was trying to protect: myself, my sister, or maybe both of us. Maybe it was just embarrassment.

But now, I'm thankful I had the foresight to prepare her for the tornado that is Marin. Thankfully, Emma is sharp and resourceful. As soon as she saw my sister on the security cameras I installed shortly after Marin left Alfie on my doorstep, she messaged me immediately and refused her entry.

My house is impenetrable, and there is no chance of Marin climbing the new ten-foot iron gate I installed at the same time as the security cameras anyway, because she looks like skin and bone with not a thing about her suggesting strength to scale my fortress.

"You know you can talk to me, Paige, and tell me anything." Max offers himself up as a sounding board. "You know me, and anything you say won't go outside of this car. I promise."

"Thanks," I reply quietly, understanding his need to be curious, but I value discretion when it comes to my personal affairs, and while I trust Max, I'm not ready to divulge anything. Not unless I have to.

"I'm right here if you need to talk."

I close my phone quietly and return it to my workbag.

I have a camera installed at the bottom of my driveway, covering the entrance to the house, and watching my sister screaming and shouting at the camera gives me anxiety. She's relentless, and she's making my heart race faster than a racehorse.

I sigh, laying my head back against the headrest of Max's limited edition Ford GT that most likely cost the same as my house, and stare out into the distance, watching the traffic pass by in a blur.

"You shouldn't be taking me home, Max."

"Why not?"

"Because we are representing opposing sides, husband and wife, Tate and Stella Young, and we shouldn't be spending any time together socially during an active case. It's unethical and a serious conflict of interest."

Max ignores me and proceeds to make a call. He's a law unto himself sometimes, carving his own path and making his own rules.

"Hey, Max." A female's voice floats through the in-car speakers.

I roll my eyes. He's most likely organizing a booty call for the night. Talk about inappropriate timing.

"Hey, Stella, how are you?"

Oh, I was wrong; he called Stella Young, and now I feel like an idiot for assuming the worst.

"I'm good. Any updates on the child custody proposal?"

"Yes. And it's all very positive. Ms. Bradshaw and Mr. Young are happy with the terms we sent."

Max turns right where I point for him to do so.

"That's great." She sighs with relief. "I just want this to be over."

"It will be soon. Don't worry, Stella." He clears his throat confidently as he drives down the winding streets toward my neighborhood. "I'm calling for a reason. I just wanted to let you know I'm currently in the car with Ms. Bradshaw. She had a family emergency during our meeting to discuss your child custody proposal. Her car is still in the garage, and I'm taking her home. Full disclosure, I wanted you to know. We haven't discussed your case outside of the office, we're not socializing, and I am loyal to you. I promise there is no wrongdoing. Do you trust me?" Max looks my way and offers a gentle smile. It's warm and stirs something inside me that feels similar to how I felt the night at The Velvet Rooms when I shared a kiss, and did so much more with someone I barely knew.

"Max." Stella almost laughs down the speaker. "Of course I trust you, and please pass on my regards to Ms. Bradshaw. I hope everything is okay."

"She's listening right now."

"Thank you, Mrs. Young." I pick at my nails, nervous about

how close we are to my house now. I'm not ready to face Marin, but I have no choice.

"Oh, please call me Stella."

"Thanks, Stella."

"Speak to you tomorrow, Stella." Max rounds up the call and hangs up when she says goodbye.

"That was easy." He pushes his car a bit harder, making the engine sound like it's snarling, with the high-pitched, sharp turbo whooshing during acceleration that sounds more like a scream than a roar.

"Thank you for the lift and for calling Stella. I appreciate it more than you know." He saved my ass and my job. Unless the case is settled or closed, it's against the rules for us to meet outside a professional setting, and I will need to call Tate and explain the same thing to him that Max just told Stella. I'll do that later.

First, I need to deal with my unruly sister.

I'm ready to talk now. "I have something to tell you." I may as well prepare Max for what's around the corner.

"Is this about the screaming woman on your screen who looked like she was about to pop a vein in her neck?" Ah, so he did notice. Great.

"Yes. That's my sister," I finally admit.

He sounds surprised when he asks, "You have a sister?"

"Yeah."

"I didn't know that."

"Not many people do," I tell him, trying to sound chipper, but inside I'm dreading seeing her for the first time in years. She didn't even have the decency to say hello, or even explain herself when she left Alfie on my doorstep.

"Is there a reason for that?"

"She has problems." It's weird how two people can be

created from the same couple and yet be so very different. "Addiction," I say non-specifically.

"I'm sorry to hear that."

"So am I. My poor parents gave up on her a long time ago." As did I.

"Are your parents nearby?" he asks, using this moment of forced closeness as a chance to ask me everything. I don't usually talk about my life, ever. But oddly, there's a sense of relief in opening up to someone who doesn't really know me. It feels safer, somehow, and I find myself appreciating how kind he's being, even though I'm often on edge around him: sharp, guarded, maybe even a little cruel. But to be fair, I give back exactly what he gives me, so I can't really blame him for how things have been between us.

"They live at an independent living community not far from here. They visit me when they can, and I visit them on the weekends with Alfie, her son, who they adore. Oh, if you slow down here," I tell Max. "My neighborhood is third right, and my house is the one with the wailing banshee outside of it, about halfway down on the left."

My description of my sister makes him laugh and for the next few minutes, we cruise in comfortable silence until we finally arrive outside my house in front of the gates that are doing their job of keeping Marin out of my house and away from Alfie.

"Is there anything I should know before I get out of this car?" He unlocks the doors of his fancy car while I have a stare-off through the windshield with my sister who looks madder than a chef with a broken stove.

"She's mean, has a real sting in her tail, and is permanently angry with the world."

"Just like you sometimes then?"

Smiling nervously, I run my clammy palms down the fabric of my skirt. This is not the time for jokes, but I appreciate his effort to lighten my heavy mood. "You never give up, do you?"

"I'm just fucking with you, and you're too easy sometimes."

He's right; I play right into his hands often.

It's not like Marin can hear us, but he drops his voice anyway. "You don't look like her if that's any consolation."

"That's because she doesn't even look like herself." Not anymore. Marin was once a beautiful woman, curves in all the right places with the rosiest of cheeks, which Alfie has inherited. But now she's a shadow of her former self, skin and bone and in need of a good hearty meal. She also used to look well put together, but now she looks dreadful, terrifying even. There's no other word for it.

Marin storms over to Max's low car and lays her hands on the hood, staring at us in challenge. Nostrils flared, skin flushed, jaw taut, she looks wilder than a bull that's seen a red flag.

"She's seething and I don't know what she will do to your car." I don't trust her. She's disrespectful with other people's belongings, and every day she wakes up in fight mode. In another life I hope she finds peace because she sure as hell never found it in this lifetime.

"It's just a car, Paige. It's easily replaceable and fixable. What's her name? I'll talk to her before you get out of the car."

"You don't need to do that. I'm a big girl, Max." I don't need saving.

"It's not up for debate. I'm telling you, not asking. Stay in the car." He presses the power button off, killing the noisy engine. "I still do a lot of pro bono work in my free time. Trust me, I've dealt with worse characters than your sister in the middle of the night."

I can't believe he still offers free legal services. Now that I have Alfie, callouts in the middle of the night are just a distant memory, but I would love to help individuals avoid harsh penalties, jail time, or get into diversion programs. Divorce might be my and Max's specialty, but it doesn't mean we can't help people who need us the most.

Whoever ends up with Max as their supporting counsel should feel like they struck gold. He might be my nemesis, but he's a brilliant lawyer.

This new side I'm seeing of Max today is completely unfamiliar to me. I never imagined he was capable of being compassionate. Maybe I never allowed myself to see it because I never truly gave him a chance. I know he comes from a wonderful family. I've met his mother many times, and even his father before he became ill, so it makes me wonder why I didn't believe Max could be just as good as they are. Now I can't understand why I never gave him a fair chance in the first place, or how we even ended up as enemies.

"Her name is Marin, but you can go, Max. I'll be fine." I'm a bag of nerves but I don't want him to know that as I reach for my workbag.

He stops me from making my move, wrapping his fingers around my wrist. It's the first time he's ever touched me, and I'm not shaking him off for reasons I can't explain. "Sorry." He removes his hand when he realizes what he did. "I'm not leaving you with her. She looks like she's eating bullets and about to fire them out of her mouth in your direction." He scratches the rough scruff on his face with his other hand, something he does often. "Now, do as you're told and sit tight until I tell you to leave the car."

"Okay." I'm never this agreeable, but dealing with Marin by myself can be overwhelming; Max can be my buffer.

"Good girl." Max winks at me, in that pantie-melting way

only he can pull off. He's devilishly handsome and that grin of his always looks dirtier than it should. Or perhaps that's my crazy brain making observations it shouldn't be.

He opens his door and is out of the car before I can make any further arguments to stop him.

"Hey, Marin." He greets her casually like she's his long-lost friend. "How are you?" He shuts the door, muffling Marin's salty response.

"Who the fuck are you?" She spits venom his way with such force, eyeing him suspiciously, narrowing her eyes, watching him, then studying me before taking her hands off Max's supercar and standing to her full height.

Marin doesn't live in the real world. Not that Max's car is anything close to normal, but Marin lives paycheck to paycheck and can barely get by. There's no way she could ever understand or appreciate the cost of his sports car. Max comes from serious wealth. Old money, and it shows in every part of his life. Penthouses, sports cars, yachts. He and his brothers don't just have one of each; they own several between them. Their lifestyle is as unfamiliar to me as it is to Marin, but at least I understand how they operate. She doesn't.

My sister and I couldn't be more different. That's been obvious since she became a teenager. While I stayed in and studied, Marin was out partying, never caring about curfews or rules. She's been testing our parents' patience since she was old enough to talk back. I never did. I had too much respect for them, and I knew exactly what they gave up to put me through law school.

That's why I keep people at arm's length when it comes to my personal life. In my career, I know what I'm doing. I'm confident and in control. But personally, it always feels like I'm walking through a minefield. And Marin? She's the biggest challenge of all.

Right now, she's challenging Max.

"I'm Max," I hear him tell her through the glass and metal barrier. "Paige's friend."

"Boyfriend, you mean," Marin snaps back, hackles up, ready to go to war. "Landed herself a rich prick in a suit."

He denies her accusation with a subtle gesture, holding his hands up. "No. I work with Paige, that's all. We just want to talk but I won't let Paige get out of the car unless you give me your guarantee you will be civil to your sister."

"What are you, her bodyguard or something?" She wipes her nose with the back of her hand then scratches at her arm. Three rounds in rehab and not one of them worked. I saw what she was like the last time she entered rehab. It wasn't pretty, and the way she clawed at her skin is reminiscent of the way she's behaving right now.

"I'm your sister's friend, that's all," Max assures her.

More like his frenemy, but I'll take whatever he'll give me today because dealing with Marin by myself is wearying. I'm trying to keep my head above water, but I'm tired and feel like all my stuffing has been punched out of me.

I'm not just running on fumes; my tank is empty.

"I'll play nice." Marin's hand movements are agitated; she's a far cry from the driven and dedicated teenager who once dreamed of being a dancer on Broadway. That all changed during the summer before she was supposed to attend the School of Theatre and Dance, but she never even made it to her first day. Yes, she still dances because, boy, can she dance, but her dream of becoming a superstar is long gone. Instead, she dances for unmentionables in a strip club, who take advantage of her, use her like a toy, and then discard her once they get what they want.

Max does a gimme gesture with his hand, telling me it's safe to join them.

I inhale a deep breath, put on my brave pants, and get out of the car, putting up my lawyer shield to protect me from her unjustified wrath.

"How have you been, Marin?" I ask, my voice devoid of emotion as I close the car door. If only I could run to her and throw my arms around her, but Marin doesn't do emotional reunions and hugs aren't her thing.

She ignores my question and asks me her own. "When the fuck did you get these?" She points to the gates with her finger.

"Not long after you left your son on my front porch." I fold my arms across my chest, feeling like I want to punch something as rage weaves through my bloodstream. In her current state, she's not fit to be a mother. "He was six months old, Marin. You left your own son outside, alone, without knowing if I was even home." I still can't believe she did that, and I see the confusion in Max's eyes as he tries to understand that horrific information.

Marin's downturned mouth is full of arrogance as she mirrors my stance, folding her arms across her front before popping a hip. Her next question makes my spine bristle. "How is the rugrat?"

"His name is Alfie and he's thriving." Cute as hell, and the love of my life. "Do you want to see him?"

"Nah, I'm good." She shrugs, moving from one foot to the other, hopping about like the asphalt is much too hot for her to stand on in her thin-soled tennis shoes.

God give me strength. She's so nonchalant and dismissive of Alfie's existence, but I'm glad she doesn't want to see him because it means I still have all the evidence I need to support the adoption, and it's stronger than ever.

"I'm adopting him." I know she won't put up a fight. Taking responsibility for her actions has never been one of her strengths.

She claps her hands mockingly. "Good for you. Paige the do-gooder."

There's something in her coldness that cuts deeper than anger ever could. I can't make sense of how easily she brushes off anything to do with Alfie. I'm no do-gooder, I'm doing what's right.

"Can I ask you who Alfie's father is?" I've never asked her before, couldn't find it within me to go there, but with Max standing on the other side of her, as if we are two bookends with her in the middle, I find the confidence to finally push for an answer. Catching her off guard when she's least expecting it might work in my favor.

"Some rich judge fucker from Pacific Heights. Geoff Holmes?" she replies straight off the bat.

Christ, she doesn't even know his name, but I do. "It's Griffin Holmes," I tell her, unable to look Max in the eyes because he knows exactly who Griffin is. Everyone does.

He's a superior court judge and holds the highest-paid judicial position in San Francisco.

"Was he a client at Caspers, the place you worked at before you relocated to Las Vegas?" I hate exposing her true profession to Max this way. Everyone knows Caspers is a strip club, and I'm loath to ask about Griffin as he's someone I respected and held in high regard. Now I'm not sure who the hell to trust anymore. Griffin's wife is the sweetest woman I've ever met. How could he do that to her? What a cheating prick.

When Marin still lived here, she worked in that seedy strip

club, more like a brothel, in one of the worst areas in the city. I can only assume that's how she met Griffin. She was beautiful once, and I can see how he would be attracted to Marin, but selling her body for drugs has come at a cost, and she now looks twenty years older than her thirty-five years. I can't even begin to imagine what type of place she works at in Las Vegas.

Shaking and jittery, she struggles to stand still, her eyes darting everywhere like she's a rabbit caught in the headlights before she replies, "Yeah, he was a client. He told me to fuck off when I told him I was pregnant with his baby. And when I threatened to rat him out to his wife, he just laughed in my face and told me he had ways of making me disappear."

This is the most she's ever told me, and I have to stop myself from asking more questions, which I have a million of. I know it's pointless to ask her anything else because she often lies to get what she wants, and she could be lying about Griffin too. Only a DNA test would prove it.

"Are you taking note?" I look to Max to make sure he's listening and I have a witness.

"Heard every word," he confirms. I'm grateful he's here today. As luck would have it, fate is apparently on my side. I'm thanking the stars.

I'll continue to make sure that little boy is provided for. I don't need Judge Griffin Holmes' support, but knowing who Alfie's father might be could work to my advantage if the adoption faces any hiccups.

"What happened to Las Vegas?" Why is she back?

"I'm done with Vegas. Too hot."

More like she's broke and too stubborn to admit it.

"Have you been to visit Mom and Dad?"

She turns her body away from me, and I know she hasn't. Marin is the queen of avoidance.

"I'll let them know you were here," I tell her, already picturing the sadness in their eyes when I mention she visited me today.

"Let's not pretend they care, Paige." She fake-laughs, making her sound like she's demented.

They care deeply about her, but the hurt she caused after her last failed attempt at rehab broke them and nearly bankrupted them as well. That's when they decided to sell our family home and move into a retirement complex. It's the best decision they ever made, and now they have an incredible social life that even I envy. The plus side is that Marin can't access the complex without permission, which keeps my parents safe and Marin away forever.

I cut to the chase. "Is it money you're after? Is that why you're here?"

She doesn't even take the time to reply, as if she already had it scripted. "It's just a little, enough to help me get back on my feet, you know?" Marin says quickly, her words tumbling over each other. She pinches her fingers together, leaving a narrow inch of space, like she's measuring something delicate or harmless when she's the most toxic and harmful person I know. "I'm not asking for much, really. Just a bit to tide me over. I've got this new place I'm moving into, and I'm short on the rent, but a couple of friends are gonna come through, they just haven't yet. Should be any day now."

She shifts from foot to foot as she talks, her eyes flicking between me and the ground. Marin has never been shy about asking for money, especially not from me, and it doesn't seem to faze her that I've already given her thousands, but today she seems different. Worse. Embarrassed.

"How much?" Max beats me to the question.

"Five." She bites her lip before finishing her sentence. "Thousand."

"Five thousand?" I gasp, completely taken aback that she thinks I don't have bills, a nanny and a child to pay for.

She knows I have the money, because I'm one of the top-paid senior divorce attorneys in the city, or she wouldn't be here. While part of me wants to give her the money, I don't see why I should. I'm not working my ass off for her to blow it all on... well, I can only imagine.

"It's like a drop in the ocean for you, Paige. You can more than afford it. How much was that get-up you're wearing? Those boots alone probably cost a thousand bucks."

I'm seething now. How fucking dare she question what I spend my hard-earned money on? But I don't let her see or hear how annoyed I am. "At least the way I earn my living is legal and above board." Shit, I shouldn't have said that; it's a low blow, even for me.

Max breaks the standoff I'm having with my sister. "You're not getting five thousand, but I'll give you..." He pulls his wallet out of his back pocket of his dress pants and proceeds to count out three thousand dollars.

Who the hell has that kind of money in their back pocket? That's insane and is probably more like pocket change to Mr. Moneybags.

"No." I step forward to stop him as Marin rushes over to him and tries to snatch it out of his hands, but Max pulls it back from her. "What are you doing?" I ask, anger climbing my throat, making my voice sound strained and gravelly.

"You only get this on one condition." Max addresses Marin, ignoring me completely.

"I can't make any promises," Marin snarks back, placing her hands on her hips.

"Well, tough shit, that's the deal."

"What do I have to promise?"

"When you visit the next time, it's for one reason only."

"Oh, yeah, what's the reason?" She sounds like a brat.

Max responds without hesitation. "To get help. Proper help. Not some halfhearted promises to try rehab. If you show your face here again, it's to get clean. Properly. Once and for all."

"I've already tried that. Three times," she screams at him in frustration. The tendons in her thin neck bulge out, and she flashes him her crooked, broken teeth that make me wince. Her thick hair is long gone, replaced with wispy blonde strands that look like they haven't been washed in weeks.

All I want to do is run to her, comfort her, tell her I still love her even after she sold Mom's engagement ring, and that I forgive her. I want to help even when I know she doesn't want it.

If I invited her into my home, offered her a shower, she'd refuse to come into my house anyway, which is probably just as well. If it's not glued down or fixed to a wall, then Marin will swipe whatever she can get her hands on to pawn.

I lost my sister to addiction, and I hate that for all of us. Especially Marin, because living the way she is isn't living; it's surviving at best.

Max stares her down, which I've seen him do numerous times before in court and to me specifically. He's so bold and masculine, sexy.

Hell, no, now is not the time for those thoughts, Paige.

But there is something about the way he's leading this conversation that makes me want to jump his gorgeous bones and kiss that perfect cupid's bow of his.

What the hell is wrong with me?

Down, girl.

Max holds firm, locking his eyes with Marin until she finally agrees. "Okay. I promise never to come back."

Her words make my already broken heart shatter into pieces.

Marin has no intention of accepting help, not from me, not from our parents, and not from any rehab facility. What remains of her now are just memories of us playing in the treehouse Dad built in the big oak at the edge of our backyard. I still believe the sister I knew, the one who was kind and full of heart, is in there somewhere. But she's buried so deep that without Marin's permission to bring her back, it feels like a hope I have no right to hold on to.

Faster than a firefly's flicker, Marin tries to snatch the three thousand bucks she doesn't respect from his grasp yet again, looking happier than a Cheshire cat.

"Not so fast." Max stuffs the money back into his wallet. "You'll get the money for the rent but I'll pay your landlord directly."

"That's not fair." She wails like a baby. "You changed the rules."

He ignores her tantrum and adds, "And if you give me your address, I will have provisions sent to your place once a week. But I'm not giving you any money to enable your habits."

Oh, he's good.

"No." She stamps her foot against the ground.

"What's your address?" Max asks, unfazed by her brat-like attempts to get her own way as he pulls his phone out of the top pocket of his suit jacket, ready to take notes.

"I'm not giving you it."

"It's that or nothing." He's so cool, calm, and collected, I'm in awe of the way he's dealing with her. Looking up from his phone, he has a stare-off with Marin, a battle of wills where there is only one winner. Him.

"Fine," she agrees eventually. She gives him her address, which is in one of the most run-down areas of the city.

I'll never disclose to my parents where she is staying; all they'll do is worry even more than they already do.

"Are we done?" she asks Max, looking displeased and pissed off that she didn't get her own way.

"Yes." Max nods in acknowledgment, closing his phone down and tucking it back inside his top pocket.

"Cheers for nothing, rich guy." With purpose, she storms away without a wave goodbye, ignoring I even exist, and begins walking back along the avenue, disappearing around the corner.

I sigh and hang my head in shame at her ungratefulness, whispering, "I'm so sorry. I will repay you the money."

"You don't need to do that." Max's voice moves closer to me. It's low, sounds familiar, but my brain is too tired to figure it out. "It's what friends do for each other. Consider it a gift."

Before I can stop them, tears spring from my eyes, and I begin to bawl, something I haven't done in years.

Keeping my head down, I cover my face with my hands and I wail for Marin, for Alfie, my parents, me. For Max's thoughtfulness and for what he just did for my sister.

I know she'll never change. I can't stop the sadness from overwhelming me, my shoulders bouncing up and down as I really let go.

"Let it all out." Warm, thick arms wrap themselves around me as I bury myself into Max's firm chest and I crumble in his arms. It hurts to breathe, hurts to think about where Marin will be this time next year. My baby sister is slowly killing herself and there are no laws I can press upon her to stop her from doing it.

With all his strength, Max holds me up, holding me against his giant frame. "I've got you, Paige. I've got you."

16

PAIGE

I'm relieved he's here because if he weren't, I know I'd be on the ground, broken and crumpled in a heap of grief and despair. I can feel the scream rising in my chest, but it chokes itself into sobs instead. He doesn't say much, but what he does say is soft and steady and it wraps around me like a warm blanket even as I tremble and shake and fall apart. He tells me he's not letting go and somehow, I believe him.

I hate that it's Max Hart holding me together. I hate it because he's just a colleague, and he's smug and frustrating and everything about him makes my skin itch with irritation, but right now, he's everything I need. I never wanted him to be the one I'd fall into, but here I am pressing my face into his chest and clinging so tightly to the front of his suit that my fingers ache. I sob like I did the day my grandmother died. Loud, raw, aching cries that pull from somewhere too deep to understand.

But this is worse. So much worse. I'm mourning my sister like she's already gone. Like she died. But she didn't. She's still here and that's what makes it so unbearable. She's breathing. Walking. Existing in the world. But she left me long before this moment. The sister I knew has been slipping away for years, and now with those final words, with that promise she gave Max, I know she's really gone. She meant every word. She's not coming back. She won't ask for help.

My tears soak the open neckline of his shirt. My chest heaves and I feel like I'm falling through space with nothing to grab but him. I don't want it to be him. I don't want to need him. But I bury myself in him anyway because I have no choice. He's the only thing holding me upright.

Silently, we stay like this, him and me on the street, outside the front of my house as I lament until I have no tears left to cry.

"Let's get you inside." Max finally breaks our stillness and kisses the top of my head. He must realize what he did when he goes stiller than a statue.

The way he's holding me, keeping me safe, is the best feeling in the world.

That night at The Velvet Rooms was the first time in years that I had felt the warmth of a man's touch, and now that I've experienced it, it's sparked a need within me to have that feeling again. I miss it. Crave it and want more of it. Need it like my lungs need oxygen. I feel like precious cargo in his arms, and I'm not sure I want to leave. And the kiss on my head? It was an accident, a spontaneous reaction. It meant nothing. But still, it was nice, and it serves as more proof that Max Hart isn't the big, insensitive brute I made him out to be in my mind.

"You smell nice." I inhale another whiff of his aftershave before arching my neck back and looking up at him. The notes remind me of the scent my date in the dark was wearing. Amber, black pepper; it's woodsy and citrusy.

Flashbacks of that night shutter through my mind like a cinematic carousel. The pieces unfolding, whizzing around, sliding together in fragments that don't make any sense.

There's no mistaking it; he smells like Mr. Fox.

It can't possibly be him.

He's the last person I would want it to be.

You're lying to yourself, Paige. Admit that you're attracted to him.

My inner hussy winks at me as any sensible reasoning I have left packs up and leaves, while the bad girl within gives me a virtual high five and is already picturing our wedding.

Max gazes down at me, our eyes locked in a quiet intensity.

He isn't just handsome, he's the kind of man who makes my brain pause, like time itself forgets to tick forward when he enters a room. He's intense, powerful, and ridiculously infuriating in equal measure, and he's more than just his looks. He carries himself with a weightless confidence only he's capable of. Even today he was unshakable.

My eyebrows dip as I recall it's the same word the mysterious Mr. Fox used to describe himself. This is getting out of hand and I'm being ridiculous. It's not him.

Although I could do with someone like him in my life. Someone calm and steadfast.

What the hell am I thinking? Stop it. Stop it. Stop it.

"You smell nice too," he counters, keeping his tone soft and low.

"It's called Vanilla Sex," I reveal. Maybe I'm testing my theory to see if he reacts.

Max's eyes twitch at the corners, highlighting the faint lines there. I'm not sure if what I said made his brows dip, but they do, low in confusion, maybe, or something close to concern, recognition perhaps. Whatever it is, I ignore it and shake my head at the absurdity of our conversation and my stupid thoughts, but I'm grateful for the move away from talking about Marin.

"My perfume name sounds better than my actual sex life. If I had to give that a name, it would be called non-existent." I try joking to lighten the tense atmosphere around us. Also, I didn't have sex with the guy from The Velvet Rooms, and it's partly true.

My run-in with Marin has definitely made me a bit of a blabbermouth. The last thing I want him to find out is how lacking my sex life is. Talking to Max about my sex life isn't just inappropriate; it's completely out of character. Sure, we play our little games, bantering with words like we always do, and we're good at it. We tease each other, push buttons, and wind each other up. And yes, we make assumptions. But we never get into the details. Not when it comes to our personal lives.

"I don't believe that for a minute. I bet guys are beating down your door, begging you to go out on a date with them."

"You'd be wrong about the beating down the door part." Cat tells me I'm too fussy. I think she's right and the only reason I managed to let myself go with a stranger was because I was in the dark and couldn't make any judgments about what he looked like.

I felt him, though. His broadness, how huge he was. Similar to Max's build now I come to think about it. And the things he said and the way he made me feel, he seemed perfect, which Max is not. Far from. He's a player. A Casanova in the flesh. Isn't he?

"Have they been beating down your new gate then?" he suggests.

"Not that either." Compelled, I rest my hand on his chest, my fingers grazing the soft hairs that are peeking out of his unbuttoned shirt. His pec flexes from my delicate touch. The athleticism in his body is admirable and he must spend hours in the gym defining his solid muscles. He feels a lot like... Mr.... *It's not him... Stop it.*

"How long has it been?" He goads me into sharing specifics about my sex life.

He doesn't seem surprised when I tell him, "Four years." I have no idea how we went from crying my eyes out to talking about my dead sex life. I think I should stop talking now. "Thank you for today." I realize Max is still holding on to me as I stare into his blue-gray eyes that feel warm and inviting instead of their usual "fuck off, Paige" look about them.

There's a shift in the air, something unexplainable that feels almost tangible as he lifts his hand and runs his fingers down my face, wiping away the last of my tears with the pad of his thumb. It's too much and yet not enough all at once. I could stay —I want to—but I need to break whatever this unexplainable energy that's whirling around us like a cyclone is. "I should go." Neither of us moves.

"I've never told you this before, but I think you're really beautiful."

My cheeks flush with heat from his weighted stare and unexpected compliment, my heart fluttering in my chest like a hummingbird.

He adds more heartfelt praise. "And you're the smartest woman I know. Just don't tell my mother I said that."

A nervous laugh breaks free from my lips. I hope he's not throwing words of admiration around like confetti because he thinks I'm desperate for sex and that I would ask him to tear off my clothes and beg him to break my dry spell. Surely not. I park that thought and convince myself that he's simply trying to make me feel better.

What Max doesn't know is that my secret tryst at The Velvet Rooms is enough to keep me going for another four years. It has to. Yes, more time with Mr. Fox would have been nice but I didn't fill out the Hook Me Up form the club sent me because Alfie needs me more than I need sex. Companionship would be nice though. Someone to share my nights with. Weekend walks would be great too, and sex would be a bonus—the icing on the cake—but an actual relationship? Let's just call it what it is and say there aren't many men out there looking for single women with a baby. I've accepted that. It is what it is.

"You have pretty lips, Paige."

I welcome that feeling of familiarity again, the one I thought I could touch earlier. It feels like a living, breathing thing, it's so real.

What is that?

"Nothing can happen between us, Max," I tell him when all I want to do is press my lips against his, to feel his lush lips on mine and experience what it's like to spend the night with the infamous Max Hart. To kill my curiosity. That's all.

"I know that, but it doesn't make me want you any less, Paige."

Under my hand, his heart beats strong and steady beneath the fabric of his dress shirt.

He wants me.

Don't fool yourself, Paige. The man's a walking horndog in heat. He wants every woman he lays eyes on.

I remove myself from his arms, my hand sliding down and off his hairy chest that's peeking through the open neckline of his unbuttoned shirt as I walk quickly toward his car to grab my workbag. I need to get out of here before I do something I'll regret, like lose my job, though I would never actually let that happen. I care too much about my career to risk it, and screwing Max Hart for one night of passion isn't worth it.

Although, maybe that already happened and I just don't know it.

Or maybe I'm wrong.

Stop confusing yourself. Move faster, Paige.

As I lift my bag off the floor of the car, the strong scent of his aftershave hits me all at once again as I dip my head inside the car. The strong waft of it invades my nostrils, sparking even more memories from that night in The Velvet Rooms.

My hand stills on the handle of my bag as I inhale another deep breath. It's not just similar to Mr. Fox's aftershave, it's the exact same scent.

Oh. My. Fucking. God.

I glance up through the windshield to find him looking straight at me while my brain works at double speed making a list of all the things Mr. Fox told me.

Has his own business. Desk job. Tick. Another tick.

Has a brother. Max has three. Tick.

Same age as me. Tick.

Unshakable. Confident. Tick. Tick.

I help people end things so they can start a new beginning. That's code for divorce lawyer, there's no question in my mind. Tick.

He said he'd been with more women than he'd care to admit and that he keeps things casual. Max is a walking red flag when it comes to relationships. Double tick.

Hairy chest. Tick. I'm looking at it right now with my own eyes, and I felt it too.

Six foot three. Tick.

Oh no. It can't be him. It just can't be.

I lift my bag off the floor, clumsily banging it against the seat and center console. Closing the door of the car much harder than I intended, I flee toward the security pad on the wall to gain access to my house as my mind begins to unravel, recalling every tiny detail from that night. My heartbeat kicks up a notch and shifts into overtime.

It can't be him. It can't be him. It just can't be him, I chant inwardly, keeping my head down, unable to make eye contact with him because his "you have pretty lips" and "you're beautiful" comments combined with all the facts I pieced together thirty seconds ago have me spiraling more than I appreciate. I rub my nose nervously and throw him a finger wave from over my shoulder. "I'll see you soon. And, eh, thanks for the, you know, ride, and giving Marin money."

It can't be him. It can't be him.

"Paige," he calls out to me.

My trembling fingers stop midair as I'm about to press the first digit of my security code. "Yeah?" My voice sounds three octaves higher than it was before.

"Do you have a tattoo on your ankle?"

Shit.

Shit.

Shit.

I hesitate. "Um..."

I don't get a chance to answer when he asks another question. "Have you ever been to The Velvet Rooms?"

Holy hell.

I clench my eyes shut, scrunch up my face, and lie through my teeth. "No. See you at the next meeting with the Youngs. And thanks again." My words come out in a rush, high-pitched and panicky. I need to get out of here. Stat.

Snapping my eyes open, I lunge for the security pad, jabbing at the numbers with a trembling hand, once, twice, each wrong code fueling the rising panic clawing up my throat. On the third attempt, the gates groan open, and I run out.

Relief crashes over me like a wave, but it doesn't slow me down. The sharp echo of my heels pounding against the asphalt is the only sound chasing me up the driveway; well, that and the chaotic storm of my thoughts.

I feel him watching. His gaze burns into my back as I get closer to home. I don't dare look back, not yet, but when I finally do, he's still there. Unmoving. Eyes narrowed. Hands buried in his pockets. Legs spread wide as if he owns the whole damn neighborhood.

He knows.

Yet another piece of the puzzle snaps into place. Nathan said he and his brothers were discussing a case, Hunter versus Hare. The fox and the bunny.

Mr. Fox is Max Hart.

And I'm the bunny that got caught in his trap.

17

MAX

Standing at the bottom of Paige's drive, I text my brother as the metal gates begin to close, stopping me from running after her. I want to chase after her, I do, because I have a billion facts I need to check, along with a billion questions I need answers to.

ME

Send me the list you made earlier.

COLE
Only if you ask nicely.

ME

Just send me the fucking list, I'm not in the mood.

It's her.
Bunny is Paige Bradshaw.
I know she is.
And she does have a kid. His name is Alfie. He's not hers but her sister's, and she's taking care of him for her while still holding down her job and working manic hours, all while her

sister does who knows what with who knows who. It's no wonder she's been late for meetings and looks like she hasn't had a decent night's sleep in months, because she hasn't.

My memory flips back to the email she sent me weeks ago as I stomp to my car and get in but don't start up the engine.

You know for someone who is supposed to be a well-connected insider, I'm surprised you don't know what has made me late for the last six months. I guess the secretaries don't tell you everything.

No, they don't, because they would have told me if they knew she had a baby.

Cole's note arrives, and I click accept to add it to my app and read down the list, my eyes and brain consuming every item.

Virgo constellation tattooed on her ankle because it's her star
sign. It glows in the dark under UV light, and she said it
looked different in daylight.
Forty.
Helps people to untie knots.
Could be a divorce lawyer.

My brothers worked it out before I did. She *is* a fucking divorce lawyer.

Desk worker.
Blonde.
Blue eyes.
Took a mask by mistake.
Has a kid.
Nicknamed Bunny.
Wears Vanilla Sex perfume by Tom Ford.

That last one stands out like a sore thumb. She's told me that twice now, and I don't think she even realized she did. Or maybe she did, and it was a test to see how I'd react. Does she know?

> Single for four years and abstinent for the same length of time.

She confirmed that again just minutes ago.

It's her!

While my fingers get busy and start scrolling down my contacts list on my cell phone, my mind gets to work trying to figure out what the hell I want to say when I text her.

I get straight to the point with an accusation.

ME

You lied to me.

PAIGE

I don't know what you're talking about.

ME

I'm not a fool and neither are you. You know exactly what I'm talking about. I know who you are. You were at The Velvet Rooms the same night I was.

PAIGE

Seriously, Max. I don't.

ME

Did something happen to Alfie that night? Was he sick?

My message changes from unread to read in a flash and as the minutes pass, she doesn't reply but my fingers are already typing another message.

ME

You can run but you can't hide forever.

I look up from my phone and stare through the bars of the metal gate at Paige's sleek, suburban home. With a frustrated sigh, I begin to doubt myself because maybe I got this all wrong. But I can't have done. There are too many similarities for it not to be true.

If it's not her, then... "Jesus Christ." I run my hand down my face, annoyed at myself because I told Paige Bradshaw I thought she was beautiful and that she had pretty lips, and then I asked her if she went to a sex club, which she's probably looking up right this very fucking minute and now knows I have.

Fuck. Shit. Fuck.

I slam the palm of my hand against my steering wheel and instantly regret it. "Sorry, baby, I didn't mean it." I rub the dashboard of my new car then pat it.

To hell with it, I admit defeat and press the start button to fire up the engine. One last glance at my phone before it connects to my car leaves me feeling hopeless, but when I shift my car into reverse, another text message arrives.

I brace myself for yet another push back from her, but a lazy smile shapes my lips as I read the preview once, then twice before opening the text to make sure my eyes aren't deceiving me.

PAIGE

The hunt is half the fun.

She quotes herself verbatim from our conversation in the dark at The Velvet Rooms.

It is her.

Game. Fucking. On.

Let the chase begin.

Until she puts a stop to the hunt.

> **PAIGE**
>
> But we are two opposing lawyers representing a couple and we work at different firms. It's not only unethical but unprofessional.

It's over before we've even began.

Pity. Paige Bradshaw, the ice queen, gave me the best blow job of my life and the way she came all over my fingers is a memory that has imprinted itself into my brain, and I think about it every morning I jerk off in the shower.

Our meetings will never be the same again. Hell, I'll never be able to look at her lips in the same way again, the very ones she wrapped around my cock and sucked me like she was the queen of fucking blow jobs.

I still can't believe it.

There was more to it than just the blow job; she made me feel. What exactly?

More. Everything.

Regardless of what she says, we're far from done. Not even close because in a few weeks, the Youngs' divorce will be finalized and then, little bunny, you better fucking have your sneakers ready, because I'm coming for you.

Although I don't think I can wait that long.

18

PAIGE

What made me send that text? I slide my cell phone into the pocket of my silk blouse, forcing the fabric to droop from the weight of it.

What on God's given Earth was I thinking?

It was a moment of insanity.

A glitch.

I can't take it back either; can't unsend or erase it.

He knows who I am.

I know who he is.

Not only did I suck the dick of a man I've loathed since the day I met him, but I liked it. Loved every hot minute.

This is terrible.

Possibly the worst thing to have ever happened to me professionally and personally.

It was good, though. Great.

He made me come so hard with just his fingers while I had my tongue shoved down his throat.

"Oh my God." I lay my hand over my chest where my heart is beating faster than a mariachi band beneath it.

"Everything okay?" Emma, my nanny, walks into the hall I haven't been able to move out of, looking concerned with a bright-faced Archie resting on her hip, his cheeks pink, and he's smiling with excitement to see me.

"Peachy." I feign happiness, shooting her a fake smile and waving at Alfie.

"I saw what happened on the camera. Who's the guy?" she asks.

"Work colleague." Six-three, blue-gray eyes I crave, and has an impressive dick, with great fingers and knows what to do with them. An involuntary burst of laughter breaks from my chest and I have to slap my hand over my mouth to stop it.

"Are you sure you're okay?" Emma eyes me suspiciously.

"I'm fine. I'll be fine. My sister, you know, she makes me crazy." I corkscrew my finger around in the air next to my temple. I feel unhinged. Delirious.

Why me? Why him?

Oblivious to the chaos zooming around my skull, Emma informs me, "She was outside for ages before you arrived, Paige. I'm so glad you had the gates in place to keep her out."

That's exactly why I had them installed in the first place. "We're safe. And you know what to do if she shows up again. You did the right thing messaging me." Unless Marin has a change of heart, she won't be back. And I'll be repaying every cent of Marin's rent and supplies Max said he would pay for. Nope, not happening. She's my responsibility.

"I saw you crying on the camera. I'm sorry she upset you."

Oh, great, Emma saw my breakdown on the app too.

What a day.

"I'll be okay," I say, checking myself out in the wall mirror and running my fingers under my eyes to wipe away my smudged mascara.

Marin will always be my sister, just not the one I grew up with. Addiction took her somewhere dark, a place I didn't follow her into. I'll never be okay with her choices, but I accepted the truth long ago. This is the path she's on, and I can't change it. I still love her. I just have to let go.

Besides, without her, there would be no Alfie, my delicious little pudding chops who brings me so much joy and love.

I turn on the balls of my feet and push my shoulders back. *Don't let anyone see you're struggling, Paige.* Shoulders back, tits out, chin up.

"Hey, baby. Wanna come to Momma?" I might be his aunt by blood, but I'll be his mom by heart and law soon enough. I do a grabby hands gesture, beckoning him to me.

Alfie extends his little arms to move into my embrace, and within seconds he's snuggling into my chest. "How has he been today?" I ask Emma.

"He's eaten lots and we've spent most of the day in the yard."

I plant soft kisses on top of his thick hair; there's so much of it. I need to take him for his first haircut soon.

"You should get an early night, you look tired today, Paige."

"I plan on having a hot bath then doing exactly that."

Emma waggles her finger at me. "Promise me once he goes down to sleep, you will do that."

"I promise." I roll my eyes at her bossiness. A glass of Chardonnay might also be on the menu; I need it after today's revelations. "You can go now, if you want, Emma." Coming home earlier than planned feels luxurious and a little reckless. Many of my colleagues do it, but it's not something I usually do. Having more time off is something I should do more of because I love nothing better than spending time with Alfie. He's already changed so much in a few months, and I'm missing out on the best part of his life. I can't afford not to work. Not only have I become used to the luxurious life and home I built for myself, but with Alfie in my life now, I have schools and college to plan and save for.

Emma hastily looks around for her bag, which she locates and scoops off the floor.

"I don't suppose you could take me to the garage in the morning to pick up my car? Please." It's been in three times in the past six months. If the dealership would admit there is a fault with it then I would be happy, but they're dragging their heels, and I might need to threaten taking legal action if they don't sort it out once and for all this time. It's only seven months old.

"No problem. What time?" Emma is a dream.

I look upward, mentally picturing my calendar. "I'm due in court at nine thirty, so eight? Would that work?"

"Perfect. I'll see you then."

"Thanks, Emma." I don't know what I would do without her. If only she did the housework too, she'd be the perfect woman. Looking after Alfie is a full-time job and it feels too much to ask her to do my laundry and clean as well. I'd pay her of course, but I much prefer her sticking to being the nanny, nurturing Alfie in the best ways possible.

I never did get around to hiring a housekeeper. I make another mental note to do that tomorrow after court and mark it as urgent.

"Have a great night. Bye, little man, see you tomorrow." Emma pinches Alfie's cheek, causing him to throw her a lazy smile, and he bops her on her nose with his pointer finger in an affectionate gesture. The two of them share a special bond I will forever be grateful for. I trust that girl with my life and my boy.

He buries himself into my chest again, which he's done since the day he arrived here. It's as if he's clinging to me for dear life and never wants me to let him go. Don't worry, buddy, I won't.

"Get some rest, Paige." Emma squeezes the top of my arm before leaving through the front door.

"Will do. Bye," I shout after her as she disappears out the door. "It's just you and me, Alfie, what are we going to do?" I should really clean the house but to hell with it. I press Alfie to my chest tightly, enjoying the smell of his fresh lavender shampoo. "Would you like to watch Nemo?" No reaction. "Or Lightning McQueen?" Nothing. "What about Buzz?" Alfie flings his head back and grabs my face with both hands. "You want Buzz on?" He loves *Toy Story*. He starts hopping up and down in my arms with excitement.

Great. "All I have to do is call Tate then we can settle on the sofa together and watch a movie." I can't remember the last time I sat and did nothing.

It was longer than six months ago.

"Right, you sit here." I park Alfie's bum on the leather sofa and pass him his Buzz Lightyear plushie to keep him content while I scroll the menu on the streaming service to find his favorite movie. "Do you think you'll be an astronaut when you grow up? Or maybe even a cowboy?" I look down at him and smile, my heart full of love. "Just don't be a lawyer. Long hours but it pays well." He just looks at me like I have three heads. "Maybe think about that one. But your daddy has a big brain." He's a goddamn judge of all things. "I can see you working things out in that clever head of yours, little fella. I think you have a big brain like him too." The way he solves problems is not only clever but also cute. Imitating me brushing my hair the other day was adorable.

Now that Max knows about my sister and Griffin Holmes, I might ask him how I go about confirming Alfie's parentage. It won't be easy. Griffin will push back, I already know that, so I need something more concrete than an untrustworthy addict's word that he's the father.

I continue scrolling through the television menu until I find what I'm looking for.

Alfie points at the screen and makes a little bu-bu noise, telling me which one he wants on when I highlight the icon for the movie. Then he slaps his hands together haphazardly with overenthusiasm.

"Buzz." I raise my hands in the air and Alfie mirrors me, making him look even cuter. Thank you, Disney, for bringing so much joy into my boy's life.

I hit play and settle myself next to Alfie, wrapping one arm around him, locking him into my side.

Moments like this I will treasure forever. He's such a contented child, and I know that for the entirety of the movie he'll sit like this with me. It's unimaginable what would have become of him had Marin not left him with me.

Her abandoning him was a blessing. He's mine now, and once those adoption papers are finalized, no one can take him from me.

Once I see that Alfie is engrossed in the television, I take my cell phone out of my blouse pocket and call Tate Young to explain the situation with Max driving me here today.

He immediately picks up, and I inform him that I had a family emergency this afternoon and my interaction with Max was unavoidable and round the call up as soon as Tate thanks me for calling him.

"Well, that's one problem solved, Alfie."

Now how do I solve an even bigger one?

The huge and inescapable one: Max Hart.

He's my enemy.

My masked date.

It was meant to be nothing. A fleeting moment. A one-night enigma I'd never have to think about again. No names. No faces. No consequences.

But now I know.

It's him. The arrogant, ruthless attorney I'm toe-to-toe with in yet another nasty divorce case.

And suddenly, I can't stop thinking about that night. The sound of his voice in the dark. The way he made me laugh even when I can't bear to be in the same room as him sometimes. The way he made me feel.

Awkward doesn't even begin to cover it. How am I supposed to keep a straight face across the courtroom table, pretending I don't know exactly what he tastes like? Pretending I don't want to find out if it would be even better without the masks?

It's wrong. It's reckless. It's impossible.

And yet... I can't stop imagining what would happen if we broke every rule again.

What a mess.

I pick Alfie up off the couch, pushing my hands under armpits, and turn him to face me, letting his legs bounce up and down on my knee. "What do I do, huh? Do you think I should tell my work or keep my mouth shut?"

Alfie blows me a raspberry, covering himself and my silk blouse in saliva, looking really pleased with himself.

"Was that a no?" I blow him a raspberry back, which makes him smile widely, and he mimics me, blowing another one back, but much louder this time.

"Okay, okay, I get it. I'll think about it." And if I do tell my work, then I'll have to deal with the consequences.

A text arrives on my cell phone and when I look down, the name across the screen makes my heart jump in my chest. Max.

MAX

We need to talk.

That man is like a mind reader.

I place Alfie on my lap and turn him toward the TV, holding him securely with my arm wrapped around his waist.

With one hand, I open my text and tap my screen to reply.

ME

There's nothing to talk about.

What happened happened, and we can't change it.

MAX

I have things I want to say.

ME

I don't.

MAX

I'll call you later.

ME

Don't.

MAX

For once, Paige, will you just go with the flow?
Please?

I take my time to reply. After all, he did say please.

ME

Okay

MAX

Good girl ;)

Oh God, why does his text sound so sexual?

It's what he said to me in the car too, and it did things to me that made my center quiver, soaking my panties.

Max Hart is the devil. The worst kind, the one who feeds you his cock, then stands there grinning down at you while you beg for more.

I hate him. I want him.

And that truth is the worst one of all.

19

PAIGE

I'm soaking in the tub in the hottest water I can withstand.

I'm covered in the bubbliest bubbles, and all the tension that was making my muscles ache has finally left my body. I'll be a new woman when I get out. A shriveled one though, because I've been in here for over an hour.

I lift my wine glass from the bath tray and finish the last of it before placing it on the floor.

It's indulgent of me, drinking on a work night while bathing in my freestanding polished concrete tub covered in expensive bubble bath foam I treated myself to last month. But it's exactly what I needed. Bliss.

I check the baby monitor screen again before I close my eyes and lay my head against the bath pillow.

As I draw a long breath, my mind drifts to my sister. I haven't yet figured out how to mention Marin in my next talk with my parents. They deserve to know she's alive, has a place to stay, and isn't out on the streets. What I can't give them is real reassurance about her safety because I don't have that information. When she gave Max her address earlier, I made sure to memorize it. At some point, when I'm not with Alfie, I plan to drive by and check out the place. I don't expect it to ease my worries or bring me any peace; it's more about curiosity than anything else. Still, it might be something I can tell my parents—just a small bit of good news. Not that there's much when it comes to Marin.

A few more moments pass by, and just as I'm considering getting out of the bath, my cell phone rings, echoing through the bathroom, the loud chimes bouncing off the walls.

I lunge for my cell phone that's resting on the bath tray to kill the ringer. A nervous energy buzzes through me the minute I set eyes on Max's name, and I answer it.

"What do you want?" We can't keep doing this. We've already crossed the boundaries that should never be stepped over.

"I wanted to check in, to make sure you're doing okay after the run-in with your sister." His smooth voice does things to my stomach I don't appreciate because I shouldn't want him. It's the wrongest kind of wrong. But my body isn't getting the memo and is betraying me from every direction.

"I'm fine." I keep my response brief and to the point.

"Good. Good." The silence stretches between us for longer than I'm comfortable with. "What are you doing?"

"I'm in the tub."

"Hit accept." He's such a bossy bastard.

But wait, what?

I remove my cell phone from my ear and roll my eyes when I realize he's requesting a video call. "I'm not accepting." I press my cell phone against my ear again.

"Do it."

"No."

"Paige. Just fucking accept. I want to see you."

God, he's annoying. If I hang up he'll keep calling me back until I accept a video call with him.

I prop my phone up on the molded cradle on my bath tray and hit the button that makes his face fill the screen.

He's wearing nothing but a pair of shorts, and he's covered in a faint sheen of perspiration. It looks like he's been working out, every muscle gleaming under the dim light of what appears to be a gym. Handsome has never looked so sinful. He's so tan. And a ten; he's a big fat fucking ten out of ten.

"Hey, beautiful."

"Stop calling me that." I'm not accustomed to him being nice to me; it's weird, but also ego boosting. Still alien though.

Being careful not to flash my boobs, I sink myself lower into the water, using the bubbles to camouflage them.

"I'm just being honest." He wipes his brow with a virgin-white towel before dabbing his face.

"Well, don't be. I preferred you when you were being a dick to me."

"You know that's not true." And there's that devilish grin again that spreads warmth at the apex of my thighs.

This is getting out of hand, and I need to put an end to this. "Well, it's been great talking to you. You've seen me now. As you can see, I'm busy." I push my hand out of the water to end the call.

"Don't hang up. Please don't." When he says please like that, all sad puppy dog eyes and downturned mouth, how can I refuse?

I let out a sigh, pretending to be bored with the conversation when what I'm really doing is eating him up with my eyes, committing every one of his sinewy muscles to my memory bank.

I give in and drop my hand back into the water, letting him know I've changed my mind.

"Thank you. I wanted to talk to you about that night."

The night that changed everything between us.

I couldn't think of anything worse. The person I initially assumed was a total stranger turned out to be the most insufferable and arrogant man I work with. Nice dick though, I'll give him that. He's got a nice face too, and a body I would like to spend more time getting better acquainted with.

"What specifically do you want to talk about?" I ask, acutely aware of how intimate this is. He's practically naked, and I am completely naked beneath the water. We're breaking rules and getting too close for comfort.

We broke protocol the minute he filled my pussy with his expert fingers that made me come so hard I almost passed out. What we had was so much more than intimacy; it was exposure combined with trust that I never thought existed.

"I want to know why you didn't fill out the follow up form."

I tell him the truth. "I have Alfie. He's become my priority. I barely have time to take a pee these days; that night was the first night I've had off in months. I don't know what I was thinking. I thought I was ready to have a little fun and start dating, but I was kidding myself."

He lifts his chin in acknowledgment, and I can tell he's itching to ask me something else as he stares at me down the camera. Eventually, he does. "The night at The Velvet Rooms, did you like me?"

"Yes." There is no point denying it.

"Did you plan on meeting me outside?" He wipes his sweaty brow again with his towel.

"Yes." That's also the truth.

"But Alfie became unwell?"

"Yes. How did you know?" I scratch my head in confusion, raising my shoulders out of the water slightly in a small shrug.

"The hostess at the door told me a few things. You had blue

eyes, blonde hair, your kid was sick and you took a mask by mistake."

"All true." The bunny mask is still lying on my dressing table, a constant reminder of our unforgettable night.

"How is Alfie now?"

That's sweet of him to ask. "He had chicken pox that night, but since then, he's been fine."

"That's good news."

"He's teething now though." That's a challenge. "The life and times of being a mom. This is all new to me."

"I can't believe your sister had a baby with Judge Holmes."

"Neither can I. How do I prove that?"

"DNA."

"But how?" My question comes out fast.

"Court order."

"I was hoping a conversation might do the trick."

He silently signals no, dismissing me. "The guy is practically untouchable. Have you spoken with him before?"

"Once." At a benefit dinner. "Without his DNA, how do I prove he's Alfie's father?"

"I would start with CCTV from the place your sister worked. Then you could show Griffin and see if that's enough to get him to agree to a DNA test?"

That's a great idea. "Will they still have the footage after all this time?" Do strip clubs have CCTV? I shudder at the thought of having to watch the playbacks. That's a hard pass.

"They will. Or someone will know if he's a regular visitor. All you need is one or two witnesses to confirm if he was there and you have all the evidence you need to schedule a meeting with him. You will wait months to see him though, or I can ask Nathan to have a quiet word. Nathan knows him very, very well and plays tennis and golf with him often."

"He would do that for me?"

"I would do that for you." Why is he being so nice?

"Thank you."

"Say the word and I'll talk to Nathan."

"I'll keep that in mind, thank you."

He does a slow shoulder roll as if stretching out his muscles. "So, you're a mom now?"

"Yeah. Instant mom, just add zero childbirth, zero prep, and a lifetime of commitment. It's been a whirlwind, and the scariest but most rewarding thing I've ever experienced. Being responsible for such a tiny person is crazy."

"You're a good person, Paige. There are not many people who could do what you have."

"I'm doing what any decent person would do." He's a part of Marin I can hold onto forever, something I can't do with her anymore because my sister is long gone. And Alfie is family, my flesh and blood, and he belongs with me. "I'm adopting him," I state.

"Yeah, I heard that earlier." His brows shoot up in surprise. "You're an incredible woman."

I shake my head in disagreement. "I'm not." He wouldn't be saying that if he'd seen me within the first few weeks of Alfie's arrival. Late nights, no routine, tears, Target runs. My mom and dad moved in for weeks until we managed to get Alfie into a routine, then they helped me hire Emma. Poor baby was just as frightened of us as we were of him. Probably more so.

"You are incredible," he counters. "We don't see in ourselves what others see in us. I see greatness within you."

"But you don't like me." He can barely stand being in the same room as me. He puts up with me because he has to.

"That couldn't be further from the truth, Paige. You can be annoying as fuck, but I don't dislike you, not even a little."

I'm not sure if that was a compliment.

He changes the direction of our conversation. "Now you know it's me from The Velvet Rooms, do you still feel the same way about that night?"

"If you mean, do I still think about it and like what we did, then yeah, I do." I'd do it all over again if I had the chance. The fact that it was Max somehow makes it feel even more special. I like a man who really knows how to please a woman. But it was more than that; I felt safe with him. It will never not be weird, though. "And you?" I ask, needing to hear what's on his mind. I'm nosy as hell and desperate to find out if he actually enjoyed it. He sure wasn't complaining at the time.

There's not even a hint of hesitation when he replies, "It's all I've thought about."

Warmth spreads within me at his confession.

"I'm glad it was you, Paige," he adds.

My cheeks pinken to a deeper shade than they already are from the heat of the bath water. "This is crazy." I've spent hours trying to make sense of how it was him in the room that night. Everything tilted once I figured it out. It wasn't a faceless stranger. It was him.

"It was the best fucking blow job I've ever had."

His directness makes me forget my left from my right, every skin cell tingling with amazement. "That can't be true." Max has apparently been with more women than I've had hot dinners which, to be fair, there haven't been many of since Alfie came along. Every meal and cup of coffee ends up cold anyway. Okay, bad example, but you get my point. I know his type.

"I'm not lying." He flexes his muscles subtly down the camera. "It felt like there was more going on. Something real passed between us. I just need to know if you felt it too."

He studies me as I consider his raw honesty, which I hadn't

expected. "I don't know. Maybe." There was. "Something did feel different, but I've been trying not to read too much into it. And it's not like anything can happen between us, so we move on, right?"

"Do... you... want anything to... happen between us?" I've never known Max Hart to be tongue-tied.

"Do you?"

"I asked you first." His penetrating blue-gray gaze studies my face. The intensity in it makes me reconsider what I'm about to say next, because that look, those muscles, his confidence has me wanting to jump through the phone and tell him to do whatever he wants to me. Lick me, spank me, chase me, fuck me into next year, and kiss me again like he did at The Velvet Rooms.

As confidently as I can, I say, "In another life, maybe. But here, now? You're a lawyer on the other side of this active case, and not just this one but many cases. We're not just two people from rival firms; we're bound by ethics and rules we both signed up for and agreed to live by." It's what I swore to and have always upheld. "We're not just complicated, Max, it's forbidden, messy. Impossible. No matter how much you want to ignore that, we both know we can't." And it's not just bad timing; the truth is, we can never go there. Not ever. "For you, I think I would be just another plaything. A fling. Nothing more." Another name in his little black book. "And I value my career more than anything. I know you do too."

"And yet, I still want you."

He wants me.

It's not that simple. "You can't have me."

"We'll see." He licks his lips and grins, as if mentally running through a scenario only he's privy to.

"There is no we'll see, Max. We are never. Going. To. Happen." What part of that is he not getting? "Also"—I point to myself—"single mom, with a baby, over here. Settling down isn't your thing." The last time I checked, Max doesn't do commitment. Or babies. I raise a finger to clarify the point I'm making. "Not that I'm saying I want that. I don't. I just know you. Know how you operate. And honestly, Max, you and I, it's never going to be anything more than two people who happen to work together sometimes. What happened was a random hiccup, a fluke, nothing more. It was an accident. A chance encounter. Never to be repeated."

I meet his gaze, steady and sure, almost predatory, as if he's imagining what I look like beneath the bubbles in the tub. "You know," he starts, "pushing me away only makes me want you more."

"You're unbelievable." And exhausting. But something stirs inside me, something reckless that wants him to chase me down, to hunt me through the trees. It makes me feel feral. Untamed. Alive. And it's everything I shouldn't want. "Bye, Max." I reluctantly reach up to end the call.

"It's not goodbye, Bunny. It's only the beginning. Call me when you're in bed. I want to show you something." On a wink, he hangs up before I get the chance to do it.

I let out an infuriating sigh.

He's impossible to deal with. And annoying.

"Unbelievable," I ramble to myself.

Tonight, he looked so sexy. Handsome. Too handsome for his own good, but he's the most exciting thing to happen to me in such a long time.

From day to day, my life is hectic, full of love, purpose, and helping people. But somehow, it's still painfully mundane.

A smile shapes my lips.

Let him chase. Let him pursue me until the stars burn out. I'll just keep telling him exactly where to go.

But first... it's not a bath I need, it's a cold shower I need to cool off.

And I'm not calling him when I'm in bed so I drop him a text to tell him so.

He can think again.

MAX

I'll call you instead. I know how you love the chase. *fox emoji*

ME

Oh, I do love the chase... especially when I'm the one setting the traps. *bunny emoji*

MAX

Traps? For me?

ME

Only for foxes who think they're clever enough.

MAX

And if I catch you?

ME

Catch me? Careful what you wish for... I bite.

MAX

Good, I like a little danger.

ME

Then keep chasing.

20

PAIGE

I'm just getting comfortable in my bed and rolling over onto my side when my phone begins to ring again.

"You have got to be kidding me," I say under my breath when, once again, Max's name appears across the screen, but this time he's gone straight to video call.

Exasperated and curious, I hit the accept button, knowing I'll regret it.

"What the hell do you want at this time of the night, Max?" I wanted to get an early night as I have court in the morning.

"I told you I wanted to show you something," he says, sounding breathless, his camera facing away from him in what looks like his bedroom maybe. It's dark, sultry, glass everywhere, and looks like the standard penthouse apartment I knew he'd have. I almost roll my eyes at his predictability.

"Will you get on with it then? I'm in bed." I'm annoyed and flustered; us talking like this so late is inappropriate.

As was the drive here today, the way he kissed me on the head, then there was the bath-time call, and let's not forget The Velvet Rooms. Jesus Christ, we are breaking all the rules.

"I thought you'd never ask." His camera moves downward, to reveal his feet, toned legs, strong thighs, and then... Oh my fucking God, his fully erect cock that his hand is wrapped around and he's stroking.

"You're naked." I shoot up in bed and rake my hand through my hair in shock.

"I like your hair down." He ignores the flip-out I'm having, continuing to stroke himself up and down at a leisurely pace. "Wanna have some fun, Bunny?"

"No, I, God that's so hot... No," I whisper when he rubs his thumb across the head of his dick. And now, for the first time, I'm seeing it, and it's even nicer than I imagined. It's big, not overly long, but he's thick and smooth. It's perfect.

"You sure?" His voice turns dark; dangerous, almost. "It's not like we would be breaking any rules, is it? It's just a call. You won't be touching me, because I'm going to fuck myself with my hand while watching you, and you're going to make yourself come for me."

As much as I want to tell him to stop, I can't bring myself to hang up either as a deep ache pulses inside me, the rush of arousal evidence of how turned on I am as he moves the camera closer to the head of his cock. I lick my lips, remembering what he tastes like as precum leaks from his tip.

"Do you have a vibrator, Paige?"

"Yes." My answer is automatic and flies out my mouth in record time. "No. No. Max. This is wrong."

I've never had phone sex before, and I'm not about to start, but holy shit, this is hot.

"Paige." My name on his lips sounds more like a warning. "Find your vibrator then take off that sexy little camisole you have on and if you're wearing panties, or sleep shorts, lose them now."

My eyes widen, my mind working at one hundred miles an hour, all my sensible reasoning going out of the window when I reach for the handle of the drawer on my nightstand. "I'm wearing a silk negligee; I'm not wearing any panties." What the hell am I doing?

"Let me see you." He struggles to get his words out.

"Two seconds." It's shameful how quickly I respond, immediately placing my phone face down on the bed so I can remove my negligee. I then lift my vibrator out of the nightstand.

I burst out laughing when I realize my vibrator has a set of little rabbit ears made for my ultimate clit pleasure.

"What are you laughing at?" he asks, his voice strained.

"My vibrator is called a rabbit." I lift my cell phone off the mattress.

"It sounds perfect. Show me. Show me all of you."

My nipples pucker, tightening to hard peaks as he strokes himself a bit faster, his groans deep and addictive. I can't stop watching him.

I know I can put a stop to this, but I don't want to. Any last remaining sliver of sense and reason flies out the window as my bad girl takes the wheel, and God help me, I want this, crave it, like sin begs for secrecy.

"This is our secret." I watch with fascination when he bucks his hips, digging his heels into his mattress. "No one ever needs to know, Bunny."

Well... when he puts it like that... I slide down the bed, peel back the comforter, revealing myself to him, fully, for the first time. The exposure sends a rush through me, sharp and electric... but laced with fear. It's bold. It's bare.

"You are fucking beautiful, Paige."

I lift the camera away from me and move it down my body, my boobs, and pussy, on full view, for his eyes only.

"Switch your vibrator on," he tells me, his voice raspy and breathless when he continues to fuck himself with his hand. "Then slide it between your pussy lips for me."

I do as he says. This isn't like me. I never just obey like this. What the hell am I doing? But the truth hits hard and clear: I'm doing it because I want to. No other reason. Well, there is; it's because it's with Max. This madness. My mind knows better, but my body, it won't listen, it wants him.

My vibrator buzzes when I switch it on and press the button on the second setting, the one I prefer. It's faster and will make me come quicker, not that it will take much; I'm already wet and ready, needing to come.

I slide the toy between my pussy lips, making sure he can see everything I'm doing. "Oh God, yes," I pant when the vibrator hits my clit.

"Slide it back and forth for me, Paige," he moans.

"Will you come for me, Max?" I ask seductively.

"Oh fuck, yeah."

"I want to come together." At the club, we came separately, but together will be the ultimate high.

"Then push that vibrator into your sweet pussy." He spits on the palm of his hand to lube himself up, then he grips himself, moving with smooth, deliberate strokes, knowing I'm captivated by every move he makes.

"I'm imagining my vibrator is your cock," I tell him.

"My dick is thicker than your vibrator."

He really is.

"Now fuck yourself for me. And make sure those bunny ears do their job."

I slide the smooth pink toy inside of me with ease because I'm so wet, and when the rabbit ears cover my already swollen clit, I arch my back off the bed and close my eyes, losing myself in the pleasure.

"Ah, Max," I cry.

"You better have your eyes open and be watching me." His strong, bold voice is enough to know I should listen, so I do as I'm told and open my eyes. He pumps himself with growing urgency, and I wish I could touch it.

"Do you know what you do to me?" His groans grow louder.

"No. Tell me," I beg, panting as the sparks of an oncoming orgasm dance around the edges of my thighs and deep in my core.

"You make me so hard for you. I want to lick your pussy as if my life depends on it." His strokes get faster still. "I want you to sit on my face while I fuck you with my tongue." He rubs his thumb over the glistening tip of his cock. "Feasting on you as you come all over my lips."

"I'm so wet for you." My mouth hangs open when I push the toy further into my body. It's a pleasurable stretch as I imagine it's him sliding in and out of me.

My back arches when the little ears vibrate harder against my clit.

I watch his hand glide back and forth as I imagine the head of his cock down my throat. He tugs faster again, making a slapping sound against his heavy balls, and I can't take it anymore. "I want to taste you," I pant out.

"You want me to fuck your mouth and come down your throat again?"

"Yes." I love his dirty talk.

"Would you like me to lick your pussy? And use my tongue to fuck you?"

"Uh, yeah, please." I squirm under the weight of his words. "I want you to do that."

"And I want to fuck you so hard, I will ruin you for any other man," he growls. "You are fucking mine."

This man is fucking filthy, with a body made for sin, and in this moment, I don't care about who we work for, what this means for us or even the consequences as I chase my release. I just want him.

"I'm going to fuck that sweet little pussy of yours. You hear me? It's all mine."

His words are my undoing. The turbulence of our passion reaches its peak. "Oh please, now, Max, yes," I cry out. "I'm gonna come."

"Come for me, Bunny. I want to hear you say my name."

With his name on my lips, I come. So hard.

Body jerking, curling my toes into the bed, I hold my breath as pleasure rips through my body, making me feel dizzy.

He calls out my name. My eyes are locked on the screen, watching him as he shoots his load all over his hand and rock-hard abs.

I want to lick him, taste him, and touch him. This is torture of the worst kind.

My breaths come out in rapid, shaky stutters, moaning as the life-changing orgasm cascades, vibrating in waves across my skin, deep in my core, and all through my body.

I've never come so hard before. My skin feels alive, electric, tingling with pleasure.

"Paige." He draws out my name in a worshipful tone, stroking himself much slower now.

For a moment, there is nothing but the sound of our soft breaths as we slowly come down together.

Eventually, he breaks our silence. "Give me a minute while I clean up."

I'm left staring at a black screen, unable to comprehend what just happened between us.

I slowly remove the toy from my body, switch it off and lay it on top of the bedsheets.

I chuckle to myself while waiting for him to come back. Holy shit. I've never done anything like that before. I might want more. That's a lie; I do want more.

Faint footsteps and shuffles alert me to Max's return. Swiftly he flips his camera to face him and time seems to pause, my stomach doing back flips with nervous excitement. Lying on his side now, he grins at me, giving me a glimpse of his ripped torso and handsome face.

I should feel embarrassed but I'm not, I'm here for every moment. It's the kind of wrong that feels too right to run away from: I couldn't walk away even if I tried.

I mirror his position and rest my free hand under my cheek, holding my phone in front of my face. "That was... unexpected." I struggle to hide the blush that's spreading up my neck.

His expression is all heat and sin, his mouth turned up in a smile that's full of mischief. It's pure trouble and full of danger and his look says he knew I couldn't resist him.

"I liked that." I look at my dopey eyes, my face slightly dazed on the camera screen.

"I fucking loved it. I love watching you come and hearing you say my name. You're so beautiful." He reaches out to the screen as if he's trying to touch my skin. "You're so fucking hot."

"We can't do that again." My blissful state dissipates when I bring us back to the reality of our situation.

He chooses to ignore my concerns when he shoots me a playful grin. "You're wrong about that."

"I'm not. This was a once in a lifetime, never to be repeated event."

"You said that when you were in the tub earlier about The Velvet Rooms too, but that didn't stop you fucking yourself with your vibrator for me."

He's right, I'm not good at standing my ground when it comes to him anymore. "God, you're annoying."

"So you keep telling me." He winks at me, and it makes him look even more sinful. "But you like me, just admit it." His blue-gray eyes challenge me to tell the truth.

"No."

"You can keep denying it, but the way your body reacts to me and the way you said my name when you came tells me otherwise, Bunny."

"Oh, fuck off with the bunny thing." I sound madder than I am, because I'm not mad. I feel better than I have done in weeks. Satisfied.

"Thanks for tonight, you're such a good little bunny. We are doing that again," he says with authority, smiling like the devious bastard he is.

"I'm not picking up the next time. This stops now." I sound less than convincing because I want to do it again.

"I'll make it worth your while," he counters.

I want to, but...

"You know you want to. Night, Paige." He hangs up, leaving me staring at my cell phone.

He's planning something.

For a change, I'm on the back foot while he's scheming away in the background.

Shit, what door did I just open?

The door to hell, and for some stupid reason, I willingly walked right through it.

21

PAIGE

I run my eyes around the large ballroom inside one of the most expensive hotels in San Francisco and suppress an eye roll as one of the partners at my firm wraps his arm around his secretary's waist, confirming my suspicion: they are sleeping together. I wonder what his wife would have to say about that.

"Good afternoon." Max's voice startles me, making me jump and causing my coffee to slosh around in the cup I'm holding on to like a lifebuoy. I hate these events.

"What are you doing here?" I audibly groan, unable to make eye contact with him.

A week ago, we had phone sex.

I had phone sex with Max Hart.

The worst part of it: I enjoyed it. It's atrocious the way my body deceives me around him. Fucking traitor.

Every time he's called me, I've declined the call because I don't trust myself.

And goddammit, why did he have to be here today? I didn't see his name on the list of attendees.

Uninvited, he pulls out the chair next to me and sits down. "I could ask you the same question. You never come to the monthly lawyers' lunches."

I'm only here for one reason. "I was hoping Lauren Stark would be here. And don't get too comfortable, I'd much prefer it if you sat at the seats over there." I point to empty chairs around the table directly opposite.

"Why?"

"Because I don't want you sitting here."

With no intention of leaving, he moves his chair closer to mine then says, "That's not what I meant. Why do you want to speak to Lauren Stark?"

The way he ignores me, makes my teeth itch with annoyance. He's irritatingly aloof and wafts of sin and something I might want to taste again just to confirm if hell feels as good as it smells.

I avoid his stare that feels like it's burning into my cheek, my eyes staying fixed to the dozens of men and women in suits. "I wanted to speak with her informally, outside the office, to discuss a case. I'm hoping to gauge whether her client might consider joint custody if we agree to full spousal support. So far, she's remained firmly opposed to granting her husband any custody, understandably, given she found him in bed with her best friend."

"I fucking hate the infidelity stories we hear in our jobs. It's made me lose all faith in humanity and relationships."

"Me too." Unable to resist, I finally lock eyes with him, summoning all my bravery, and instantly regret it.

It's unfair to be that handsome. That raw intensity about him stirs feelings I know I shouldn't have.

I'm a confident woman; I am immune to his charm.

Who am I kidding? I can already feel myself unraveling. That expensive suit he's wearing only makes him look like he belongs in a photoshoot for Giorgio Armani. Polished, composed, every thread stitched with certainty. Meanwhile, I'm held together with caffeine and wishful thinking, trying not to give away the fact that I'm coming apart at the seams.

"Separation is fucking brutal." He shudders as if it gives him the jitters.

I let out a long, heavy sigh. "Just another day in the life of a divorce lawyer, Max."

"Marriage never ends well."

"Your mom and dad are still married," I point out.

He shakes his head, dismissing me. "They might be married, but since Dad moved into the memory care home, well, let's just say it's not what they hoped their retirement would look like."

My heart contracts, hating how deflated Max sounds. I heard rumors that his father had Parkinson's disease and was now in full-time care, but I wasn't sure how true they were. Idle gossip isn't really my jam, and I stay away from our staff kitchen at break times to avoid the chin-wagging.

"I'm sorry to hear about your dad, Max." I mean it. His father was an incredible lawyer and someone I admired and looked up to. Max and his brothers are just as impressive, if not more so. Combined, they are a tetrad of lawyer brilliance that makes even the toughest of judges sweat.

He juts his chin up in acknowledgment, his eyes full of sadness. "My mom visits my dad every day."

"Till death us do part." For sickness and in health. For better or worse. His parents got a bum deal, which is so unfair.

He suggests morbidly, "They should change wedding vows to be 'until we get divorced' instead."

"My mom and dad are still married." They are the only couple in my family who have stuck together through thick and thin.

"Those marriages are few and far between. Rare these days."

He's right.

He swivels around in his seat, sitting sideways and now staring straight at me as if he's searching my soul for an answer. "That's so fucking depressing. Remind me why we became divorce lawyers again?"

I want to ask him who styles his hair. No one wakes up looking like that by accident. It's a sea of messy waves, infuriatingly perfect, and all I want is to run my fingers through it... again.

Like a magnet, the pull toward him is strong and inescapable, and I find myself mirroring his actions. As I stare at his gorgeous face, I realize all the extreme levels of disdain and hatred I've ever felt toward him aren't there anymore; it's changed into something completely different. Admiration, lust, desire... Oh, no, this is bad. *Focus, Paige.* "We do what we do because we love it, Max."

"My client lost full custody of his dog today. I don't love those days."

"Poor guy."

"Poor dog. I think the judge was more of a cat person." His grin is playful and inviting.

Laughter bursts from my chest at his stupid joke that catches me off guard.

He smiles wider. It's cocky and masculine, and makes him look like he won the goddamn lottery. "You should smile more. And I like this little dress you're wearing today." He flicks the metal pull tab at my neckline. "You're kind of illegal-looking right now."

My pulse quickens with forbidden longing.

"Thanks." I blink once, then twice, as the distance between us shrinks, and the room around us blurs into a hazy mess.

"Did you enjoy the other week, Paige?" he asks in a huskier tone.

"Yes. You know I did." I don't think I could've been more obvious. I said his name as I came, hard.

"So why haven't you picked up my calls?"

"Because it's wrong."

"Don't care."

I hate the way he disregards my concerns, railroading my thoughts, knowing it won't take much to twist my arm to change my mind.

He chews up what space there is between us, his mouth finding the shell of my ear. "Presidential suite." He places a keycard into the palm of my hand; his warm breath tickles my skin. "I checked the attendance list and I knew you'd be here today. Don't argue with me. See you in an hour, Bunny."

And with that, he's gone, leaving nothing but a cloud of aftershave behind and a surge of desire igniting through my core.

Presumptuous bastard.

My fingers tighten around the room keycard so hard that they make my knuckles turn ghostly white.

When I leave this event, I'll hand the card to reception.

I look down at it, uncurling my fingers from around it as it burns a hole in my resolve.

I'm not going.

Maybe I will.

Shit.

I'm definitely going.

22

MAX

I'm sitting on the chair in the darkened room of the presidential suite in the hotel, drinking yet another whiskey.

It's been over two hours, and it's time I faced the truth: she's not coming.

My fingers tighten around the glass, and my stomach knots with self-hatred for thinking she would.

Fuck.

What an arrogant idiot I've been. She doesn't even like me, so why would she show up?

She has no reason to.

And on top of that, we're representing opposing sides in an active case.

This isn't just awkward; it's completely inappropriate. I'm not only being insensitive; I'm also being unprofessional. Something I never am.

Paige was right not to show up. She's the better person.

My move was a bold one. Too bold. Even for me.

I put my glass down on the side table and reach for my suit jacket as any last bit of hope I had slips from my fingers.

And that's when I hear it. The click. The opening of the handle and the sound of the door being pushed open.

She stands there, a silhouette against the corridor light behind her, the contrast stark in the dim room.

It's Paige.

"Hey, Mr. Fox."

Fuck.

She's here.

23

PAIGE

"Hey, Mr. Fox," I say softly as I enter the presidential suite, the lights from the corridor illuminating every contour of furniture in the enormous space.

With one hand on the door to hold it open, I pause at the threshold, caught somewhere between the pull of what's right and the lure of something reckless. Stepping inside would go beyond a mistake; it'd be a deal with the devil. One I'm willing to accept.

Only for one afternoon, though, nothing more.

It's a one-time thing to scratch the itch and get each other out of our systems.

Eyes pinned on him, I stare at a motionless Max, who looks surprised to see me, sitting on a leather chair on the other side of the suite. With no lights on in the room, he appears dark, menacing, and his features and rich brown hair almost look black against the closed white drapes behind him.

A smirk pulls at my lips.

Ah, so he wants to replay the game in the dark again.

I like it.

Might love it, actually. The wetness pooling between my legs is evidence that I want him.

My hand uncurls from around the door handle as I move fully inside the room, taking the first step into hell. If we get caught, we'll be burned to cinders.

The anticipation and danger of it all pulses through me so hard I'm surprised he can't hear the blood pumping through my veins.

Slamming shut behind me, the door automatically locks, plunging us into semi-darkness.

"Bunny." Max's smooth voice holds a rasp of excitement. "I didn't think you'd show." He doesn't move from where he's seated.

"I didn't think I would either." I sat in the bar for over an hour weighing up my options.

To be good or not to be? My inner bad girl won.

"I'm so fucking happy you're here."

Sure he is.

We're about to explore the forbidden one last time.

Then we'll shut it down.

"I only have four hours." I lied to Emma and told her I'd be held up in meetings at the last minute, something I never do.

This is reckless of me and careless of us. Most of our work colleagues are still downstairs in the bar labeling today as a working lunch, and if anyone caught us, it would be game over for both of us, yet I'm still here.

"Four hours will never be enough with you." His deep voice is crisp and clear and full of intention: he wants more than just today.

"Well, it will have to do." It's not completely dark in the room as the afternoon sun shines through the edges of the drapes, creating a halo of light. What we're about to do is far from angelic. There's enough light for me to see his smirk and the firm grip around the arms of his chair he's glued to.

I drop my workbag onto the floor and step away, removing my suit jacket and letting it fall to the ground before reaching up to unzip my dress. From neckline to hem, I slowly, provocatively unzip each of the interlocking teeth of the zipper, easing it down inch by painfully slow inch, letting the fabric loosen and slip from my shoulders like a whisper, pooling at my feet. I step out of it with my eyes fixed ahead, daring, inviting. I can feel the heat of his approval as Max watches every movement I make.

Wearing nothing but my matching silk and lace lingerie, and sky-high heels, I'm petrified. I'm no longer in my twenties. Yeah, I work out and look after myself, but I'm curvier than the women I've seen him photographed with. I'm more hourglass with love handles you can fill your hands with than a gazelle-type model.

Running his pointer finger along his bottom lip, back and forth, rhythmically, hypnotically, he assesses me as I stand before him completely exposed.

I step toward him one more time, but he stops me in my tracks when he tells me to, "Lose the lingerie, leave the heels on."

I raise one eyebrow in challenge, my body aching for his touch.

"Now, Paige." His impatient tone suggests I should obey, which I know I will as I'm powerless here. I'm powerless against him when we are like this together.

As seductively as I can, I slip my thumbs into my barely there string panties and slide them down my hips and legs before removing them completely. In a last-minute decision, I throw them his way, and as if he was expecting me to do it, his light-ning-quick reaction has him catching them, balling them into his fist before lifting them to his nose, where he inhales a deep breath and lets out a desperate-sounding groan.

"Now the bra." He stuffs my panties into the pocket of his dress pants, his eyes never leaving mine as he licks his lips. His gaze drops down my body, appraising me lazily, unlocking an unfamiliar feeling within me.

Lust, pride, longing? I'm too busy reaching around my back to unhook the clasp and slip the delicate fabric off my shoulders to give it any more energy. Holding my bra out to the side, I drop it to the floor dramatically, getting carried away in the moment. The way his eyes travel across my body, lingering on my pussy and boobs, make me feel wanted, the deep throb between my legs now pounding much harder than it was before.

I'm desperate for him to touch me.

"C'mere." He crooks his finger at me, beckoning me to move toward him, and when I'm only a step away, he tells me to kneel.

As he points to the floor, he spreads his legs wide to make room for me.

Unquestioningly, I bend down and rest my knees on the deep carpeted floor.

"You know what to do. Don't make me spell it out for you, Bunny." His strong commanding words are a complete contrast to the softness of his hand he's running down my cheek.

When he runs his thumb over my bottom lip, I open my mouth and slip it inside, then suck it. Hard. Twisting my tongue around it, reminding him of what I did at The Velvet Rooms.

It takes less than a second for him to reach for my hand before rubbing it over his hard length. "Feel what you do to me, Paige."

"Mmmm," I hum around his thick digit and give his cock a firm squeeze.

"Fuck, yeah. Now take my cock out." He pulls his thumb out of my mouth.

Like the good little bunny I am, I willingly obey, removing his shoes and socks first, then make light work of his belt, fly and button of his dress pants. He lifts his hips off the chair to help me get rid of them entirely then, grabbing the collar of his shirt, he pulls it up and over his head, throwing it on the floor.

I lick my lips, preparing myself to taste him again. It's what I've imagined doing since our first encounter.

Teasingly, I brush my hands up his legs which are covered in soft hairs. He wasn't lying when he told me he was hairy all over. He feels amazing, and warm, hard; everything I could ever want in a man.

When he grabs the base of his cock, I lean in and open my mouth wide and waste no time, greedily pulling him into the back of my throat.

"Holy fucking shit," he almost roars.

To hell with going slow and limbering up. I want to give him an even better blow job than I did the first time.

He grabs the sides of my face and fucks my mouth, making me gag when he goes too deep, but I don't stop; instead, I suck him harder, bobbing my head back and forth, moaning because I'm enjoying every scorching-hot minute of it.

As I dig my nails into the skin of his thighs, he suddenly pulls his dick out of my mouth, holding his cock at the base and grins down at me.

Desperate to explore his body again, slowly I run my hands up his thighs then abs, making him flinch and moan from my touch. "Do you want more, Paige?" He taps the head of his cock on my lips, painting them with precum, transferring my lipstick onto his head. I push my tongue right out of my mouth and lick the underside of his cock, flicking the thick vein of his shaft.

I grin up at him, and his eyes are full of desire when I lick his length from base to tip, flicking it again using the tip of my rigid tongue.

"Do you like sucking my cock?"

I nod and pull him into my mouth again, making him fling his head back with a deep groan. "Oh, fuck, baby, you're so fucking good at that."

Swirling my tongue around his head, I suck and lick, making him thicken in my mouth. He won't last much longer unless I stop.

"You're fucking perfect, Paige." He looks down at me with admiration and something twists in my chest, making it burn from the closeness growing between us.

He pulls my hair out of the bun it was in, unraveling my long hair. Then he gathers it into his hand and grabs hold of it, creating a ponytail before arching my head right back. His dick falls out of my mouth, and I'm gasping, panting, needing more as my arousal coats my thighs.

"I want you." He crashes his lips against mine, invading my mouth with his tongue. It's a rough kiss, desperate even, as his fingers grip my hair tighter. It's a painful pleasure I want to chase and want more of.

His other hand moves between my legs, and I groan when his thick digit slides between my lips, then he pinches my clit between his deft fingers. I widen my legs for him, kneeling upward to prevent him from bending so far down.

Repeatedly, he works me into a frenzy, rubbing my clit with his fingers. My body is completely on fire and about to burst into flames, and I moan in ecstasy when he pushes his finger inside of me, then another easily, because I'm so wet.

"Can you take another?" he asks, mumbling against my lips.

"Yes," I gasp, panting like the needy little bitch I am.

He adds another, stretching me in pleasurable, painful ways.

"Fuck. You are so wet." With my hair still wrapped around his hand, he pulls me off his lips using my hair, arching my neck further back, staring down at me in the dim light.

"Now, are you going to come for me like a good little bunny?" he rasps.

"Yes," I pant. I'm almost there.

With his thumb he rubs my clit with purpose as his fingers fuck me much harder this time, setting off my orgasm. I call out his name as I shatter around his thick digits. My muscles contract around him, my body shaking and humming with delight, soaking his hand with my orgasm.

"Good fucking girl." He keeps moving his fingers in and out of me, much slower now, over and over, massaging my inner walls, pulling every last piece of pleasure from my body.

Max covers my mouth with his lips, swallowing my moans of ecstasy as I continue to fall apart.

He slips his tongue into my mouth, and a rush of desire sends goosebumps across my skin as our kisses grow more urgent. We clash fiercely, gasping for air, our tongues and teeth tangled together. Heavy breaths and low groans spill from us as the intensity builds.

"I fucking need to be inside you," he rasps between kisses, removing his fingers from my dripping wet core, pulling a regretful moan from my chest. I'm already missing the feeling of fullness.

I clasp his face between my hands and tell him, "I want to feel you inside me." It's wrong of me, of us, to be doing this. But I need him, and my mind and body aren't giving me any choice. They're overriding any rational thoughts that are telling me we shouldn't be doing this. "I need to see you, all of you." I want to see what I felt in the dark and what I saw on camera.

I want to see his muscles and explore the deep divots and undulations of his incredible hard body.

His answer is a quick command. "Stand up." Then he's on his feet, lifting me into the air.

On autopilot, I wrap my legs around his waist, toeing my shoes off behind his back, making them land with a loud thud against the floor. I thread my arms around his neck as he carries me with ease as if I'm a feather, striding into the lit bedroom, his cock easily finding my pussy.

I lower myself onto his cock as he walks, teasing the tip. He's rock solid and much thicker than his three fingers. Hell, I hope I can take him.

"Condom, Bunny," he affirms, looking over my shoulder to see where he's going. "Such a needy little thing. Do you want my cock that bad?" He chuckles darkly.

So bad. But shit, where is my mind at?

"I'm not on the pill, Max." I have no need for contraception; that was, until today.

With ease, he lifts me off the head of his cock and lays me down on the bed, reaching past me, the crinkle telling me it's a condom. "Move up the bed," he whispers in my ear.

I shuffle up the mattress while he stands at the foot of the bed, and with fascination, I watch as he rips the condom, my eyes dropping down his athletic physique. And holy shit. If I thought he had a nice body on camera, it's nothing compared to the real thing.

"Spread your legs for me," he demands, rolling the condom on then stroking his cock as he stares at my pussy when I bend my knees, resting my feet on the bed, doing as he asks.

"Fucking beautiful." His voice lulls me into relaxation. He's told me dozens of times he thinks I'm beautiful, and I think I'm starting to believe he really means it and it isn't just a pickup line of his.

Like a lion stalking his prey, he crawls up the bed toward me, and I spread my legs even more to accommodate his huge frame.

Hovering over me, I look up into his eyes, my hands embarking on their own adventure, exploring every hard muscle of his body and causing goosebumps to scatter across his tan skin. I skate my hands over every luscious part of him, not missing an inch of his incredible physique. He's buff and huge compared to any man I've ever been with. His body feels exquisite, and he's all man, which I find intoxicating.

One time with him might not be enough to satisfy this need I have inside me. It's greedy, needs feeding and wants to consume him in the way I want him to consume me.

As I move my hands farther down his body, my urgency takes over and I wrap his hard cock in my hand and glide it through my fist. I can't wait any longer for his thickness and length to be inside me.

He hisses at my touch as I stroke him up and down, then he lowers himself and brushes his lips over mine, and I grip his cock harder this time, which he seems to like, and makes his brain freeze. He stops kissing me, his mouth open against mine, on the verge of losing control.

I wrap his waist with my legs, guiding him toward my wet center, letting him know my intentions.

"Paige," he breathes against my lips, a soft sigh escaping him.

He doesn't need to say what he's feeling, I feel it too. This unspoken pull, and unexplained connection, as we tip the scales between restraint and surrender.

"Fuck me," I whisper, barely able to string a sentence together.

In one hard thrust, Max fills me up, gloriously stretching me. We both groan at the same time, knowing we can't go back, can't take back our forbidden actions, or this moment that I will remember for the rest of my life.

"Shit." He lays his forehead on mine. "You feel so fucking good, baby."

"It's Bunny, not baby, to you," I tease, shifting my hips to push him into me more.

He smiles lazily then kisses me, fucking my mouth with his tongue as he begins to move and expertly fucks me, undulating his hips in waves.

My body comes alive with every move. And it's wrong of me to want him, but doing this with him feels so right.

He doesn't like you as much as you think he does; this is just fucking around, a way for you to get him out of your thoughts.

Something shifts in the air between us and when he lays his forearms on either side of my head and fucks me like he owns my body, all I see is him. I can no longer keep ignoring the connection we have.

But you have to, Paige.

"I don't want to ever stop doing this with you," he pants, moving his hand to grab my ass as if needing more leverage. His cock fills me in pleasurable ways, rubbing my inner walls, teasing another orgasm from me.

With his other hand he pulls at my nipple, rolling it between his fingers, then pinches it, making it harden.

He moves his mouth to my other nipple, continuing to fuck me into the mattress, much faster now, as he sucks my nipple into his hot mouth. I rock my hips against him, fingers clutching the back of his neck, silently begging for more. His mouth devours my hardened nipple, lashing it with his tongue before biting and nipping just enough to make me gasp. Then he shifts to the other, lavishing it with even more attention, drawing out a moan I can't contain.

I silently plead for him to head north and kiss me again. But instead, he continues to flick his tongue over one hardened nipple, then the other, teasing and biting at it before capturing it between his teeth again. The sharp jolt of pleasure shoots straight to my pussy.

"Fucking beautiful," he murmurs against my skin.

He runs his tongue around the edge of my nipple, slow and deliberate, before taking it fully into his mouth. Then he bites, much harder this time, and the sudden spike of sensation nearly rips a scream from my throat. It's almost too much but I never want it to stop.

"Kiss me," I beg as I claw at him.

When he reaches my lips, we attack each other's mouths as he really begins to fuck me.

"I won't last," he pants, shaking his head. "Your pussy is so fucking tight."

Thank you, Pilates, for pelvic floor exercises.

"Give me everything you've got," I beg him as the ferocious pent-up tension builds as he rocks and thrusts furiously back and forth, moving in and out, his heavy balls slapping off my ass. It's everything I know I've been living without and everything I'm missing in my life.

I grab his sculpted ass, slamming his thick cock into me, deeper, my neck arching back as pleasure floods my body. He takes this as an invitation to bite my neck, licking and sucking on it, sending my senses into overdrive.

A whimper leaves my lungs and I dig my nails into his flesh when the head of his cock rubs my G-spot.

I don't care if this only lasts a few minutes; I need to come. I need him to come.

Now.

"Max." His name comes out of my mouth in a hiss.

"Jesus fucking Christ." His fingers grip my hip with bruising force, and I wrap my legs tighter around him as he drives deeper with every earth-shattering thrust, each one stealing the breath from my lungs.

I reach up and thread my fingers through his hair, pulling the strands at the back of his head, and guide his mouth back to mine.

"Fuck me faster, Max." I arch my back and let out a long moan as a wave of pleasure crests through me, which he senses.

"You're close. Your pussy is clenching my cock."

"Yes," I hiss.

He hammers into me at lightning speed when his cock hits my G-spot again, once, then twice and a third time, and my orgasm erupts through my body. A shockwave of molten heat tears through me as I tumble over the edge of pleasure, a surge of indescribable bliss flooding every inch of my skin. I come undone and the release I feel is otherworldly as a kaleidoscope of color bursts behind my eyes, my moans bouncing off the walls of the suite we're in.

My body is buzzing. Alive.

The sexual tension that's been simmering between Max and me for hours—no, days; months—finally shatters as I surrender to him, letting him fuck me through my orgasm.

Like a backdraft waiting to explode, we've been smothering our need for each other, locking our feelings away. The heat between us has been building, unbearable and unchecked, and all it took was the smallest breath of air to ignite the wildfire we've become.

My orgasm doesn't stop; it rises again as he pushes me quickly into another wave of pleasure.

Breathing harder, we pant against one another, mouths open as I yell into his throat to fuck me like he's never fucked anyone else.

I clutch his solid, sweat-slicked body, unwilling to let go. My skin hums, alive with sensations I haven't experienced in what feels like forever, but honestly, nothing has ever felt like this. It's raw, electric, like we were meant to find our way to each other.

Our impending release hovers. It's volatile and near combustion as he drives into me with wild urgency. The massive bed slams into the wall, but neither of us cares who might hear; we're too far gone. I feel unhinged, unbalanced on the edge of something explosive.

Desperate, I drop my legs and dig my heels into the mattress, thrusting my hips up to meet his. Sparks shoot up my spine, radiating through my core and thighs. My body trembles, the pressure mounting, higher, higher, until I break, shattering beneath the weight of it all.

I come again.

And he comes with me.

He roars my name like it's the only word that has ever come out of his mouth and it feels a lot like ownership.

Breathless and trembling, our bodies clench, grind, and convulse in unison as the high slowly fades. He moves within me in dreamy, lazy strokes until he stills completely, relishing the quiet afterglow.

I'm overwhelmed with contentment, a deep, aching happiness. Tiny sparks of ecstasy shimmer across my hot, sweat-slicked skin as he presses soft, reverent kisses along my neck and shoulder, and I melt into him like warm liquid gold.

No one has ever made me feel the way he does.

He's stirred something primal inside me, a desire I thought had long gone quiet.

Now that he's touched me this way, I know I'll never be the same.

He's awakened my need for more.

And he may have ruined me, for anyone else, forever.

24

MAX

Having cleaned up and got rid of the condom, I walk out of the bathroom and stride into the bedroom.

I'm glad I was wearing a condom; that thing was full.

I don't think I've ever come so hard.

Don't get me wrong; I've been with women, not as many as people would think, but still, today was new for me. There's something bigger at play than Paige and I just having sex. It felt... Fuck knows. Different? Fucking amazing.

Climbing back onto the bed, I pull back the covers and slide in beside her, lying on my side to face Paige who looks half asleep and has that whole just-fucked look about her that softens her often stoic features she paints on.

"Are you okay?" I brush her hair off her face as she gives me a dopey-eyed smile.

"Yeah."

"You look tired." It's more evident to me now that I'm paying attention to every little thing about her.

"Recently, I'm always tired."

I take a chance to ask her something I'm desperate to know,

and I might be taking advantage of her while she's in the post-sex afterglow, but fuck it. "Tell me about Alfie and what happened." I don't want a CliffsNotes version; I want the whole story.

With no stone left unturned, Paige tells me everything—from Marin's addiction and when it all started to her leaving Alfie on her front porch, which I struggle to understand. But Marin must have been desperate, and she knew Paige would look after him. She left him in safe hands. Hands that I never want to stop touching me. *Not now, Max.*

"And now you're adopting him." It's more of a statement than a question.

"Yeah."

"You're a formidable woman." Strong and confident she might be, but she's also surprised me with how kind she is. I don't know why I didn't see it before. Although she's been showing me snippets of herself during negotiations that benefit everyone, specifically when there are children involved.

"I'm also a busy woman." I already know this; you have to book months in advance to schedule settlement conferences with her.

"And here I thought you were an ice queen who ate the hearts of small children for dinner. Turns out, you have a heart after all."

She bites back without hesitation, "And you're still an asshole." I can tell from the hint of humor in her tone she doesn't mean it. She adds, "I'm just..."

"Guarded, I know, I get it." I see that now. "You don't trust easily."

"I work in a very male-dominated office. It's dog-eat-dog. Or man-eat-man."

"How many women are partners at Moore & Associates?"

"Not enough. Two."

"Two? That's fucking ridiculous. We have more women than men in the office." I rest my face on my hand against the pillow.

"And that's why your firm is so successful. The women are keeping you and your brothers in check," she says, staring deep into my eyes.

"You got us all figured out, huh?" I give her ribs a gentle poke and think about my next question. "Why didn't you accept Nathan's job offer?" There's more to it than just hating me, and I bet she doesn't hate me now, not after I made her come three times.

"Because at the time I was planning to open my own firm, then Alfie arrived and..."

"Fire clashes with firework factory."

"Yeah. Something like that. And it wasn't a complete disaster; I mean, all I had to do was put my plans on hold because I had a job, and it's a great one that offers me the stability I need until I revisit that option again. I've had to adjust my life to accommodate Alfie, and it's been difficult at times. Instead of opening my own law firm, I'm considering things like moving to an area where the best schools are and saving for college for him. It's a minefield. Scary too."

It's all the things I never considered, and maybe I could help ease her financial worries. "Whatever Nathan offered you I will double it. We have daycare too if you ever needed it, plus dental and medical cover and our pension scheme is top tier." It's one of the best.

"You can't double his offer." Her eyes widen in shock.

"Yes, I can. It's my fucking firm. Cole might be a little bit scared of you though." That makes her laugh.

"Yeah, I seem to have that effect on people. First impressions and all that. But this job has made me develop a thick skin. And

I don't trust many people. Maybe that's because of my ex, who cheated on me, too."

"He was a fool."

"I was the bigger one for suspecting and not doing anything about it." She thinks for a minute and tiptoes around her next question, dropping her voice to a whisper. "Have you ever cheated on anyone?"

"Never. The last woman I was in a serious relationship with turned out to be someone I couldn't trust. We lived together for a while, but then she became ruthless in her pursuit to sell more newspapers, using unethical practices."

"You dated a journalist?" she asks in surprise.

"Yeah. Julie Hanson."

"Oh my God, I saw that on the news. The paper she worked for was shut down. You dated her?" she asks again, sounding shocked by this revelation.

"Unfortunately. But we dated years ago." I thought she was the one. How wrong was I? "When she started sharing with me the things she was doing at work to get a story, I asked her to move out. She did, eventually, but not before she sewed dead fish into the bottom of my curtains and stuffed my mattress with fish guts. She was fucking crazy."

"Holy shit." Paige gasps, amusement dancing all over her face.

I can laugh about it now; I didn't at the time.

"Oh, it gets better. She gave my new car a paint job."

"That's wild."

"There's more, but I won't bore you with the details. Let's just say there was a restraining order in place." Not anymore because she's in prison for hacking celebrities' phones, using their personal conversations and emails, even photos, to bribe and extort them. "I'm well aware of thinking someone is one thing and they turn out to be someone different altogether." Although I think I've done that to a degree with Paige. She's beautiful in every sense of the word.

"She was a wolf in sheep's clothing."

"Exactly." I'm surprised she didn't hack my phone too; there were plenty of opportunities for her to do it. To this day I have never understood it, and the only answer I have ever been able to come up with still doesn't make sense to me: that she did love me like she said she did. But how could she have when she subsequently went on to try to damage my career, publishing fake stories about me and my firm?

"I heard the last woman you dated was Juliette, the influencer. You seem to have a thing for women with similar names," she teases me. "Julie, Juliette."

I have a thing for someone who goes by the name of Paige. "Juliette wanted something I couldn't give her."

"Is that code for she wanted to settle down and have babies?"

How the fuck does she know that? "Maybe."

"Definitely."

"Okay, you got me, so I'm a commitment-phobe." That's what my brothers call me.

"So instead, you screw around."

I scowl at her because that's an assumption she's made. "I know that's what the gossips would have you believe, but I promise you I haven't been out on a date or slept with anyone since Juliette and I broke up, and that was months ago."

She stays quiet before she summons the courage to ask me, "So you don't do things like booking presidential suites every week, then?"

"This is a first for me."

"Me too."

I clear up any other assumptions she's made about me. "And I've never dated the opposition."

"Neither have I. But we're not dating, Max."

Such a fucking pity. "Are you sure I can't persuade you?" Maybe another orgasm might help to convince her.

"We can't. You know that. And I can't stay."

I roll over to check the time on my cell phone. "We still have a couple of hours left." Enough time to make her come again on my cock, tongue, fingers...

"Well, you better make the most of your time, because after today, that's it, Max. We can't meet up again like this."

"Okay." I climb on top of her and gently roll her onto her back.

"I mean it," she admonishes.

"I know." I murmur the words as I plant soft kisses down her neck, trying to pull her mind away from her insistence that we should never do this again. I continue my slow distraction, pressing my lips to her collarbone, taking my time, not missing a single inch as I travel lower. My teeth gently tease her nipple, drawing a gasp from her as I lick it with my tongue, before I move to her stomach, kissing along her soft curves, savoring the warmth of her skin. Finally, I settle between her thighs, covering her pussy with my mouth.

She grabs hold of my hair and pushes her clit against my tongue as I flick it then suck it into my mouth.

"Why do you have to be so good at that? It's not fair that you work for the opposition." She bucks her hips, grinding her pussy against my mouth to chase her release, writhing and moaning, her whimpers building when I insert a finger inside her wet heat. I massage her inner walls as she digs her nails into my scalp, sending shivers down my spine. Unable to take my eyes off her, I look up and watch her fling her head back, and whether she likes it or not, I know she's enjoying everything about our illicit affair.

"If only we could do this every day." She sighs in a blissed-out state.

If I have it my way, we will be.

I'll make her feel so good, she'll forget she ever hated me.

"We could do the same tomorrow," I suggest.

"You know I love the way you push me to be bad, Max." Another moan escapes her lips. "Don't ever stop chasing me."

Her command makes me smile against her pussy.

If I knew she wasn't into it, I wouldn't pursue her like a starved animal, but with her permission, and the way she just gave me the green light, I will because she's the one in control here, not me.

And I know she likes nothing better than being caught.

Only the thing is, I thought I was hunting her, but from the minute she moaned my name, she had me on a leash all along.

25

PAIGE

MAX

Good morning, Bunny.

ME

Stop texting me.

MAX

The Blue Bay Hotel, today, 1 p.m.

ME

I'm not coming.

MAX

See you then.

ME

I've told you; I won't be there.

MAX

Room 309. Pick the keycard up from reception.

ME

Have fun with your hand.

Chewing my fingernail, I pace the floor behind my desk and stare at my phone as the hustle, bustle and low hum of chatter of the office continues outside my office door. Luckily for me my colleagues are blissfully unaware that I'm currently having an existential crisis.

It's been hours since Max sent me his text demanding I meet him for lunch today, and he still hasn't responded to my reply where I declined his invitation.

Who the hell does he think he is telling me what to do?

I won't jump when he says how high. I won't bend and stretch for him, not for anyone, although... I love the chase, want him to keep pushing because it shows me he wants me, makes me feel alive, and I love it.

When he grabbed my hair and pulled my neck back then told me to come for him yesterday as he fucked me from behind, I did. Willingly, I cried out his name as I came all over his cock.

That familiar cocktail of emotions spirals once more. A mix of excitement combined with the happy buzz of adrenaline fizzes through my veins like a shot of pure electric energy from the rush of our illicit encounter. It's forbidden. Barred. But it was so good. Great fucking sex.

I stop pacing and throw my phone onto the pile of papers covering my desk, and place my hands on my hips as I eye the ceiling, considering my next move.

I made it very clear yesterday that our time in the presidential suite was a one-time deal and that it would never happen again. What part of just this once did he not understand about yesterday?

Oh, I know what it was... it was probably something to do with me telling him never to stop chasing me. What the hell was I thinking?

It was a slip-up at my end, a miscalculation in my judgment. I had way too much coffee at the lawyers' lunch. That's all it was. And the guilt, holy shit, the guilt I felt as soon as I left the hotel consumed me to the point that I was unable to eat any dinner last night.

Angrily, I swipe my phone off my desk and re-read his text messages again.

"Arrogant fuckwit," I grumble under my breath.

I send another text, ensuring he gets the message this time.

ME

Acknowledge my text. I can't make it.

You are so annoying.

The read receipt glares back at me. It's time stamped and everything. It took him milliseconds to read it, meaning he has our conversation open.

ME

I can see you've read my text, answer me.

I check the time for the tenth time: 12.30 p.m.

Oh, screw it. I lift my workbag off the floor and slide my phone inside then check my reflection in the glass walls of my office. What the hell am I doing? I don't need to look good for him. I already know I look great today in my black leather pencil skirt and white blouse. "Spicy" is how Emma put it this morning.

"I'll be back by two." I storm past Edward, my new legal secretary, flicking my long hair over my shoulder. Yeah, I'm wearing it down, and not because Max said he liked my hair down; no, it was because I didn't have time to pin it up.

That's my excuse and I'm sticking to it.

"Have a great lunch," Edward calls out to me as I walk toward the elevator.

"Oh, it won't be." It will be frustrating, and Max will be hideously maddening.

This is the only way he'll listen to me. An in-person explanation is best.

And if he doesn't get the message this time, then maybe I'll have to file a restraining order against him.

Why didn't I think about that before?

I chuckle deviously to myself.

I would never do that but maybe it's the only way to keep me away from him.

But that's not what I want either.

This morning I even made a visit to the doctors to have the contraceptive pill prescribed.

It was a moment of madness, clearly. I even popped the first one in the car, because the doctor said this type of pill only needs two days to kick in. Two days, and suddenly there are no excuses. No safety nets. Just me and this hunger I can't seem to tame.

What have I become?

A dirty little slut who craves Max Hart's dick, that's who.

And God help me, I want more.

My head might be saying stop, but my body and heart crave his touch—the heat of his hands on my skin, the weight of his lips crushing mine, and the way he says my name like it belongs to him. It makes me feel things I never thought were possible.

I have no control over my emotions anymore when it comes to him, and no matter how hard I try to fight it, every breath, every beat of my heart drags me closer. Closer to the edge. Closer to him.

And the truth? I don't even want to resist.

26

MAX

I'm standing behind the hotel room door as Paige storms in, annoyance bouncing off her so hard it's tangible.

As I've told her before, she's too easy to wind up, and I knew that ignoring her text messages would provoke a reaction. I suspected she would show up today, using it as an excuse to confront me face-to-face and try to justify why we shouldn't keep going, to end things between us. I won't let that happen. She has no idea how determined I can be. And she wants it too, or she wouldn't be here. She just can't bring herself to admit it to me. I've been the enemy for too long and it's screwing with her head how much she likes me; how much we like each other.

"Can't stay away, huh, Bunny?"

She lets out a startled scream as I wrap my hand around her wrist and push her against the wall, pinning her there, causing her workbag to hit the floor with a thud as the door closes, locking us away from the rest of the world.

"Max." My name comes out of her mouth in a delicate whisper. She might be shoving my shoulders as if trying to push me away, but there's no strength behind it or any fight. She isn't fooling anyone. She wouldn't be here if she didn't want to be.

"We can't, Max."

I run my nose along hers, her sweet breath heating my lips that are desperate to kiss her once more. "But you're here now, it would be a shame to waste the room."

"I guess." Her chest heaves up and down, in and out, as if she's already breathless. The anticipation is almost too much for her to withstand, and she's agonizing over what her mind is telling her but what her body refuses to believe.

Gliding my finger over her bottom lip, I drag it downward, moving my touch to her chin, her neck, brushing my fingertips over her clavicle, then between her cleavage, making her breath come out in uneven stutters.

My hands find her waist, desperate to feel her shapely hips again that I'm completely obsessed with before I shimmy her sexy leather skirt upward, inch by painful inch.

"We shouldn't, Max." There's not a hint of believability in her tone as she allows me to slide the form-fitting slinky leather all the way up to her waist, my cock thickening in my boxers.

"We should," I counter, slipping my fingers inside the tiny triangle of fabric at the front of her lace panties. When I push my fingers between her pussy, my smile tiptoes around the corners of my mouth when I discover she's already wet.

She can spin any story she wants, but I see through it; she wants me. Wants this and is turned on by the excitement of our clandestine dalliance.

When I gently rub her clit, she cries out, gripping onto my shoulders, her back arching in response.

She's already so close.

Do I know this is wrong? Of course I do. But can I stop

myself from wanting her? Never. Now I've had a taste of her, she's all I've thought about, dreamed about.

I was lying to myself, believing that four hours with her yesterday was enough. I need more, want more, crave her soft moans and whimpers, crave the way she smiles when she comes, crave the gentleness of her touch and lips on mine. Whatever she'll give me, I want it all.

And she might object again today, tomorrow, and the next day after that, but there's no substance to her words. Her resistance is long gone.

Her eyes meet mine, and I already know what this one means. It's the one where she looks firm, almost domineering, but I can see the cracks, her resolve wavering, a softening that reveals how close she is to giving in.

"One more time." I nod confidently, her defenses beginning to subside as she tilts her hips, rubbing her clit against the palm of my hand while I circle her wet entrance, making all the blood rush to the head of my cock with the need to be inside her.

She tries to straighten herself with dignity, but she has to bite her lip to stifle her outcry, her body relaxing in my arms. "One more time," she answers, gasping as I push a finger inside her wet heat, her walls gripping my digit, pulling me needily into her body.

It won't take long before she's coming all over my fingers then my cock.

I watch her intently, her mouth dropping open in silence when I curl my finger inside her and rub the area that makes her come lightning fast, which I discovered yesterday.

"Make me come, Max."

"Not yet." My mouth swoops in to kiss her tempting mouth, our hungry tongues touching each other as if they are long-lost lovers. I suck her tongue into my mouth as I remove my fingers from her wet center and lift my hand to our mouths.

Giving her no time to think about what I'm doing, I press my finger against her lips as I let go of her tongue from between my teeth then tell her to, "Lick."

Without hesitation she sucks my finger into her mouth, sucking her juices off my digit, twirling her tongue around it, ensuring she tastes every last drop. My dick pounds harder, growing thicker as precum leaks from the tip as her expert mouth sucks me illicitly in the same way she did yesterday.

When she pushes my finger out of her mouth with her tongue, I plant a soft kiss on her lips before dropping to my knees, lifting her leg on top of my shoulder, my mouth now perfectly aligned with her pussy. I spread her lips with my fingers, my mouth watering at the thought of tasting her again. "You have such a pretty pussy, baby." She tastes sweeter than honey.

I look up as she looks down, a sinful smile dancing across her lips as the air around us becomes heavy with need. The thrill of us doing this together again swirls around us in a mix of passion and desire. We hate each other—sorry, we *hated* each other, couldn't stand to be in the same room as one another, or even bear to breathe the same air, like a couple on the brink of divorce, seeing only our worst traits, but now, there's banter, a shift to flirtatiousness from the barbed conversation we once had. It's transformed into chemistry and attraction that makes the fiery tension between us stronger with an air of vulnerability about it. We might work together professionally but our bodies work even better together between the sheets.

Her moans burn with lust. "I need you inside me," she says, tilting her hips with impatience.

Fuck yeah, she wants this.

"Not yet," I say again, turning my head to the side to kiss the skin of her inner thigh, and finally when her body is almost trembling with need, I kiss her pussy, making shots of euphoria fly out of her mouth.

"Oh fuck, yeah, harder, Max."

I lick her clit with my tongue, flicking it much harder like she wants me to this time. I know she's loving every minute as she threads her fingers through my hair, pushing my mouth against her pussy much harder as I thrust my tongue into her entrance. She flings her head back, forgetting how close she is to the wall and bangs it. But she doesn't care and does it again as she arches her back off the wall, holding my mouth against her pussy to keep me there.

"Fuck yeah," she pants with need, making me chuckle. Her cursing is the best sound I've heard all day.

She's usually so stern; watching her come apart like this on my tongue is not only amazing but proof of how far we've come —from enemies to this.

The woman who once glared at me like I was her personal nightmare is now trembling, letting me touch her in ways she would never have allowed me before; I wouldn't have dared to. It's addicting, the way her body melts under my hands, how she clutches at my hair as if she can't believe this is happening.

And honestly? Neither can I.

I never thought I'd crave her this way, or that I'd learn to read every breath, every gasp, every plea. But now, tasting her surrender, hearing her swear like she might break, it's the sweetest victory I could ever ask for, and I don't want to ever give it up.

I take a moment to look up at her. Eyes closed, she's grinning, completely lost in the moment as I eat her out like my life depends on it. She's so fucking beautiful. The strong muscles of her thighs contract as I drag my finger through her folds, making her suck in a deep, sharp breath as I work her body possessively.

Sucking her clit into my mouth, I flick it with my tongue, which has her bowing her back even more and digging the heel of her stiletto into my shoulders and back. I hope she scratches and bruises my skin with her sharp pumps deep enough to leave a scar. I want her branded into my skin.

I thrust a finger inside of her while continuing to lick her clit until she's moaning and writhing, pushing her hips and holding my face against her pussy as her pleasure coils through her body, dragging her closer to the edge of her orgasm.

She's on the edge, about to shatter, and I flick her clit faster.

"You taste so fucking good, baby," I pant, thrusting another finger inside her before sliding them in and out, and adding a third, stretching her to get ready to take me again. I'm so desperate to be inside her, my cock eagerly pounding and ready to fuck.

"Max," she cries out when I curl my fingers inside her, her legs beginning to shake.

Her walls twitch around my fingers and I whisper against her pussy, "My cock is so fucking hard for you."

"Make me come, then fuck me, Max." She reaches down and cups my face so tenderly that for a fleeting moment this feels like so much more than just sex and hooking up in secret. It's intimacy unlike anything I've ever felt. It's raw, consuming, and so fucking real. There's no masks or darkness to hide us, no walls, and no biting words to keep each other at a distance. Just skin and heat and the unspoken truth that somehow, against every odd, we chose this.

Or maybe, it found us in the dark that night at the club.

She clings to me like I'm her anchor, and maybe I am, because right now she's mine too. The world fades around us, and I'm relishing, memorizing every sound she makes, every shiver, every ragged gasp that says she trusts me. That she wants me.

After everything, all the closing statements in court, our arguments, the fierce rivalry to win court cases, the pent-up anger splitting hairs over property, child support, and alimony for our clients, this is what's left: a bond so intense it threatens to undo me. Ruin us.

Every woman before now was insignificant, because this, here, right now, is all that matters, and we are so hot together, we could start a forest fire.

I feel wild and so turned on, every hair on my body standing to her attention.

Her hips are rocking, telling me she's desperate to come, so I pick up the pace and lick her swollen clit much faster now, sliding my fingers back and forth for her to chase her release she so desperately needs, working her body. I wish we had been doing this for years, not days.

What the fuck took us so long?

Between my fingers fucking her dripping-wet pussy, and my tongue lashing at her clit, I send her into sensory overload, focusing all of my attention on making her feel good and forget any other man but me.

"Fuck, Max," she moans, her breathing becoming labored.

And when I suck her clit again, her fingers painfully pull at my hair so tightly I wonder if she'll pull every strand from my scalp.

Pleasure crashes through her when she cries, "I'm coming," barely able to catch her breath and letting out a long groan.

I take my time, allowing her to come down from her high, my fingers slowly moving in and out of her drenched pussy as she rides out the last wave of her orgasm.

I kiss her clit one last time, causing her to jerk, before removing my fingers from inside her.

She releases her hold from the vise-like grip of my hair. I'm hoping that she does the same again because I'm already addicted to the pleasurable pain I want more of.

I glance up, and when her eyes hit mine, she shoots me a satisfied smile as I lazily smile back. And there it is again; the intimacy. The warmth and happiness.

"You good?" I ask tentatively.

"Can we do that again tomorrow?" she asks, biting her bottom lip as I rise to my feet.

Quicker than a match ignites, I've undone my pants, rolled a condom on, lifted her into the air, wrapped her legs around my waist, and filled her soaked pussy with my cock.

"I think that answers your question." I fuck her up the wall, her nails digging into my back.

"This is bad." She stares at me through her lashes; her thoughts caught somewhere between taking a leap into sin with me or stopping this altogether. "I want you."

"Me too." Being bad never felt so good.

"Tomorrow will be the last time," she pants, lying to herself and me.

"Last time," I parrot, knowing it won't be.

27

PAIGE—THE NEXT DAY

MAX

Hotel Ridge, 1 p.m. today.

> **ME**
>
> Okay.

MAX

No arguments? Are you sick?

> **ME**
>
> Fuck off.

MAX

Oh, there's the caustic comeback that makes me hard

> **ME**
>
> Go away, I'm busy.

MAX

See you later.

> **ME**
>
> Can't wait.

What the hell did I tell him that for?

Can't wait?

Oh... maybe it's because I can't.

This isn't just terrible, this is a disaster.

If I go to hell, I'm taking him with me.

* * *

Two Days Later

MAX

Hotel Zaptos, 2 p.m. today. I'm in court this
morning, so I won't be able to come earlier.

ME

Okay. I'm taking the afternoon off.

MAX

How long do we have?

ME

Until 7 p.m. And I went on the pill. I'm clean if
you are.

MAX

You went on the pill?

ME

Yes. Don't read too much into it, I have heavy
periods.

That's a lie. One of the many I've been telling recently.

MAX

That will be a first for me.

ME

Me too. I can't see you for the next few days, so make it memorable.

MAX

Brace yourself, Bunny.

28

PAIGE—A WEEK LATER

"Good afternoon." I smile at the host in one of the fanciest restaurants in the city. It's not my usual choice to have a meeting with a new client over lunch, but according to Edward, it's what the client insisted on. "Reservation for Bradshaw. I'm meeting my client, Mr. Smith."

"He's already arrived. This way, ma'am."

A flash of confusion crosses my brow as I look around the empty restaurant.

"Quiet day?" I ask.

"Mr. Smith booked the entire restaurant for your meeting, ma'am."

"Excuse me?" I follow the host to the back of the restaurant, noticing his stiff posture as he ignores me.

Wait... is "Mr. Smith" just a cover name for someone ridiculously famous?

This has happened several times before. Last time, a big movie producer used an alias to set up a meeting with me to ask if I would take on his messy and very public divorce. It was around the same time as Alfie arrived, and because my life was so hectic and the case was so public, I turned it down and sent him to Max. I've seen those cases play out on television, and the last thing I wanted was for my private life to be plastered all over the news.

"Mr. Smith, your appointment has arrived." The host steps aside to reveal a smug-looking Max sitting at a table tucked in the back of the restaurant, and I can't help but smile as my stomach flutters.

Max stands up as I approach, a slight nervous energy in his movements. He's never booked a restaurant before, and yet here he is, casual like it's no big deal. He reaches out, brushing a stray strand of hair behind my ear, then leans in slowly for a kiss. Before I can stop him, his lips are on mine. It's soft, gentle, almost hesitant. Unexpected. Everything about this moment feels surprising.

I should pull away, but I don't. Instead, I let the thrill of being here together, so openly, make my heart race as his lips brush against mine.

"We shouldn't be doing this," I gasp, stepping back just enough to catch my breath.

"No one's looking," he murmurs, a playful smile tugging at the corner of his mouth.

"They have staff, Max," I whisper, voice low, eyes darting around.

He waves a hand dismissively. "Stop stressing, my friend. Merrick owns the place so we have nothing to worry about. Today, there's only one server, one host, and one chef. Just for us."

"For us?" I raise an eyebrow, incredulously.

"Yes. Lunch."

I shake my head, smiling despite myself. "This is completely over the top, Max. And extravagant."

His eyes soften. "I wanted to spend time with you."

I glance around again, voice dropping. "We usually do that in hotel rooms."

He steps a bit closer, his tone quiet but earnest. "That's not enough. Quick escapes aren't my thing anymore. I want more than that. I want to be with you."

I look up, surprised, almost breathless. "Like a couple?"

He pauses, then shrugs with a small, almost shy smile. "Maybe." Then, changing the mood, he asks softly, "Are you hungry?"

"Starving," I admit, feeling the tension shift.

He offers his arm, a gentle invitation, and together we walk toward the table as if we are two people stepping into something new.

"Then let's eat," he says, almost sounding relieved that I didn't put up a fight like I usually do. He informs me, "They make the best mezze platters here; we should order two." He gestures for me to sit down. "Then you can tell me all about what you've been doing the past few days. I missed your Alfie updates, and did you get the flowers I sent?"

"I did." Oh, yeah, so there are flower deliveries to add to the list of sweet things he's done for me. And now this.

He booked the whole place. For me? For us? God, this isn't just about stealing a few hours anymore. This isn't some dark corner where no one knows our names.

He cleared a room, shut out the rest of the world, as if he wanted time itself to stop for us. What does this mean? He's not hiding us away in the shadows; he's giving us light, giving us space. It's dangerous. And intoxicating.

This is more than sex. It's more than stolen touches and whispers in the dark. It's him telling me he wants more and that I matter.

And that scares me more than anything... because I'm starting to believe him, and beginning to realize I want more too.

29

PAIGE—FOUR DAYS LATER

"Do you like my cock?" he asks. His eyes turn dark as I watch him fucking me from behind in the hotel mirror.

"Yes." Too much. My nipples tighten into hard peaks when he grabs them, pinching them between his expert fingers, fondling them, then squeezing them tightly between his fists.

"Hands on the wall."

I do as I'm told and brace myself against each side of the mirror on the wall.

"Good girl," he growls, moving his hands from my tits to my hips, digging his fingertips into my flesh.

"Max," I cry out, pushing back as he fucks me with wild abandon.

"Don't ever tell me we're stopping this."

Catching his eyes, I smile wickedly at him in the mirror. He was pissed when I told him yesterday that we should stop this. I want to, but I just can't seem to help myself when it comes to him.

"Never," I cry out as he fucks me so deep, forcing me to stretch up onto my tiptoes.

"You're pussy feels so good."

His dick feels so good, it's as if it was made for my pussy.

Reaching around to my front, he rubs my clit. Pinches it, then spanks it, rendering me speechless.

I rock my hips, fucking him, moving in time with him, back and forth with the need to find my release as he strikes into me from behind.

He slides his finger down my backside, spitting on it as he slips his thumb into my tight, puckered hole while hammering into me faster. I push back again, meeting every punishing thrust.

"Oh, fuck, yeah," I cry out, my back arching in response, my core pulsing.

I've never done this with a man before. My historically bland sex life—who am I kidding?—my *barren* sex life is a thing of the past. Everything we do together is so fucking hot and I might never want to stop, although one day, I know we will. We have to.

"Relax," he instructs, pressing a kiss to my shoulder. There's this odd feeling of pressure at my back hole. It's not unpleasant; if anything, it's different, nice.

With his other hand still on my clit, he spanks it again, as he pushes his digit deeper into my back entrance, and with one more slap of my clit, I come.

He comes, roaring my name, the thick veins in his neck popping out of his skin, his pulse pounding in it as every muscle in his body is taut as he fills me with his hot seed. Going on the pill was the best decision; with nothing between us, I feel every twitch and pulse of his cock.

Together we come undone. Our bodies work in perfect harmony with one another.

Gentle bubbles of happiness and pleasure fizz across my skin.

What was supposed to be a one-time thing has become so much more. I don't even know how to label us anymore. Whatever it is, it's wonderful and terrifying. But while part of me longs to dive right in, another part fears I'm in over my head.

Max moves in and out of my body slowly, emptying himself inside of me fully and ushering me out of our dizzying ecstasy.

Looking at me in the mirror from over my shoulder, he trails gentle kisses along the curvature of my neck once more.

In this moment, there are unspoken words and things that neither of us is willing to admit: we couldn't stop this even if we tried.

"Same time tomorrow?" he asks, his expression full of satisfaction.

"I thought you'd never ask."

30

PAIGE

"Good morning, Paige."

"Morning, Edward." I stride past him, feeling achy all over from the rigorous sex at lunch with Max. It was better than any gym workout, and I swear my flexibility is better than it was before. I can now easily put my legs up by my ears without feeling like my hamstrings might burst when Max leans on my legs to push them back further.

It's so deep when he does that and the stretch feels so good.

"How are you today?" Edward asks me.

"I'm great." I feel fantastic. Sex is amazing, Alfie is great, work is busy, and I now have a new secretary who has made my work easier. I'd been managing and using temps for way too long because I was planning on leaving. Since the curveball that is Alfie entered my life, and since I've finally accepted I won't be starting my own firm until I can afford to, I finally took the plunge and hired a full-time secretary. It's just as well he's here because I've started to lose focus on work. If I thought I was busy before, I'm so busy now that I skip lunch.

"There's a parcel on your desk," Edward tells me, pointing

through the door of my office to my desk, while focusing on whatever is on the screen of his computer.

"What is it?" I ask curiously, feeling confused because Edward opens my mail.

"I don't know; it arrived ten minutes ago. It was delivered by courier and marked personal, so I left it for you to open." He drags his attention away from his task and looks around before lowering his voice to say words that shock me to my core: "You know, people in the office are starting to talk."

I widen my eyes in shock, then try to compose myself. "Talk? About what?"

"You, and where you go at lunch. They keep mentioning that you never used to do that and how they all think you have a new man. Plus"—he uses his head to point at my office—"you received another bunch of flowers the other day from Mr. Fox. Patricia in accounts read the card before you arrived the other morning."

Damn you, Max Hart, for your careless romantic gesture.

And damn us for coloring outside the lines. I have to tell Max to stop sending me flowers, or better still, to stop sending me text messages of where we are meeting next.

Even more so, I need to stop sending him messages asking him where and when we are meeting. He's become the thing I swore I would never allow him to become: my fix, my person, the one that stirs emotions in me I promised myself I'd never invite.

"I don't have a new man." I wave off the accusation. Technically, we're having fun. Nothing more. He's not my man. It feels like he is though.

He stares me down. "Even if you did, I have your back, Paige. I've been telling them you have meetings."

"Do they believe you?"

"I don't think so."

"Shit," I hiss under my breath, and I glance around the office but no one is looking at me.

"You know, it would only take one call to the florist to find out who sent you those flowers."

My chest feels too tight, like my own skin is trying to rip itself open.

Edward suggests, "Have him send them to your house instead. That might be a better idea and would stop the chins wagging." He winks like a conspirator then goes back to whatever he was doing on his computer.

"Thanks, Edward." I step inside my office and close the door behind me.

People are talking about me.

I rub my fingertips into my temples.

This is getting out of hand.

Edward is massively protective of me and discreet, and he has eased my workload tenfold; choosing him was the best decision I've made this year.

On the flip side, sleeping with Max Hart might be the worst one.

But that still hasn't stopped me from going back for more, though.

It's been months since our first hookup in the presidential suite, and I almost hate myself for it, but I've seen him nearly every day at lunch. It's crazy to think we can keep this up, but my self-reasoning tells me that we aren't, and never have been, discussing the Youngs' divorce case, so it's fine. Everything's fine.

It's not fine.

It's far from it.

The case should have been closed weeks ago, but after Stella Young pushed for Tate to have more custody of the children—probably to mess with his weekends, which he planned to spend golfing and going out on his boat—and so we are still weeks away from settling the Youngs' divorce.

When all I want is for it to be over, then I won't feel so guilty.

After hearing what the office is saying about me, it makes my decision easier today. Max will hate me for it, but I've given it a lot of thought and at lunch, I'm telling him that this will be the last day I meet up with him. We can't keep doing what we're doing. I'm not lying this time.

Becoming romantically involved with him during a divorce case is a serious ethical breach. If anyone were to find out, it could explode into a terrible scandal for both of us.

Something I never want to happen.

So it stops. Now. Today.

We draw a line under the desire that keeps pulling us back together like magnets. This is our ending.

I stare at the mini black box edged in gold that's sitting on my desk and drop my workbag on the floor as worry is replaced with curiosity. I take a seat behind my desk and pick up the box that looks more like a gift than anything work-related before removing the lid, revealing a smaller black perfume box surrounded by black tissue paper. I lift it out of the box and read the words on the front: *Tom Ford, Fucking Fabulous.*

My eyebrows furrow in confusion as I open the box to reveal a black perfume bottle inside.

There is only one person who this can be from. Max.

I recheck the box to confirm it's from him and I smile to myself, excitement rushing through my veins when I find a small note tucked beneath the black tissue paper.

Holding the card between my fingers, I read it, then burst out laughing and have to cover my mouth to quiet the loudness.

My beautiful Bunny,

Please replace your old perfume with this new one. Your sex life is no longer vanilla... it's Fucking Fabulous.

Mr. Fox x

There is no denying it; we're more than enemies with benefits. We're crossing into relationship territory. Why did he have to be so nice? Why couldn't he have just kept being the alphahole fuckboy I thought he was?

Instead, he's kind-hearted, funny, sweet, and he's the best lover I've ever had, always putting me first during sex. He never finishes before I do. In his eyes, that's non-negotiable, and I'm here for it. Actually, I *was* here for it. We're past tense now, not present after today.

"Shit," I hiss under my breath, eyeing the perfume. He's twisting my wrist, making me reconsider ending our midday trysts.

Popping the lid off the perfume bottle, I pump the atomizer a couple of times to draw the fragrance up the dip tube, then spray it on my wrist. I inhale the strong scent, drawing the notes into my nostrils, instantly lifting my mood.

"God, that's nice." I spray it on the pulse points of my neck then a little more over the fabric of my dress.

It's unsettling how much he knows about me in such a short time, but he's taken the time to ask questions and really explore my life because we've spent countless hours together, uncovering every detail of our bodies and every chapter of our childhoods and lives both inside and outside the court. From the sports he plays to the cars he drives, I know everything about him, just as he knows everything about me. He even knows when I lost my virginity. It was prom—absolutely dreadful with a guy named Vincent who turned out to be a one-pump chump, which Max found hilarious.

We talk and share things about each other's lives. It's an intimacy that goes far beyond the surface. Our physical closeness opened the doors to our emotional truths and personal histories, some of which we've never shared with anyone else. When we are together, we're vulnerable, sharing our bodies and memories. The bond that's building feels unique and comforting, scary too because I share parts of myself with him that I hide from others.

I bend down and pull my cell phone out of my workbag to text the man who is chipping away at my ice queen heart... His words, not mine. If only he knew, every time I'm in his orbit, it flutters wildly like a beast in my chest, as if it's trying to break free from my body.

> ME
>
> Thank you for the perfume.

I almost add a kiss on the end of my text then reconsider it and send it without one.

> MAX
>
> You are most welcome. Did you like it? x

> ME
>
> It's beautiful.

> MAX
>
> Just like you. x

Fuck that infuriating man and that damn kiss.

As my fingers hover over the keyboard, I'm unsure if I should send my next request. I don't want to, but we need to before we get in any deeper than we already are.

Develop feelings... if I haven't already.

I hit send before I have any more time to inwardly debate.

ME

Can we meet up today, but just to talk?

MAX

Don't tell me, you want to end things? Again? x

I hate how well he knows me; it's as if he's living inside my head sometimes.

ME

Yeah.

MAX

No hotels today. Meet me at the airport near Watsonville. I'll send you the directions.

ME

That's miles away. I have work to do.

MAX

Forget work. See you soon. And think about us, Paige. I know what I want. I want you. Meet me today, though, let's have some fun together.

Why is he always so diplomatic? Oh, I know why, because he knows if he gives me space and time, I will change my mind yet again.

ME

Are you going to tell me what we're doing?

MAX

No. Can't wait to see you.

Another text from him arrives right after his last one.

MAX

I miss you every day I don't see you. x

Ditto, Max. Ditto.

* * *

I drive into the parking lot at a private airfield I didn't even know existed, and there he is.

Max.

With his strong arms crossed tightly, the midday sun highlights every corded muscle in his forearms.

Ankles crossed, he's leaning with relaxed confidence against yet another sports car—a Lamborghini, I think, glossy and black as a panther ready to pounce.

Designer sunglasses shield his eyes as he surveys me, the airfield behind him. Dressed in jeans and a spotless white T-shirt that matches the pristine white of his sneakers, he looks effortlessly relaxed, while I suddenly feel overdressed in my royal-blue work dress.

And holy freaking shit, he's the sexiest man to have walked Planet Earth, I'm sure of it.

Max uncrosses his ankles as I pull up beside him, the parking lot almost completely empty.

I turn off my car, then open my door to get out of my black Range Rover. My fully equipped SUV has never felt so dull compared to his supercar.

"What are we doing here?" I move to him and stand between his uncrossed legs.

Pulling me into his arms, he rests his hands on my hips. "Skydiving."

"I'm not skydiving," I shrill, mildly panicking.

"No? Well, I am. You can join me or watch me. It's up to you."

I look up at the sky just as a small plane is taking off. "Do you go up in that?"

It's so tiny, I'm not sure it looks safe.

"Yes. Are you scared of heights?" he asks with a slight hint of mockery in his tone.

"I'm not scared of anything." That's not true. He scares me because meeting him here today feels like an official date.

Relationship territory. My earlier thoughts appear in my mind.

"Then jump with me."

"Have you done this before?"

"Dozens of times. My brothers might be all work, work, work and no play, but I like doing both."

"You've done this dozens of times?" Once is too much for me.

"It's a hobby of mine."

"What else do you like doing?"

"I take Lidia here"—he taps the door of his car—"to the race-track most Sundays. I bungee jump wherever I go on holiday, and the next thing I want to try is base jumping."

I hope he has great life insurance. "You are certifiably crazy." I laugh at his absurdity, also because he named his car.

"Crazy about you." He possessively pulls me closer and kisses me breathless. Every nerve ending erupts with the certainty that I'm falling for this insanely gorgeous, kind, and powerful man.

"What if someone sees us?" I whisper against his lips.

"No one I know comes here, and besides, everyone is working."

"Edward told me today that people have begun to talk at work." I could even hear the whispers behind my back and could feel the heat of their stares as I left the office today. "You can't send any more gifts or flowers to the office."

"I'll send them to your house then."

"That's not what I meant."

"Stop fighting us, Paige." The worry I see in his eyes every time I try to push him away is back, and I hate that I'm the one who put it there.

"I don't want to lose my job, Max."

"What about me? Do you want to lose me?"

I can't even lie. "I don't."

Maybe I should just take the job at Hart Law. It would make everything easier. But what happens to my career if Max and I implode?

That's a hell of a leap. I mean, we're not even dating. It's just sex. Right? "You're not going to lose me, baby. You've got me." His arms around me squeeze me tightly. "After the Youngs' case closes, then we figure out how we make us work."

"Is that what you want?" I ask tentatively. It feels like the question that could change everything.

"Yes... more than anything. I just don't know how we'd do it if you were to continue your job at Moore & Associates."

I feel the same and have thought the same. "So, we just keep doing what we're doing, for now?" I ask, petrified of ever having to give him up.

He nods with a gaze so intense it feels like he's touching me everywhere. "In the meantime, we need to keep us a secret, for the Youngs' sake. I don't want anything about us coming out that will affect their case."

"We've never spoken about them." I look around the lot again. "We're in a very public place."

"Like I said, no one comes here that I know. Chill, baby."

This is getting too serious, so I change the subject. "I don't want to jump."

"Come and watch me then." He stands to his full height, threading his fingers into mine.

"I can't believe you skydive for fun?"

"What can I say, I love the rush. I love being reminded I'm alive." His grin is reckless and dazzling, the kind that makes my stomach somersault. He swings our joined hands between us, like we're just two ordinary people on an ordinary day, even though nothing about this feels ordinary.

"Promise me you'll be safe," I say.

He laughs, a deep, warm sound that vibrates through me. "That sounds like you care about me, Bunny. But don't worry I know what I am doing, although I do have to sign a waiver, because there are no guarantees."

That makes my stomach turn in a different way. I'm already worried about his safety, confirming his accusation. I care about him. Too much. It's almost dangerous.

I roll my eyes, pretending to brush off my concern.

He pulls me closer, tucks a loose strand of hair behind my ear, and kisses me again. For a second, the buzz of a distant plane is the only sound between us.

"Bye, Lidia." He nods toward his sleek black Lamborghini, an obedient servant waiting to fulfill his thrill.

I burst into a fit of giggles like a lust filled teenager. He's unlike anyone I've ever dated. Oops... we're not dating.

"Let's do this." He tugs me along behind him, his steps quickening, driven by the buzz of adrenaline he's always chasing just out in front of him.

My heart's already racing faster than any supercar. "What are we doing after this?"

"I'm taking you out for an early dinner at the Rolfstone."

That's a Michelin-star restaurant.

Yeah, this is a date.

A crazy, unpredictable, only-he-could-plan-it kind of date.

31

MAX

Disappointment washes over me when I see Cole's name pop up on my screen with his text message. I was hoping it would be Paige.

COLE
Are you free for lunch?

ME
Not today, I have plans.

COLE
Again?

ME
What do you mean, again?

COLE
You've been sneaking out for lunch without me for weeks. Are you dating?

ME
No.

COLE

You sure?

ME

Yes. Now fuck off, I'm busy preparing the new settlement for the Young case.

COLE

You'll be glad when the Young case is over.

ME

Why?

COLE

Then you'll have a bit of a breather from Paige. That is, until the next case you go head-to-head on.

ME

I'm warming to her. Turns out she's not the ice queen I thought she was. She's bright, sharp, and not what I expected. She's incredible.

COLE

Did you have a lobotomy since I saw you last?

ME

No.

COLE

So why are you being nice about her?

ME

I'm not, I'm just telling you how good she is at her job.

COLE

We all know that, Max, but what you said sounds personal and has nothing to do with work. Do you have a thing for Paige?

ME

No.

COLE

Are you sure about that?

ME

Yes. I have to go.

COLE

Sure you do. Have a good *lunch*.

32

MAX

I'm sitting at the back of the courtroom waiting for my case to be called when what sounds like a fucking circus bursts through the courtroom doors.

Every head whips around, even the judge's, to see what the hell is causing all the commotion. I freeze, momentarily stunned.

It's Paige. Paige, holding a baby in her arms. Alfie, I believe; it has to be him. He looks like the photos she's shown me of him, and he's wailing, red-faced and frantic. But it's not just that. Her hair's down—Paige never wears her hair down in court—and she looks completely undone.

Disheveled. Exhausted.

She's juggling a stroller, awkwardly pushing it down the gallery aisle with one hand, Alfie clutched to her hip with the other, her workbag barely hanging from her shoulder. It's chaos, and she's in the middle of it, and somehow, I am too.

"Sorry," she apologizes, as she gasps for breath.

"Ms. Bradshaw?" The judge addresses her. "What is the meaning of this?"

"I'm sorry, Your Honor... my nanny... she called in sick... and my car... is at the garage." She struggles to get her words out, then covers her mouth with her hand as if she's sick herself. "And I'm... Oh, God... I think I might throw up..." She doesn't finish her sentence as Alfie continues to cry in her arms, sounding unhappy and disgruntled.

"This is a courtroom, not a daycare, Ms. Bradshaw. Sit down or get out." The judge points to the courtroom doors.

Paige holds her stomach as she tries to bounce Alfie up and down on her hip to soothe him. "Your Honor, I have a case on this morning's docket. I'm sorry, I... I'm not feeling well, but I had to come..."

Judge Balfour stares at her. He's stern, but I can tell how concerned he is. "Ma'am, slow down."

Paige pants, bouncing Alfie over and over, unsteady on her feet, and struggling.

"What case?" the judge asks matter-of-factly, peering over the top of his glasses.

"Forbes custody matter."

The judge eyes the baby, then signals to the bailiff. "Please assist Ms. Bradshaw. Ms. Bradshaw, do you need medical attention?"

"No, I'm fine, really." She sways on her feet slightly, gripping the stroller for balance, and I'm on my feet in seconds. Shit, she's going to topple over with Alfie in her arms.

Much firmer now, Judge Balfour booms, "Court is in recess. Ms. Bradshaw, sit down now, let's get someone to help you."

She doesn't need someone, she needs me; they both do. I'm running to her, by her side and scooping a screaming Alfie out of her arms as the judge finishes his sentence.

Taking Paige's hand, I gently usher her to a seat and tell her to sit down.

"Hey, hey, little fella. It's okay. You're okay," I coo, trying to settle a distressed Alfie. He's not sick; I think he's sensing Paige's unwell state and hysterical morning.

According to Nathan, babies pick up on things like that, which is why he has Arianna working minimum hours. He doesn't want her or the baby being stressed. See... he's a fool for her, as I am for Paige and her little boy, whose sobs have begun to die down, his little chest stuttering as he gulps in fresh air.

"You don't look so good, Paige," I tell her. She looks green.

"I feel terrible." Her eyes roll back into her head as I snuggle Alfie into my chest without a care that he's covering my new suit in snot and drool.

"We'll call you a cab, Ms. Bradshaw." The bailiff appears by my side.

"I'll take her home. She knows me and trusts me. We've worked together for years, and I know who to contact at her office to inform them she's unwell." Luckily, I brought my RSQ8 today. I had a different kind of court date planned with my brothers after work. Looks like tennis will have to wait. "Do you think you can walk to the front of the building, Paige?"

"Maybe." Her reply is faint.

I lay the back of my hand on her forehead. "You're burning up." She feels clammy. "I'm going to take you home, okay?"

"Okay," she replies. I know she's sick, or she'd be fighting me and telling me to go fuck myself.

"Find me a rear-facing car seat for the baby, he's only one." I look at the bailiff. "From anyone, and I'll have it returned as soon as I'm finished with it. And here are my car keys. Can you retrieve my car from the underground parking lot and bring it around the front? It's a burnt orange color, gold wheels." I hand him my key fob for my one-of-a-kind sports car. "Push the brake pedal and the start button to start it." With seven hundred brake horsepower, it's a beast of a car. I hope he loves taking her for a spin.

He smiles as if reading my mind. "Yes, sir. Give me five minutes and I'll meet you out front."

"And can you grab my briefcase and pop it in the back seat of my car, please? I would be very grateful." I point to where I was sitting in the gallery.

"Of course, sir." He leaves without another word, taking my briefcase with him as he exits the courtroom.

I look at the judge and give him my name, then request for my case and Paige's to be rescheduled.

"Approved, given the circumstances, Mr. Hart. I'll reschedule the hearings."

"Thank you, Your Honor."

Awkwardly, because I'm not good with wriggling babies, I place Alfie into his stroller, struggling with the clip to secure him. "There we go." I look up at Alfie, who is all big watery eyes and snotty nose. He shoots me a huge smile, showing off the only two front teeth he has, as if he's grateful for my calm in his chaotic morning. He's cute.

"C'mon, buddy, let's get Momma home," I tell him, noticing he's still wearing his pajamas from last night. How she managed to even get herself dressed is anyone's guess.

Paige isn't just tenacious; she's feisty and wouldn't ask for help unless she's about to keel over, just like she is this morning, clearly having caught the bug that's been doing the rounds at work. Sounds like her nanny did too.

"Momma." Alfie looks up at her, pointing his chunky digits at her.

"Yeah, Momma." I mimic back and point to her too.

"Ohhh, Momma isn't well," she grumbles, a faint smile

tugging at the edge of her mouth, doing a shitty attempt at feigning happiness.

She's usually the picture of class and control: elegant, immaculate, untouchable. But today, she looks nothing like that. Pale, disheveled, swaying even while sitting down.

I need to get her into bed.

Normally, that thought would come with a smirk and a dirty punchline. But not now. Not this time. Nope, this time, it's not about bending her to my will; it's about holding her up, keeping her safe. Nursing her, not ruining her.

Picking up her workbag, I throw it over my shoulder and round the stroller, getting ready to push it, something I've never done in my life, but how hard can it be? Surely it's just like riding a bike.

Threading my fingers into Paige's, I urge her to stand up. "C'mon, Paige. Let's get you home."

She takes my hand without question.

I don't care if anyone sees us because this isn't about work. She's unwell and struggling today; she needs me, and I'm going to be there for her. Forget the case we're working on together; this is more important.

"Atta girl," I say once she's on her feet, and I guide her back up the aisle toward the exit, steering Alfie's stroller with one hand. "I'll have you home in no time." That's if I can manage to steer this damn stroller that's testing me, its wheels rolling this way and that.

She leans her head to the side and rests it on my shoulder. If she was firing on all cylinders today, she wouldn't touch me with a ten-foot pole in public.

Pathetic of me perhaps, but I like that she needs me today, and I was here for her.

Slowly, the three of us move out of the courtroom, through

the cavernous building and down the steps that lead us out of the Superior Court.

Within minutes, the bailiff, whose name I didn't catch, arrives in my car, the engine purring like an angry tiger. Fuck she sounds nice.

"How many cars do you have?" Paige asks, all delirious and woozy sounding.

"A few." Ten plus a motorcycle. Which reminds me, I haven't been out on my Yamaha YZF-R1 in months. It's about time I took her for a ride. What can I say, I like fast cars, bikes, throwing myself out of planes and off cliffs, bungee jumping; I do anything that shoots my adrenaline into hyperspace and beyond.

A halfhearted "Your car is really cool" comes out of Paige's mouth.

Under normal circumstances, she'd be scolding me for being a show-off and fuck knows what else, but today she likes my car, and I'll hold on to that, knowing she's being honest and not hiding behind her sarcastic comments.

She likes me, I know she does, she just can't bring herself to admit it. I know she hates herself for liking me. I'm the opposition. The competition. And that doesn't sit well with her.

But that's okay. I have a plan to change that.

Too soon perhaps? Probably.

Do I care that I'm being hasty? Absolutely-fucking-not.

Alfie claps his hands as we arrive at my car and starts chanting, "Ca, ca, ca."

I look over the stroller, down at him. "Do you like Max's car?"

"Ca, ca, ca." He bounces up and down in his stroller. "Man's got great taste." I chuckle and turn to Paige who is trying desperately to smile, but her resilience is fading fast.

"Right, let's get you in the car first, Paige."

The bailiff steps away from my car and points to the seat he has already installed for Alfie, which needs to be returned by the end of the day, and he informs me there's a sickness bag in the side pocket he also placed there.

"What's your name?" I ask him, digging my wallet out of my pocket.

"Cliff."

"Well, Cliff, you saved my life today, so thank you." I pass him two hundred bucks for his kindness then ask him to watch Alfie while I buckle Paige into the passenger seat of my car.

She doesn't put up a fight because she has nothing left in her. Next, with ease I surprise myself by placing Alfie in the car seat in the back, securing him, and double-checking that the car seat buckle is locked in place.

"Well, would you look at that, Alfie. Max did it." This parenting thing is a piece of cake. One day I'll tell Nathan I got it the first time, unlike him when they went to buy one. Arianna said he almost lost it in the store because he couldn't figure it out. Old fucker.

Alfie claps his hands as if congratulating me on a job well done. Yup, he's cute.

When I shut the door, sealing Alfie inside, I'm surprised to see Cliff has already collapsed the stroller and is stuffing it into the trunk along with Paige's workbag, and another bag I noticed was haphazardly tucked under the stroller in the storage basket.

"You've done this before." I laugh, scratching my head. I wouldn't have a clue how to fold the complicated-looking thing.

"I have five kids."

"Wow."

"Yeah. Wow." Cliff chuckles before patting me on the shoulder and tells me the car key is in the center console. "I hope she recovers quickly."

Me too. I hate seeing her suffer.

"Thanks, Cliff." I couldn't have done this without him.

I jump into my car, adjusting my rearview mirror to get a better look at Alfie's reflection on the car seat handle mirror. He seems right at home in the back.

Turning my head to check on Paige, I discover she already has her eyes closed and is half asleep. Good, she needs to rest.

I flick the turn signal to indicate I'm merging into traffic, check my mirrors before pulling away from the sidewalk, and when I press the gas pedal, Alfie starts making car noises, which makes me laugh.

"Brrrrrmmm. Brrrrrmmm." He makes motor noises with his mouth.

"You like cars, Alfie?" I ask, knowing he won't answer.

He babbles excitedly. "Brrrrrmmm. Brrrrrmmm." I glance at him in the mirror and laugh again as his chubby cheeks puff out, as he continues to mimic the engine's growl.

He's lucky to have Paige in his life. He's such a happy soul, and I know that's all down to her.

As I drive toward Paige's house, I can't help but think about how natural this feels. Paige in the passenger seat, baby on board. Not something I ever thought I'd want. I'm a free spirit; commitment's never been my thing, but somehow, this feels right.

33

MAX

"What time is it?" Paige sits up too quickly as I walk into her bedroom. "Oh, God, I moved too fast." She places her hand on her head and lies back down. "Why does the room keep spinning?"

"That's because you've barely eaten anything for three days."

"Three days? What? No. I've never taken a full day off work before, why three? This is terrible. And why are you still here? I thought I told you to call my parents."

"They were here again today to check on you, but they've been and gone."

I called them on Paige's cell phone as soon as we got to her place, and they came right over. They believed me when I told them I was her boyfriend. She'll hate me for that, but she's hated me for worse, so whatever.

They helped me put Alfie to bed on the first night Paige was sick, showed me how to change diapers, make a bottle, and bathe him. I managed just fine by myself tonight.

They were determined to stay, but I refused to let them. I couldn't risk either of them getting sick. Having a dad in a memory care home, I know how vulnerable he is now that he's older, and his immunity isn't what it used to be. I didn't want to risk Paige's parents getting sick either. If it was bad for Paige, I can't imagine what it would be like for them.

And like I said before, this baby stuff is a piece of cake. I'm doing great. If there's a competition for the best dad—well, not dad, but you know what I mean—then I'm winning this shit, and I'm going to give Nathan a run for his money. I've had court cases harder than this.

I place a fresh chilled bottle of water on her nightstand, then the baby monitor, and sit down on the edge of the mattress.

"Where is Alfie?" Paige asks, moistening her lips.

"Sleeping."

"Why? What time is it?" she asks groggily, her voice weak.

"Nine o'clock at night."

"I've slept all day." She sounds disbelieving as she tries to pull herself up again, but I'm right here to help her this time, propping her up with pillows behind her. "Thank you. This is so embarrassing. I feel like a baby."

"Oh no, Alfie is a dream to look after; you're worse than a baby," I joke, teasing her.

"Shut up." She rests her head back on the fluffy pillow and closes her eyes, blowing out a breath. "I think I puked my entire life up."

"You sure did." I honestly thought I might need to take her to the hospital when she was retching so hard. "Do you think you can walk to your bathroom to brush your teeth tonight before bed?"

Nodding slowly, she confirms she can. "Yeah. I want to take a shower. I feel disgusting." She pinches at the neckline of her T-shirt and pulls a repulsed face.

I lay my hand on her forehead to check her temperature. "Your temperature has come down." She's over the worst of it.

She pops one eye open and looks at me suspiciously. "What are you after?" she asks. Her voice sounds rough, like it's been dragged through gravel. Her throat must hurt from being sick multiple times.

"What do you mean?" I ask.

Opening her other eye, she glares at me. "You've been taking care of me and Alfie for days. You're after something."

"I promise you, I'm not." I care about her. Not that I can bring myself to tell her that because I'm baffled by it myself.

"Mmmm," she hums, not believing me. "I need to pee."

"You should get up and take a shower now."

A long sigh leaves her throat. "I should." As she tilts her head to the side, I can tell she wants to ask me something but can't bring herself to do it.

"Do you want me to help you?"

Her shoulders drop in defeat. "Yeah, could you, please? To make sure I don't fall or hurt myself. I feel so weak."

"Give it a couple of days and you'll feel like yourself again."

"I hope so. When Alfie had it, he bounced back and was chasing after the next-door neighbor's cat; well, crawling after it."

"He did the same today."

"You were in the yard?" Her lips part in surprise.

"Yeah. He loves the inflatable kiddie pool."

"Did you fill it up?"

"Yeah, I found it in the garage."

"You've been in my garage?" She quirks an eyebrow questioningly.

"Yeah. I built the backyard playset that was in there, too. That thing is fucking huge. When did you get it?"

Narrowing her eyes, she takes some time to answer. "Ages ago. I just never got around to building it."

"Well, it's done. Alfie loves the swing and the window on the playhouse. He's in plastic heaven." He thought it was hilarious when I played peek-a-boo with him this afternoon through the window. "I can move it if you don't like where I put it. Your backyard is enormous." I understand why she bought the plot. It's like a jungle at the far end—plants, trees, bushes, with a hidden fenced-for-safety pond. It feels like a secret garden down there.

She glares at me before looking past me. "Where is Max Hart and what did you do with him?"

I shake my head, aware she's having a hard time understanding why I'm helping her. Trust me, I am too. This feels strange for me, and I don't understand it any more than she does. "I know this might surprise you, but I am nice." Not only have Paige and Alfie shown me what I have been missing from my life, but I no longer believe that relationships or babies are not for me. I want both, all of it, with them.

"Only when you want something in return," she snaps back at lightning speed, but there's a hint of a smile and sarcasm in her biting tone, and I know she's starting to feel better. Also, she doesn't mean it. She's not fooling anyone.

"There's my fork-tongued Bunny." Oh, how I've missed her.

Her pale cheeks fill with color at the use of her pet name, and I kind of love how shy she is about what we did all those weeks ago in The Velvet Rooms. Deep down, she likes what we did, loves it actually, and she hasn't exactly put up a fight to bring an end to us. Every time she wants to, she changes her mind.

She wants me and us, and all she needed was a nudge that got us where we are today.

I've missed her touch the last few days, missed our conversations and secret rendezvous. As soon as she's feeling better, she'll be coming all over my tongue quicker than she can scream my name again. Doing both at the same time would be preferable.

Leaning over, she picks up the water bottle from the night-stand and drinks half of it. More than she has managed in days. "God, that tastes good. I think I'd like that shower now, please."

I lift my ass off the mattress and peel back her cream-colored comforter to help her get out of the bed.

"I'm not wearing any panties," she gasps, looking down at her holey college T-shirt she's clearly had for years.

"It's not like I haven't seen it all before."

Her cheeks turn even darker.

When we had phone sex, I watched her push her vibrator in and out of herself while I jerked off. I've also had my tongue inside her pussy as she's sucked my cock at the same time, in the best sixty-nine I've ever experienced during one of our many lunch hours. I'm not embarrassed; I don't know why she is. We're consenting adults, and it's hot as fuck watching and listening to her fall apart every time we fuck.

Pulling at the hem of her shirt, she holds it down to cover herself as she swivels around on her butt to get out of bed as ladylike as she possibly can.

"Take it easy," I tell her, offering my hand for her to take. She's weak and still needs another day of rest to recuperate.

"Thanks." She lays her hand in mine.

I give it a reassuring squeeze, encouraging her. "Slowly come up onto your feet."

Gingerly, she does, and when she's upright, I place my other hand around her waist so she can use me for support, and I lift the baby monitor off the nightstand to take it with us as we pass.

"Thanks, Max."

"I've got you, baby."

As if she's in disbelief, she shakes her head.

"What?" I ask as she takes her first few steps toward her ensuite.

"Just you."

"What about me?"

"Well, you know. This is weird."

"Weirder than us meeting in secret and having sex and dates? Don't tell me you haven't enjoyed it."

She snorts, then winces.

"Are you okay?" I immediately go into panic mode.

"Yeah, my stomach muscles are sore from all the vomiting."

Thank God it's just that. "You'll feel better tomorrow." And she'll be back to biting my head off, calling me an asshole. I live for those moments.

What can I say, I'm a sadist. Obviously.

"Almost there." I guide her into her adjoining bathroom and tell her to sit down on the edge of the toffee-colored polished concrete tub. Paige Bradshaw has expensive taste. Her house is sleek and cool as hell. Marble-topped furniture, chandeliers, glass everywhere in creams and gold, plush cream carpets—it's warm and inviting and feels like home. Unlike mine. Having lived here for a few days, I'm now seriously thinking about changing all the gray and black in my penthouse to a similar palette as Paige's.

Turning on the shower, I set the temperature knob ensuring it's not too hot, then let it heat up, laying my hand under the water to test it.

"It's ready." A soft hiss fills the room as water patters gently against the tiled flooring of her giant wet room.

"Thanks." She runs her hands through her hair, which she's taken down.

"Your hair is really long." I sound like a chump; it's not like she doesn't know that already. I mean, it's her hair; of course she knows that.

She pulls her hair to her front and examines the ends. "I had a few inches taken off it last month."

The same color as Rapunzel, her hair is all shiny and golden, like spun silk, and must take her ages to dry it. "I like it," I admit. Love it actually and love curling it around my hand, licking her neck and arching it back as I fuck her from behind...

My cock bounces in my boxers.

Not now.

What the fuck is wrong with me and this woman?

I'm here, in her house, under her roof with the same woman who has claimed to hate me for years, and yet, no matter how hard I try, I can't seem to stay away. I know, deep down, she does in fact like me or she wouldn't have spent hours between the sheets with me and risked her position at Moore & Associates.

Every minute of every day, I find myself thinking about her and wondering what she's doing and who she's with. Over the last couple of weeks, she's started to let her walls down—not completely, but just enough to let me inside and take a look around, sharing parts of her day, her childhood, things that Alfie has learned and that make her smile.

I've loved taking care of Alfie over the past three days. Loved her parents too.

Most of all, I love the way Paige challenges me; every cutting remark, every deflection only pulls me in deeper. She pushes me back, but all it does is make me want to get closer. I want to peel back every layer, take my time learning everything about her, discovering the parts she hides and the ones she doesn't even know she's protecting.

And that little boy she's raising is a fucking delight. He's funny and smart, and I could be wrong, but I swear he said my name today. It sounded more like Ma than Max, but I'll take it.

He may not have had the best of starts but Paige is doing a fantastic job and giving him a life he deserves.

Griffin Holmes might well be his father, but he doesn't need him.

With Paige at the helm, he's flourishing.

I admire the way she's changed her life to accommodate Alfie into hers. She'll make sure he never wants for anything anyway. His nursery is a testament to that, as well as the nanny she hired and the home she's fully baby proofed. I almost ripped my fingernail off trying to figure out how the kitchen cupboards opened. They're not just baby proof, they're also adult proof.

"Emma will be back on Monday," I inform her. "I told her to take the rest of the week off or until she feels better. She called your phone. I hope you don't mind me answering it."

"Not at all. Thank you." She shoots me a small smile.

"You said it was your nana the day you were in my office when Marin arrived unannounced, but what you really meant was your nanny, am I right?" Why did she lie?

"I didn't want you to know." Looking deflated, her shoulders slump.

"Why not?" I rest my ass on the vanity unit and cross my legs at my ankles, folding my arms around my front.

"Because until the adoption goes through, I keep thinking he's going to slip through my fingers. Like he could be taken from me at any moment. What if Marin comes back and says she wants him after all? I just thought... the fewer people who knew about him, the safer it felt. My heart couldn't handle it. People asking about him if he wasn't mine anymore." She trails off, her eyes dropping to the floor, voice barely a whisper.

Paige might put on a strong front, but she has insecurities

and confidence issues just like the rest of us. "It would break your heart," I say. She's fucking breaking mine. Seeing how much she loves Alfie makes me admire her even more. Saintly doesn't even scratch the surface; she's a fucking goddess.

"I wouldn't survive it. I love him."

"I know you do. But no one is taking him from you, Paige. Marin won't fight you." From what I've seen with my own eyes and heard about her from Paige, her sister only cares about herself. "When does the adoption come through?"

"The paperwork was filed months ago, all my background checks have been done, they waived my home visit due to my position as a lawyer, and now we wait for the court hearing, which is in a month."

The hot water begins to fill the bathroom with steam, creating soft spirals that resemble little sprites dancing through the air.

"You have nothing to worry about, Paige. It will go through."

"I know, but there's always that tiny"—she pinches the air between her fingers—"sliver of what-ifs that you can never predict. Marin could mess it all up at the last minute."

I don't think she will. "Paige, look at me."

She looks up and stops picking at her nails, looking fragile and nothing like the woman who sat in my office, cool and composed, calling me and my brothers "egos in suits."

"The offer is still on the table. Just say the word and I will ask Nathan to have a quiet word with Judge Holmes. His DNA in exchange for a signed NDA to guarantee your secrecy in exchange for a seamless adoption." It's really that simple. All she needs is leverage.

Her eyes widen as if she had never considered that, but I've given it a lot of thought the last few days.

"It's a good plan but let me think about it. My head's still a little fuzzy."

It's a no-brainer, but I admire her caution. It's a bold move, one that could work in her favor, but she needs time to think about it properly. To consider all her options.

"Let's get you in the shower." I push myself off the vanity unit and help her to her feet. "Shout if you need me." I turn to leave once she's steady.

"You're not staying?" she asks in slow-spaced words.

"Do you want me to?" My brows knit together. I'm surprised she hasn't already kicked me out the bathroom after invading her house, like a vampire without an invitation.

She nods, once, just a fraction—I almost don't catch it—then twice, much firmer this time. "Can you help me? Or do you not want to get sick?"

"I'm past caring about that, Paige. Also, stomach bugs have never bothered me. I seem to have a stomach of steel. When my brothers got sick, I never did. I never got chicken pox either. I'm apparently immune."

Without words, I accept by pulling my T-shirt up over my head and pull off my gray joggers, taking my boxers with them.

What we do when we meet up in hotels feels different compared to being in her personal surroundings.

This is intimate and really pushing her outside her comfort zone.

Completely naked now, I wait for her to make her move.

34

PAIGE

I'm clearly still delirious.

I asked him to join me in the shower. Naked. Together. In my house for the first time.

I'm still unwell; there's no other explanation. I should be telling him to pack up his things and go home from fear of getting caught by anyone from my work. Not that anyone from work has ever shown up at my house before but you just never know.

Because this is wrong, and at this point, there is no rule book; we're making up our own rules.

If you don't discuss the Young case, you're in the clear, Paige.

Yeah, keep telling yourself that. You're both coloring outside the lines and you know it.

There's doubt there in his eyes as he considers his options, but he surprises me when he grabs the back of his T-shirt and pulls it up and over his head, removing it from his body.

As if he's carved from the finest Italian marble, he's not just sculpted; he's criminally hot. It's as if someone designed him to be illegal in every state. And no matter how many times I've seen him naked, it still feels like I'm seeing him for the first time all over again.

He then removes his joggers, taking his boxers with them, and locks eyes with me as if they are glued to mine, challenging me to go next.

For a brief moment, I drop my gaze to his semi-hard cock, and I let out an involuntary "Oh" that has him chuckling.

"I'm a man and you're beautiful. My dick gets hard when I'm around you. Ignore it, because there's no guarantee it won't get any bigger or will go away."

I'm hoping that it doesn't go away. However, we can't go there. To do the sex stuff. I'm too exhausted. But still, his dick is always nice to look at. And I like knowing I make him hard. And he called me beautiful again. I really seem to have a thing for that.

Maybe this is a dream. And if it is, someone better shake me awake because I'm about to get in the shower with the devil in a suit I spent entire days fantasizing about destroying in court. That was until the day everything changed when he booked the presidential suite.

We've been reckless and dangerous with our decisions.

But here we are, standing on the edge of the fire, ready to burn yet again.

It's not until Max says, "Your turn," that I realize I'm ogling him, perving over Max freaking Hart. The man I have loved to hate for as long as I can remember. The same man whose dick I've spent hours sucking, begging him to make me come. He's also the same man I've spent hours arguing with in and out of court. Come to think of it, foreplay would be a better name for it. It was the prequel to the best sex of my life.

"I already know what's under that T-shirt, Paige. I've seen you dozens of times."

"Did you undress me?"

"No, you did that yourself."

"Right."

"While I was in the bedroom with you, and your mom."

"God give me strength." I cover my face with my hands, feeling embarrassed with how out of it I was.

"You're beautiful, Paige. Every fucking inch of you is beautiful, and that heart of yours is what I like about you the most."

Well, when he says things like that, it really makes me want to tear my clothes off for him.

Wrapping my fingers around the hem of my Yale T-shirt I've had since law school, I pull it all the way up to my waist before lifting it over my head, exposing every part of me.

And all under the roof of my house. We've more than crossed the lines now. This is personal.

"See, that wasn't so difficult now, was it?" His hungry eyes drop down my body before moving up again to meet my gaze. "Now brush your teeth, and I'll meet you in there. I'll help you wash your hair." He strides toward me, grinning as he passes and gently pats my ass. A slap would be too much in my fragile state, and I appreciate how considerate he's being.

I've never had anyone wash my hair before. This is new. Different. Nice even.

Like the good little bunny I am, because for some reason, I can't seem to say no to him, I brush my teeth and feel instantly better.

Tentatively, I join him under the rainfall shower that flows from the ceiling, letting the water cascade down my body and wash away the past few days. I allow the warm water to soak into my skin, easing my stiff shoulders and achy back muscles from retching. I haven't thrown up for several hours, and I'm praying I won't again. I don't think my body could take any more.

Under the water, Max turns to face me. His eyes flick between mine, quiet and searching, as if he's trying to read what I'm not saying. Then he reaches up, fingers threading through my soaked hair, gently brushing it back from my face with a tenderness that takes my breath away.

He kisses my forehead softly. It's sweet, unexpected, and wrong; we shouldn't be doing this, he shouldn't be here, in my house.

"I withdrew from the case," he says as if reading my mind.

"What case?" I ask, searching his face for an answer, already knowing it. Surely not.

"Young versus Young."

"You did what? You can't do that." I won't let him.

"I already filed the motion this afternoon. My associate's taking over. She's sharp, she'll catch up fast. And Stella agreed. She's satisfied."

"Why? We're practically at the end."

"You know why, Paige."

And there goes that silence again that happens between us more often than I would like, only this time it's longer than usual and makes my heart gallop in my chest like a racehorse.

I throw him a shy smile because I know what he means.

Then he confirms it with confidence. "We can't keep pretending the tension between us isn't there. We can't deny what happened in The Velvet Rooms or our secret rendezvous. If anyone saw us together in a conference room, it wouldn't take a genius to realize there's something between us." He presses his forehead against mine.

It's such an intimate gesture, he's unraveling me piece by piece. I hate that he's right, and I will never look at him in the same way again, but what's the rush?

"You should have waited until the divorce is finalized and the case is closed."

"I can't wait that long."

It's only a few weeks. Although the courthouse clerk misplaced the court papers, and we might be months away from settling the Youngs' divorce, rather than weeks as we had hoped.

Closing the small distance between us, he wraps me in his arms and whispers in my ear, "I don't trust myself around you. I can't fucking stay away. I don't want to, and I know that if you didn't want me here either, you would have kicked me out of your house whether you were sick or not, and you know it."

"You sort of invited yourself into my life." I still can't believe he's here.

He nuzzles into my neck. "You gave me the code to get in."

Of course I did; it took me several attempts to remember it in my fevered state.

His fingers thread into the hair at the back of my neck before he says, "Tiptoeing behind backs, dancing around, and pretending that I don't want you is out of the question. I don't want anything preventing us from exploring whatever this is. Withdrawing from the case was the right thing to do."

He's insane.

My usual sharp mind struggles to keep up with his next confession. "I'm doing the only thing that feels right, so we don't fuck up our careers and get ourselves suspended, or worse, disbarred."

That's a bit extreme, as it would be dealt with in-house in the first instance, but I understand his concerns. They're the same as mine.

Max adds, "This is the only choice that feels right. If we keep going like this, we're risking everything. Our careers, our names, everything we've worked for. I can't live with that, and I can't keep lying to my brothers either. But what matters even more is you. I won't let anyone drag your name through the mud or question your integrity because of me. You've built something incredible, and you're the sharpest, fiercest divorce lawyer I've ever known. Hell, half the time I'm in awe of you. I'd hate myself if this cost you even a shred of the respect you deserve. I want you. I want us. Me, you, and Alfie."

There's so much promise behind his words that it also scares me shitless. We have no idea what this is, and he's already making plans to be with me, by the sounds of it—plans I haven't agreed to. To be a family. He's so bossy, masculine, and... I might just like him making decisions for me. Lately, I've been making life-changing choices that impact not only my life but Alfie's, and I know adopting him is the right thing to do. My mom always taught me to trust my gut, and that's what I'm doing.

"I'm the guy who follows the rules." I know he is. "And yeah, what we've been doing feels incredible, Paige, but it was still wrong of me to push you into secret dates. The truth is, you had me wanting more. I wanted to see how far you'd go, what you'd say, if you'd admit that you liked me." He continues. "I know you're just too damn stubborn to tell me. And maybe that makes me a greedy bastard for needing to hear you say it, even if it was by having phone sex with me to confirm what I suspected initially."

It's true what they say: actions do speak louder than words. He heard everything I didn't say that night.

"I've already told my brothers I'm at your place. Eli dropped off a bag with my clothes. And they know I dropped the case we're on opposite sides of."

"You told your brothers about us?" I pull away from our closeness, my mouth open in shock.

"Yes and no. I just told them I was here and not to ask any questions. They got the message."

That means they know. They aren't stupid. "Please tell me you didn't tell them about The Velvet Rooms?" Mild panic rises in my throat, which is sore from vomiting repeatedly.

He shakes his head silently in refusal before saying, "No. I would never hear the end of it if I did. Doesn't mean they won't figure it out, though. We talked about you—well, Bunny—together. We made a list."

"You made a list?"

His eyes widen as he nods, mischief flickering across his lips. "I was getting their help to figure out who you were. They knew it was you before I did. The clever fuckers. Once they see your tattoo, well, then the bunny will be out of the trap." His smirk is diabolical and full of trouble.

"No way." This is terrible. Then another thought hits me. "Then they'd know I went to a sex club?"

"Correction. It was one time; you're not a regular."

Which means they also know I haven't had sex for four years too. How embarrassing. I'm the practically-a-virgin woman they were talking about in Max's office when I walked in.

World, swallow me whole.

Annoyingly, compared to my drama-filled monologue, he's a wall of calm when he tucks my wet hair behind my ear. "Now, will you relax? You're overthinking it. Just chill out, switch off your brain, and let me take care of you, please."

Well, when he says please like that, he makes it difficult for me to refuse.

In silence, he washes my hair twice before he lathers my body in soap. I luxuriate in the way he leaves not an inch of my skin untouched. From my arms to my legs and stomach, and yes, he even washes me down there too. The weird thing is I let him.

I've been running about like a headless chicken for as long as I can remember and it feels nice to be taken care of for a change. It feels good. I might want this every day.

I close my eyes and bask in the warmth of the water that makes me feel all fuzzy and renewed, the citrus scent of the shower gel filling the air and the kindness of his touch adding to this new experience. He's surprisingly gentle, and when he respectfully rinses the last of the soapy suds from my body, he kisses my shoulder, then along my collarbone, moving up my neck. He's bold but not too daring and simply cares for me like he promised.

Throughout our shower, his cock remains hard and it's difficult not to look, or touch it. I mean, it's right there, and for the life of me, even though I've been sick, I still want to drop to my knees and suck him dry to thank him for helping me and Alfie while I've been laid up in bed. I didn't think Max was capable of thinking about anyone else other than himself. Turns out I was wrong about him, although he could be doing all of this to simply get inside my panties again.

Then why would he stay here for three days taking care of Alfie, cook soup from scratch—which he did yesterday, though I couldn't stomach it—and hold my hair back when I puked? Why would he do all that when no one was watching, when there was no one to impress but a sick woman and a kid who barely knows his face? Shockingly, it sounds like they've become firm friends in my absence, and it doesn't sound like Alfie has missed me at all. However, I've missed his snuggles and the silly way he sneezes then laughs at himself like he's the world's top comedian.

"How has Alfie been?" I ask, staring at him in awe.

"He's amazing," Max replies with such a genuine heartfelt

tone I know he means it. "Tomorrow you can give him all the cuddles you missed out on."

"I don't want to give him my stomach flu," I groan.

"If he gets it, we deal with it together."

We deal with it together.

Max is blowing my mind over and over again.

He adds, "It's doing the rounds at our firm."

"There's no escaping it. Emma gave it to me. Sharing is caring."

"I never get stomach bugs. I already told you, I'm immune." He pats his stomach.

I thought he was joking but clearly Max has a strong invulnerable body as well as strong abdominal muscles; figures.

"Never?" I ask curiously.

"Nope." He sways his head in protest. "Alfie likes me by the way."

"Keep telling yourself that." Alfie likes everyone.

"Your mom said I was a natural with him."

"I'm sure she did." Handsome is very difficult to disagree with, and Max is the epitome of it.

"He loves Buzz Lightyear."

"He's obsessed with him." If Max keeps this up, I can see myself becoming obsessed with him; that's if I'm not already. I might be. Just a smidge. More like a lot, but whatever.

Max adds more observations. "And *Cars*. He loves that too."

"That boy is either going to be an astronaut or a Formula 1 driver."

"Sounds like my kind of man. Fast everything," he says with a twinkle in his eye.

"Does that include fast women?" Jealousy punches my gut.

While Max has made his intentions clear with me, us, that

he wants to dive into what's unfolding here, there is no escaping his past. He's had a couple of serious relationships, one of which was years ago. And kids? He's far from the settling-down type. What kind of spell did Alfie cast to win him over? Maybe it was his smile that did it, or his giggle, or maybe it was his full-on gibberish he does with perfect inflection that makes him sound like he's giving an in-depth TED Talk that won Max's heart.

He's not just here for Alfie, I know this. It still doesn't stop me from doubting him.

I'm not his usual type. I have a kid. What we were before, rivals with benefits, has totally changed. We're no longer hooking up in hotels just to get whatever it was out of our systems. Now, I'm completely head over heels for Max and can't stop thinking about him.

I also admire how ballsy he's been, inserting himself into my life because he likes me and wants to explore whatever this is. He's crazy.

What's even crazier is he quit the Youngs' case. Without asking me first. It's as if he already knew I wanted him. Not that I've admitted that to him because this could fizzle out as fast as it started. However, this feels different, feels right. Perfect.

He wraps his arms around my waist. "You're wrong about me liking fast women. The type of woman I like is feisty and comes with a side order of takes no shit." He pats my ass, something he seems to love doing.

"Oh, yeah?"

"Yeah, I like one in particular. She doesn't put up with my bullshit, and she challenges me to be better." Confusion wrinkles his brows.

I think that comes as a surprise to him, and I don't think he knew what he wanted until now.

"For the first time in my life, you, Paige Bradshaw, are all I want."

"That can't possibly be true," I whisper, disbelieving.

"Well, believe it, baby, because I'm here right now, with you, with Alfie, and there's no place I'd rather be. Although it would have been an epic sleepover if it hadn't been for the sickness stuff, because that was... well, at one point I thought you were going to puke your internal organs up." He grimaces and shudders as he recalls how unwell I was. "It was fucking brutal."

"Trust me, I know. It felt like the purge." Like a demonic sickness expelling my body.

He's seen me at my worst and yet, he's still here.

What a head fuck.

"It's time for bed. You need to rest." He kisses me on my forehead again. It's going to take some time getting used to how caring he can be.

I let out a huge yawn that makes Max turn off the shower and wrap me in one of my cream fluffy towels, cocooning himself around me in a giant hug.

I'm so tired I could sleep for a month.

"Now, where is your hairdryer?"

I look up at him. "I can dry my own hair."

"Are you sure?"

"I'm sure." He doesn't need to do everything for me. I feel much better now.

"Okay, well, while you dry your hair, I'll change the bedsheets. Where do you keep them?"

I didn't realize billionaire playboys knew how to change bedsheets, and that's why I'm still staring at him in disbelief.

"Will you sleep with me tonight?" I ask. I don't want to be alone.

A flash of humor crosses his face.

"I'd love to."

And for the first time since our secret affair began, he sleeps in my bed, wrapping me in his arms and snuggling close all night, and it's the best sleepover a girl could ever wish for.

35

PAIGE

"How are you feeling?" Max asks as soon as my feet touch the floor in the hallway.

"Better. The best I've felt in days." He was right; a good sleep was all I needed. My eyes drop down and then back up at his athletic physique that I've spent hours licking and kissing.

Wearing nothing but his boxers, he looks completely at ease in my house. Too comfortable. Whatever he wears, he always looks so damn fine. "Could you not find any clothes to wear this morning?" I ask.

He answers me with a cheeky smirk instead of words.

He's delicious and if he's not careful, when Alfie goes down for a nap, I might blow him just so I can have another taste.

"Where's Alfie?" I ask, feeling bashful in my own home. Waking up with Max in my house is opening my eyes to a whole new world. A preview of what life would be like if he lived here.

Shut up, Paige.

"In his highchair." Max kisses me on my cheek, then holds out his hand for me, which I take willingly, allowing him to guide me into the kitchen.

My heart expands in my chest at the first sight I've had of my little cherub in days. "Hey, baby." Max releases my hand when I pick up speed and sit down in the chair next to Alfie's highchair.

"Momma." Alfie grants me a gummy smile, banging the tray of his highchair with his grubby, crumb-covered hands.

"Have you missed me?" I've missed him. So much.

He points at Max. "Ma."

Yeah, he hasn't missed me. The traitorous monkey. He's an adorable one, though, so I'll let him off, and from the smile on his little face, I can tell he likes Max as much as I do. He's a great judge of character, maybe even better than I am. Alfie liked him from the start.

Max really is something else, though, someone I know now to be loyal and caring. In every sense of the word, he's a great man.

"Is that Max?" I point at him, making Alfie babble back at me as if saying yes. "Has he been looking after you?" I kiss Alfie's temple over and over, inhaling his baby scent, as he stuffs toast into his mouth, watching the iPad Max has set up for him on the dining table.

Max would make a great daddy.

Oops, where did that thought come from?

"Mmmmm," Alfie hums to himself, enjoying his breakfast as he squishes his buttery toast between his fingers.

"What time was he up at?" I ask Max. I slept through his usually loud morning chatter. That's very unlike me.

"Six."

"I'm sorry, he usually sleeps later than that."

"It's the time I get up every day. I don't mind." He shrugs, moving to my stove. "I made you some oatmeal." The steam from the pot on the stove billows into the air. "It will give you some much-needed strength and line your stomach."

He thinks of everything.

"That's so kind, thank you." It's then I notice how tidy the house is. "Did you clean?"

Nodding in reply, he adds, "And I did your laundry. It's all ironed and put back in your closet." He grins at me and I find it impossible not to return a smile.

But wait, what?

I bite my lip and look away. I hate that he's seen how disorganized my home life has become, and I'm ashamed of myself. I feel like I've taken advantage of his trusting nature. I've got my shit together, just not all at once.

"You have a new housekeeper starting on Monday," Max informs me.

I snap my head back his way again when he announces that.

He points to the house phone. "I called the numbers that were by the phone. I just assumed you hadn't managed to arrange for one to start yet. The business is called Gem & Shine. I vetted them, and it all checks out. Good references too." He continues to surprise me. "I also called your work after you got sick to let them know I had to bring you home. I spoke to your new secretary; he seems nice."

He's organized my life for me while I've been in bed for days.

How many times can I keep thanking him?

Lost for words, I watch him move around my kitchen with ease as if he owns the place, pouring the warmed oats into two bowls, one for him and, I assume, one for me, adding sugar on top, more for my benefit, I think, to boost my sugar levels.

He strides confidently toward the dining table in only his boxer shorts, and I find myself ogling him again as he sets my breakfast down on my placemat, then his own, and tells me to eat.

Without question, I do, digging into the sweet creamy oats, completely stunned by how natural this all feels.

If anyone were to peer through the window and see Alfie by my side watching *Finding Nemo*, and Max sitting across from me, they'd think we were... a family.

Strangely, that doesn't scare me.

"What day is it today?" I ask, mumbling around my food I can't eat fast enough. I've lost all sense of time.

"Saturday." Max rests his spoon in his bowl, his eyes blazing through me, unspeaking in a prolonged look. "Do you feel well enough to go out today?"

I already feel better, the food in my stomach warm and full of nutrients and energy that I need to recover.

"I do." What does he have in mind?

"Well enough to come to a wedding with me?"

"As your plus one?" Holy shit, this is huge.

"Yeah."

"I can't, I have Alfie."

"Your mom and dad are taking him for a sleepover tonight."

I can't keep up. "When was that arranged?"

"Yesterday. To give you another night to recover because I can't take care of Alfie tonight."

"Right." I would never expect him to do that for me. Also, I'm well enough to look after Alfie myself; I don't need my parents to take him tonight, although I won't be able to stop them, as they'll be excited about having him overnight.

"So, will you come with me today?" Max asks with so much expectation in his tone.

"Who's getting married?" And why doesn't he have a date?

"Nathan and Arianna."

"What? No." I drop my spoon against the side of my bowl,

causing the crockery to chime as it clatters. "I can't go to your brother's wedding." Then they'll know. Everything.

"I'm no longer working on the case. It should be fine. No one from Moore & Associates will be there today."

Panic crawls up my throat, my pulse racing through my veins. "It should be fine? I still need to tell my work, Max."

"Do it Monday."

"Do it Monday," I mimic him, shaking my head. This fucking guy. I know I have to.

"And if it all goes to shit, you'll come to work for us. Simple."

He makes everything sound seamless. But what about my reputation? And will everyone think I'm losing my edge if I'm sleeping with the competition? And what about my privacy? Max is never out of the tabloids because he's dated so many celebrities and has become one in his own right. That lifestyle is not something I want or need. It's bad enough when I represent celebrities' divorces. I hate the questions and the intrusiveness into my personal life.

Although... I stare at Max across the table. I have someone who would protect me from all of that. He's someone I could depend on to take care of me and Alfie. He's proved that over the last few days.

"Do you have a dress you could wear?" Max asks.

I have dozens of dresses to choose from. "Yes."

"So, you'll come? That's if you feel up to it?" There's so much hope in his voice; how can I refuse?

And the truth is I want to go; I would hate for his plus one to be anyone other than myself.

Nope, that's not happening. It's me or no one.

"I might not last the whole night, and I definitely don't feel like drinking any alcohol today," I admit, on the brink of accepting.

"Is that a yes?" His extraordinary eyes shine brightly, and his mouth, suggestive and softening, breaks out into a leisurely smile.

I think it is. "Yes."

Without missing a beat, he lists what's happening today. "We leave here at ten. Pack a bag, you can stay at my place tonight. We need to get ready there too as my tuxedo is there. I'm one of Nathan's best men today. My brothers are too." He sounds excited about that, his face lighting up, making his eyes sparkle.

"Okay."

What a rush.

I'm going to a wedding as Max Hart's date.

And I'm going to meet his family.

This feels a lot like we are taking the next step in our relationship.

And again, that doesn't scare me. It should because gradually he's been breaking down my defenses, and I've been letting him into my life little by little. I mean, look at him now—he's pulled up a chair at my dining table and seamlessly become a part of my life.

"Eat up." He points his spoon at my bowl. "You'll need your strength for later."

I grin, feeling the butterflies in my stomach. "Is that your way of telling me your family is a full-contact sport?" I tease.

"Nope. But I am."

Oh, boy, I'm in serious trouble.

36

PAIGE

Apparently, Nathan and Arianna's wedding is a low-key affair today. Family and very close friends only.

I'm neither, which makes me an official wedding crasher.

The only small caveat is that I was invited last minute, but still.

Inviting me to share such a special day with his family is not only wonderful but also a bit overwhelming. I'll be spending the entire day with them, and being so close shifts Max and me from just sex into something completely different.

I don't even know what to label it as.

"It's just a date," I think out loud, having a conversation with myself in the mirror on the wall in Max's master bathroom that is the same size as my bedroom. It's ridiculously oversized, with one of the best showers I've ever had the pleasure of experiencing.

As soon as we finished breakfast, in record time, I chose a dress, packed an overnight bag, and was in Max's car before I changed my mind about today.

My choice was made easier when my parents arrived earlier than expected and assured me he was in good hands. They have a full day planned with ways to keep Alfie entertained. That boy is so spoiled.

My mom informed me they had plans tomorrow afternoon and wouldn't be bringing Alfie back until later, and told me to take my time returning and, most importantly, to have fun.

For the rest of the day, I'm not a mom or a lawyer. I'm just Paige and I'm going to luxuriate in playing hooky from my usual routine to be Max's plus one, and I'll spend the night at his place, which puts my house to shame.

Situated on the top floor of one of the most prestigious units in the city, his penthouse boasts panoramic ocean views, a private elevator, a rooftop deck, a gourmet kitchen, high ceilings, and glass everywhere that lets in an abundance of light. There's marble and bespoke furnishings that scream wealth. It's ridiculously over the top, and I think I might be in love with it.

On the way to his apartment, he called his mom to tell her he was bringing me today. Without any fuss, she simply asked my name, added me to an adjusted table plan, and that was it. Simple. No fretting or stressing, just a relaxed, "I'll tell the staff to update the plans." If it had been anyone else, I can't imagine it would have been that easy, but his parents own a ranch they turned into a wedding retreat where the wedding is happening today, and with ease, they just slotted me in.

I'm not family, and yet, without question I've been whisked away to spend the day with them.

Looking at myself in Max's bathroom mirror, I reapply my lipstick for the third time, fretting over what shade to wear. It was red first, then pink, and now it's more of a subtle beige pink. "Boring?" I ask myself, examining my lips and scowling at myself in the mirror.

"You look anything but boring, you look good enough to eat." Max steps inside his cavernous bathroom wearing his tuxedo, which fits him to perfection.

I whip around to face him, my eyes eating him up. "You look..." Handsome, gorgeous, godlike, fuckable... *C'mon, Paige, think of something.* "Great." His tailored tuxedo isn't wearing him, he's wearing it and owning it.

Confidently and with purpose, he walks up to me with a look that tells me he approves of my one-shoulder midi dress in powder blue. Made of soft crepe, it's not only sophisticated but also elegant, with the asymmetric neckline perfectly framing my decolletage. This is the part of my body Max seems to love kissing the most. Surprisingly, he's left me to get ready on my own today and hasn't even tried to have sex with me. I appreciate the space; it feels like we've entered something more meaningful. It's more careful. More intentional. It's as if he's trying to respect me in a new way, or maybe he's unsure of what we are, too. There's a quiet between us that wasn't there before—an ease of sorts. It's thoughtful, tender, respectful. I guess we're still figuring each other out, and maybe today is just what we need to help us do that.

Max's piercing eyes size me up from top to bottom, the strong tic of his jaw pulsing beneath his perfectly groomed beard that frames his strong jawline.

"Will I do?" I whisper.

"Oh, you'll more than do." He stands in front of me, toe to toe. "I really want to kiss you but I don't want to ruin your lipstick."

"I don't mind." It needs a hint of pink; I was about to change it again anyway.

Closing the distance, he traces his finger along my bottom lip before lowering his mouth to mine. He kisses me softly once, then twice, before cupping my face with his warm hand and angling his mouth for a deeper kiss. It's a blazing kiss that ignites something in my heart that makes me weak at the knees and has me imagining what spending every day with him would be like. Our kiss goes on forever. It's slow and sensual, long and deliberate, bone-tingling and dreamlike. No matter how long it lasts, I know it will never be enough. He slides his tongue inside my mouth, his hungry lips tasting minty from his toothpaste with hints of amber from his aftershave he's sprayed on his beard.

I never knew kisses could feel like this: so all-consuming and addictive.

I thread my hands into his hair at the back of his neck, unconcerned with messing it up. No matter how many times I've done it in the past, it always looks effortlessly styled to perfection.

Nerves dance low in my belly, because I know once we end this kiss, it's time to go.

I may have met his brothers hundreds of times before, but somehow it feels like this is the first time I'm genuinely meeting them. Today, I'm not just a last-minute addition to the guest list; I'm stepping right into the middle of their private day, their family's moment. It feels intrusive, like I'm crossing an even bigger line than Max and I did all those months ago. And yet, he wants me there. That means something, doesn't it? Or maybe I'm reading too much into it.

Whatever it is, I push it to one side and forget about it as I lose myself in him as Max's talented mouth sends powerful sensations to build below my waist, drowning out my uncertainty about today.

"Max." I love saying his name. I've said it so many times, he almost feels like he's mine.

He pulls away from our kiss and presses his forehead against mine. "As much as I want to keep going, we really have to leave or we'll be late. If we are even a minute late, Arianna said she would chop all the Hart men's balls off." He presses his crotch against my stomach, letting me feel how hard he is as my heart pounds in my throat.

"Well, we had better get going then if you want to keep them." I quite like sucking them while giving him a hand job. He seems to have a thing for that and always comes much quicker when I do. "I just need to reapply my lipstick." And touch up my makeup around my mouth too, no doubt.

He nods. "You look beautiful."

"Thanks. You suit a tux." I wiggle either side of his bowtie between my fingers, being careful not to screw it up. He looks so refined, his classic watch peeking out from under his cuff just enough that it hints at both his wealth and stature.

With his hands on my hips, he coaxes me to turn around to face the mirror before he says, "We look good together."

We do. Like we are meant to be.

The significance of what he's saying weighs heavily on my shoulders because I can't believe that for all these years I've hated him. I hate myself for not seeing him, all of him, which is staring back at me in the mirror.

Monday can't come quickly enough. That's when I'll inform work about Max and me.

What do I tell them? We're together, dating, what exactly?

"Ms. Bradshaw, would you consider dating me? Officially?"

I swear this guy's always in my head.

"I think I might like to try that." I'd love to do it more than anything, but with a baby and having never dated since Alfie arrived, I have no idea how to make it happen. Screw it; with babysitters, Emma, and my parents, I'm sure I'll figure it out.

Doubts seep into my mind, rising like a river flooding an unsuspecting town.

Will he get bored of me? Annoyed when I can't make nights out or make last-minute plans?

He told me he was a commitment-phobe, and I can't help but think this might just be another fling for him.

"I have a baby," I state, getting the doubts out of my mind, wanting to be honest.

"I prefer nights in."

"I can't make last-minute plans because I need to find babysitters."

"Anything last minute will include Alfie."

Okay, that makes me feel better.

"You're a commitment-phobe," I blurt out, feeling stupid about my insecurities. But he can't just swoop into my life, and Alfie's, then decide after a few weeks he's had enough of me.

"And you hated me. People change."

"You don't have to change for me."

"I don't think you understand; I want to." He pauses briefly before adding, "For you." He softly kisses my exposed shoulder, ghost-like. "For once, I know exactly what I want. You've shown me a side of life I didn't know existed, something that feels like home. And I want to turn that into reality. With you."

Emotion bubbles in my chest, my eyes welling up, and I have to shake my head to stop the tears from falling, taking a deep breath to hold them back.

I'm utterly speechless, stunned, as he presses another kiss on my shoulder and releases my hips. "I'll leave you to reapply your lipstick. You have two minutes, baby." He leaves me staring at the doorway he left through.

Like a clever fox, he hunted me with patience, injecting excitement into my once dull life. Then he switched on his spell binding charm, and I, the bunny, finally stopped running because I couldn't resist being caught. He, the fox, burrowed his way into my heart.

There's no escaping him now.

He's got me.

37

MAX

I'm standing in a line, shoulder to shoulder with my brothers at the front of the recreation room of Dad's memory care home, waiting for Arianna to arrive with my dad, who is giving her away today because she doesn't have any family of her own.

After today, she'll officially become one of us. A Hart. While we can never replace the family she lost, I hope we are enough to make her feel like she's always been part of us.

"You brought Paige Bradshaw as your date?" Cole asks through the side of his mouth, sounding shocked.

"Yeah," I answer, knowing I'm about to be hit with a barrage of abuse.

"But I didn't bring a plus one because you and Eli said you weren't."

"It was a last-minute decision." I wanted to ask her for weeks; this morning felt like the right time to ask.

"Shut the fuck up, will you?" Eli snaps, keeping his voice low, his exasperation evident.

"You brought Rainbow Bright?" I ask Eli, amused that he doesn't look so happy about that. Her hair is soft pink today, fading to purple at the ends. I actually love how bold she is and how she doesn't give a fuck, and she's so relaxed, unlike Eli.

"How many times do I have to tell you? It's Sapphire," Eli grits out between his teeth. "And she just invited herself, something about how she wants to immerse herself in our family values or something equally as stupid that has fuck all to do with work. I mean, how will her being here today help the staff conference? And look." He angrily pulls out a clear stone from his top pocket. "She even put a crystal in my jacket pocket because it will make me feel calm and align my chakras, which is a pile of shit. How the fuck will a crystal calm me today when all she does is wind me up? She's annoying."

Unable to contain ourselves, Cole and I burst out laughing. Sapphire has really gotten under his skin.

"You need another dozen of those crystals to calm you down, that one isn't working," Cole teases, trying to mess with him more.

"Will you three knuckleheads keep your voices down?" Nathan bites back, making us straighten up. "You're like fucking children."

I chuckle out loud again. Nathan's been on edge for weeks, but today I think he might blow a blood vessel if things don't go to plan.

I lean forward and eye him. "How are you feeling?"

"Fine." He lifts his chin confidently, but I know he's nervous and feels a little out of control today, which he hates.

"You've nothing to worry about." I reach past Eli to my left and pat Nathan on his forearm, the same strong arm that pummeled me at tennis last weekend.

His shoulders drop at my reassurance, his features softening. "Thanks." He blows out a breath before looking my way. "So, you and Paige?"

"Yeah." I'm as shocked about it as everyone else.

"She's Bunny?" I knew he would work that out.

"Yeah." It's a dick move if I deny it. "I figured it out last week," I lie.

"You're fucking kidding?" Cole sounds even more shocked than I was when I figured it out.

"Deadly serious," I reply.

Cole says what's on his mind. "Only you could show up at a sex club and end up leaving with the most gorgeous woman there. That's a talent."

"You think she's gorgeous?" That's news to me. He's scared of her, yeah, but I didn't think he found her attractive. And I thought he liked Libby; maybe I was wrong about that.

"I have fucking eyes." Cole leans his head to the side, moving closer to me, and whispers, "Is she as domineering in the bedroom as she is in court?"

"Fuck off." I'm not sharing personal details with him. When she was just a stranger and we didn't know who she was, I shared everything I knew about her and what happened in the dark. But now that I know who she is, I'm respectful and would never divulge what we do behind closed doors.

My reply seems to amuse him. "Wow, it must be serious. You're all closed off and shit."

"Yeah, well, she's..." I peer over my shoulder at where she's sitting behind me, and I almost melt on the spot when she beams at me and gives me a little finger wave, looking a billion dollars even though she's been unwell for days. "...everything."

Everything I didn't think I wanted, or needed, or would crave to the point I can't stop thinking about her, but here I am, lust drunk and so fucking high I feel like I could fly.

I turn my head around to the front again, clocking Judge Griffin Holmes sitting next to his wife.

Shit, I forgot he was invited today, but this might work in Paige's favor. Maybe I can talk to him later, discreetly. If I time it right, hopefully without Paige knowing. Today, I want her to have a day away from her responsibilities just having fun. Most importantly, I want to open up my personal life and family to her, show her who we really are, and let her see that there's a place for her and Alfie with us if she wants it.

"She's it," I say in a tone that's filled with awe.

Cole claps me on the shoulder. "Hell, if you're saying that, and you've only known she was Bunny for a few days then she must be something special."

"She is." I'm as surprised about it as he is.

I look to my left and then my right to find my brothers grinning at me as if saying, *This is new.*

It is. And it should be scary as hell, but I'm running toward her, not away.

The wedding celebrant clears her throat, signaling Arianna's arrival. "May I invite everyone to stand as we welcome the bride?" The classical music starts, prompting us to stand at attention.

"Here we go." Eli grips Nathan's forearm. "We love you, brother."

"Oh, stop or you'll make me cry. Look at my beautiful babies." Mom appears like magic having helped the caregivers to wheel my dad in on his fancy wheelchair that assists him now.

Harmoniously, the four of us watch Arianna walk down the aisle, her hand on my dad's arm as he uses the electronic joystick controller with his other hand to slowly steer himself toward us.

She is seven months pregnant and glowing, and happiness radiates from her as she moves closer to her forever... my brother.

While I'm happy for him and his soon-to-be wife, my chest tightens with sadness as I look at my dad. He's a shadow of his former self. Once an intimidating lawyer, Parkinson's and dementia have stolen the greatest man I've ever had the privilege of knowing and working alongside. He taught me to be bold and brave and to always, always do the right thing.

I hang my head in shame.

I've been such a fool, letting my dick overrule my head. I need to tell my brothers that I've been meeting with Paige in secret throughout the active case we're on opposite sides of. For months. I lied to them, said I had only just figured out who she was, but I've known since the day we made that list in my office all those weeks ago.

We not only compromised our clients' interests, but we also risked being disciplined by the bar.

Forcing myself to stand up straighter, I lift my head, pushing my thoughts aside for now, and focus on Dad and Arianna.

For the first time in a while, Dad is smiling up at Arianna, then he moves his gaze to us before finally landing on my mom, who looks overwhelmed, dabbing the corners of her eyes with a tissue.

It's been such a long time since I've seen him look this happy; I should know because I visit him almost every day.

And the way he's looking at my mom... full of admiration, longing, and love... it's the same way I see Nathan look at Arianna... the same way I look at Paige.

38

PAIGE

Apparently, my stamina is much stronger than I gave it credit for. It's almost ten o'clock and I'm still at Nathan and Arianna's wedding.

Greedily, because I could eat a fridge full of food today to make up for lost time, I ate the entire gourmet meal. That was some of the best food I've ever tasted. I even managed to have a glass of champagne and feel surprisingly good, despite how unwell I've been.

For the millionth time today, I look across to Griffin Holmes' table, watching his wife casually talk to Max's mom. With no sign of him, I can only assume he's helping Max and his brothers to carry out whatever prank they have planned for the newlyweds.

I've considered talking to Griffin several times, but every time I've thought about approaching him to question him about Marin and Alfie, something in my gut stops me. Now is not the time to cause a rift. This is Arianna and Nathan's special day, and I'm not about to ruin it.

"Have you enjoyed yourself today?" Max finally returns.

I can only imagine he's been messing with Arianna and Nathan's two-story treehouse where they are sleeping tonight. Amongst the trees, there are another ten of different sizes and designs that Max's mom has built on the ranch grounds. A ranch I had never known existed until today.

It's beautiful, with pastures that go on for miles, a complete contrast to the city that's less than an hour away.

Max takes the seat next to me when I tell him, "I've had a great day. Your family are incredible." They made me feel welcome. "I love how you included your dad today." After the ceremony, the reception was moved to a grand and elegant marquee inside the ranch grounds. Max might have implied it was a small affair, but I don't consider a couple of hundred people a small one. When we returned from the family and very close friends-only ceremony, all the guests were waiting inside the marquee to greet the new Mr. and Mrs. Hart.

The Harts are so extra, without being overly garish with it; they are stylish, and everything about today has been pure class.

"At the heart of everything is my dad," he says, sounding sad. "And without him, today wouldn't have been the same. We were fortunate that he was having a good day today. Some days he isn't... he's just not the same."

"Do you miss him?" I place my hand on top of his.

"Every day. I miss him sitting in the big office Nathan is now in. I miss asking him for advice, but most of all, I miss Sundays sitting on Mom and Dad's porch, shooting the breeze."

Sorrow and pain knot inside my stomach. "I'm so sorry, Max." I can't imagine what it must be like to watch your father disappear in front of you, changing into someone you no longer recognize.

He lifts my hand to his mouth and kisses the back of it. "Thank you." He changes the direction of our conversation. "I saw you dancing with Cole."

"I think he's warming to me." He asked me to dance. Twice.

"He told me he's so scared of you that you make his balls jump up inside of his body."

I throw my head back and let out a great peal of laughter. "No way." I cover my mouth with my hand.

"Yes, way. You used to make my balls shoot up inside my body, too. You still make them do that, but only because I come so hard when you suck my cock, baby." He licks his bottom lip while staring at mine.

"It's Bunny to you, remember?" I whisper, leaning in and moving closer to him. I haven't kissed him since we were in his apartment earlier. He's been too busy talking to family and friends, taking care of his mom, and dancing with her. Then there were the speeches from each of his brothers, which went on forever but were hilarious from start to finish. While he sat at the front table, I watched with hearts in my eyes throughout Max's heartfelt speech.

I hate to admit it, but I can see myself falling for him; that is, if I haven't already.

"Come with me." He stands up to his full height.

"Won't they care that we've gone?"

Max glances at the dancefloor filled with people enjoying themselves, shaking and moving to the incredible live band that has had everyone on the floor since the first dance. I notice Griffin Holmes has returned to his seat, confirming my suspicion that he was helping Max and his brothers.

"They won't even notice we've left." I answer my own question. No one is paying any attention to us.

"Let's go."

We run across the field toward a barn and burst through the double doors clawing and kissing each other until we can't wait any more.

He clumsily searches for the switch on the wall, banging the door behind him as he finally finds it and flicks it on, flooding the barn with low, warm lighting.

I've never fucked in a barn before. With my lips firmly planted against his, I side-eye the space to discover boxes and boxes of supplies and liquor stacked high on racks along either side of the walls.

"It's a storeroom. No one comes in here." He unzips my dress and removes it from my shoulder, stripping me, letting it pool around my feet. He scoops me into his arms like he's done dozens of times and walks hastily across the barn then places my ass on a giant table in the center of the room, our breath hotly mingling with desperation.

My hands move fast to undo his fly as he removes his bowtie and throws it on the floor. Then he undoes the top buttons of his shirt, tugging it up and over his head, waving it around when it refuses to come off his wrists because his cufflinks are keeping his sleeves in place tightly.

Eventually, he throws it on the floor, his expensive-looking cufflinks along with it. He drags my panties to the side and lines his ready-to-go hard cock at my entrance, rubbing his head up and down my pussy lips. "Have you missed me, baby?"

I'm sure he calls me baby just to piss me off. "Yes."

He pushes the head of his cock inside of me painfully slow, tugging down the cup of my bra, squeezing and caressing my tit gently at first then rougher, rubbing the pad of his thumb across my nipple, making it harden from his touch.

I widen my thighs to receive him and shift my hips to push

his cock into me some more, being bold and showing him how much I've missed his touch. Having someone like him in my life, caring for me and Alfie in a way no one else ever has, makes me want to show him how much he means to us.

He's the perfect man.

With a firm punch of his hips, he drives into me, stripping away everything but the sheer need to have him fill me up, and the way he's stretching me feels heavenly. It's always felt like he was made for me. Eyes locked, the whole world could go up in flames but in this moment, with him, like this, I wouldn't care.

Max grabs my hips, digging his fingers into my flesh so hard I know he'll brand my skin with his fingerprints.

His gaze drops to where our bodies join, and he watches as he pushes himself in and out, inch by pleasurable inch.

He throws his head back and lets out a sound that's closer to a roar as I clench tightly around him. I look up at him, taking in every inch of his sculpted muscles and defined abs, my mouth watering at the sight.

"Fuck," he groans. "Your pussy is mine."

He's right, my body belongs to him and no one else. There is no one else for me.

Max presses his fingertips deeper into my skin, and as we find our rhythm, his pelvis rubs against my clit as we move together in perfect synchronization.

We both cry out in pleasure at the same time he widens his stance to give him more power behind his thrusts, teasing my orgasm to make an appearance.

I lay back on the table, wrapping my legs around him, digging my heels into his ass, urging him to fuck me harder, letting my long hair flow off the tabletop and onto the floor.

"I need to come," I moan.

He really loses it and fucks me up the table with rough hip thrusts.

"Milk my cock, baby." He grabs my hips and pulls me onto his cock at the same time he moves back and forth frantically.

He grunts, his thrusts becoming frantic as I squeeze my tits and pinch my nipples hard.

"Fuck, yeah, come for me," he orders, the corded muscles of his body tightening when I clench my inner walls around him.

He's about to blow, and the veins in his neck thickening, his skin turning red from pent-up frustration, he growls, "Jesus fucking Christ. Come." His voice thunders as if in pain.

His cock thickens inside of me.

And that's it for me. I tip over the edge, my orgasm weaving its way through my body, and I cry out as it crashes through me. "Ah, fuck." With my body on fire, I shudder, my pussy clenching around his cock, thrashing and moaning as I lose control, pinching my nipples until they're aching with pleasure.

"Good girl," Max grits out, punching his hips into mine, his heavy balls slapping off my ass as he moves in immoral ways.

With one final pummeling thrust, he lets out a deep guttural groan and explodes inside of me, his cock pulsing and his body twitching as he jerks out the last of his release.

He fills me with his hot ropes of cum, and every one of his muscles is taut as his orgasm takes over his body. Our sweaty bodies, our breaths, our orgasms merge together, creating our own brand of surrender.

I can barely recall a time when I loathed him. That seems like it was so long ago now.

He lowers himself, pressing his firm abs against me, molding himself perfectly to me as the slightest move he makes has tiny aftershocks pulsing through us.

"I want to do this forever with you," he says, planting soft kisses along my clavicle before moving to my lips.

"Me too." I could spend hours exploring his hard body and never get bored.

A long groan of pleasure vibrates in his throat when I run my nails down the contours of his back.

Panting, coming down from his high, he releases his grip on my hips, his chest rising and falling. He slowly pulls back from our skin-on-skin embrace, locking his gaze with mine as if trying to etch this moment into his soul.

Grazing my temple with his thumb, he presses a soft kiss to my lips again, a tender juxtaposition to the way he just fucked me.

With his heart beating in time with mine, he tucks a lock of my hair behind my ear and I take the opportunity to kiss the rapid pulse on his wrist. I want to know what he's thinking when his brows dip. It's quick but I see it.

"Paige... I..." A burst of laughter and high-vibe chatter stops him from finishing his sentence.

"We're naked." I chuckle, throwing my hands over my boobs to hide them.

He grins down at me and slowly slides his cock out of my body. "They won't come in." He leisurely eyes me. "Fuck, you're so beautiful." He slides two thick fingers into my wet center, and I let out a sharp hiss as he pumps them in and out before spreading our combined wetness over my clit, sending waves of pleasure surging through my core again. Everything he does makes my body feel like it's been set ablaze.

Looking up at me through his lashes, he smiles before he says, "You're all mine."

"I'm yours," I confirm on a husky moan.

I'd agree to anything at this point. Because the way he's

touching me feels impossibly sinful and I never want him to stop. I arch my back off the table, writhing against his talented fingers.

Mind, body, heart, and soul, I willingly surrender myself to him to cherish like a keepsake. And boy, does he take care of me all night and the next day, in his apartment, on his rooftop terrace, in his bed, shower, and hot tub, where he completely worships me.

39

PAIGE

It's Monday morning, and even though my muscles are sore and my body aches all over from the bedroom gymnastics Max and I did over the weekend, I'm excited to jump back into work and catch up on everything I missed last week.

I also have a meeting with the chief legal officer later to inform her that I am dating Max Hart.

To put it mildly, I'm terrified. Having never dated another lawyer before, this is a first for me. I don't know how this will go or what they will suggest moving forward to prevent Max and me from crossing paths on a case again. Because we've represented clients adverse to one another—not just several times, but dozens, so many I've lost count.

Elenor, our founding partner's secretary, taps on my door with her knuckle. "Good morning, Paige, could you come with me please?" As usual there's no smile from her; she's all business and always has this air of uptight stiffness about her, and her perpetual expression is hard and stern.

I follow Elenor through the sea of desks and bustle of the

office, down the long corridor that leads to Dalton Moore's
office.

"He's waiting for you inside." Elenor motions to the door for
me to walk through.

Well, this is new.

Perhaps I'm finally being made a partner, as I've wanted for
all these years.

"Please close the door and take a seat, Ms. Bradshaw."

Feeling nervous for no apparent reason, I shut the door and
take a seat on the opposite side of his desk.

Today, Dalton looks older than when I started here. Strong
and confident still, yes, but he's aged significantly over the years.
Running a successful law firm is taking its toll, but I'm sure I
heard a rumor that he was considering retiring next year.

With his elbows on his desk, he steeples his fingers in front
of him and looks at me with suspicion. "I'm going to get straight
to the point, Ms. Bradshaw. It has come to my attention that you
have been fraternizing with the opposing counsel during an
open case."

My heart falls into the pit of my stomach, and I gaze at him
in despair.

As my stomach twists into knots, he continues. "Having
romantic relations with someone you are working against is a
significant conflict of interest as well as highly unethical, Ms.
Bradshaw, and therefore I am sorry to be the one to inform you
of this but we have decided to relieve you of your position here
at Moore & Associates." His words are well scripted, confident,
and slowly drawn out.

I'm unable to speak. All I can do is stare at him, while tears
blind my eyes.

"After consulting with our chief legal officer about your situation, I have decided not to report you to the Office of Chief Trial Counsel this time, to avoid any repercussions on our part. The last thing we want is a scandal or an audit that could damage the firm's reputation. However, due to your connection with the opposition, I have no choice but to let you go to protect the integrity of our work. I hope you understand."

I gulp hard, hot tears slipping down my cheeks. "I was going to tell you today."

"Well, Ms. Bradshaw, someone beat you to it."

"Max Hart isn't working on the case anymore; he withdrew."

"But you were seeing him in an intimate way before he did." Dalton turns his computer screen toward me and scrolls down through the folder of photos and CCTV footage of Max and me together.

I can't deny any of it; they are all time-stamped and dated, revealing my truth.

"I'm so sorry." I shake my head back and forth, feeling completely defeated. I've never been fired from a job before, and suddenly, I feel dirty and seedy. Our secret hotel hookups no longer feel exciting or fun; instead, they tarnish everything I thought Max and I had, turning memories into regrets and making me question if it was worth it.

It wasn't worth the risk of losing my job.

"Ms. Bradshaw, as a way of keeping this to ourselves, I ask that you please sign this NDA to ensure your confidentiality." Dalton slides the document across his desk in my direction.

He's serious about not wanting to cause a scandal. I don't blame him; I would do the same if it were my firm.

I take the pen he hands me and quickly sign it, not reading any of it, my tears blurring the words and ink across the parchment.

All I want to do is run and get as far away from here as possible. I'm so embarrassed.

Dalton continues in his monosyllabic tone. "And in return, mainly as a goodwill gesture, because I know you now have a little one to take care of, I would like to give you six months' pay upfront to help ease the transition. That will give you plenty of time to find a new position at another firm." He takes the signed NDA and replaces it with what looks like a reference. "To help you, Ms. Bradshaw." He confirms my suspicions. "You're a great lawyer, Paige." He addresses me by my first name, something he never does. "One of the finest. And I am sure you won't struggle to find another position."

I brush the tears off my cheeks, desperately trying to pull myself together, my throat aching in defeat, contracted with all the things I should have said months ago but didn't.

Just when I think he's done, he drives the knife deeper into my heart. "Just don't screw your next position up or screw the opposition."

I'm filled with humiliation, my cheeks turning hot and crimson. I can barely look at him. "I won't." My voice is small as I take the reference.

"You're free to go. HR will be in touch to finalize the details."

I'm on my feet and making my way to the door just as he finally twists the knife for the last time. "Be careful, Paige. Griffin Holmes is not a man to be messed with."

I shake my head in confusion. "I don't understand."

"Stay away from him, Paige. That's all I'm saying." I didn't speak to him at the wedding, and I've never had any contact with him, so what does he mean? "And please tidy yourself up in the bathroom before clearing out your desk. Without a fuss, preferably. You know how the tongues like to wag. And don't take what doesn't belong to you, Ms. Bradshaw. We have security cameras everywhere."

Heartfelt. Gee, thanks. As if I would.

I nod, and with nothing left to say, I leave, my head spinning at a hundred miles an hour and feeling utterly sick to my stomach. Wiping away any mascara from under my eyes, I straighten my shoulders, donning a mask of confidence, and make my way to my office to pack up my belongings. Fuck going to the bathroom to clean myself up; I want to get out of here as quickly as possible, my embarrassment transforming into simmering anger.

Griffin Holmes. What the fuck did Dalton mean?

I busy myself by putting the last of my things into a box, and just as I'm about to put on my jacket, an email zooms into my personal inbox on my phone from the adoption agency.

To: Paige Bradshaw
From: Helena Dexter
Subject: Update on your adoption process: upcoming home visit and additional information

Dear Ms. Bradshaw,

We hope this email finds you well. We wanted to update you on the next steps in your adoption process. Following our last message, the adoption agency has changed their decision and will conduct a home visit as part of the ongoing assessment. Please be aware that someone from our team will contact you to schedule this visit; however, it may be several months before it occurs, as scheduling and staffing issues can cause delays.

Additionally, we have recently received some new information relevant to your case. Currently, we are reviewing the details, which may potentially impact the timeline of your adoption process. We will keep you updated as we gather more information and work to move things forward as smoothly as possible.

Thank you for your patience and understanding during this time. Please feel free to reach out if you have any questions or concerns.

Best regards,

Helena Dexter

I read the email again.

Months.

Months?

What living hell did I step into today?

My temples throb like a pulse as I'm overcome with despair, the shock of defeat immobilizing me. I can't think or see straight.

A demon has it in for me today.

It's then a name pops into my head.

Griffin Holmes. He's the demon.

Typing fast, I forward Max the email from the adoption agency and a CliffsNotes version of why I've been fired, asking him to call me as soon as he receives my email, as I'm heading home. I also include the code to my security gate so that he can easily enter my house in case he forgot it from last week and he decides to drop in.

Then I'm darting out of my door without saying goodbye to Edward, storming through the office, as Elenor, Dalton's secretary, does her best to subtly escort me out of the building. But with my belongings stuffed into an archive box, it's more than obvious I've been fired.

I lift my chin, refusing to let the burn of humiliation scorch my skin.

If Griffin Holmes wants to break me, he'll have to try harder because as I step into the glaring sunlight outside, one thought thunders through my mind: this is not the end of me or my career.

Not by a long shot.

40

PAIGE

"You're home early." Emma sounds surprised to see me as I walk through the door only having left a few hours ago.

"I got fired." God, that hurts. I'm the girl who graduated from Yale Law School with honors. Rule follower, perfect attendance, spotless record; I do everything by the book and yet here I am, out of a job because I had sex with Max.

We were stupid to think we wouldn't get caught.

We broke every rule we promised never to break. We made an oath. Then we tore every one of them to shreds. We let our bodies betray us, answering a call we swore we'd never answer.

"Oh." Emma's eyes widen. "Oh," she says again, as if hit by a sudden thought, her mouth forming the shape of an O.

"Your job is safe, you're still hired," I say, my voice lifeless. To hell with pretending I'm okay. I feel broken.

I had already decided to keep Emma on; she's too good to lose and Alfie loves her. With six months' salary to tide me over, I'll find a new job, or maybe this is the push I needed to take a leap of faith and start my own law firm.

I dump the box of my belongings on the floor and toe off my

shoes before untying my hair from its ponytail, then I dig my fingers into my scalp to relieve the tension.

What a fucking day. The worst I've ever had.

"Alfie is taking a nap. He was fussy; I think his gums are sore from teething," Emma informs me, worry written all over her face as she assesses me. "Are you okay?"

"Not really." I pull a faint fake smile. "You can go, Emma."

"Are you sure? I can take Alfie out for the afternoon once he's woken up."

"No, it's fine. Come back tomorrow." I tag on the end a small, "Please."

Tomorrow. It's my first day since leaving college of being unemployed. I'll do whatever it takes to keep a roof over my head; I'm not going to become homeless too.

As Emma gathers her things to leave, Max bursts into my home looking frantic and beside himself, his hair messier than usual and eyes darting everywhere.

"What happened, Paige?" he asks, sounding breathless, wrapping me in his arms and hugging me so tight my lungs might burst.

From over his shoulder, Emma mouths, *See you tomorrow*, disappearing quietly out of the door as I break down in his arms, yet again. Much the same as the day he comforted me when Marin was here, swaddling me like a baby as my life lies around my feet in tatters.

My heart can't take any more.

He lets me weep, lament, as I fall to pieces in the arms I never want to let me go.

"I was going to tell work today, Max." I sob, my hot tears making my eyes sting.

"I know you were," he coos, rubbing my back with his hand, trying to soothe me, but it doesn't work. "Me too. I was going to tell my brothers that we've been meeting in secret since the day we made the list in my office. They think I only found out last week it was you at The Velvet Rooms."

"We were stupid to think we wouldn't get caught." I cling to him, burying myself into his neck.

"It's all my fault. I shouldn't have pushed you the way I did," he admits, but that's the furthest thing from the truth.

"I wanted to." I did, and no one ever makes me do anything I don't want to. I'm not that weak. I wanted Max and I have no regrets about that.

"Come and work for us," he offers.

"No." Ethically, that doesn't sit right with me. Screwing the opposition is one thing, but screwing the boss to get a job is a different thing entirely.

I've already broken rules and codes of conduct I never thought I would to satisfy my needs; I won't do it again.

"Dalton warned me when I left that I was to stay away from Griffin Holmes." My words come out in stuttered breaths.

Max stiffens around me, and after a while, he pulls out of our embrace. "Say that again, Paige." He holds me at arm's length.

"Dalton said, 'Be careful, Paige. Griffin Holmes is not a man to be messed with.' Then he went on to warn me further. 'Stay away from him, Paige. That's all I'm saying.'" I quote him verbatim, wiping my snotty nose with the back of my hand.

All the blood drains from Max's usually tan face as he steps back and begins pacing my hallway floor. "Oh, my fucking God," he says, clawing at the ends of his hair. "Motherfucker," he roars, running his hands down his face, dragging his features downward.

"What?" A dull ache of foreboding looms over me, and I get

the sense Max is about to tell me something I'm not going to like. "Max?" I shout loud enough to wake Alfie.

His mouth opens in horror before he tells me, "I spoke with him at the wedding."

"Who?"

"Griffin."

"Why? What about?" A suffocating feeling grips my throat as I realize what he's implying. "Oh, my God. What did you do? Tell me you didn't mention the adoption or Marin."

He closes his eyes, dropping his head in shame, confirming what I already know. He did.

"Do you have any idea what you've done?" I seethe, all the blood rushing to my head.

"I thought I was helping. I asked him if he could make the adoption go through quicker." His voice sounds strained as we begin to spiral.

"You screwed everything up, Max. I lost my job because he sent photographs and video footage of us together at every hotel we checked into. To my fucking boss. Where would we be now if Griffin had sent them to our clients? Our reputations would be in tatters, Max." Mine already is. And it wasn't just a suspicion I had, I was right about it being Griffin. Having never mentioned him before, there's no other reason why Dalton would warn me away from him. "I'm now getting a home visit from the adoption agency because they received some new information relevant to my case." I wrap air quotes angrily around my words. "The person who sent that information was Griffin fucking Holmes." I spray spit out of my mouth, angrier than I've ever been, rage pumping around my veins at Mach speed. "How dare you interfere in my life," I grind out.

He flinches at my scalding fury. "That's not what I was doing; I was trying to help."

"Instead, you screwed everything up." My life is falling apart around me while I'm coming apart at the seams. "What did you say to him?" Tears stream down my face, but I stand firm, ignoring them as I question him like I would a witness on the stand.

Max runs his hands through his hair, once, twice, before he finally tells me. "I asked him if he knew Marin. He said he'd never heard of her." He points to somewhere far off in the distance.

I fold my arms in front of myself; my defenses are up and I'm ready for battle. "Of course he wouldn't admit that; she's a sex worker, Max." And an addict. "Then what?"

"Then I told him what Marin told us outside your house that day, which he denied again and said he wasn't Alfie's father. However, he mentioned he would look into the adoption as a favor, but there was no guarantee he could help."

And now he's using Alfie's adoption as a threat—to show me how powerful he is. He's the most influential judge in San Francisco and capable of anything. "Do you really think the adoption agency will allow Alfie's adoption to go through if I don't have a job with no way to support him?"

"I just offered you a job," he shoots back, his voice a sharp bite.

I bark back, "You can stick your job offer up your ass. I will never work for you. I can't even bear to be in the same room as you right now." I don't want to be anywhere near him. Tears continue to stream down my cheeks, my throat aching and my temples thumping from all the stress of today, the last few months, everything.

Max and I glare at each other: Me shooting virtual daggers at him while he looks at me with so much pain etched into his expression that tells me he knows he fucked up. Good. Let him choke on that guilt.

"I'm so sorry," he finally says, his voice cracking. I believe him. I know he's sorry, but still, he destroyed everything good in my life.

"Get out of my house," I grit through my teeth, anger swelling in my guts.

"Paige." He steps forward, but I stop him in his tracks with my hands, signaling for him to back away.

"Please get out of my house. I never want to see you again."

The look of devastation on his face cuts my already shattered heart to ribbons. "Paige, don't do this."

"Don't do this?" I mimic mockingly, my tone chaotic and rising with every word. "It's a little too late for 'don't do this.' I wish I had never gone to The Velvet Rooms that night, wish it wasn't you, wish I had never met up with you all those times. You pushed yourself into my life, pretending to care about me, and Alfie. But the reality is, you don't care about us or you wouldn't have spoken to Griffin behind my back. I never asked you to do that and now you've fucking destroyed my life. And his." I point up the stairs, gesturing to Alfie who is now crying. "You might be reckless with your life, throwing yourself out of planes without consequence, but that's not how I live my life. So, do me a favor, Max, get the fuck out of my house and never think about me again. I know I won't be giving you a second thought." That's not true but for all our sakes, I have to forget him and move on with a new plan. The first one being, how I turn Alfie's adoption around.

"Paige, please listen to me," he begs, his voice trembling, breaking in places, and coming out in short, sharp bursts. "I know I ruined everything, but if it's any consolation, I don't regret The Velvet Rooms or our lunches together—none of it, except talking to Griffin. If I could go back in time and change what I did, I would. I'm so sorry, Paige. Please, baby, you have to forgive me."

Is he joking?

"Forgive you? I fucking hate you." I don't hate him. "Now, leave or I'm calling the cops." I place my foot on the first step of my stairs. "I was doing just fine before you entered my life. I may not have had a picture-perfect show home that's always tidy, but it's full of love and happiness. My life was uncomplicated before we started whatever the fuck this is." I motion to the space between us. "I guess the chase was always part of the excitement for you. But you got me. You've had your fun, and you can move on to the next woman." Damn, that's painful. "I don't need you, Max. I don't need anyone. So, please, just leave me alone and see yourself out. I have a baby who needs me and a job to find so I can support him. Goodbye, Max." Then I run up the stairs, away from the man I wanted to spend every hour of every day with. Instead, he broke my heart, broke me, shredding any possibilities of me having a family to call my own.

Dashing into Alfie's room, I lift him out of his crib and into my arms, soothing him to settle him down.

He instantly stops crying when he realizes it's me, and when I bop his nose, he looks happy to see me, his cute smile melting my shattered heart.

He's the only good thing in my life.

While I pull him close to me, and bounce him up and down, I watch Max out of Alfie's bedroom window drive erratically out of my gates, his car roaring through the neighborhood and out of our lives while I bite my bottom lip to conceal my sobs as grief rips through me once again.

He lost me. I lost him. The man I'm completely and utterly smitten with and know that deep in my heart I'm in love with.

It was stupid of me to let my guard down too soon, and trust him with my heart, because he broke it.

But my heart will heal, and I'll find another job or start my own company if I have to, because gossip will be flying today at Moore & Associates after Elenor, Dalton's secretary, accompanied me to the lobby, and that news and speculation will spread rapidly before the day is over.

I'll come back fighting, though. For Alfie's sake. He's my family. Just him and me, my mom and dad. We don't need anyone else.

"I can't lose you, Alfie. Please don't leave me," I whisper.

I won't survive otherwise.

41

MAX

Radio silence.

That's what my brothers are giving me right now as they stare at me from across my dining table in my apartment, waiting for me to explain why I gathered them here urgently.

If I thought Nathan was mad about me calling him just as he was about to leave for his honeymoon, or "babymoon" as Arianna called it... fucking babymoon... pft... he's going to go nuclear the minute I tell him about me and Paige.

"Spit it out, you have ten minutes, Max," Nathan snaps, resting his arms on the table and locking his fingers together.

I drag my hand down my face. "You know how I asked to be removed from the Youngs' case last week?" I start.

He nods. "Yes."

I clear my throat nervously. "It was because I discovered who the woman at The Velvet Rooms was."

"It was Paige, you already told us that on Saturday, and you did the right thing removing yourself as soon as you found out last week," Eli jumps in.

I shake my head. "That's the thing. I didn't find out last week."

Nathan's eyes widen with shock as he works out what I'm about to confess.

"I've known for months and we've been sleeping together for months." My posture goes limp, my bones dissolving away at the shame and enormity of what we did.

They all shout at me at the same time. "Jesus Christ." Cole. "What the fuck?" Eli. "What the hell were you thinking?" Nathan.

Cole fires another question at me. "Is that who you've been sneaking off with at lunch?"

It's what he suspected weeks ago in our text conversations.

"I wondered where the hell you were going. And what about all the afternoons you've been off?" Eli asks.

Shit, he's noticed too.

"I've been with Paige." I come clean.

"Why the fuck have I not noticed?" Nathan asks, looking puzzled. He's usually very observant.

"Because you've been organizing a wedding and have a baby on the way," I state, feeling stupid for pointing it out.

He glares at me and I shrink in my seat.

"Is that why you are never off your phone now too? You're always texting." Eli reveals how closely he's been watching.

I nod, unable to talk. I'm so ashamed, and the room goes silent. Eventually, I say, "We just sort of happened." That's partly true. I made the move, but she didn't exactly turn me away. She wanted it all, wanted me. In the same way I did. The chemistry between us was undeniable, and there's no way we could ignore it.

"Right, your dick just sort of slipped out of your pants? Yeah, I can see how that happens," Cole scoffs sarcastically.

Eli injects himself into the conversation again. "Are you out of your damn mind? Sleeping with the enemy while you were in the middle of a case is a line I never thought you'd cross, Max. You've compromised everything Dad built. Do you realize how bad this looks if anyone finds out?" He slams his hands on the table, then pushes his chair back and paces the floor angrily. "You've opened us up to a lawsuit if your client challenges the agreed divorce settlement."

I bite back. "Only if Stella Young claims she was unfairly treated and our relationship influenced her settlement." She'll never know if we don't tell her. My brothers will never allow that. They'll be contacting her as soon as they've read over the court documents to make their assessment. "Paige and I never once spoke about the case outside of work." We were too busy exploring each other's bodies.

"And how exactly do we prove that?" Cole asks, sounding pissed at me.

"You have my word."

"That's not enough, and you know it, Max." Nathan shakes his finger at me. "You put all of us at risk." He begins listing every rule I've broken. "Professional conduct, professional disgrace, malpractice, breach of ethical duties, loyalty, and confidentiality."

"I know, I know." I hold my hands up in mock surrender, feeling stupid as fuck, panic threatening to swallow me whole.

Cole asks, "If you knew, why did you do it?"

"I just... I... I don't know." I don't have an excuse. The only thing I have is that I wanted her, and I wanted to find out if the connection I felt between us was real and true. It was. It is. But my brothers will never accept that.

Nathan arches his neck back and eyes the ceiling, as if he's unable to look at me. Any minute he's about to really lose it.

"You don't fucking know?" he asks slowly, a time gap between each word.

Of course I know what I did. I wanted her, and I went after her, even though it was reckless. At first, it was all about the thrill and the sex, but then something changed between us. Paige and Alfie ended up taking permanent residence in my mind and my heart. It caught me off guard. I didn't see it coming, and it surprised me, too.

"I'm sorry," I say. Two simple words that I'm not sure they will believe from me right now.

Eli steps up to the table and places his hands on the tabletop. He leans forward, looking intimidating. "Sorry doesn't cut it and we can't let that slide. You're suspended, effective immediately. You're out until we decide if we can ever trust you again."

I'm paying the price for choosing her over my brothers and their punishment is fair.

"There's more," I admit.

"More?" Cole asks, looking even more shocked.

"It involves Griffin Holmes, Paige, and Alfie," I inform them.

"Who's Alfie?" Nathan asks curiously, jumping in quickly. Clearly, Eli never told Nathan or Cole about Alfie, who I was holding when he stopped by Paige's the day she took ill at court.

"Paige's sister's baby. Paige is adopting him." Well, she was until I fucked it up. I have to fix this. Stat.

Nathan tilts his chin up, squinting. "What does that have to do with Griffin?"

"He's Alfie's dad," I say, then pause. "That's what Marin, Paige's sister, claims. On Saturday night, I pulled Griffin aside for an off-the-record conversation. This morning, Paige was fired from Moore & Associates. She also received an email from the adoption agency saying they'd gotten new information about her case, and it will now take several months to go through the

courts. That doesn't make sense— the adoption was nearly finalized, just a few weeks away from a decision. Now they're
backpedaling, and I think it's because I asked Griffin if he could
do me a favor and push it through faster. I also asked if he could
make sure there weren't any holdups. Paige believes Griffin got
her fired and sabotaged the adoption." Paige was right— in his
heartless, roundabout way, Griffin is showing her not to mess
with him.

"Griffin wouldn't do that." Nathan's expression grows hard.

"I think he's capable of anything." I jab my finger against the
tabletop to make my point. "Griffin threatened Marin, told her
he could make her disappear. But no one's going to believe her;
she's an addict, and she used to work at a strip club." Paige
would never want anyone to know that, but my brothers are a
wall of discretion; they would never share that information.
"Griffin went to the strip club for his entertainment. With Marin.
And today, when Paige was fired, Dalton Moore warned Paige to
stay away from Griffin Holmes. Dalton had fucking video
footage from the hotels Paige and I had been meeting up in, and
photos. In twenty-four hours, Griffin managed to get all of that
information. He saw us at the wedding together and went out of
his way to try and destroy Paige's reputation." I don't care about
mine. All I care about is her. "Dalton even made Paige sign an
NDA to keep her mouth shut about us so as not to cause a
scandal or trigger an audit." This is a fucking disaster and bigger
than both of us.

"What did Griffin say to you when you spoke to him, Max? I
need all the details." Eli joins us back around the table.

"He didn't say much after I asked him if he could help. He
laughed, patted me on the shoulder, wished me well, and told
me not to believe fantasist addicts who work in strip clubs, but
he would see what he could do about Alfie's adoption. But the

thing is, I didn't tell him about Marin being an addict, nor did I tell him about what she did for a living. He gave himself away." He'd clearly had one too many whiskeys. I don't think he even realized what he said.

"Shit," Nathan gasps, knowing he's caught between friendship and family loyalty.

I can tell Nathan is struggling with this. Griffin has been a good friend of his for many years.

"How do we prove Griffin is Alfie's dad?" Cole asks.

Eli's sharp mind jumps into action. "DNA? From Alfie. Can you ask Paige for it? And which treehouse did Griffin stay in on Saturday night at the ranch? Ask Mom if the sheets have been washed yet. If not, I know someone in forensics who owes me a favor. I can ask him to sweep the treehouse at the ranch."

Fuck, that's a great plan, but it's Monday. Mom's team are nothing but efficient; the sheets will have been laundered for sure. "That's not even legal," I state.

"We're not going to court with whatever we find, Max." Nathan jerks his head back, his face turning thunderous. "We're going to play him at his own game. No one fucks with my family."

What does Nathan have planned?

"Call Mom. Now." He points to Cole, then points to Eli. "And you, call your forensics contact, and you." He turns to me next. "I need Marin's address and then call Paige."

"Paige broke up with me." It was over before we got to experience how good we could have been together. Paige hating me hurts more than I ever thought possible. "I can't ask her for Alfie's DNA." She loathes me.

"Didn't you just stay there?" Deep in thought, he steeples his long fingers together.

"Yeah."

He holds my gaze, and I can tell he wants to chop me up into tiny pieces. Instead, he's helping me when what he really should be doing is firing my ass, removing me as a partner, and cutting me off. "And did you hold Alfie?"

"I took care of him when Paige was sick." Nathan's brows fly up to his hairline in surprise. I would tell him I could give him a run for his money but now is not the time to fuck around. "I haven't unpacked my bag yet."

"Find the clothes you wore when you were there. You'd better hope there's a hair of his on your clothes, or this could mess up our plan. Also, I need the name of the strip club Paige's sister worked at."

"Caspers," I confirm. "And I have Marin's address. I know where she's living because I'm paying her rent."

My brothers all stare at me in shock. "I did it for Paige."

"Do you love her?" Nathan asks.

I let out a heavy sigh and remain silent. I do love her; she's the only woman I've ever loved, but I can't say it out loud, not when I've never even told her, and probably never will now. "She said she never wants to see me again." My chest tightens. "Just... fix the adoption. That's all I'm asking. Fix what I screwed up. Please."

Nathan lifts his cell phone off the dining table. "You'll step back, no work, and let us fix the mess you made."

"Who are you calling?" I ask, my voice low and defeated sounding.

"Dalton. Then I need to call my wife to explain why we're delaying the babymoon she was excited about. Don't be surprised if she wants to tear your spine out through your mouth. And you're damn lucky we have our own jet and I can easily change the flight schedule."

I groan. There's another name to add to the list of women who hate me.

"Arianna loves me." I try to make myself feel better. After she helped me uncover the lies my journalist ex-girlfriend fed her to try to bring down my family, we became close. She's perfect for my brother. I admire the way she handles his grumpy ass. She's the only woman I know who could do that.

"Arianna might be the only person who loves you right now. I can't fucking believe what you've done."

"Neither can I." I pulled the trigger on my own life, dragging Paige down with me into chaos.

Nathan swipes and taps on the screen of his cell phone before holding it to his ear. "Go." He points at me. "Alfie's hair. That's what we need." He holds up his hand, stopping me when I'm about to respond. "Dalton, good to hear your voice. How long has it been?" Dalton replies, making Nathan fake a laugh as he scowls at me and points his thumb over his shoulder, instructing me to leave.

I remove myself from around my dining table, feeling like I've been dismissed from the principal's office, like some naughty teenager who's been caught smoking around the gym block.

I'll never tell anyone how bad I feel or how much my heart hurts. Admitting that would make my love for Paige real, and I'd rather tear out my own heart and bleed silently than do it. The weight of it all bores down on my chest as I walk down the hallway toward my bedroom. I lost her. I ruined everything.

My hand presses against my chest as I struggle to breathe.

Clutching the fabric of my shirt between my fingers, I rip it open, making the buttons fly everywhere, angry at myself for thinking I was some sort of hero.

No excuses. I messed up, and I'll own it.

While I might not be able to fight for Paige and Alfie, my brothers will. For me.

I lift my overnight bag off my bedroom floor, glad I didn't have time to wash it over the weekend.

Unzipping it, I frantically pull everything out and examine each piece of clothing, trying to find one of Alfie's blond hairs, searching each one methodically.

"Shit." I throw a T-shirt on the floor when I come up short. It's hopeless. We have nothing.

Defeat overwhelms me as I plop myself heavily on the edge of the bed and rest my elbows on my knees.

If Paige loses Alfie, I... I can't even bring myself to imagine what that would do to her, and I would rather die than watch that unfold.

I swipe my bag off the bed angrily and throw it across the room. As it lands with a thud, a flash of something white bounces out of it, making my brows dip in confusion.

Tilting my head to the side, I lift my ass off the bed and march over to a white scrap of cotton I don't recognize and snatch it off the floor.

As I unfold the fabric between shaky fingers, a devious smile spreads across my face. It's Alfie's filthy white bib. Clearly it got mixed in with my dirty laundry. It's drenched in his drool from teething and it's pure DNA gold.

Griffin Holmes. Watch out. My brothers are coming for you.

God knows why they are helping me, because I don't think they'll ever trust me again.

42

PAIGE

"Wow," Cat says after I've given her the unedited version of events that led me to be able to go for walks in the park midweek with Alfie.

I push and pull Alfie's stroller back and forth. He's sound asleep, and I don't need to soothe him. It's a habit more than anything.

Cat and I are sitting on one of the green benches that overlook the brightly painted Chinese Pavilion on the other side of Blue Heron Lake in Golden Gate Park. With the sun blazing down on us, the ducks quacking now and then, and the gentle hum of wildlife surrounding us with their unique songs, I almost forget how heartbroken I am.

For the past two weeks, my life has shifted from hectic to peaceful, and I've completely immersed myself in everything about Alfie. I didn't think it was possible, but each day that passes, I fall more and more in love with that little guy.

My heart might have shattered the day Max left my house, but Alfie is helping to piece it back together. Gradually, bit by bit, I know I'll be okay. It's just going to take longer than I expected to get over Max, and that tells me everything I need to know: my feelings run deeper than I ever admitted, deeper than I even realized.

"Why didn't you call me sooner?" Cat asks before taking a sip of her iced coffee from her clear to-go cup, sliding her sunglasses back on to shield her eyes from the sun.

"I didn't want to talk to anyone." I even gave Emma time off with full pay to give me some space. I can't afford to be frivolous, but I need time and space to heal, get my life in order, and consider what my next move is.

"And what about the adoption agency, any progress with them and update of time scales?"

"They won't budge on their decision and told me I have to wait for the home visit, which they could spring on me at any time." Sounds more like a test than following protocol. As if they're trying to catch me in the middle of doing something illegal.

Fuck Griffin Holmes. And fuck Marin for putting us all in this position in the first place.

I drove past her place the other day, and despite all my willpower, I couldn't bring myself to knock or even get out of the car. Seeing where she lived, I wasn't ready to face whatever was behind that door or the things she's hiding inside. There's already too much uncertainty and worry in my life, I just can't handle any more.

Regardless of Max's offer to pay her rent, she may have already left town. Marin's a floater, a nomad, a ghost slipping through lives without leaving a trace; except that is, for a baby.

Which reminds me... the check I sent Max to cover Marin's rent still hasn't been cashed.

Goodie do-gooder. He doesn't need to take care of Marin for

me. Throwing his money around, thinking he can solve world peace or something.

Kind of him though.

Remaining quiet, I'm deep in thought, something I do a lot of now, when Cat asks, "What's the plan, Paige? You need a plan."

I hate to admit it, but I do. I have responsibilities, and still I haven't even attempted to look for a job. That's not what I want.

Edward, the best secretary I've ever had, called me last week to check on me, genuinely concerned about my well-being. He never dug too deep, asking only how I was and when I'd get a new job, and to keep him in mind since he loved working for me.

If he knew I'd been screwing the opposing counsel in the middle of a live case, he wouldn't be asking that. It did, however, tell me that he had no idea why I was fired. If he knew, he may not have asked to be my legal secretary again. Still, hearing that so many clients have been calling around, refusing to work with anyone else other than me, was a nice confidence boost.

"I think I want to set up my own firm." It's time. "But I need an office." It will make me look bigger than I am. Rent is ridiculous in the city but if I am serious about it, I need to either ask my mom and dad for help, or make a call to the bank to ask for a loan.

"I have an office you can use," Cat offers cheerfully as the birds chirp and twitter around us. "We use it as a storage room, but it can easily be cleaned out. It's wasted space, to be honest, and would make a great gift from me to you for a business start-up." She extends her hand as if passing me a present.

I scoff, shaking my head. "I can't let you do that."

"You're not, I am offering, and you need it, so that's final. Give me a week to clear the space and get a desk and phone line set up for you. And you"—she waggles her finger at me—"sort out your business name, register the business, then set up your social platforms. I can have someone in my IT department create a website for you. Easy."

When she puts it like that, it does sound easy. "I feel like a charity case," I admit.

"It's not charity, it's what friends do for each other." She shuffles along, moving closer to me on the bench, and threads her fingers through mine. "Remember when I caught Bryce screwing my secretary, and I lived with you for months until I found a new place?"

"You're my friend, I would have let you live with me permanently."

"That's exactly the point I am trying to make. We are friends for life and I love you, Paige. The office is yours."

I will never be able to return the favor. "Thank you," I say, her kindness forming a lump in my throat.

Unable to keep it together, I weep aloud, unraveling in the park as life continues around us. I'm usually so well put together, but lately all I've done is cry. It's ridiculous, really. Cat wraps her hand around my shoulder and rocks me side to side, tucking me into her tightly, laying her head on top of mine when I rest it on her shoulder.

She lets me cry until I have no more tears left, wrapping me in her cocoon of comfort.

"The tears aren't just about the office, are they, Paige?" She shoots from the hip. Cat knows me better than anyone.

"I miss him, Cat. It hurts so bad." I fist the fabric of my summer dress over my heart. "In here."

"Have you heard from him?"

"He's called me every day." I live for those moments.

"And?"

"I haven't picked up." I'm too chicken shit, and I'm still angry with him.

Almost every day, he sends bunches of roses in different colors, each accompanied by a handwritten note with apologies and expressions of how much he misses me and Alfie.

When I returned from the hairdresser's the other day, I arrived home to a delivery: the shiniest, coolest Lightning McQueen ride-on motorized toy car, complete with flashing lights and buttons on the steering wheel that make it sound like the car is alive and talking. Alfie's eyes lit up the moment he saw it, and for a second, my heart ached because he knew exactly what would make Alfie smile.

"Oh, Paige." She sighs, pressing a kiss to the top of my head, probably leaving a big red lipstick mark on my much shorter, fair hair. I had several inches cut off last week. It still feels strange booking weekday appointments at convenient times, but that's something I'll be doing more often once I have my own business. From now on, I'm making my own rules. And I'm sticking to the professional ones I took an oath on.

And I will never, ever, break them again.

I've learned from my mistakes.

"Maybe you should talk to him," she suggests.

"I think we're past that, Cat." I shrug dismissively.

"He clearly wants to explain himself, and maybe listening to him will help. Also, you should consider switching your output mode off and flicking it to receive mode, Paige. You have a habit of railroading every argument, sometimes."

"I do not," I counter, jerking out of our embrace.

Cat lifts her iced coffee to her lips and smiles against the rim of her cup. "You're about to do it now."

My shoulders drop in defeat. "God, I hate how right you are sometimes."

"All I'm saying is, hear him out."

I shake my head. "How do you forgive someone who stopped Alfie's adoption from going through?"

"The clue is in what he said to you on the day everything blew up, Paige," Cat replies casually.

I push my sunglasses up to rest on top of my head and dry my tear-stained face with my hands. I'm so glad I didn't wear any makeup today.

Cat explains what she means. "Max thought he was helping. He thought he was doing the right thing."

"But he destroyed everything," I counter.

"Are you even listening to what I'm saying? Why would he send you perfume, look after Alfie for days while you were sick, or fix your leaky kitchen sink?"

God, yeah, he did do that when I was lying in bed.

"And why the hell would he do your laundry, hire a house-keeper, and build Alfie's playset? Or invite you to his brother's wedding?"

"I don't know."

"It's so obvious, Paige."

"Is it?"

"He loves you."

"He doesn't love me." I shake my head violently, brushing off her crazy theory.

"Then why would he approach the highest-ranking judge in San Francisco to ask for help?"

"Because it was Alfie's father?" It seems that everyone I spoke to at the adoption agency and the top adoption lawyer in the state couldn't help me overturn the decision made weeks ago. Griffin is not only a powerful man but also dangerous—a heart-less bastard.

"God, you really can be dim sometimes, Paige." She pauses, turning to face me fully. "It doesn't matter who the highest-ranking judge in the city is, it could've been Brad fucking Pitt for all it's worth. Max went to the only person he believed could help you, and that just happened to be Griffin Holmes, Alfie's father. But Max couldn't have predicted that he would be so callous. What Griffin did was put you and Max in your place, to show you who was boss, and that was out of both of your hands. Max tried to do the right thing, for you and for Alfie, but he could never have known Griffin would pull what he did. What Max did wasn't malicious."

It takes a minute for my brain to catch up. "You're right," I whisper.

"I know!" She throws her hands in the air as if she's cheering for my revelation. Alfie jerks in his sleep but doesn't wake up.

"Sorry, Alfie." Cat smiles, tapping the handle of his stroller.

"It's too late now."

"It's never too late." She swipes her hand through the air, dismissing me. "Anyway, I'll let you think about what I've just said and while you do that, I need you to drive your ass to my office block now, to look at your new office. Make sure it meets Paige Bradshaw Esq.'s standards, then we need to make a plan to get your website designed, have a phone line installed, design business cards, and move you in."

"I have Alfie."

"Darling, I have staff." She pushes her designer sunglasses up her nose. "They'll entertain him while his mommy gets to work."

"I'm not his mommy yet." Not officially. That feels so far out of reach now.

"Yes, but starting your own firm means you're one step closer —job stability, a beautiful, loving home, financial security, and no criminal record. Although the things you did with Max in The Velvet Rooms sound criminal," she teases to lighten the mood. "And for God's sake, will you please stop beating yourself up? You met a hot guy in an exclusive sex club who just so happened to be the guy working on the same case as you, and he figured out it was you. So, you broke some work rules, had a little fun, and hell, girl, you had some great sex, by the sounds of it." She playfully punches the top of my arm. "And you got fired, but screw them, you don't need Moore & Associates." She flips the bird in the direction of my old office, causing me to chuckle. "Now you can charge double, if not triple, what you were making working for them. I don't call what Max did destroying your life, Paige, I call that divine timing. He did you a favor."

For the first time in two weeks, a mix of strength and confidence filters through me, and I rise to my feet, psyching myself up, ready to face a new challenge. "I'm setting up my own law firm," I state, wrapping my fingers around the handle of Alfie's stroller.

"Yes, you are."

"And Alfie's adoption will go through." I have no control over their final decision but I'm willing to do whatever it takes.

"Hell, yes it will." Cat pushes herself to a standing position. "You've got this."

I might not yet.

But I will.

43

NATHAN—ONE WEEK LATER

I take a sip of whiskey, mainly to calm my nerves, then rest my back against the seat, flicking glances between Cole and Eli. No Max, though. He's on week three of his suspension.

We decided that a month would be enough for him to reflect and learn from this situation. Officially, we've told the staff that he is taking a month off, and we will stick to that explanation.

I'm unusually nervous about today because I have no idea how it will go. Knowing what I know now about Griffin Holmes is more than enough to make my stomach twist in knots. I thought he was one of the good guys, but it turns out he will do whatever it takes to keep his power, including sacrificing his son and his safety to protect himself, using him like a pawn rather than a person in his own personal game of chess.

"How long have we been friends, Griffin?" I ask, looking around the almost empty country club where I invited him to play a round of golf today.

"Too long." He places his knife and fork together on top of his plate then rubs his swollen stomach. The fucker ordered the most expensive lobster on the menu.

"So, you trust me?"

"With my life, Nathan, you know that." He laughs, sounding cock sure of himself, but I'm about to blow his charade to pieces.

"Oh, you shouldn't have done that, Griffin," I say as Cole slides an envelope across the dinner table we are sat around. "Not when you fucked over my own flesh and blood."

"I don't understand." He can play the fool all he wants, but he's not fooling me or my brothers.

"Open it." Eli points to the envelope. "I'm sure it will all make sense."

Suspiciously, Griffin darts his gaze between me and my brothers, who are flanked on either side of me, before he slides the envelope off the table and opens it painfully slow.

His nostrils flare as he cautiously pulls out the evidence from the crisp white envelope my brothers spent hours gathering.

My voice is steady and bold as I tell him what he already knows. "What you will find there is the DNA results confirming you are, in fact, Alfie Bradshaw's father. His mother worked at the strip club on 6th Street." I pause to chuckle. "I don't know why I'm telling you this; all the photographs of you two together at the club are right there. There's also a disk inside with hours of footage of you two together. You seem to have a thing for blondes, which is news to us all, especially when your wife is a brunette."

It's amazing what money can buy you these days. In this case CCTV footage and photos dating back not just months but years.

"Although I understand why it might be easy for you to cheat on her, dividing your time between here and Sacramento provides a solid alibi to hide your indiscretions. Tell me, what would she say if she knew what you were doing when you were 'working' here? Mmm?"

During my time as a lawyer, I've never played dirty. After today, I don't intend to do it again.

Griffin tries to hide his annoyance with a long, fake sigh, but I can see it in his brown eyes; they are clawing at me like talons. He shoves the DNA results confirming Alfie's parentage, along with the photos, back into the envelope to hide them. "What do you want?"

"Revoke your instruction to block Alfie's adoption," I order firmly. He paid Paige's caseworker an obscene amount to delay it. "Set the wheels in motion and approve the adoption. Personally."

"And if I don't?"

"Then the footage of you with all of the women you've been cheating on your wife with gets sent to her, the national newspapers, and Katie Ross." I smirk. "She's a close friend of mine and owns SFN, the news channel. I'm sure they'll be very interested in how many times you've visited the strip club." He's a faithful and loyal customer, visiting every week without fail. Watching girls strip is one thing; it's another to go all the way and pay for sex like he does.

A red rash climbs the skin of his throat. Through a tight jaw he asks, "Anything else?"

We've got him.

I reply, "There's a copy of those documents along with the video footage in a safety deposit box only my brothers and I have access to. Push the adoption through, send us the original court documents once it's done and only then will I send you the name of the bank they are being held at, along with the code to access the safety deposit box."

The things I do for my fucking brothers. It's what they did for me when Arianna and I split up.

Admittedly, I would have moved faster to help Max, but I

wasn't about to let my wife down or cancel our honeymoon, denying her the babymoon she spent weeks planning. While I was away, Cole and Eli handled all the investigation and dirt digging. I just showed up today and played my part. It was pure luck that Eli's contact found one of Griffin's hairs in the shower cubicle of the treehouse he spent the night of the wedding in at Mom's ranch.

Griffin Holmes might be the Chief Justice of the state Supreme Court, but he fucked with my family and I won't stand for that.

I may need another vacation after today.

"And just so you know, Griffin, we double-checked the case Max and Paige were opposing counsel in, and there was no bias involved. At Hart Law, we do everything by the book. Max was suspended for a month, but what you did to Paige Bradshaw to get her fired is deplorable." He's off the Christmas card list, according to Arianna. "Now, do we have a deal?" I sit forward, resting my elbows on the table, and steeple my fingers against my lips.

He glowers at me, his lips thin with anger, a layer of perspiration beading his brow. "Yes."

"Oh, one more thing." I hold my finger in the air. "You will see to it that Alfie is well provided for in the form of a trust fund for his education. You will also provide Paige Bradshaw with child support until Alfie finishes college. I'm sure you know people who can track Paige's bank details to transfer the money to. You know a lot of people, Judge Holmes; I'm sure that won't be difficult."

There's no way Paige will willingly accept Griffin's help, and she would never give him her bank details. She's too proud. But it's what she's entitled to—what she needs to support Alfie.

Griffin has more than enough to support her and Alfie's child support will be like pocket change to him.

It's a sneaky move on our end and she can kick and scream all she wants, but if she doesn't want it, she can save it in another trust fund for him.

"Are we finished now?" he asks sharply, his eyes almost black and blazing with fury.

"There's a car outside waiting to take you home," I inform him coolly, my muscles loosening, the tension leaving my body. It's not over yet, but I guarantee by tomorrow it will be.

I know Griffin and he'll do anything to make this go away.

He rises smoothly from the chair and places his napkin on top of his plate. "Gentlemen." He nods, shifting his gaze between the three of us. "It will be sorted by midday tomorrow."

"Thanks, Griffin, it's been a pleasure doing business with you." I hold my hand out for him to take but he shuns my olive branch gesture and without a second glance, he leaves the clubhouse with his head hanging in shame.

"Call Max," I tell Cole. "Tell him it's done."

As soon as he finishes the call, Max appears from where he was hiding.

"Thank you," he says, looking lost, heartbroken, even. I know that look. I've worn it myself, and it's hell. The truth is, the suspension wasn't just about the rules. It was about giving him space to breathe, to heal. We all knew his case was clean, that everything would check out, but letting it slide? That wasn't an option. Not because we wanted to punish him, but because trust between brothers has to mean something. And he broke it.

He sits opposite me and clears his throat, running his hands through his hair, which I know he does when he's nervous. "I can never thank you enough for what you all did for me." His eyes dart around the table.

"It's time you face some hard truths, Max. What you did wasn't just reckless; it was selfish. This isn't about work or the firm; it's about family. You lied to us. You even lied to Cole when he asked if you were seeing someone in a text. You hid lunches. You hid the truth. You've sat at home for three weeks because you couldn't be honest and you couldn't keep your personal life separate from your work. You didn't just make one mistake—you risked your career, a case, and our reputation. We grew up believing we could always count on each other. No secrets, no lies."

Eli steps in when I finish what I have to say. "You know we would do anything for you but you couldn't even give us the truth."

"It won't happen again, I promise. All I want is for you all to trust me again."

"You broke the bond we built." Cole's words cut deep.

Max might be close to Eli and me, but he's closer to Cole, and knowing how much he hurt him will sting.

"What's worse is that it wasn't a mistake; you made a choice," I add.

"I know. Trust me, I know," Max replies, holding his hand over his chest, which is something Eli said he's been doing since the day in his apartment. He's hurting. I get it, but it will ease soon.

Cole leans forward and locks eyes with Max. "Don't ever shut us out again."

"We're brothers," Eli says.

"And that means something," I add.

"We're family," Max states.

"And don't you ever forget it." Mom appears as if from nowhere and sits down next to Max, lifting his hand into hers.

She places her other hand on the table, motioning for us to take it, which I do, along with Eli and Cole.

Her smile softens us all as she looks at each of us. "Now you listen to me." She squeezes our hands. "Your bond as brothers is everything. It's even fiercer and stronger than the blood that bonds you. The world out there will try to break you down; make you turn on each other. Don't let it. You were raised to stand shoulder to shoulder, no matter what. Life is too short. Please don't waste the precious time you have in this world fighting because it's the one thing that can tear you apart. And nothing, no one, no case, no mistake, no pride, is worth losing each other over. Remember that. Always."

"Mom," Max says almost inaudibly as he reaches out to hug her.

"Your heart will heal, and your brothers will forgive you, Max. One step at a time, though. You need patience, sweetheart." She pats his back, then kisses him on the cheek.

Fuck, I might cry.

"I love you." She grabs his face, squashing his cheeks together before shifting her gaze to us. "I love you all. Now stop this madness, take the afternoon off, and come for a late dinner. All of you. Arianna is already on her way to the ranch."

Ah! So that's how Mom knew we were here.

"Maybe you could play some tennis before the sun sets," my mom suggests as a way for us to start repairing our brotherhood.

We now have two strong Hart women to contend with.

Maybe a third if Paige ever forgives Max.

"I'd like to play tennis," Max says.

"Me too," Cole agrees.

Eli next. "I'm in."

Then I add, "And me."

I keep my mouth shut, but my thoughts are loud.

Tomorrow, maybe this will all be behind us.

I pray Griffin keeps his promise then maybe Max can move on, and Paige with him. If that's even what they want. But the way Max looks when her name comes up? That's not a man planning to let go. That's a man not *ready* to let her go.

44

PAIGE

"Mommy's home," I yell with a smile on my face, happy to be home. It's only been two days since I moved into my new office space inside Cat's office building, but I've had a great day. I even signed another client today and, on the drive home, I wondered why the hell I didn't set up my own firm years ago.

Dropping my workbag on the floor, I pull my arms out of my dress jacket and hang it on the coat hook at the bottom of the stairs. It's almost impossible to find an empty hook, and I really must sort our jackets out soon.

"Hey, Emma's out for a walk with Alfie."

A male's voice, the one I have come to know so well, makes me jump, and I spin around on the balls of my feet faster than the crack of a whip.

All my happy feelings turn into... well, they're still happy because Max is here, in my house, standing in the kitchen doorway, but the tightness in my chest is a mix of annoyance and confusion... attraction? Whatever it is, it's dizzying.

"What are you doing here?" I ask, flabbergasted by his magical appearance like he's Houdini. The scary thing is he looks right at home here in my house. Comfortable, even though he's nervously running his hands through his wavy locks, something I've witnessed him doing often and done myself dozens of times.

"How did you get in?" I ask, puzzled by his magician's act.

"Emma."

When I called Emma to tell her my plans she was here the very next day to take care of Alfie while I set up my new office. She missed our little munchkin as much as he missed her.

I'm glad Emma let him in. In hindsight, changing the code on my gate after I told Max not to come back seems like such a childish thing to do now. "Where's your car?"

"I parked it down the street. I didn't want to scare you off."

"You didn't need to do that." I would have opened the door to him. I've been desperate to see him and thought about him every day.

Painfully handsome, he's all tan skin and thick biceps stretching the short sleeves of his white T-shirt, the threads looking close to tearing. I can tell he's been working out—a lot.

"How have you been?" I ask, because I'm desperate to know.

"Good."

I'm teetering on the edge of throwing myself into his arms or throwing something heavy at him for doing what he did. For risking it all. His career, mine. For me. For Alfie.

He tried and failed, and I should thank him. Really, I should, but I can't bring myself to admit I was wrong.

Hurt clouded my judgment, and I acted rashly, refusing to hear him out. At the end of the day, he was just trying to help. How can I be mad at him for that? Cat was right; I should be mad at Griffin. He's the one to blame.

"You cut your hair," he says, more of a statement than a question.

I reach up and touch the ends of my shorter hair. "I needed a change."

"It suits you. You look beautiful." There's so much melancholy in his tone when he says, "You haven't answered my calls."

"I didn't know what to say." That's the truth. I was too embarrassed.

He nods, looking everywhere but at me. "My brothers suspended me."

"I'm so sorry, Max." He'll be devastated by this; he's as wedded to his work as I am, more than our clients are to each other.

"I have a week of suspension left." He looks downward and scuffs the toe of his sneaker against my caramel-stained wooden flooring.

It's a fair punishment, and his brothers were right to suspend him. I think Dalton firing me was a bit harsh, although I have no idea what Griffin threatened him with if he didn't.

"Cole and Eli went through the court documents that were filed for the Youngs' divorce and didn't find anything unethical or any favoritism to either party with the settlement."

There was nothing to find, but I understand why they did it.

"That's great news." And a relief. I knew there was nothing to worry about but still, I was.

There's a long pause between us, both awkward and soothing. Time seems to stretch, as if we don't want the moment to end.

Eventually, he lifts his head. "I have something for you," he says, passing me a large envelope that's thick and official looking that I didn't notice he was holding. I was too busy looking at his face.

I move forward and examine it intently. "What is it?"

"Alfie's adoption papers. The court finalized it this morning."

"What?" My hands start to shake as I reach for the envelope. This can't be real. I look up at Max, then down at the envelope, and back to his face again to make sure this isn't some sick joke.

He gives a small cough to clear his throat. "Inside you'll find details of Alfie's trust fund. You will act as trustee of the fund until Alfie becomes eligible to receive it. And you will also receive monthly child support from Griffin Holmes until he finishes college." I'm about to refuse his financial help when Max interjects. "You don't have to use it. Put it away, save it, for Alfie, for whatever he needs. It's done, Paige, so don't argue."

I heed Cat's advice and keep my mouth shut, listening to him rather than arguing, eager to catch every detail. This is the best day of my life. Of Alfie's life.

"He's mine?" I ask in disbelief, my eyes turning watery and blurring my vision.

"He's yours, Paige."

"You did this for me?" I whisper, my emotion about to bubble over. I shouldn't be surprised he did this for me. He's a good man, steady, dependable, and he's shown me over and over that he wants nothing but the best for me and Alfie.

"I fixed what I broke, Paige. Well, my brothers did. I couldn't sleep at night knowing how much I fucked everything up."

"You didn't."

"I did." He shoves his hands into the pockets of his jeans, nibbling on his bottom lip, the ones I've kissed numerous times. He seems to think for a second before saying, "My brothers spoke to your sister and she agreed to go to rehab, but since they spoke to her, her roommates said she left for Vegas."

"She's not one to be tied down." Emotion rises in my throat as the enormity of everything he just told me sinks into my mind. It's almost too much all at once. My legs feel like Jell-O.

"And that's what I came here to tell you. So, I'll be off now."

"Okay." I nod, following him to my front door. Every cell in my body wants to pull him back, keep him here, and more than anything, I want to throw myself around him and thank him, but something stops me.

I hurled so many cruel words at him the last time he was here, words I can never take back. I told him I'd never forgive him, but the truth is, I do. I forgive him.

He changed everything for me and made the adoption happen, made it effortless, all for my sake.

How could I ever repay him for that?

The truth is, I can't. What he's done is beyond measure.

"See you around." He does an awkward salute-type gesture and smiles shyly as he opens the door.

"Max," I shout after him.

"Yeah?" His face lights up, hope flickering in his eyes.

"Thank you. For this." I lift the envelope packed with documents that hold Alfie's future inside, my heart hammering with relief and gratitude. I'm eager to call Mom and Dad to share the good news.

He hesitates, then meets my gaze. Keeping his voice low and steady, he blows me away when he says, "For what it's worth, what started out between us turned into something I didn't see coming. I'll admit I liked the secrecy too. But most of all I liked spending time with you. Getting to know the real you was the best part of my day." There's a small pause before he adds, "You were everything to me." A faint smile pulls at his lips. "Bye, Paige."

Completely stunned, I can't move or speak. I can barely breathe as I watch him walk down my driveway and through the gate at the same moment Emma comes back inside, pushing Alfie in his stroller after their walk.

Max stops to speak to Alfie, bending down and saying something funny that makes Alfie giggle, waving goodbye to him before he leaves.

And with one final wave, without looking back at me, he's gone.

Please, don't go.

And yet, I let him walk out of my life once more.

There's no chance he will ever forgive me after all the things I said.

And he used the past tense when he said, *You* were *everything to me.*

He moved on.

45

MAX

It's my first day back in the office and for the last hour, Louise has been bringing me up to speed.

Louise thrusts a divorce petition into my hands. "Unfortunately, Erin called in sick this morning, and I'm afraid she can't attend the first four-way settlement conference scheduled for today. I've read through the documents—everything is straightforward, and all is being divided equally. No children."

"That's a first." I place the paperwork on my desk.

"And if you leave now you'll make it." She checks the time on her watch.

I fucking hate being thrown in at the deep end. "But I haven't read over the case."

"I just told you; it's a simple division of everything. And if needed, you can skim read it before the client arrives. Go on, shoo."

"What? Now?" I check the time.

"You know what the traffic is like. If you leave now, you'll have enough time to read through the case."

"Where is it?"

"Howard Street."

"I'd be quicker walking." I could use some fresh air. My head is already full of information; it's near to breaking point.

"Well, you had better get going then." Louise pushes herself up to a standing position. "It's good to have you back."

"It's good to be back."

Having spent the last four weeks working out, binge-watching TV series, and doing little else besides a few tennis matches with my brothers, I've barely left my apartment. So, yeah, now that I'm back at work, at least I'll have something to distract me.

It might only be four weeks since Paige ended things with us, but it feels like a lifetime.

I miss her. And Alfie.

I miss the sound of her laughter, that unexpected warmth I never thought she had, until she showed me the real her—a strong, passionate woman, full of love and unwavering strength, fiercely protective of her little boy.

When I saw her last week, I was excited to see her, eager to find a flicker of hope in the ruins I created. It was there, but I could tell she was doing everything she could to stop herself from asking me to stay.

Seeing her again was a cruel reminder of everything that had slipped away from me. I wanted to tell her how I felt, to somehow make her understand that despite everything, I wasn't ready to let go.

As soon as the adoption went through, pushed by my brothers, who've been my rock through all this chaos, I knew that was the end of us, marking a definitive line. It was a bittersweet moment, and honestly, I don't know what I would do without them. Without their support, I'd be completely lost.

Gathering my briefcase, I slide the case file inside, the snap of the lock clicking sharply in the quiet humdrum of the office.

"This is the address, the firm's called Central District Family Law." Louise hands me a neon-pink sticky note as I pass her desk. I pause, scanning the building number on Howard Street, fixing it in my mind before handing the note back.

Central District Family Law? I've never heard of them, and I usually know everyone in this field. They must be new. Small, maybe. I typically handle high-profile divorce cases, and this sounds like a more modest operation.

"See you after lunch." I nod and wave her goodbye.

Time to focus. Time to throw myself into the first case and rediscover a part of myself through work again.

With purpose, I step out of the office and into the bright city lights, onto the busy sidewalk. I pull on my sunglasses and feel the weight of the day ahead. The warm San Francisco air brushes against my face as the city hums around me, but inside, I feel empty. Without her in my life, everything has lost its meaning. I can't even remember who I was before she came along.

With time, my brothers say, I'll get over her.

But how long does heartbreak really last?

Every tick of the clock feels like it's stabbing my heart. And there is nothing I can do to dull the pain, each day blending into a blur of painful memories and a future that no longer exists with her and Alfie. The ache often catches me off guard, like right now—the weight of missing her is crushing me, and I don't know how much longer I can carry it the way I have.

Finally, after walking up and down the street several times, I step through the entrance of a building I don't think I'm supposed to be in. The sign above the door says Golden Glow

Health, so I am definitely not in the right place, but the number is correct.

Confused, I push my sunglasses on top of my head and wait for the receptionist to finish her call.

"Good morning, sir," she greets me when she finishes.

"Morning. I think I'm in the wrong place." My eyes flick back up to the sign above reception. Yup, I must have memorized the wrong building number, something I never do. Typical.

"Is there a law firm nearby? Central District Family Law?"

"You're in the right building, sir. Central District Family Law is on the fourth floor. They haven't put up the sign yet."

Relief rushes through me. "I thought I was going crazy."

"No, sir. If you take the elevator to the fourth floor then it's conference room two, second room on the right. Your client has already arrived."

"Thank you." I'm in the elevator and on the fourth floor within minutes.

Pushing open the door to conference room two, I'm greeted by Erin's client. "Mr. Parker?" I ask. Having never met him before, I have no idea what he looks like.

"Yes." The jolly man stands up to greet me, puzzlement lining his brow as he shakes my hand.

"Unfortunately, Mrs. Springs is unable to make it today due to illness. I'm Max Hart. I'll be representing you at today's meeting on behalf of Hart Law." I check the time on the wall clock and curse inwardly. Having spent too many minutes looking for a sign with the words Central District Family Law on it, I lost the time I needed to read the case notes before today's meeting. I'm winging it.

I walk around the table and take a seat next to Mr. Parker as two females walk through the door chatting happily with each other, and for a second, time stops. The ground seems to move beneath my feet.

It's Paige.

Paige is here.

Today, she looks even more beautiful than my memory ever allowed me to believe.

Slowly, I rise to my feet, and for a moment that feels frozen in time, we lock eyes across the room.

As she stands before me, I soak in the warmth of her presence, grateful to exist in her orbit, if only for a fleeting second, because I can't stay. I can't be here.

Whatever cruel game the universe is playing with me today, I'm not in the mood to take part.

"Are you representing Mrs. Parker?" I ask her, my words slow and drawn out.

"Yes." She looks as shocked as I am.

"Of Central District Family Law?" Is that who she's working for now?

"It's my firm."

"Right." I pick up my briefcase from the chair beside me. "I'm afraid, Mr. Parker, you'll have to wait for Mrs. Springs to return. I can't represent you today. Ms. Bradshaw, please coordinate with Mrs. Springs to reschedule this meeting."

My eyes never leave Paige's as I force out the words I never imagined I'd say.

"Why not?" Mr. Parker demands, clearly baffled.

"Because I'm in love with Ms. Bradshaw," I say, my voice steady even though my heart pounds in my chest. "And that creates a conflict of interest."

Paige's pupils widen in shock at my confession. It's the first time I've admitted the truth, even to myself, and I can see precisely why it would hit her like a tidal wave.

Eventually, I break our gaze and turn to Mr. Parker. "This is highly unorthodox, Mr. Parker, and on behalf of Hart Law, I sincerely apologize. You will not be billed for today, nor will your client, Ms. Bradshaw."

Without waiting for a reply, I leave.

I told her I loved her and I have no regrets.

46

PAIGE

"Are you okay?" Warbled words rush through my ears as if I'm underwater. "Ms. Bradshaw?" Someone shakes me out of my daydream, adrenaline flooding my body.

"He loves me?" I ask on a gasp, my feet firmly glued to the floor.

"Did you not know?" Mrs. Parker counters, sounding amused.

"I... I... I didn't." I blink rapidly, fully coming out of the shock of his confession. "Can we reschedule?" I have somewhere I need to be.

"You should go after him," Mr. Parker suggests.

"I should."

"So, what are you waiting for?" Mrs. Parker's hand lands firmly on my shoulder. "Go."

A wide grin spreads across my face, causing my cheeks to ache from the stretch. "I'll call you!" This may be unprofessional, but I don't care. He loves me.

I'm already half-running in my heels, barely keeping my

balance as I bolt out of the conference room, my heart pounding so hard, my body feels like it's vibrating.

I frantically scan the corridor and realize he's already gone. Panic shoots through me as adrenaline floods my veins, and I slam the elevator button on the wall, cursing when the display shows it's stuck on the top floor.

"Screw it." I slam through the fire escape door and take the stairs two at a time, my heels clattering, sounding like gunshots against the concrete.

As I burst onto the street, the warm San Francisco sun hits me, blinding my sight, and I have to use my hand to shade my eyes. Up and down the street, my eyes dart through the midday crowd, searching...

There.

That familiar head of hair, fingers combing through it the way he always does.

"Max, wait!" I call, my voice breaking, as I sprint after him through the thrumming chaos of Howard Street, weaving between suits and tourists, refusing to let him slip away. "Max!" I shout again, raising my voice even louder.

Through the crowd of bobbing heads, I catch a glimpse of him again, and to my shock, he turns around.

Then I'm running, shoving past annoyed people, ignoring their angry curse words at me as I desperately push my way through.

Max starts walking toward me, hesitant at first, then breaks into his own run, and we collide somewhere in the middle of the sidewalk, chest-to-chest, breathless.

I throw my arms around his neck, barely noticing his brief-case crashing down onto my foot. It doesn't matter; none of it matters.

"I love you," I blurt out, words tumbling over each other, unstoppable. "I love you so much."

An irresistibly devastating grin curves his lips.

I cast my mind back to all the times he's looked at me in the same way. He's so devilishly handsome and flawless. He's caring, tender, and generous. He's the whole package.

"I'm not perfect," I tell him. "I make mistakes, say things sometimes that I shouldn't, I don't listen when I should, but the biggest mistake I ever made was not telling you how I feel about you."

"I've missed you." His ocean eyes lock onto mine. Still smiling brightly, full of triumph, he says again, "I love you, Paige."

I reach up and rake my fingers through his perfectly groomed locks that I will never get bored of touching as the city around us moves in a blur, like we are in our very own time tunnel.

"You are everything to me, Paige, and I love Alfie." His hand cups my face.

My eyes fill with tears of happiness. "I know you do. I felt it and I saw it with my own eyes. The way you took care of him for me, and the adoption." I shake my head in awe at what he did. "I will never be able to thank you."

"I think I might have an idea." He winks cheekily at me, making my heart fill with contentment and happiness.

There's my beautiful man.

He dips his head and kisses me, softly at first, but it's been weeks since we last kissed, and I've missed him. I'm done waiting. My tongue plunges into his mouth with shameless greed.

Our kiss is messy, frantic, downright filthy, desperate, and hungry. And God, it's absolutely perfect. The way his rough beard tickles my chin has memories flooding my brain of every time we've done this.

Together we soar, reconnecting in the best way possible as our illicit kiss risks getting us arrested for indecent behavior.

He grins against my lips once more. "I love you, baby."

"It's Bunny to you, Mr. Fox." I know he did that on purpose. But how I've missed that nickname and want to hear him repeat it.

"I think I've loved you since the first night at The Velvet Rooms," he says, his voice steady and confident. "I never meant to hurt you, and every day I've regretted what I did."

"It's in the past, Max. I messed up too, and I'm sorry."

"You have nothing to apologize for."

I'm about to argue with him, then I remember my new rule. Listen.

"Every single day I hoped we'd find a way back to each other, Paige. I just didn't know how. But I love you, so much. I can't bear another day without you."

With his hypnotizing mouth, he kisses me again. It's even better than I remember, blowing every one of my brain cells into smithereens because the way he kisses me turns my mind to goo.

"What are you doing this afternoon?" I ask completely breathless, already canceling all my meetings for the rest of the day.

"You."

That's the most perfect answer I could ever hear.

47

PAIGE—ONE YEAR LATER

"Alfie's sleeping." Max creeps into my bedroom—sorry, our bedroom, because Max lives with me now—on his tiptoes as if not wanting to wake Alfie up.

We haven't moved all of his belongings into my place yet, but we will soon. We'll be forced to do so once the sale of his penthouse goes through. After that, we need to figure out how to accommodate his numerous cars. We've already discussed building a house together; hopefully, we can find land big enough to include a garage to house ten cars plus a motorcycle.

I still have to pinch myself sometimes to remind me that this is real and that Max would rather move into my home that is a quarter of the size of his.

He walks across the bedroom, wearing nothing but his black boxers, making my mouth water.

He's so fit, and tight, and big... in all the right places.

To say it's been a crazy twelve months would be an understatement.

Starting my own firm didn't last long, and now I work for Hart Law. Don't ask; it felt right, and that's all I'll say about my decision. Well, it's also because they are the top law firm in the state, which might have influenced my choice. And I got offered the job before Max and I were a thing, so there's no nepotism.

It feels good to co-counsel with Max. No longer do we work against each other; we work with each other, in the boardroom and bedroom. Nathan was right; together, we're a force to be reckoned with. Now we are representing one of the wealthiest actors in Hollywood; he's going through a messy divorce with his wife. Once we finalize this divorce, there's no doubt more celebrities will be lining up to ask for our help.

"I hope he sleeps all night." Max crosses his fingers and pulls a silly face that has me laughing.

"Fingers crossed." It's been the hottest summer on record, and he's been unsettled at night for the last week.

"He did say dada, as if he understood me when I asked him if he would sleep all night." Max laughs at our quirky little dude.

Max strides over to the dresser across the room, yanking open the top drawer and rifling through its contents. I can't quite see what he's pulling out—his broad back blocks my view. But honestly, that view alone is enough to make my mouth go dry. Those sculpted muscles he's flexing might be my new favorite obsession.

"I was thinking," he says, his voice dropping low and rough, "we could have a little fun tonight."

A thrill shoots straight through me.

"That depends on what kind of fun," I manage, breathless, my heart pounding. What is he planning?

Then he flicks off the side lamp, plunging the room into darkness for a heartbeat, before switching on a black light that bathes everything in an electric, sinful glow.

A rush of excitement nearly sends me spinning off the bed.

When he finally turns around, I gasp.

He's wearing the same fox mask he wore on that first night at The Velvet Rooms, the one burned into my memory forever.

"Where did you get that?" I ask, breathlessly.

He smiles wickedly. "I might have called in a favor from Cat."

Under the black light, the blue outlines of the eye holes glow with an otherworldly menace, making him look wild, dangerous, and irresistibly sexy.

He tilts his head, slow and predatory, studying me like prey.

Without a moment's hesitation, I pull my T-shirt up over my head and roll onto my side before opening the bottom drawer of my nightstand and pull out the bunny mask I kept from that very night.

A dark smile curves his lips. "Bunny."

I slip my mask on, heart hammering. "Mr. Fox," I say, dropping my voice now wearing nothing but the mask, and my tattoo that's glowing under the black light.

He stalks toward me, shadows dancing over the neon lines of his mask.

"Don't be scared, little bunny," he growls, the same dark promise he whispered that very first night.

But I'm not scared. Not even close.

I'm safe. I'm happy.

And he was worth every single risk.

We were worth it.

If you had asked me this time last year where Alfie's adoption would be, I never would have predicted this. Not only am I officially Alfie's mom, but having Max Hart's name on his adoption certificate would have felt like an impossible, ridiculous dream. But last month, Max asked if he could adopt Alfie as his own, and to say I was shocked to my core would be an understatement. I cried, he cried when I said yes, and we've already started the paperwork to make that happen.

It's surreal to say the least, but it's all real.

And if I had to do it all over again, I'd break every rule in the book, twice, just to spend the rest of my life with him.

Something I fully intend to do.

If breaking rules means saying yes to eternity, then so be it because I'm going to ask him to marry me.

Then Max will be mine, and Alfie's. Forever.

* * *

MORE FROM VH NICOLSON

Another book from VH Nicolson, *Breaking His Boundaries*, is available to order now here:

https://mybook.to/BreakingBackAd

ACKNOWLEDGMENTS

First and foremost, my deepest gratitude goes to Boldwood Books. This adventure has been nothing short of extraordinary. Every lesson, every moment, has been enlightening, and I've never been more thrilled about what's to come.

Publishing a book truly takes a village, and I'm beyond lucky to have had such an incredible team beside me. To my brilliant editor, Megan Haslam. Thank you for your unwavering support, and steady guidance. To Jennifer Davis, I'm so grateful for your copyedits. And to Susan Sugden, thank you for your incredible proofreading skills.

A huge thanks to Lori Jackson for designing such a breathtaking cover; it's everything I could have hoped for and more.

To my amazing husband, Paul, your constant encouragement and unwavering belief in me means the world to me.

To my talented beta readers, Nicki, Lizzy, Rita, Lynn, Casey, and Carolann, your thoughtful feedback, as always, has been priceless. Thank you for pouring your time, energy, and enthusiasm into my work; you keep my creative fire burning bright.

To my street team, I'm endlessly appreciative of your tireless efforts to share and celebrate my books. Every post, every mention, every kind message lifts me higher.

To the book bloggers, Bookstagrammers, and BookTokers, thank you for your boundless creativity, your gorgeous graphics, and the fun, engaging videos you make. Your love for books shines so brightly, and I'm so lucky to have your support.

And lastly, to you, the passionate romance reader, thank you from the bottom of my heart. You're the reason I get to wake up every day and do what I love most. Your support means more than words will ever capture.

ABOUT THE AUTHOR

VH Nicolson is a Scottish author of spicy romance fiction. She was born and raised along the breathtaking coastline in North East Fife. For more than two decades she's worked throughout the UK and abroad within the creative marketing and design industry. Married to her soulmate, they have one son.

Download your exclusive bonus content from VH Nicolson here:

Visit VH Nicolson's website: www.vhnicolsonauthor.com

Follow VH Nicolson on social media here:

- facebook.com/authorvhnicolson
- instagram.com/vhnicolsonauthor
- tiktok.com/@vhnicolsonauthor
- bookbub.com/authors/vh-nicolson
- pinterest.com/vhnicolsonauthor

ALSO BY VH NICOLSON

The Billionaire Boys

Lincoln

Jacob

Owen

The Billionaire Hart Brothers

Breaking His Law

Breaking His Rules

Boldwood
EVER AFTER

JOIN BOLDWOOD'S
**ROMANCE
COMMUNITY**
FOR SWEET AND
SPICY BOOK RECS
WITH ALL YOUR
FAVOURITE
TROPES!

SIGN UP TO OUR
NEWSLETTER

HTTPS://BIT.LY/BOLDWOODEVERAFTER

Boldwood

Boldwood Books is an award-winning fiction publishing company seeking out the best stories from around the world.

Find out more at www.boldwoodbooks.com

Join our reader community for brilliant books, competitions and offers!

Follow us
@BoldwoodBooks
@TheBoldBookClub

Sign up to our weekly deals newsletter

https://bit.ly/BoldwoodBNewsletter